Dead Man's Contract

Dead Man's Contract

ЛЖ

Jack Alun

Bright Pen

A Bright Pen Book

British Library Cataloguing Publication Data.
A catalogue record for this book is available from the British Library

ISBN 978-0-7552-1587-4

Authors OnLine Ltd
19 The Cinques
Gamlingay, Sandy
Bedfordshire SG19 3NU
England

This book is also available in e-book format,
details of which are available at www.authorsonline.co.uk

Life can only be understood backwards …
Søren Kierkegaard (1813-1855 AD)

I am a simple man, not a solver of riddles.
Terence (195-159 BC)

Prologue

'It seems so long ago now. I used to be a maker of documentaries, a tele-journalist; anyway, some kind of corporate freelancer. Not because I didn't like people, but I hated to be owned by them.

'For a long time I'd been filming in conflict zones around the world – some big ones and some that people never got to hear of. There was always plenty of work because at any one time there are as many as fifty different wars going on in the world. But I never thought I'd end up killing someone.

'On this occasion, we'd got permission from the Bogotá government to be placed with a platoon from the 3rd Division of the Colombian Army, which had been deployed to a remote region in the south-west of the country, near the border between the provinces of Narino and Cauca. And we were pretty pleased about it. But what we didn't realise was that the permission we'd received was ring-fenced. That, from the point of view of the Aribe-led government, we were their tool – to be manipulated into producing a propaganda whitewash. To show how the security situation in the country was completely under control, and the FARC insurgency in particular. An insurgency which'd been declining anyway since the nineties, when the group became more interested in making money from narcotic crops than in overthrowing right-wing oppression.

'Later, we learned that government forces were strong

in Narino and Cauca, making a serious clash with the rebels already unlikely. We accompanied patrols, which led us through the relative calm of army-held territory. At other times, filmed the large bonfires on which we were told recently confiscated coca plants were being burned. They expected us to tell the world, especially the U.S., that the war against the rebels and the rebel-controlled drugs trade was going well.

'As soon as the impossibility of fulfilling our assignment, of capturing any images of the conflict, became apparent, we requested a return to Bogotá. But we were entirely dependent on the army for transport. And the next time the platoon was due to be supplied wasn't for several weeks. And no-one would or could give us a precise date.

'The officers tried to encourage us to keep on filming. We were allowed to film every part of the soldiers' daily lives – apart, that is, from them doing any fighting.

'So the first week went by and we spent time and money collecting nothing of much interest – some routine patrolling, polite questioning of villagers and, of course, the numerous bonfires. And certainly most of the soldiers loved being in front of the camera. But with the absence of any action or adrenaline rush, the crew and myself became frustrated to the point of screaming – mostly at each other.

'One afternoon, the three of us were sitting in the corrugated shell of a building, which passed itself off as the local bar. Doing what we usually did in periods of boredom and inactivity, which was to get drunk – to a man. Or, more exactly, to two men and a woman – a soundman, myself and Frederica, a camera-operator who we called Freddi.

'She'd been working with us for years and was a real pro – with an eye for a shot and a devil-can-fuck-himself attitude in dangerous situations. She stood only a little over five feet tall and was well fleshed without being fat. Her hair, which she tied back, was brown and shoulder-length and got matted again as soon as she'd combed it. She was one of those people who never got fazed by problems, which made her good to have around. Feminine, in the conventional sense, she was certainly not – her clothes were practical, shapeless and seemed always several sizes too large. At work, she wore big T-shirts and loose combat trousers and donkey jackets and her only concession to dressing up was a big sweater and jeans.

'Slowly the over-priced booze began to work on us and numb the boredom. The bar owner was grinning at the promise of more takings, as his battered cash box filled with our money. It was by now the middle of the afternoon and my head felt like a merry-go-round. I was beginning to suffocate. I felt I needed to be in the fresh air before I exploded, before another day passed in a blur of alcohol. And to be doing something. The only problem was, I had no idea what it was that I wanted to do.

'Perhaps intuiting what I was thinking, or feeling the same way herself, Freddi got to her feet. She was totally wrecked like the rest of us. Obviously angry, it took a while before we could work out what she was trying to say. To get up off our arses and go out and do some filming with her. That she'd had it with that stinking dump and wanted to get her body into the daylight and be doing something useful.

'But it seemed I was the only one who was interested in joining her. Not just because of the drink or monotony, but curiosity at what Freddi had in mind. Normally meticulous and organised, more used to being directed, here she was speaking at the top of her voice and urging us to do something, something crazy. The alcohol coursing through her veins, she was up for anything. Anything that meant not having to spend another minute in that hole of a bar.

'After collecting her camera, she met up with me again in the camp's compound. Parked unattended a little way off from where we stood was 'our' Kaiser Jeep M715. We had been assigned a driver we could call on when we wanted to use it, but only if three or four other military personnel accompanied us. We were never permitted to leave the ramshackled town without the express permission of the *teniente*, the officer in charge of the platoon. Only today, we didn't intend to ask permission of anybody.

'To the west of us was a river, which marked a sort of unofficial frontier, the limit of area under total government control. The day before, while out with one of the patrols, we'd come across a ford which the officer in charge, the *subteniente*, had forbidden us to cross. That evening the *teniente* came looking for us to explain how the land on the opposite side of the river had already been cleared of rebels during a campaign known as the Plan Patriota – which had been undertaken with the aid of the U.S. So what purpose could possibly be served by going there? As far as he could see, none, as the Colombian army now completely controlled the area. We had his word for it.

'It would have been easier if we'd taken something smaller, like the more manoeuvrable Willy MB that stood beside it, but the sheer power of the one-and-a-quarter ton M715 was too appealing to resist. The keys had been left in the ignition. It would make light work of the ford over the river, which we were already driving towards.

'I know now that, as the person responsible for the crew's safety and welfare, I should've been exercising my judgement, shown better leadership. But the alcohol and adrenaline pump had already combined to obliterate commonsense.

'As we drove along the uneven track parallel to the riverbank, I shouted at Freddi to get her camera working. She wound down her window. Then suddenly, for no reason, we began laughing, laughing as if what we were embarked on was the funniest journey in the world. We were like kids laughing at nothing and everything at the same time.

'At the ford, I wrestled the wheel of the M715 hard to

the right and jolted the vehicle violently into the water. Spray from the tyres splashed up and it took all Freddi's expertise to keep hold of the camera. As we crossed, she cursed me, having to feel around in the metal alloy case at her feet for a cloth with which to wipe the camera lens, as she bounced in her seat.

'On the far bank, I nosed the M715 up out of the river and towards a narrow track that mirrored the one we'd just driven along on the other side. As soon as we'd crossed, we arrived at a sort of T-junction: right would take us back in the direction of the town and a terrain we were already familiar with, left would take us farther away and into the unknown. The latter was riskier, but risk was what it was all about and, if we got lucky, maybe, just maybe, it would make the whole of our wasted trip worthwhile.

'We made the left turn and Freddi got busy with the camera, at once falling silent as she filmed the way the sunlight fell in columns between the canopy of trees, like so many searchlights illuminating the ground beneath. A contrast that made the shadows and the tree trunks seem darker. Somehow, it seemed to intensify the silence our presence was shattering.

'We were still having the mother of a good time, but despite ourselves I could feel a tension beginning to grow. Perhaps that was why, as soon as the vehicle began to collide noisily with the branches of foliage that had strayed across the narrow track, I began to hoot at the top of my voice. A strange goose-like noise, broken by a series of yelping sounds. Freddi quickly understood and stopped filming and joined me in the "who gives a fuck anyway?" cacophony I was creating.

'Then came the shot. I heard a sharp slap or snap and felt the wind of the bullet pass through the cab of the vehicle before it smacked through the window next to me. Something landed in my lap – probably a piece of glass. Freddi made a coughing sound, I assumed with the shock.

'Then panic took over. I accelerated down the track for twenty or so metres before suddenly braking hard and skidding the vehicle over the soft ground, sending the back end of it smashing against the trunk of a tree. Instantly, I reversed, jolting back into the undergrowth, as it crashed and snapped around us. The second or two the Kaiser sat there racking on its suspension, a second bullet punctured the roof of the cab above our heads and punched a round hole through the centre of the windscreen. More bullets smacked against the vehicle's bodywork. I hit the accelerator to get the hell out of there.

'Scared and sobering, the drive back along the track took all my attention. Now and then, I heard another bullet strike the vehicle. Then as we drove farther away, they stopped. Not until we reached the ford leading back across the river did I become aware of the sounds coming from Freddi – inarticulate sounds. And when I turned to look, she was clutching her face, blood oozing between her fingers and the backs of her hands and arms.

'It took every last bit of concentration I had to angle the Kaiser down the slope onto the width of the ford that would take us back across the river. I felt the glass fragment shift in my lap and start to slide between my legs. When I looked down to see if I could get rid of it without cutting myself, a wave of shock and revulsion overcame me. The involuntary tug I gave the steering wheel almost caused me to swerve the vehicle into the deep water flowing beside the ford. Lying there, bleeding into my jeans, was a part of Freddi's lower jaw, severed and partly shattered by that first bullet to have been fired at us.

'As she held on to what was left of her face in obvious agony, I couldn't tell whether she was choking or trying to retch. The camera, lying undamaged at her feet, was still turned on and I caught myself, for a second, wondering whether the footage it had recorded might be useable. Freddi's injury was too severe for me to help her. And although the movement of the Kaiser was causing her distress, I daren't slow down. She needed urgent help. But I could go no farther with part of her jawbone in my lap. So, taking a delicate hold of it, I picked it up and placed it in hers. I couldn't think of what else to do with it. Like Freddi, I was in shock.

'So, after what seemed like an eternity, we finally roared back into the base, narrowly avoiding getting shot by the sentries as we did so; and nearly killing a couple of soldiers, who were ambling across the compound. At the sight of the returning Kaiser, everything erupted around us. Right away, the *teniente* pushed his way through the group of soldiers gathered around our vehicle and ordered me to get out. He drew his pistol as if he were about to shoot me. He had the look on his face of a man who had nothing to lose. But there was something more urgent to worry about.

'With attention focused on me, no-one had noticed that Freddi was hurt. I began to gesticulate and speak loudly in English, only for two soldiers to be ordered to hold my arms, forcing them behind my back, as if they were restraining a dangerous criminal. But still no-one paid any attention to Freddi. I angled my head back in the direction of the Kaiser's cab and began repeating the words *el médico, urgente*, over and over like a demented parrot; until the *teniente* finally caught on to what I was trying to say and a new pandemonium broke out. Immediately a soldier was dispatched to get medical equipment, while another was sent to telephone for help. Several others carried Freddi from the cab and laid her on the ground beside the front wheel of the Kaiser. The one holding her shattered jawbone, like me, seemed uncertain what to do with it. The *teniente* stood looking down on her, still holding his pistol. You could see he was staring at the ruins of his army career.

'The soldiers who held my arms were ordered to take me to an empty wooden hut and lock me inside. Before long, the other member of the crew, who'd remained in the bar drinking, was frogmarched across the compound and locked up with me. Still pissed, he was angrily demanding to know what was going on. He'd been roughly treated by his escort. The hut we were in had no windows and a dirt floor, and outside an armed guard had been posted. He was scared.

'The last we heard of Freddi was she'd been put on a stretcher then flown by helicopter to a hospital somewhere in the north – in Pasto or Mocoa, perhaps. But as the soldiers had had orders not to speak to us, we never found out exactly where.

'A couple of extremely uncomfortable days followed, punctuated by raised voices and endless reprimands, but little in the way of food or hygiene. And we were to remain that way until the government at whatever level in Bogotá could decide what to do with us. We'd disobeyed army orders, but apart from theft of a vehicle we'd broken no civilian laws and this was causing problems.

'When the order finally came through, we were manhandled with what remained of our equipment onto the back of an old two-and-a-half ton M35 truck. Still under armed guard, we were then treated to a bone-jerking ride to the nearest airfield and flown back to the capital; where, on arrival, we were transferred to the civilian airport and escorted on to an American Airlines jet bound for Austin, Texas. We were hungry and dirty, but at liberty to leave.

'Only days later, after we'd got back to the UK, did we obtain scant news of Freddi from the British embassy in Bogotá – that she was dead and her body was in the process of being repatriated to a family in England she'd never spoken of. The rest, where and when she died, was never made clear. Not even in the few column inches it made in a couple of the national broadsheets.

'So that's it … how I managed to fuck my business and get a lovely person killed into the bargain. There was a

In his right hand, he still clutched the bundle of flyers he'd been distributing. He took one and held it out for her to read. He had to speak louder than he wanted to in order to make her hear him through the window glass of the car.

'You called me … we just spoke on the phone.'

Then he noticed that she too was holding one of his flyers. Hers was crumpled as if she'd been clutching it tightly. Or she'd picked it up in the car park after someone else had screwed it up and thrown it away. Realising he was looking at it, she held hers up to match his, a secret signal – like the halves of a torn banknote.

She turned on the car electrics in order to let down the window, so she could speak to him without shouting. As it slowly lowered, he tried reassuring her with a smile.

But what happened next he was unprepared for.

'Hello, "R.I.P". What can I do for you?'

'I need help.'

'What kind of help would that be?'

'I've been raped. … It happened last night.'

The gravity of her words contrasted with the quiet matter-of-factness of her voice. But her big hazel eyes began to swell tears, as from deep down a suppressed emotion rose to the surface.

'You must call the gendarmes immediately.'

Then he stopped himself. Idiot. He suddenly comprehended why she'd contacted him. Why she couldn't go directly to the police herself. He pointed to that part of the flyer that listed his professional services.

'I understand. You'll need me to do the translating for you? We'll drive there right away.'

'No.'

He was confused.

'You don't need a translator?'

'No, I don't want the gendarmes.'

'You can't allow the bastard that did this to you to get away with it.'

11

'The bastards will get what's coming to them. But not this way.'

He registered the use of the plural 'bastards'; then waited for her to continue. But she didn't. None of it was making sense.

'Listen, I don't get involved in physical violence. The "R.I.P" on the flyer is designed to grab people's attention, that's all. If you want to get even with these men, I'm not the person you're looking for.'

'You're wrong. That's not what I want. I just need somewhere to go, to stay for a while. I need time to think. Whatever you charge, I'll pay it. I'll pay you double.'

'Keep your money, that's not what I do. If you want somewhere to stay, try the tourist office. They speak English. But in my opinion you ought to go straight to the gendarmerie. Not just for your sake but to protect other women from these bastards. I'll come along with you and I don't need paying for it.'

'You're not listening to what I'm saying.'

'They'll also call a doctor to examine you.'

'I don't need the gendarmes and I don't need a doctor. I just need you to listen.'

'I think you're making a mistake. What about HIV? You'll need checking over.'

'Listen. And don't look so angry. Okay, okay … I know you're trying to do your best, but I'm the one who knows what's best for me.'

'So tell me what it is you want.'

'Like I said, I'm looking for somewhere to stay that's quiet and with no neighbours, and a little off the beaten track. Somewhere that can't be seen from the road. Where I can work things out.'

'That could be most places round here. You've got a big choice.'

'Where do you live?'

'I don't rent my house out.'

'That wasn't the question.'

'About fifteen or so kilometres from here. Why?'

'In the country?'

'Yes.'

'Quiet?'

'One neighbour about half a kilometre away.'

'Alone?'

'Quite.'

'Then it's a small house.'

'It's big enough.'

'What, two, three bedrooms?'

No reply.

'More? As long as it doesn't feel like we're living together, then it'll suit me fine. I'll pay you rent as well as your fee, whatever that comes to. Name your price. I won't trouble you for very long.'

'Come with me to the gendarmerie then you've got a deal. You can't be thinking straight at the moment. It's the best thing you can do. Trust me.'

'If I go to the law, those bastards from last night will get off anyway, then find a way to get to me – I know well how legal systems work. And I do trust you, otherwise I wouldn't be talking to you now. But you've got to believe me, mine's the only safe way to go. No gendarmes.'

'They can offer you much better protection than I can.'

'Do you want this job or not? Listen, I know you're trying to do the right thing, but it has to be my way or no way. If that's not clear to you, I'll look for someone else.'

'It's clear enough. But I still don't think you're right. Who else are you going to ask to help you?'

'I'll find someone, don't you worry.'

Though the threat of tears lingered at the corners of her eyes, her voice, still soft, was firm and controlled. She'd talked about using his house as some sort of refuge, and paying him money for doing so, which he could certainly use. Looking down at the helpless, beautiful face before him, his emotions became confused. His responsibility was to take this woman to the gendarmerie and to see a doctor without delay, but all of a sudden he doubted he was going to.

'Okay.'

'Try not to look so concerned. Is that your decision then? Are we going to your house or do I have to look for someone else to help me?'

'It's your decision. You know how I feel about it.'

'Then I've already decided.'

'I'm in a black Jeep Grand Cherokee. Wait here. I'll drive over and you can follow me out of town. It's a market today, so stay close.'

#

Getting away from Villefranche-de-Rouergue in late July had taken them far too long. It was a Thursday, market day – a good time to search for clients, but bad if you were hoping to get somewhere in a hurry. Weatherworn farmers clogged the tiny roads, their cars built before the invention of speed, their driving wavering between indecision and eccentric. And mixed in amongst them, the summertime tourists, assertive, confused, and searching for parking places, trying to insert their too-big modern estates or SUVs into spaces marked out for nothing much bigger than a supermarket trolley or the little Citroën C1 that was following close behind his battered Grand Cherokee. And everywhere else rambled pedestrians, who for that one day only seemed to own the roads.

As they sat in the traffic, her agitation at the slowness of their progress grew worse. It was not until they'd climbed away from the town and the air through the open window of the Jeep at last grew cool, that he noticed her beginning to relax. The farther they travelled, the more the tightness in her shoulders eased and left her face. But the firmness with which she gripped the steering wheel remained – as if clinging to it ensured she'd be safe.

He observed her in his rear-view mirror with a sympathetic curiosity. But he didn't have to be the world's premier psychiatrist to understand that, after what she'd been through, it'd be a long time before she'd be able to trust anyone again. And certainly not a man.

But then another thought occurred, which begged the question: if trusting men from now on was a problem for her, and God knows he could understand why, then what was she now doing following him along a strange road in the middle of the French countryside? Him, a total stranger who'd been handing out cheaply printed flyers in a supermarket car park? Certainly, it wasn't his trusting face. That'd already taken too many existential and physical buffetings to make him look anything other than he was – damaged property, best to be avoided. Or 'R.I.P.', the witty name he'd given his company – attention-grabbing, but in her present state not exactly reassuring.

If physical protection was what she was after, sure he was still reasonably fit for his age; but then the gendarmes were the professionals and better equipped to protect her than he was. And where was the wisdom of hiding herself away in his house? A totally reckless decision that caused him to think she was more psychologically damaged than she appeared. On top of that, the only thing she knew about him was the name that appeared on the flyer.

But the name was a saga in itself, full of family aspirations and pretensions. While young, he was conscious of the power of an insignificant punctuation mark; of the unearned superiority it implied and the way it singled him out from others. So he dropped it. But on official documentation, it still remained – John Cariol-Jarret.

Again, he examined the progress of the red Citroën C1 hire car in his rear-view mirror. Shortly, they would have to make the right turn on to the track leading to his house. Though more relaxed, he wasn't sure how much she was actually concentrating on driving. Her eyes were fixed on the middle distance, seeing but not assimilating, her attention absorbed by an inner world. He thought of sounding the car horn to warn her of the forthcoming manoeuvre, but the thought it might frighten her stopped him. A hundred metres before the turning he slowed to a crawl and began to indicate.

#

The old Jeep Grand Cherokee bounced along the rough farm track, creaking on its well-worn suspension. But Jarret's attention was focused on the little red Citroën C1 following behind. It covered the ground easily, swaying over the potholes, gently negotiating the two tight bends on the descent to the house, which on Google Earth resembled a flattened zed. It followed like a dutiful dog, not too close and not too far away, until they reached the roughly cobbled courtyard and parked side by side in the shade of a huge walnut tree that spread its shadow along the side and roof of a squat, stone barn. Beside which, looming solidly, stood a large grey stone house – east-facing. It too cast a shadow that during the afternoon would creep across the courtyard until it travelled to the spot where the two cars had parked.

Jarret creaked open the Jeep door and crossed to the little red bubble that'd been following him. As he did, the young woman emerged to meet him, her long blonde hair flowing from one shoulder to the other and back again. He could see now it was darker around where it clung to her head than at the sides and wondered whether this was an expensive coiffure or whether the sun had bleached it as it slowly grew. She closed the car door softly behind her. As she stood upright, her hair flowed back to reveal her smooth forehead and high cheekbones.

'So, what do you make of it?'

'It's not the Ritz, but it'll do.'

'It'll do? You don't know how proud that makes me feel.'

'I didn't mean it like that. It looks nice. It's just a little foreboding.'

'But is it what you're looking for?'

'Like I said, it'll do. What do you want me to say? It's perfect.'

'If you've an alternative, I suggest you go to it.'

'It was you, not the place.'

'What do you mean by that?'

'I'm good with people and when I saw you in the car park I had an instinct. I could tell that ...'

Jarret waited for her to finish, but she didn't.

'Have you got somewhere you can hide my car?'

'I can park it in the back of the barn here and arrange it so that it's not easy to find. Are you sure you don't want to take a look around the house first?'

'I assume no-one saw us arrive. Perhaps you'd better hide the car now.'

'Then take one of the chairs there into the shade. I'll be gone for a couple of minutes. I'll show you round after.'

The old farmhouse was folded within the undulations of the French countryside, not far from the tiny village of Solac. Six years ago, Jarret had bought it as a holiday-home-cum-hideaway in the beautiful valley of the Sérène, named after the modest tributary which ran through it. Trixie, his then partner, had planted two lines of buddleia bushes at the back of the house to attract the butterflies. The following summer their long purple flowers were covered with a kaleidoscope of moving colour. One day, they discovered one that had flattened itself against the lintel above the back door. Its wingspan measured about ten centimetres and it had marks on its wings like eyes. It reminded Jarret of a death's head and so was probably a moth. It was that day, he remembered, that Trixie christened the farmhouse Le Papillon: the butterfly. And to all – except the oldest of the inhabitants of the area, who continued to call it by its original name, La Roque – that was how it became known.

The few people who Jarret had ever allowed to visit him would odds-on miss the sharp right turn from the road onto the partially hidden farm track, the first hundred metres of which he shared with his neighbour, Didier Brosard, a pig farmer, living beyond the two small hills that divided their properties. If the wind was in the wrong direction, the air could become ripe; otherwise Didier, Yvette, his wife, and their pigs and chickens were friendly and very private. They made perfect neighbours.

In many ways, though, they were the imperfect couple. Yvette was curvaceous, well-fleshed and attractive, whereas Didier was lean and sinewy, with narrow shoulders and an almost unintelligible local accent. Yvette certainly couldn't be called stylish, but her clothes were always colourful, matching and at least paid lip service to the twenty-first century. Didier was a ragbag of check shirts, shapeless jeans and hideously patterned sweaters. His cap was fixed permanently to his head and his face lost beneath permanent stubble. They were still childless, but very much in love.

It was only when Jarret saw them dancing that he got it: moving as one across the wooden floor of the village hall – spruced and almost shining, him erect, her beautiful – as they stepped and twirled to the rhythms of the dance. In the music of those evenings, they were transformed.

Jarret had had plans for developing Le Papillon and the land around it; but, apart from two large lawns, a small orchard and a half-finished swimming pool, most of them had come to nothing. Obliterated by the bureaucracy of the local planning authorities or, more usually, the blur of a morning hangover.

Though over the years the house had been worked

on, the barn had remained untouched. Embedded stones protruded erratically through its earth floor. Strands of ancient spiders' webs hung from dust-encrusted beams and the remnants of old straw lay in musty heaps against one of the walls. Abandoned tools, rusted farm machinery and worm-eaten feeding troughs compounded the impression of decay.

The wooden double doors groaned as Jarret opened them wide. The car was tiny, but just fitted the narrow entrance. He had to turn on the headlights to see his way across the gloomy interior and avoid colliding with the scattered debris. Carefully, he steered towards the back wall, the car's shiny new paintwork – only three thousand kilometres on the clock – gathering dust as he went. Halfway in he stopped, got out and dragged an ox plough from its ancient resting place in the far right-hand corner, then parked the car in the space he'd created.

Removing an old stained tarpaulin from on top of a rusting generator, he slid it gently over the C1's shiny red paintwork. Next, he collected together a pile of rotten planks and laid them carefully against the back of the vehicle, before placing a bucket on its roof and beside it a length of corroded hosepipe. As he closed the double doors, he looked back to survey his handiwork. In the gloom and beneath the old tarpaulin, the car could have stood there for fifty years.

When Jarret returned, she was sitting in the shade of the walnut tree. She'd removed her shoes and her feet were resting on a chair in front of her. Though she still looked fatigued, leaning back there with her eyes shut, she appeared to have relaxed. But as she heard him approach, her body tensed and a look of alarm spread across her face, an expression that was quickly replaced by a wide smile.

Her eyes searched out his.

'Finished?'

'I don't think anyone's going to find that in a hurry.

Before we go inside, how about we formally introduce ourselves?'

'Formal introductions – wow! What's wrong with telling each other our names?'

And with that she slipped on her shoes and got to her feet. Then, holding her hand out well in front of her, her palm held flat in a parody gesture, she moved towards him.

'I'm Alicia and pray, kind sir, who might you be?'

The change in her behaviour was sudden and took him by surprise. Now she seemed to be making fun of him. Her smile was fixed and had settled comfortably into the laughter lines around her eyes and mouth. He felt nonplussed as he took her hand, searching his mind for a clever reply. But none came.

'Jarret.'

She gave his hand an exaggerated shake. And she was laughing. But whatever the joke was, he didn't share it.

Alicia – it worked! If she'd have invented it, it couldn't have suited her more. He found himself having to repeat it out loud.

'Alicia – that's a beautiful name.'

He'd said it slowly, so it hissed as it slid off his tongue. He could almost taste it.

'It's a name. I could've chosen a better one. My parents knew how they wanted each of their daughters to turn out and for me Alicia was their template.'

Daughters – but he let the reference drift by without comment. There would be time for talk later.

'Jarret – so what's your first name?'

'You can call me John or Jay, if you prefer. You ready to take a look inside?'

His voice sounded husky from the clouds of dust he'd kicked up in the barn and his nose and eyes were still crusted. All of a sudden he felt self-conscious and brushed at his clothes and hair. As they made their way towards the house, a thought occurred to him and he stopped in mid-stride.

'Your bags! I left your bags in the car!'

But she looked unconcerned. Just patted the large leather bag that hung from her shoulder.

'This is all I've got. I've no other bags with me. That's another reason why I wanted to hire you. Coming to stay here is a temporary solution. I can tell you now, but what I really need you to do is to collect my suitcase for me.'

He hesitated before replying. In Villefranche, she'd talked about wanting him to find her somewhere to stay for a while. Talk of a suitcase was a new departure.

'Where exactly do you mean?'

'Not now. I'll tell you later. There'll be plenty of time. First, show me the house.'

He'd not noticed it before because all he saw before him was a victim, albeit a beautiful one, of an unspeakable crime. But now, he realised, she'd started giving him orders.

The façade of the farmhouse had been left largely as it was when Jarret had bought it. Only the inside had been transformed. The big wooden beams, stone walls and colonnades had been revealed and cleaned and stood in vivid contrast to the new electrical fittings, radiators and the gleaming ceramic of the bathrooms and kitchen.

The front door entered directly into a kitchen-dining room. Alicia stepped inside onto a red, hand-fired Spanish tile floor. At a glance she took in the brilliant white kitchen units and big, centrally positioned chestnut wood table. And heard the sigh of the heavy oak front door as he closed it behind her.

'Okay. It's not half as grim as it looks from the outside.'

She stopped abruptly in front of him. She stared down at a neat circle of dark objects arranged in the middle of the floor.

'Jesus, what are those supposed to be?'

It was barely an hour after midday, but Jarret had to reach for the light switch to illuminate the gloomy interior – a problem in old Aveyronais houses. Only in the spotlights' angled light could he make out what she was looking at. And when he did, it was all he could do not to burst out laughing. Carefully laid out in the centre of the room was a squeezed circle, almost like an open eye, of dried gourds – their reds, yellows and greens vivid against the shiny, dark floor. It was one of the downsides of not locking his front door when he was out. Didier had been to visit.

'It's only my neighbour. I'll clear them up later. First, let me show you where your room is.'

2 (Thursday pm)

He'd never been much of a gardener. That'd always been Trixie's interest, her first but not her only love. But when Didier began growing bitter gourds down the side of his old grey stone barn, Jarret was drawn to them. The strange prehistoric-looking fruit, relatives of the melon and cucumber, held a strange fascination for him. Sometimes he'd visit Didier once or twice a week just to watch them develop their reptilian curves and angles. As they slowly transformed into colours, he could more associate them with Africa or a tropical island than dangling from wire strands against an Aveyron farmyard wall.

The gourds that'd been kicked to the side of the kitchen floor he knew were purely ornamental. The pattern that Didier'd created on the kitchen floor was his idea of a joke, his schoolboy sense of humour – the size of his gourds was for him a constant source of referential amusement. Now it'd pleased him to pattern these already phallic objects to represent a female pudenda – a joke, no doubt, at the expense of Jarret's erratic sex life.

Gathering them up, Jarret placed them in ragged rows at one end of the large kitchen table. He'd think where to put them later.

When he'd finished, he began to prepare an omelette for their lunch.

Alicia had remained in her en suite bedroom at the end of the upstairs corridor. He'd put her in a room as far away from his own as possible. He thought she'd prefer it that way. It gave her her own space to be private in. And she'd seemed pretty pleased.

'This'll do me nicely.'

Then she'd opened the door to the en suite, running her eyes approvingly over a dark grey slate floor and ivory-toned wall tiles. Before returning to her lemon-painted bedroom with its one exposed stone wall and king-sized bed.

'Very nicely, indeed.'

But few of the choices of decoration had been Jarret's. They were Trixie's, his long-term ex-partner. His role had been to agree and organise the workmen to do the jobs. Hers was the taste – his contribution had been to provide the money to pay for everything. It was Trixie who had always been the homemaker and a good one. At one time she'd even harboured aspirations to be an interior designer. It'd been a perfect partnership, everyone had said so, until the time when the money stopped coming in. In his more sentimental moments, he'd tried to believe their relationship had amounted to more.

Jarret was in the kitchen beating eggs. Of the many theories concerning how to make the perfect omelette, the philosophical and practical line Jarret followed was Elizabeth David's, and her assertion was simple – if you've got a favourite way of cooking something, then that's how you should cook it. Modern media chefs might have to keep rewriting and reinventing, but for Jarret and his cookbook guru the preparation was straightforward.

Although only on low heat to warm, the olive oil in the frying pan already gave off a rich fragrance. In the refrigerator he'd placed a bottle of rosé wine. It'd been almost a year and a half since last he'd drunk alcohol. When he'd removed the bottle from his small *cave* at the back of the house, it'd become dusty, and the old key he had taken from the nail beside the door had left rust stains on his fingers. But the wine wasn't meant for him.

He laid the knives and forks and side plates on the table with a clatter in the hope that the sound would carry upstairs. Alicia was still in her bedroom. Before he'd left her, she told him she felt a wreck and asked if by any chance there was some make-up in the house. From one of the empty bedrooms along he collected the vanity case, containing various jars, bottles and tubes that Trixie had kept for their female guests to use in cases of emergency. Plus several other small items abandoned by women during their brief migrations through his house. He gave them to her. She thanked him, then told him she intended to take a shower. It was on his way out that he'd asked her if she was hungry. As soon as he left, he heard her lock the door behind him.

As footsteps sounded on the stairs, Jarret raised the gas under the heavy iron pan and watched the olive oil begin to ripple with the heat. When Alicia entered, he saw that her face had been lightly made-up and her hair freshly washed: there seemed a new glow about her. She smiled at him as she crossed to the table.

'I'm starving.'

'Sit down. It won't take a minute.'

Shortly, two omelettes slid light and steaming onto the warmed plates, the melting cheese and runny egg oozing from between their folds. Jarret placed one in front of her and offered her a bowl of green salad. A basket of freshly cut bread was already on the table. She refused the chilled rosé he'd opened for her and chose a glass of Volvic water with a lemon slice.

Outside, the shadow of the house inched across the courtyard. It was a perfect afternoon. The silence in the room was broken by the sounds of dining. The rosé, sweating with condensation, remained untouched, but the salad and the bread passed back and forth between them. Neither of them was ready to speak until they'd finished.

'That was very good.'

'Thanks. Dessert?'

'I couldn't eat another thing.'

'Coffee?'

'Nothing.'

A silence once again descended upon the room. Alicia had turned sideways on her chair and seemed preoccupied. Whatever her thoughts were, Jarret had no intention of intruding. But as the interlude stretched, he gradually grew more uncomfortable. For a brief moment he thought of reaching for the wine. But he controlled the urge, and instead collected up the plates and carried them to the sink to wash them.

Then he remembered what she'd said to him outside.

'You mentioned earlier that you'd wanted me to pick up a suitcase for you?'

'Yes.'

'I could go this afternoon if you like.'

'That would be kind. The sooner you collect it the better.'

'Where exactly did you leave it?'

'It can't be far from here. There's a village on a small hill, I don't remember the name of it. Then you go past a lake. Do you know where that might be?'

'There are a lot of villages on small hills in this area. The lake might narrow it down.'

'The name of the village could have begun with the letter B or P.'

'Pradinas?'

'That sounds like it. But I think the road it's on is towards somewhere called Narjic. I saw it on a signpost.'

'Najac. Then it's somewhere between Najac and Pradinas. What else can you remember nearby – any signs, other houses, something about the road, odd countryside? Anything that'll help'

'The name of the house, it's a joke – Manoir Ivant. The owner enjoys going round telling everyone English 'I live in the manner I vant' in a phoney German accent. It's stupid.'

'Who is this person?'

'He's called Adams and there's another man, who works for him, called Fraze. If you find the road, you can't miss the place. There's a big white sign outside. It'll be obvious.'

'I'm only going there to collect your case. Understood? Like I told you, no heavy stuff and no retribution, that's what the law's for.'

'I assure you I'm not after anything else. The case is all I want.'

'Apart from the men you've already mentioned, is anyone likely to be there?'

'Nobody – there's just the two of them. You might come across a couple of employees, but they won't cause you any trouble. I just remembered, while you're there, could you do another little service for me. If you look to the side of the house, you'll see a big garagy-type barn where the cars are kept. If you look to the right of the building, behind a bush, you'll find a wooden box with six bottles of wine in it. I'd be really grateful if you could collect those for me as well. You'll think it's stupid, I know. They're a present I bought for my father, but I'd hate to leave them behind for those bastards to drink. They cost me quite a lot of money and I'd really appreciate it. But try to make sure they're not watching you. If anyone sees you there, leave the box for later. But, if you could collect it for me, it'd make my father very happy.'

This was the most she'd said since they'd met, and the most animated she'd been. Her voice was educated but at the back of it he thought he could detect the trace of a foreign accent he couldn't quite recognise. The inflections and modulations of another language lingered, despite the care she took with her pronunciation.

3 (Thursday pm)

An ostentatious white sign to his right caused him to brake sharply, reducing his speed to a crawl. The Grand Cherokee's 2.5 diesel engine idled beneath the bonnet, emitting the deep purr of a big cat. The bold black gothic lettering on the sign indicated he'd arrived at his destination – a large arrow at the bottom conveniently pointed him in the right direction. Beneath the arrow, in smaller, finer print, was the name of the proprietor, Christopher K. Adams.

Though there were no other cars on the road around, he indicated through force of habit and entered a single-lane track. Passing beneath the shade of a line of trees, he followed the arc of a shallow valley as it gradually descended, before finally coming to a stop in a large grey gravelled clearing. An arched entrance with heavy wooden gates stood in front of a large grey house that was situated on the far side of the clearing. His was the only car parked there.

Hoping there'd be an advantage in his visit being a surprise, Jarret pushed open the large wooden gate and entered. He ignored the smart new electric bell and intercom that'd been installed beside a large wooden front door and chose a small path that led to the right of the building. Despite the pretensions of its owner, the Manoir Ivant was little more than a recently renovated farm complex, with the main house joined at the rear to a series of barns, flanking a courtyard to form a large *cour de ferme*.

By the side of the building the ground fell away sharply.

New windows had been installed in the walls of the barn, on the right-hand side of the house, which had now presumably been converted into living accommodation. Both the windows and the heavy wooden shutters which flanked them had been freshly painted a traditional blue grey and were gaping wide in the afternoon heat. The stone sills of the first two were the height of a man's chest. If the building was equipped with an intruder alarm, the open windows indicated it'd been switched off. Making it easy for anyone who had a mind to break in. Rounding the corner of the barn, he climbed the short distance to the plateau of level ground, towards a low line of rocket-shaped conifer bushes. They looked strangely out of place against the rugged countryside. As he followed the path between them and the back of the barn, he saw why they'd been planted there – as a windbreak for the large and equally out-of-place swimming pool beyond them. It measured, maybe, thirty-five metres by fifteen, with a scallop of Roman steps that led into the shallow end, not far from where he stood. On the far side of the swimming pool stood a white painted building with a pan-tiled Mediterranean-style roof, changing rooms and what at a brief glance looked like a well-equipped kitchen. Beside the pool a man was stretched out sunbathing, while another swam.

He stopped for a moment to familiarise himself with the layout. A short distance beyond the pool, the land abruptly dropped away again, flattening only when it reached a small meadow with a stream running through it. To the far left side of the meadow, within easy reach of the house, was a cottage, stone-built and halfway through having its roof re-tiled. Though scaffolding stood along one of its walls, the site was unoccupied, work having halted for the day because of the afternoon heat.

The man beside the pool lay stretched out on a wooden recliner. His tan was far too intense and preternatural to have been acquired during the sunless days of the erratic southern French summer they were having. His body glistened, as it reposed on a pale blue and cream striped cushion, not from swimming or from sweat, but from a fresh application of suntan oil. In the pool, the other man, blond-haired and equally suntanned, was breaststroking lazily towards the deep end. On the bottom of the pool, a remote cleaning device worked away tirelessly – a tiny, dark robotic box on the end of a plastic umbilical cord.

From Alicia's description, Jarret assumed the man in the pool was Fraze and the man on the recliner Adams. He was surprised to have stumbled on them like that. He'd imagined he'd confront them in the house, close to where Alicia's case had been left. But there was nothing for it now but to bite the bullet and get the whole thing over with. The dozing, oiled man on the recliner, whom he was presuming was Adams, was facing away from him. As he moved towards him, he couldn't prevent himself wondering whether Adams had applied the suntan oil himself or whether the man in the pool had done it for him.

'Mr Adams?'

Jarret's deep voice shattered the somnolence of the afternoon and made the man jump. Immediately, he sat up, half-turned and placed his legs firmly on the ground either side of the recliner, the material of his bathing trunks stretching tightly to reveal a lump of crotch. His eyes struggled to focus in the sudden glare of sunlight and he fumbled for a pair of dark glasses on the ground beside him.

'Who the fuck …?'

'Mr Adams? I apologise. I didn't mean to startle you.'

That certainly wasn't true, but he may as well start off by being polite. He could see that Adams was at a disadvantage; with any luck he could keep him that way and be away again without any trouble. He wasn't there to make accusations.

'I've come here about a little matter of some luggage.'

'What fucking luggage?'

'The luggage a certain young lady forgot to take with her when she left this morning.'

He resisted using the words "escaped" or "got away". Making Adams jump was one thing; to make accusations at this early stage in their meeting was another.

'What "young lady"? Not that slut who was staying here with us? No way. Do me a favour, if she wants to get her bag back tell her to come and collect it herself. And tell her, while she's about it, to return the things she took from us.'

'What things?'

'That's none of your fucking business. Tell her, if she returns them now, we'll say no more about it. We'll look at it as her little joke. If she doesn't, tell her she's going to find herself on the end of some big fucking trouble. No, not trouble – she's fucking dead! Now crawl back to where you came from.'

Jarret's attention was deflected by the sound of splashing at the edge of the pool. Levering himself dripping from the water was Fraze, who only moments before had been breaststroking towards the far end of the pool. The sunlight now reflecting off his wet body emphasised a muscled physique he was proud of.

Jarret wasn't aggressive by nature – if compromise or capitulation extricated him from a tricky situation, then that was the route he'd take. But he was reasonably fit looking – a hangover from his university days when he'd been quite a respectable soccer player and the visits Trixie, his ex, used to make him pay to the gym. And though alcohol had over the years taken its toll and though he didn't exactly look like a prizefighter, his physique still made others think twice before upsetting him.

'What's up, Chris?'

Dripping a trail of water, the glistening swimmer crossed to stand beside the differently glistening Adams, who had remained seated astride his recliner.

'This joker's just going, Fraze.'

'When I've got what I've come to collect, then I'll go.'

Jarret had always been stubborn, but that remark had slipped out. It was stupid and he knew it.

'Wrong. You leave here when I tell you to. Now. And don't forget to give that little bitch my message. Now sod off and tell her to come and do her own dirty work.'

Despite good sense telling him to leave, he moved to the foot of the recliner. He wanted to confront both men head-on and to better position himself should Fraze decide to act the enforcer. If he did, he'd have to make his way between the recliner and the pool edge, handing Jarret the advantage.

He felt a momentary desire to hit someone. He was angry. But Jarret took a deep restraining breath and made an effort to sound calm and reasonable.

'Look, you two got up to something last night and I'm not going to comment on it. But let's face it, you're lucky it's me here and not the police. As my client says, she doesn't want to take it any further; if that's what she wants, that's fine. I'm not going to go into the rights and wrongs of it, but from where I stand you're lucky not to be spending the next five years in jail. So, let's get this over with; tell me where her bag is and I'll leave.'

'I don't believe this. What lies has that little whore been spreading about us?'

'You had your fun last night. You've been lucky, now let's leave it there. Tell me where the bag is.'

'Hear that, Fraze? This is too much. Any fun we might have had with that bitch was at her doing. Listen to me, mister-who-or-whatever-you-fucking-are, the tart was up for it. That's what she does and that's what she's good at. We were the ones that needed to take a break. She fucked us, then when we were asleep she went. Now listen carefully to what I've got to say – before she went she removed something that belonged to me and now I want it back. And pronto. You just make sure she delivers. Tell her, her health depends on it. Is that clear to you? Okay, now you've run your little errand. You've earned your money. Now lose yourself.'

'No, not till you hand over what I came for.'

'Fraze, he's a retard. Get him out of here.'

Fraze, seemingly undeterred by his near-nakedness, moved towards Jarret, fixing on him with cold, narrowed eyes. As he advanced between the recliner and the pool, Jarret took half a pace sideways, transferring his weight onto his right leg. And prepared himself. So the moment Fraze reached the end of Adams's recliner and began to turn, he was surprised to be met, square in the chest, by Jarret's shoulder, propelling him backwards into the blue water of the pool. The glass surface exploded and he disappeared beneath it.

Summoning all the menace he could muster, he turned back towards Adams. And froze. In an instant, he felt his stomach knot and his breathing become shallow. Adams, for his part, had remained on the recliner, though now he leant back, legs out in front of him, in his hand a snub-nose revolver. The need for self-preservation cancelled out Jarret's aggression. In the interval between barging Fraze into the water and watching him sink, Adams from somewhere had produced a gun.

'Now are you understanding me, tosser? Just remain where you are.'

Jarret watched helplessly as Fraze struggled to the edge of the pool. This time it took him a little longer to get out of the water, anger and humiliation etched on his face. Jarret tensed. He knew he'd badly miscalculated. Either Fraze was going to break him into pieces or the darkness inside the revolver's barrel would soon become his. He no longer felt tough.

The first punch sank into his unprotected stomach, evacuating the air from his lungs. He doubled over, feeling the surge of pain and the need to vomit. Then his skull cracked and jerked back as a knee smashed into the side of his face, almost snapping his neck. Next a hand gripped him by the hair while another was driven several times into the side of his face. Barely conscious, he heard the voice of Adams coming from afar. Fraze maintained the grip on his hair.

'That's enough for now, Fraze. I think he understands you're not happy with him. Check his pockets to find out who he is.'

Fraze let go of Jarret's hair and roughly searched through his pockets until he discovered a wallet. From it, he removed the driver's licence and a business card, which he handed to Adams, who examined them both. Shortly, he slipped the business card into the waistband of his pale blue briefs and returned the driver's licence to Fraze, who replaced it in the wallet and snapped it shut. Then, turning sideways and drawing his arm back across his body, he frisbeed the wallet into the middle of the pool, where it floated for a moment and began to sink.

Jarret was still reeling from his beating, his head still fuzzy, as Fraze turned to him, grinning. He dragged him to the edge of the pool.

'I hope you know how to swim.'

'Petulance, Fraze. Leave it. So, is it Jarret or Cariol-Jarret? Are you up to something or are you some sort of schizo? But that's no concern of mine as long as you tell your whore-client what'll happen to her if we don't get our property back. And I'm not a comedian, Mr whoever-you-are, and this gun I'm holding is not a joke.'

After he'd finished speaking, Adams paused for a moment, then held out the snub-nose for Fraze to take from him. In the brief moment it took to complete the action, Jarret made out the interlocking circles of a logo and the word AirLite on the side of the gun. Comforting, to anyone about to die, that the manufacturer had made the product so instantly recognisable.

The gun, which Fraze now held pointing into his face, had a rubber grip. It was curious how the closer he came to death the starker his perception was becoming, and the slower the passing of time. He remained too dazed to comprehend all Adams had been saying and that, coupled with the nearness of death, made him reckless.

'What's the rubber handle for, Adams? You going scuba diving or are you just incontinent?'

'You're the one who should be pissing himself. Take the jerk back to his car and get him out of here. And no more of the grievous bodily – that's an order. I'd twist his bollocks off myself, but I think he's probably hurting enough for one day. Anyway, our Mr Schizo has got a message to deliver.'

'Tell me what she's got that belongs to you?'

'That's none of your business. Just deliver the message, otherwise this is going to get serious for everyone.'

'I'll think about it. What about my wallet?'

'The loser wants his wallet. Well, I'm not going to get it for you, and I don't think Fraze is going to get it for you, so you're going to have to dive in and get it for yourself.'

But before Jarret could move, the sole of a foot against his ribcage decided for him and he hit the water crabbing sideways. As he gasped for breath, the chemical cocktail of pool water scoured the back of his throat and nose. It took him three dives before he could locate his wallet, but at least it temporarily blocked out the sound of laughter. He swam back to the shallow end, away from where the two men stood laughing, and heaved himself dripping onto the poolside. He started to walk towards the gap between the conifers and the end of the barn.

'Hey, Fraze, why don't you give the man a helping hand.'

The walk back along the side of the house seemed a long one. His shoes squelched, his jeans were heavy and uncomfortable and his polo shirt clung uncomfortably to the contours of his bruised body. He'd emptied the water from the wallet and carried it in his hand as it was too wet to put away. Fraze pushed him in the back with the revolver to make him move faster, but his aching body and uncertain balance made that difficult. Then he heard Fraze say something to him and begin to laugh, but he no longer listened – he was too defeated for that. The only sound that reached him was the flip-flop, flip-flop of Fraze's pool shoes, and that annoyed him.

When they got to the car, Jarret turned to face his scantily clad escort. He fully expected Fraze to deliver a farewell punch or a crack across the face with the gun. He'd put money on the psycho being unable to resist it. He thought he'd make it easy for him; the sooner he got it over with, the sooner he could be out of there.

But he was wrong. Adams was the boss. And Fraze followed orders.

'Get in the car and next time send the bitch; she's tougher than you are ...'

And he laughed at the image it conjured.

'... and much more fun.'

Jarret no longer had the strength to react; the last thing he needed now was to be provocative. As he climbed up into the Jeep, it was still with the anticipation of a crack across the skull. Instead, he was startled by a shrill cry from overhead. He looked up and saw two buzzards slowly, serenely spiralling against the perfect azure of the sky. Kings of the wild countryside locked in their moveless motion.

Not until the Jeep's engine had exploded into life and he was steering across the grey gravel car park towards the road, did he start to feel secure. He accelerated and watched the rear-view mirror as Fraze receded into the distance, waving the revolver in farewell, an extravagant grin distorting his handsome face.4 (Thursday pm)

When Jarret returned to Le Papillon, there was no sign

of Alicia. But that didn't bother him. His clothes were still damp and reeked of chlorine. He didn't call out to her. He was humiliated at the beating Fraze had given him and the fact he'd returned to the house empty-handed, without either her suitcase or the box of wine for her father. But despite being clammy and uncomfortable, he decided not to get changed in case she was asleep and his moving around upstairs disturbed her. She'd looked exhausted when he left. Anyway, the time to admit his failure would arrive soon enough without him hurrying it.

He eased himself into a chair at the kitchen table. In front of him were the gourds he'd placed there before lunch. Absently he began to sort them. Not really intending to do anything with them, just to avoid thinking about what he was going to do next.

As he fingered one of the bottle gourds, he could hear Yvette's, his neighbour's, voice urging him to make some of them into nesting boxes to hang on the outside of his house. Several times she'd explained the design to him. Simple enough. But would he ever do it? He doubted it.

Dismissing Yvette's urging from his mind, he rose painfully from his chair and collected an armful of the gourds. He didn't want to have to look at them any more: they reminded him of a pleasanter time. Opening the cupboard under the sink, he piled them untidily inside. Out of sight, out of mind. He'd decide what to do with them later. Each time he bent down with another armful, the chlorine stink from his clothes reminded him of his miserable afternoon.

As he finished putting away the last few and was closing the door quickly before they all fell out, he heard a faint noise behind him. Immediately, his heart began to race. His first thought was that Adams had followed him home. Instinctively, with fists clenched, he spun around. A dark silhouette stood motionless in the doorway.

After a moment's silence, Alicia spoke.

'What the hell happened to you?'

How long she had been standing there watching him, he didn't know. But at the sight of her, he suddenly felt a weariness descend. The thought of the opened bottle of rosé still in the refrigerator became almost more than he could stand.

'I'm so sorry. I should never have got you involved in this. Forget my suitcase. Just hide me here for a while. I'll still pay you.'

But he didn't find the thought of letting her down appealing. This time he looked at her when he spoke.

'You'll get your suitcase back, don't worry. There are other ways to get into the Manoir Ivant.'

'Look at your face. Look what they did to you!'

He placed a palm against the left side of his jaw. It felt cut and swollen and growing more painful by the minute. He went to the freezer, removed one of the trays of ice cubes and emptied them into a clean tea towel, which he wrapped around them.

'I'm going to take a shower.'

'Get those wet things off and I'll put them in the washing machine for you.'

She sounded like his mother. He went upstairs to his bedroom and obediently took off his chlorine-reeking clothes and abandoned them in a pile by the bedroom door.

In the shower, he applied the ice pack to his face and then to the darkening bruises on the side and front of his body. It melted in strangely tantalising rivulets. Only when the tea towel was empty did he reach for the shower gel and start to rid himself of the stink of pool.

Forty minutes later, with hair wet and dressed in a dark blue polo shirt and a faded pair of khaki chinos, he dropped his wet clothes into the laundry basket and made his way back to the kitchen, where he'd left Alicia. The swelling on his face had gone down, though his torso was still painful.

When he re-entered the kitchen, Alicia was at the open

front door staring into the courtyard. He looked beyond her to where the angling sun highlighted the contours of the cobbles. The heat of the day had diminished, but a soft south-east breeze had kept the sky a deep Mediterranean blue. He stood quite still and watched her for a full thirty seconds, before deciding he badly needed a drink.

He spoke softly, not wanting to startle her.

'I'll put up the parasol over the table outside. Then I'll go and get us a drink.'

She turned, for a moment bewildered to see him there. Her face was shadowed with worry. She seemed confused, as if he was speaking to her in a foreign language. Then the shadow dispersed and she relaxed.

'Yeah, I'd like that. I'd like that a lot.'

'What about if I put some melon with Serrano ham and a squeeze of fresh orange, and then I could cook us a couple of tuna steaks with a green salad? Good for a warm evening and it'd help us absorb the alcohol.'

'Perfect for any evening. What do you want me to do?'

'You can set the table outside if you want to. The cutlery's over there in the drawer and the plates and glasses are in the wall cupboard above it. I'll go and put the parasol up.'

Jarret found cooking always relaxed him – chopping the food, stirring the pots, smelling the spices and herbs, sampling the dishes as they sizzled or bubbled before him. And he always enjoyed eating. Though this evening, it wasn't food he wanted but a drink.

Alicia was already beneath the parasol enjoying the coolness of the early evening shade when Jarret arrived with two plates piled high with orange-coloured melon cubes and slices of rolled Serrano ham. The breeze that rummaged through the wisteria leaves did likewise to her hair. She smiled at the sight of the food.

When Jarret returned again from the kitchen, he carried a tall green wine bottle encased in a silver cooler. Without asking, he half-filled two glasses with the pale, slightly *pétillant* wine and handed one to Alicia. They sat at opposite sides of the slatted wooden table.

'*Santé*. To a better tomorrow.'

'Why not to a better today? *Santé.*'

Relaxed by the warmth of the day and the gentle infusion of alcohol, they ate and only spoke about the food. Both were hungrier than they thought. The tuna steaks were succulent, slightly pink but not bloody, and were set off by a dribble of reduced Balsamic vinegar. They digested easily. Dessert was the offerings from the fruit bowl – peaches, apricots and a sprinkling of last year's walnuts that had fallen from the tree in the courtyard.

Alicia selected a peach and sliced carefully through its downy outer skin and yellow flesh. The fruit she halved, quartered, then cut finally into eighths. Her meticulousness and concentration amused Jarret. Until he realised her actions were not the result of concentration at all. They were automatic. That the shadow had returned and, for the present, he'd lost her again.

Worry disfigured the smoothness of her brow. He shifted uncomfortably on his wooden chair, making it creak, before taking a long sip of his wine. Tomorrow, he would definitely recover her suitcase from the *manoir*. But, for now, he needed to recover Alicia.

'Coffee?'

The switch was flicked again. And her brow cleared.

'That would be nice.'

'Sugar? Milk?'

'Neither.'

The machine in the kitchen bubbled and hissed and, before long, he returned carrying two ebony-coloured espressos. The white china cups and the steaming dark liquid they contained were like the contrast of good and evil. On the tray beside the coffees was a bottle of fifteen-year-old calvados and two glasses. When he'd given up drinking, he'd secreted the key to the drinks cabinet away at the back of a kitchen drawer and tried to forget it.

Tonight, he wasn't bothering any more.

He uncorked the bottle and poured out two glasses. Though with his body unused to alcohol, he'd probably already drunk enough. He allowed the dark flavours to play over his tongue and to loosen it. He hoped it would do the same to her. There were things he still wanted to find out.

'If you don't want to answer any questions, that's fine with me. But the more you can tell me, before going back for your suitcase tomorrow, the more I can tell what I'm up against.'

'I'm sorry. I shouldn't have kept anything from you. It was difficult for me to talk about it, that's all. If it doesn't sound corny, I already feel safer knowing that you're around. But listen, you really don't have to go back tomorrow. Not just for my sake. ... Now ask me what you want to know.'

To Jarret, that 'not just for my sake' was like asking a suicide bomber not to detonate. The calvados had aroused a false bravery. A fact he would wake in the morning to regret.

'I am doing this for you, but it's not just for you any more; after this afternoon, it's become more personal.'

She'd mentioned being corny: that was being corny. Movie talk. He knew it as soon as the words had left his mouth. Nothing but swagger. He poured himself another calvados and prayed that she didn't see him for the idiot he felt.

But rather than seeming to notice, she played along with it.

'I don't want you to get into trouble because of me.'

The second time he resisted the bait.

'The sub-species at the *manoir* – what were you doing staying with them in the first place?'

'How far do you want me to go back?'

41

'Wherever you think it begins. Unless you've had enough for this evening.'

'I suppose it started for me over a year ago. ... Are you sure you want to hear this?'

Of course he was sure. He wanted to know everything about her.

'It's a long time till it gets dark. And if you're getting thirsty, there's plenty to drink.'

'Once I had a sister called Amelia. She wasn't exactly a twin, but as close to being a twin as two children can get and not be twins. Little more than nine months separated us. As sisters we were close, but also as friends. We grew up doing everything together. We were in different classes at school, but shared a sort of telepathy that seemed somehow to keep us always connected. Of course, eventually, we left school and went our separate ways, but a day didn't pass when our mobiles weren't hot from chattering, and when we weren't talking we were texting one another. And we had no secrets – work, boyfriends, our hopes, unhappinesses. Everything. There was nothing about our lives the other one didn't know about.

'Then one day, while I was at work, I had a phone call from my mother telling me my sister was in intensive care in Lincoln. And that she was probably going to die. It was like someone had put a bomb under my little organised world. At first, the grief and fear almost paralysed me, but I managed to get into my car and drive all the way from Nottingham, where I worked, to the hospital. She was still breathing when I arrived, but in all other respects it was already too late. The person I'd known and loved all my life had been replaced by something inanimate, connected by tubes and wires to various machines.

'For the next two days, I sat with her, talking to her – as if, magically, my talking could bring her back to life.

'But she died. The respirators, the drugs, the monitoring machines – couldn't help her. And so slowly, very slowly, she wasted away and died. And do you know what, despite all the specialists and consultants and all the tests they carried out on her, no-one could tell us what she had died of.

'After that, I stopped eating, sleeping, not wanting to meet anyone or go anywhere. I stopped living, really. Only a superhuman effort on the part of my parents made me attend the funeral. Straight after, I went back to my apartment and locked myself inside. The grief was too much for me. I became inconsolable. It seemed like all the happiness I'd ever had in my life had been taken from me. It consumed me like a type of madness. Eventually, my father got a locksmith to open my apartment door. Then I was taken away to private clinic in the hope that I'd be cured.

'This was in September last year. When slowly, day-by-day, I began to rebuild the life which had effectively stopped with the death of my sister. And somehow, with a lot of help, I managed it, though at times it's still difficult not to feel incomplete. When I was thought well enough to leave the clinic, I emerged to find my apartment rented to someone else, my lease car repossessed and my job with a small public relations company gone. The firm where I worked had offered me a little severance money and my parents, acting under power of attorney, had accepted it. Apart from my sister, that job had been my life. So I was forced to go back and live at home.

'And now all this at the *manoir* happens to me.'

She looked down and away from him, her hair obscuring her face. He understood what she must be feeling.

'You've been through a lot. I'm so sorry. Maybe now I can understand why you didn't need the gendarmes. But why did you come to France?'

She didn't answer right away. Perhaps it was unfeeling of him to ask such a question. If he hadn't been drinking, he probably wouldn't have. Nevertheless, after a short time, she turned back to him to answer. Though she no longer looked him in the eye.

'My parents. ... It was supposed to be part of my recovery. They thought it would do me good to get away for a while. My father's ex-work colleague had a son who owned a big house in Aveyron. It was rural and quiet and a perfect place, my father thought, to send me on a short vacation. He had no way of knowing what it would lead to.

'Also, it's been partly my fault. I didn't want my father to tell anyone about my breakdown. I wanted to be treated like a normal person again and not an invalid. And bless him, he did what I said. Whether it would have made any difference to the way those bastards treated me ... I don't know.'

Here Alicia paused again. Her eyes defocused and she peered again into the deep, dark space that had been hollowed out inside her. But there was no cure in darkness, no resolution – Jarret understood that from experience.

'None of it was your fault; they're just criminals. You were the innocent one. They took advantage of you. Talk to me, if you want to.'

He hoped his voice sounded caring, not like that of a sick pervert. The spectre of Adams's snub-nosed pistol flashed before him – you might resist a civilised man, but you didn't resist the drugs or the violence. She mustn't feel ashamed.

'If you don't want to – that's okay too.'

Her eyes clicked into focus. But they were wilder, more evasive, as she confronted another new set of demons. Then slowly, quietly, almost in a trance, she told him the story. Lowering her head, so that her face was partly hidden by her hair to obscure whatever traces of shame or emotion. There was no hint of tears. No halt to the flow – just the sound of her voice, automaton, toneless, as it progressed through the details.

She finished as abruptly as she began, and a silence

followed as she waited for Jarret to react. But he was unable to. He was shocked. His confrontation with Fraze and Adams suddenly was nothing compared with what Alicia had been through. She raised her head, revealing her face again, and looked at him. The expression in her eyes possessed a hint of fear. As if what she'd told him had pushed him away.

His head swam with anger and alcohol. And, in his confusion, words of consolation escaped him.

When she spoke, she spoke softly, but what she said was like a challenge to him.

'Do you know enough yet?'

Again he was unable to answer.

Her body bent closer and her eyes penetrated into his eyes.

'Well?'

The precision and matter-of-fact manner in which she'd described her assault had left him confused. He was not good in situations like this. Expressions of sympathy never tripped easily off his tongue. When he spoke, it was only to prevent a curtain of silence closing between them.

'Do you know anything more about these animals?'

A pause.

'Nothing.'

'You said Adams was your father's friend's son. What business is he in?'

'I told you, I'd never met him before. Neither he nor the blond one told me anything about themselves. I only know what I told you.'

Once again Jarret struggled for words. He wanted to comfort her and show he cared. Her eyes were willing him.

'I don't know much about date-rape drugs – but it seems unlikely they spiked your drinks with Rohypnol or GHB, because if they had you'd probably have some sort of amnesia. Your recall seems too clear for that.'

'What?'

'So Adams must've got his hands on something else – the perverted, calculating bastard.'

And that was it. Suddenly, any distance that existed between her words and the event she was describing disappeared. Her emotions crashed like a dynamited building – their chaos and complexity distorting the smooth perfection of her face. Her body heaved and tears squeezed between the shut lids of her eyes. And, as in the supermarket car park, when they'd met all those light years ago that morning, she became hunched and defensive.

Though he still had no easy words of consolation, Jarret knew he'd been an idiot.

Unsure what her response might be, he rose to his feet and moved slowly round to Alicia's side of the table. Gently, he placed a hand tentatively on her shoulder, ready to withdraw it again, in an instant, should she react. But she didn't. Instead, she permitted it to remain there – a small and way-too-late gesture of consolation.

For several moments neither of them moved, until Alicia reached up and placed her left hand on top of his. And, in the eternity it took her to stop crying, he remained standing there like a statue.

5 (Friday am)

It was difficult to know whether Jarret liked himself after what had occurred. There was a fuzzy feeling in his head from the previous evening's alcohol that he was no longer used to it. As he made his way downstairs, any lingering euphoria he feared would soon be replaced by loathing and disgust. He might feel now as if he owned the world, but part of him already knew he should be carrying out its garbage. Or down on his hands and knees trying to scrub it clean.

In the kitchen, he moved like a bad TV extra, going through the motions of preparing the table for breakfast. Alicia had been sleeping deeply when he left her, curled on her left side, foetal, unmoving. The indents in her naked back had looked like contours on the map of paradise. Quietly taking his clothes from the bedroom floor, he'd slipped away and left her to her oblivion.

Outside, it was another perfect, cloudless summer day. The sun was bright but, as it was only shortly after seven, the air had not yet warmed. At four hundred or so metres above sea level, it was one of the benefits – a person was able to breathe, even in the hottest weather.

On his drive to the *boulangerie* in Solac, the light was rich with contradictions – opaque and transparent – an unfolding landscape of valleys veiled in mist and trees that cast long shadows beneath a limitless sky.

A bell sounded as he entered the little shop, but nobody came immediately to serve him. When at last he did, the baker offered no intelligible greeting; merely grunting, as he took the money for the croissants and the bread. It was too early to be sociable. Outside, the village looked as if it was posing for a travel brochure that'd never be printed. The church, the chateau and the grey stone walls emanated the illusion that time stood still.

The oven was already warm when he returned to the house. He removed the croissants from the bag and put them on a plate ready to go inside. Then, messily, he cut the baguette into thick slices. The butter and the homemade jam were already on the table. Everything, under the circumstances, he could think of to prepare a perfect breakfast was done. All he could do now was to sit and wait. A dark aroma of coffee reached him from the filter machine. He watched as the kitchen clock began to count the minutes.

#

The previous evening, Jarret had double-locked the doors and secured both the downstairs and upstairs shutters against intruders. Something he'd never normally have dreamed of doing. Alicia had remained in the kitchen, sitting at the table, waiting for him. It surprised him that, after her ordeal, she didn't want to go straight up to her room and lose herself in sleep.

So he suggested a nightcap, one for the road, before they turned in for the night. He asked her if she preferred to remain in the kitchen or go into the lounge and listen to some music. It might relax her and help her cope.

But depending on the viewpoint of the person on whom he was inflicting it, Jarret's taste in music was either erratic or eclectic. Jazz, classical, world, a smattering of pop and an unaccountable and, in most people's eyes, unforgivable addiction to Dylan. Once they'd settled in the lounge, he scrolled through his iPod and plumped for Bill Evans's 'Re:

Person I Knew', an intimate, musing, live performance, a perfect way to fade out the evening.

Alicia sank comfortably into a leather settee in the middle of the room, facing the wood-burning stove. She'd left plenty of room, but Jarret declined to sit next to her. Instead, he selected an armchair in the corner near the window, next to the stereo – a deliberate distance away from her. He'd made half a cafétiere of coffee, but when he offered her some she declined. Said she preferred his idea of the calvados. He poured two measures into brandy glasses and gave her the smallest.

The Bill Evans's concert mused its intimate spiral through the room – Eddie Gomez's bass and Marty Morrell's drumming complementing the main man's introspection. Slowly, they drifted with the music, staring into the bottoms of their brandy glasses as if, any minute, like crystal balls they'd disclose their secrets.

When the CD ended, he reached again for the iPod and scrolled again through the albums until he found Thelonius Monk's 'Alone in San Francisco'. Music that was again musing, solitary. But after only a few bars, he found it wasn't working for him. It was too discordant, too jolting, too unsettling. He sat upright in his chair and downed the calvados. He thought about seeking out another piece of music with which to end the evening. Miles Davis's 'Love Songs' maybe? But he spoke instead.

'Maybe it'd be a good idea if we got some sleep soon? It's going to be a busy day tomorrow.'

She nodded, as if in agreement, but she didn't reply.

'You'll find some of my ex-partner's clothes and things in the cupboard on the landing. Just help yourself to whatever you want. She had good taste. You might even find a nightdress there.'

'I don't feel sleepy.'

'It's been a long day and a rough one.'

'How about a refill? Perhaps that'll help me to sleep.'

49

It certainly hadn't been Jarret's intention to offer her any more to drink, largely because he knew he'd join her. And he wanted to get his head clear for the morning. Adams and his friend already held an advantage over him. He didn't want to get so befuddled that he became an even bigger pushover. On top of that, he was beginning to feel uncomfortable alone in the room with Alicia. He was unable to pinpoint quite why. He just was.

As he refilled their two glasses with calvados, he told himself they were to be the last, no matter what. A large part of the day had been beyond his control; he didn't need the evening to go the same way.

Despite the alcohol, the pain from his visit to the *manoir* and a growing fatigue made his body yearn for the comfort of his bed. But it wasn't right to leave Alicia alone. An echo of his mother's words when he was a boy sprang to mind – 'don't worry, it'll be alright in the morning'. She'd used them whenever he was upset or ill. They were a mantra, which she applied like a balm. He had the urge to do the same for Alicia. But things seldom improved by the morning, as he knew only too well, so he kept his mouth shut.

Sitting down was causing the muscles in his side to stiffen and he shifted uncomfortably in his chair. He took an ameliorating mouthful of calvados before returning his attention to Alicia, only to discover she was already staring at him. Her expression was one of concern and it worried Jarret that he might have no alternative but to sit up all night with her, when what he craved most was to rest.

But he was wrong. The concern was for him.

'You're still hurting.'

'Not really.'

'I can tell you are by the way you're moving.'

'It could have been worse.'

'But it was worse than you made out, wasn't it?'

'As worse goes – it was moderate. He could've shot me.'

'Why? What do you mean?'

As soon as the words escaped, he knew he should've kept his mouth shut. Or pretended they were meant as a joke. But he was tired and his head felt light and he could think of nothing to say, so he said nothing. But at the mention of a firearm, she'd tensed and a look of fear spread across her face. When she spoke, at last, she sounded different, urgent.

'What do you mean? He had a gun?'

If his brain hadn't buckled under him, he might have talked her out of it. But it was too late to lie. He tried a sort of jokey bravado.

'Adams had a small handgun. If he hadn't, he might've been pulling Fraze out of the pool's filter system by now.'

But it didn't make her laugh.

'Jesus!'

'They may be a pair of perverts, but I don't think they're psychos. Tomorrow, I'll just be more careful.'

'Jesus Christ! What have I got us into?'

'Hey, come on. You've got us into nothing, so there's absolutely nothing to blame yourself for. This is only because of what those deviants did to you. If I'd had my way, they'd be locked up by now. Tomorrow, I'll collect your suitcase and then it'll be all over. I promise. They won't even know I've been there until it's too late. After that you're welcome to stay in Le Papillon as long as you like. And when you want to leave, I'll make sure you get to wherever you're going. I promise that too. So don't worry, everything's going to turn out okay.'

'I can't let you take any more risks for me.'

'That's my choice. There's nothing for you to worry about.'

'But if anything happens to you …'

'It won't. They won't be expecting me to return. There were no security cameras when I looked around yesterday, which means their system is probably linked to a sound alarm. If it's a hot day like today, they'll have the windows open, so the only thing I'll have to think about is which one to climb through. So don't worry, I won't be knocking on anyone's front door.'

'I'm scared.'

'Don't be. When you get your suitcase back, you'll be free to do what you like.'

'What if they find out who you are and come looking for you?'

She'd pinpointed the weakness in their situation, especially as Adams had kept his business card. But his business card only had his business address on it, and that was in Villefranche. Jarret wasn't going to tell her about it. She was worried enough as it was.

'They won't find you here. I guarantee you that.'

It was a lie. In fact, with little research Adams could find Le Papillon any time he liked. But why would he bother? The suitcase didn't even belong to him. Anyway, he'd be better off keeping his distance from Alicia because, if she chose to go to the police, he'd be in a lot of trouble. And why would he want to come looking for that?

Only then did he remember what Adams had said about her taking something that belonged to him.

'It's only your case and wine you want me to collect for you, isn't it?'

'Yes. Why?'

'Just that Adams said you had something of his that he wanted back and that you were to return to him personally. But that would be clearly out of the question.'

'Why would he say that? He's lying. The only thing I got from him was something I didn't ask for.'

'I'm sorry. He's probably just trying to ensure that you'll keep your mouth shut. If he saw you again, he'd almost certainly threaten you. But don't worry, he won't get near you.'

'I'd like to believe that's true.'

'You're safe here. If it makes you feel better, I've got a hunting gun locked away in a cupboard. I can load it and take it upstairs with me tonight. No-one could break into this house without me hearing them. With all the shutters closed, this place is a virtual fortress.'

'Come over and sit by me. I need to feel somebody close, somebody I can trust.'

But Jarret didn't comply with her request. It'd come out of the blue. But it was an offer best declined. In the silence that followed, he felt strangely paralysed – suspended midway between decency and desire.

'Perhaps that wouldn't be a very good idea.'

'Now who's worrying? I'm not going to bite you.'

Then a dark instinct stirred and he gingerly raised himself from his chair and crossed to the settee. He sat at the opposite end of it from Alicia and looked away. Suddenly, the discomfort he was experiencing wasn't only physical. Two angels were wrestling inside him and he knew that as long as there remained a distance between them, the good one would win.

Only, Alicia rose from her end of the settee and came and sat beside him. She inclined her body against him, like a child, resting her head on his chest, her blonde hair cascading down the front of his shirt. Again he experienced discomfort. But this time physically, and he shifted slightly away, more to move her weight off his damaged ribcage than because he didn't want to be near her.

'I'm hurting you.'

'My ribs are a little tender, that's all.'

'I should move.

'No, I'm okay.'

And discomfort became replaced by another sensation. He freed his arm and placed it around her, pulling her gently back towards him until he could feel the warmth of her body merge fully with his. It wouldn't have surprised him if she'd struggled free and asked him what he thought he was doing. But she did neither.

The good angel inside him was telling him to stop before it was too late. That what had happened to her had damaged her enough already. That he should take control of both himself and the situation and not be taking advantage of someone's emotional chaos. But reaching out, she ran a finger across his chest, above the sternum, then let it slide downwards until it rested upon his stomach. He winced with pleasure.

Tilting his head downwards, he looked at her. But there was no way of knowing what she was really thinking. If her intentions were innocent, then why did they feel so dangerous? What exactly was she looking for from him? Then, as if intuiting his confusion, she swivelled in his loose embrace and looked directly up into his eyes. And for the first time since they'd met, he noticed that her hazel pupils were softened at the edges by a tinge of green.

When he lowered his face towards her, she was already pouting in anticipation of their intimacy. Still, the voice in his head urged him to stop – he was there to protect her, not to exploit her. But as his face drew closer to her full red lips, he knew the outcome would be different. As they kissed, her hair brushed his cheek and he breathed in its freshly washed warmth.

Their kiss, at first soft and tender, became long and intense.

Her T-shirt pulled easily over her head, exposing her perfect coffee pale suntan. Her slim, ribbed body and smoothness of skin made him salivate at the same time as his mouth tasted dry. For a moment she held herself away from him, allowing him to absorb her unblemished perfection. She knew she was beautiful. It was written in her face, in the loosely held jaw, the slight purse of the lips. The eyes.

Tugging at the shoulders of his blue polo shirt, she helped him as he slipped out of it. Torso to naked torso, they re-embraced – her smoothness and softness against his toughened body with its muscle and knots of dark hair. Her Beauty to his Beast.

Soon, the remainder of their clothing spread like litter across the floor – the deep cushions of the settee absorbing the changing rhythms of their lovemaking. They grappled towards climax like combatants. Then began the slow dissolve into afterglow. The silence. The realisation of what they'd done.

Later, in the bedroom, she ran a finger over his bruises and then gently brushed kisses against each of them. 'Kissing them better', as his mother would have said. And with each kiss he felt more the hero and entirely hers to command. As they'd mounted the stairs, Jarret had thought briefly about collecting the shotgun from the cupboard, but with Alicia holding his hand, he felt indestructible.

She was the most beautiful, most perfect woman he'd ever seen. Her only blemish was a dark tattoo on the smooth round of her right buttock, where the soft flesh merged with the small of her back. Two distinct letters, from an alphabet he'd never seen before, like runic symbols, inscribed in the blackest of inks. But he kissed their cruel defacement anyway and told her he thought it pretty. If it was meant to distract attention away from some other imperfection, he couldn't make one out. Except for the tiniest birthmark on the velvet flesh of her inner thigh – a scarlet pattern in the shape of a small animal. A blemish so natural it made the tattoo seem more ugly.

He didn't mean to think about it, but, close as they were, it was difficult not to notice that Adams and Fraze hadn't damaged her body in the way they had his. He was grateful, but his hatred of them was in no way diminished. The damage to her, for all its lack of outward signs, had been just as real.

\#

A loud hammering on the front door exploded Jarret's delicate but uneasy calm. Opening it cautiously, he was dismayed to find his neighbour, Didier, standing there with a larger-than-life smile revealing a mouthful of perfect but discoloured teeth. Though it was early, he was full of energy. He'd come to announce that that morning he'd slaughtered a suckling pig, almost certainly illegally, and that he and Yvette would like to share it with him. How would seven o'clock suit Jarret?

Didier's shrill voice penetrated the morning. Normally, the way his Aveyron accent mangled the French that Jarret had learned at school acted as a breath of fresh air. But in a world turned crazy, this sudden injection of normality only added to his insecurity. He liked dining with Didier and Yvette. She was an excellent cook with a head full of her mother's and grandmother's recipes, and Didier produced some of the best meat and vegetables Jarret had ever tasted. Also, he enjoyed their company. But the cold light of morning left him with no alternative but to decline.

'I'm sorry, I can't make it this evening.'

There followed a silence, in which it was obvious that Jarret's refusal had taken Didier by surprise. The expression on his face changed and he pretended to be hurt. He awaited an explanation. So Jarret felt that he had to lie and told him he was very busy, that at the moment he had a lot of clients, and that there was something he needed urgently to finish by tomorrow. Jarret had never before declined one of his invitations.

But Didier's intuition told him that something else was going on. That something at Le Papillon was not as it should be. He looked closely at Jarret to see if his friend was feeling well. Then past him into the kitchen, where the answer instantly revealed itself – a breakfast table set for two. The smile returned and he nodded slowly.

'Ah, I understand. Urgent work. You don't have to lie to Didier. I know when a man has better things to do. Now

I understand what happened to your face. Must be quite a woman. Next time, eh?'

'Next time.'

'And did you like those gourds I left for you? Very good, eh?'

'Impressive. You must teach me how to grow them some time.'

'I will, but yours will never be as big as mine, my friend.'

He began laughing as if at a very funny joke. Then a look of mock concern spread across his face.

'What's wrong, my friend? She can't be that ugly. Though sometimes the next morning you never know. C'mon, things can't be that bad.'

But Jarret lacked the willpower to tell him that they were worse, and probably about to worsen. For as they were speaking, he was almost certain he heard the faint sounds of Alicia's footsteps crossing the landing.

Right away, he experienced a sense of panic and started to close the front door. He offered Didier no word of goodbye. Then he remembered something and opened it again.

'Any chance I could borrow your van for a few hours around lunchtime?'

'More urgent business, eh? You know where it's kept. The keys'll be in it – come over for it when you like. And, Jarret ... when are you going to introduce me to this lady?'

Jarret knew that he wouldn't cross-question him as to why he wanted the van. Other people's business was other people's business as far as Didier was concerned. But the 'lady', that was another matter.

'Some time, if you're good.'

Another lie. And he slammed the door.

6 (Friday am/pm)

It was just before noon and the sun was exactly as he hoped it would be – hot, unimpeded and bleaching. The road lay before him like a river of mercury, punctuated by intensities of shadow. The stretches where there were no trees sounded like the old Renault van was being driven through water, its tyres leaving parallel dark wounds across the soft surfaces, splashing through tarmac that clung to the vehicle's underside.

Only the day before, Jarret had driven away from the Manoir Ivant, beaten and defeated. Now, he had another plan.

He stopped at a secluded parking place beneath the shade of a small copse, about a kilometre from the *manoir*. Before leaving, he'd carefully studied a *Carte Bleue* that mapped out the area in precise detail. From it he worked out a cross-country route he would take, using side-tracks and fields, which he estimated should take him no more than half an hour on foot. It would be quicker to follow the road, but surprise and safety depended on him remaining out of sight.

After checking the ground under the trees was hard enough to support the weight of the van, he steered it carefully up a small incline, at the side of the lay-by, and into the camouflaging shade of the copse. The wet spring and early summer had contributed to the density of the leaf canopy.

Wearing sunglasses and an old baseball cap for

protection, Jarret headed east along a dirt and stone track. In the midday sun, his shadow barely registered on the ground behind him. After walking a couple of hundred metres, he turned left onto a narrower track, where grass and weeds grew between ruts left by tractor tyres. He followed its gentle curve round the barbed-wire edge of a stubbled cornfield. The pace at which he moved, it'd be some time before he reached the *manoir*.

After several minutes, he came across a crumbling building, which might've once been a barn. Part of its roof had caved in and its grey stone walls were beginning to tumble into the neighbouring field. If he needed to stash the suitcase anywhere on his way back, this would be a suitable place to do it. But in case of trouble, he'd look for others.

The baseball cap was hot and made his head itch, and against his forehead already felt damp. Trixie had bought it for him before she'd left. Originally cream and with a NY logo on the front, he'd found it useful, but he'd never like it. Over time, it'd become soiled and dirty and the peak bore the marks of two oily fingerprints. As he walked, he raised the cap using a thumb and the same two fingers to allow his scalp to breathe.

It was a stupid time of day to be doing anything physical – a stupid time of year. Soon the workforce of Aveyron, indeed the whole of France, would be on their holidays, their *congé annuel*. Farmers would still be working, but not at that time of day, and certainly not at noon. But it was this precise stupidity that Jarret was counting on to get him in and out of the *manoir* without being seen. Adams and Fraze would be no exception, about to enjoy a leisurely lunch and sheltering from the sun. And the same went for anyone working for them.

At the end of the cornfield, the track T-junctioned and he turned right. After a short distance, he came across a wooden farm gate that opened into a large field of well-cropped pasture. Once through the gate, he headed for the shelter of a tall hedgerow. The field was strung out asymmetrically along the side of a fairly steep hill. At the top, if his calculations were right, he would see the *manoir*.

#

When Alicia had entered the kitchen that morning, he'd no idea what to expect. But a heavy foreboding told him to fear the worst: that he was about to come face to face with yet another of his never-ending errors of judgement. He never learnt.

He stood with the kitchen table between himself and the doorway through which Alicia was about to enter.

But it was as if the sun had risen for a second time that morning – a brighter and a more warming one than illuminated the courtyard outside. As she walked towards him, wearing one of Trixie's T-shirts, she was smiling. Not like Didier had smiled, all teeth and mockery, but in a way that released something inside him. Then it disappeared. It was what he'd been dreading. A creased brow replaced the brilliant white smile, but then she began to laugh at him. In the way that Didier had laughed at him.

'Hey, it's all right. Don't look so gloomy.'

Moving close, she took his head in her hands and kissed him lingeringly on the lips. The smell of her perfume, which had once belonged to Trixie, intoxicated him in a way it'd never done with his ex. And all thoughts of breakfast left him.

'It's okay. No regrets. I enjoyed myself last night. By the expression on your face, a whole lot more than you did.'

But as he reached out to take hold of her, she evaded him.

'What's for breakfast? After last night, I'm starving.'

'The coffee's ready. I'll put the croissants in to warm.'

'Warm croissants, sounds like heaven. Why does anyone ever eat them cold?'

As soon as they'd crisped, he plated them and placed them in front of her. Immediately, she took one and bit into the crisped, flaky dough. He looked on and sipped his coffee as, before long, Alicia took a second croissant and spooned strawberry jam on to the plate beside it. She certainly didn't lack an appetite.

He told her about Didier's visit and about what good friends and neighbours Didier and Yvette had become. But he waited until Alicia had finished eating before becoming more serious.

'Alicia … I only know you by your first name. Despite last night, we've got a business relationship. Right?'

'Despite last night!'

'What I mean is … we're friends and … we're also business partners. And I don't know who you are."

Briefly, her head rocked back with laughter, but when she spoke she was angry.

'Yeah, yeah. … You think I've not got any money to give you. Don't worry, I'll pay you in cash, not freebies.'

He felt the rebuke like a smack across the face. Money wasn't the first thing on his mind where Alicia was concerned. He'd expressed himself badly. She'd misunderstood what he was trying to say. To retrieve the situation, he backtracked.

'It's because your name'll be on your suitcase. It'd help if I knew what it is.'

The anger evaporated. It was cruel of him. Nevertheless, she took her time to reply, as if needing to consider her response. But that was absurd because one's name flows easily off one's tongue. He attributed it to the fact that he must have embarrassed her.

'Taylor. Alicia Jennifer Taylor. My father's English, my mother's French. But you won't find my name on the case. I don't think there was a label on it.'

She sounded defensive. But, for that moment, Jarret was unaware of externals. He was pleased knowing just that little bit more about her. And the French mother – that accounted for the hint of an accent in Alicia's voice that he couldn't quite place.

He returned to the subject of the *manoir* as if he'd never left it.

'The label won't matter. If it's still in the room where you left it, I'll collect it for you, no problem. But I need you to clarify one or two things for me before I set off.'

He asked where her room had been situated in the *manoir*, for a description of her suitcase. The rest he'd have to improvise when he got there. He told her also that he would leave before midday. Just thinking about what had to be done made him impatient to get it over with. It would take him a little time to walk to Didier's. And then the van he was borrowing wasn't the fastest thing on four wheels.

'Forget the breakfast things and keep yourself out of sight while I'm gone. I'll get back here as quickly as I can.'

'Just be careful; you know you don't have to do this.'

'I know.'

The air outside was heating up by the minute. He was halfway across the courtyard when Alicia's voice called out behind him.

'Just one more thing.'

'What is it?'

'You will try and bring my father's wine back? You were serious?'

'I'll do my best.'

'It'll make him … me very happy.'

He left the courtyard behind him and began to climb the path that led to Didier's. He'd bring her back the head of the Medusa if she'd asked him to.

#

From the crest of the hill, he could see the buckled and sloping grey roofs of the buildings that comprised the Manoir Ivant. From what Jarret recalled of its layout, he was approaching it from the back; he could just make out the bright red pan tiles on the pool house. To avoid the pool itself and the gable end of the converted barn, he must now veer more to the north than he anticipated.

As he descended the hill, the walking became easier. But now, in open ground, he moved more quickly until he reached a small copse at the bottom of the slope, a hundred metres or so from the south-west corner of the *manoir*. Out of breath, the cool shade of the leaves offered a welcome respite.

Once he'd cooled sufficiently, he made his way down the remaining slope towards the final field leading to the steeply banked artificial plateau on which the swimming pool had been dug. He moved quickly until he reached the part of the bank, at the back of the *manoir*, closest to the path he'd taken the day before. He lay panting in the weeds and long grass for a full minute before moving again.

At the top of the bank, he wormed his way beneath the simple three-stranded wire fence and, on hands and knees, crawled towards the conifer hedge that grew beside the swimming pool. Taking great care, he parted the branches and revealed a partial view of what lay beyond. Adams and Fraze were sitting at a circular wooden table, beneath a brightly coloured, fringed parasol. Their bodies shone from a fresh application of sun oil. Two bottles were on the table in front of them – one of red wine and the other, which had once contained Champagne, now turned upside down in an ice bucket. On the table, beside the two bottles, were a bowl of salad, an oval platter of cheese and a basket of bread. The scenario was almost better than Jarret could've wished. Alcohol had already dulled their senses.

Jarret slid back down the bank and made his way towards the side of the house, before having to squeeze through the mixed quince and hazel hedge that now blocked his path. In the shade of the granite-walled barn, he stopped and listened. With the intermittent sounds of birdsong and cicada came the drawling conversation of the diners and the occasional clinking of their plates and glasses.

As the day before, the shutters and windows along the side of the barn were all opened wide. Jarret selected one three from the corner, which was nearest the swimming pool. A stone jutting from the wall beneath it made it easier to access. Grabbing hold of the bottom of the oak-wood frame, he pulled himself up. Perched on the stone sill, he removed his baseball hat and sunglasses.

A cautious look at the dim interior revealed the room was unoccupied. Taking care not to make any noise, he lowered himself onto a well-polished wooden floor. Dust mingled with the smell of polish. In the silence that followed his entry, he became aware for the first time that he was scared.

The room contrasted with the neglected nature of the building's exterior. Another time, Jarret would've admired it – the beautiful oak floors and doors, sandblasted chestnut beams, pointed granite walls, all minimally supplemented by a rustic, hand-crafted dressing table, chair and bed, at the foot of which stood a simple oak chest. Standing to the right of the door was a fitted cupboard and beside it an en suite bathroom. If Adams had had a hand in any of the design, then Jarret would've had to admire his taste. Not to mention the size of his wallet.

The bedroom door opened immediately onto a narrow corridor. Halfway along it a window had been built into the wall to give it extra light. But it was a meagre light swallowed by a grey shadow, which shrouded the corridor like a mist. Jarret moved cautiously along it towards the outline of a door that he anticipated led into the courtyard, at the back of the main house.

The corridor ended abruptly in a whitewashed stone wall. It would have been easier if it connected with the main house, which was where the spiral staircase to the bedrooms was to be found. Adams had paid for a careful and expensive conversion job, so why the fuck hadn't he had a door built through? He obviously didn't intend the barn to be a servants' wing. It was too expensively furnished for that. So it could only be that he wanted certain guests kept separate from the main house.

In contrast, the light outside the corridor was intense. It dazzled him – but he was impatient. He turned and closed the door quietly behind him. When he noticed the woman crossing the courtyard, it was already too late. There was no retreat.

Away from the protection of the corridor, Jarret had little choice but to remain where he was, quite still, hoping she'd pass by on the other side of the courtyard without noticing him. Although the door was not far behind, any movement ran the risk of attracting her attention. But something did. Because she suddenly halted and looked straight at him – as if he'd tuned in to some mystical wavelength emanating from her beribonned brain.

Briefly, he thought about retreating inside the barn conversion and climbing out of the window before Adams found out he'd paid a second visit. He tried a friendly wave – to reassure her that his presence in the *manoir* was no cause for alarm and that he was just as much at home as she was. But he got no response; She only remained staring at him from across the courtyard.

He couldn't delay much longer and he didn't want to call out to her. And he was still undecided what to do when she put down her basket and began to walk towards him. Without the basket, she moved more quickly, but her movements were as ungainly as before.

To move her as far as possible away from where Adams and Fraze were having lunch, Jarret began to walk slowly in the direction of the main house.

As she got closer, he made her out to be a woman in

her thirties. Her coarse blonde hair had been piled back carelessly and secured with a dark ribbon. She wore a loose, shiny orange blouse that ballooned at the cuffs and a long Indian cotton print skirt that screamed 'Hippy'. He watched her, tall and heavily built, as she trudged across the large courtyard towards him.

Jarret wondered whether this was the strange maid Alicia had spoken to him about.

Before she caught him up, he stopped and turned, and smiled at her with a confidence he didn't feel. He had to take control of the conversation.

'Can I help you?'

'Hi! Warm day. Just left Mr Adams and Fraze by the pool. Going to join them again shortly. Adams said it'd be okay to pop into the house and use the phone. Need to get some garage chap to come out and check my car over. Engine's been misfiring.'

He spoke softly, making her strain to listen to the words. Also he spoke in English, a language he hoped she wouldn't understand but would connect him in nationality to Adams. In order to hear him, she tilted her body towards him. But she looked relaxed, which was good – and obviously struggling for perspective through the haze of a thousand and one marijuana-laced nights, which was better.

'Chris didn't tell me there'd be visitors this week. I never know half of anything. There're visitors when I'm not expecting any, then visitors I'm expecting don't turn up, or turn up after I'm expecting them. You can't plan for anything here. It just does your head in.'

She spoke English, with a Birmingham accent, her voice throaty and slow.

'Quite understand. Arrived suddenly. Had the idea yesterday. Driving by – thought I'd drop in and say hello. Knew Adams, er … Chris wouldn't mind. Old friend. Known him for years.'

'Suppose I should go and look for Chris and ask him

66

what he wants me to do about it. I'm not happy. I've a lot of my own things to do this afternoon without having this to think about.'

'Absolutely no need. Probably won't be staying. Just use one of the rooms to change in, have a swim and be off again once the garage chappie's had a look at the motor. You carry on with what you're doing. Chris'll call you if he wants you for anything.'

'You sure?'

'Absolutely sure. Off before supper.'

'Then I can get on with my own stuff? Do you want my husband to take a look at your car for you?'

'Not necessary. I'm sure he's busy.'

'He's a good mechanic; he's got a real feel for it.'

'Expensive motor. Still under guarantee. Best let the garage sort it out.'

'Just thought he might be of some help. I'll be off then, Mr …?'

'Read.'

'Mr Read. D'you mind if I tell you something? I don't mean it personally.'

'No. Go ahead.'

'You don't talk like normal people.'

'Thanks.'

'No, I don't mean it like …'

'I know. Goodbye, er ...?'

'Florence. My friends call me Flo; whatever you prefer. And thanks for not being any hassle.'

As she turned and walked away, Jarret sought the shelter of the main house, where from a doorway downstairs he watched her as she recrossed the courtyard. He wouldn't decide what to do next until she'd picked up the basket of laundry. If she continued towards the tiny stone cottage beyond the swimming pool, fine. If she turned instead towards where Adams was having lunch, he'd have to be gone.

But she didn't head towards the pool. Good, gullible Flo. Just hoisted the laundry basket and headed for the cottage. He'd been lucky. His muddied jeans and shapeless grey T-shirt were not what someone driving an expensive car was likely to be wearing.

Built against the back wall of the main house was an impressive double stone staircase that led up from the courtyard at either side of a large door. Traditional to the region, Jarret had seen many such staircases, but never a double one. In the past, this must have been the farmhouse's main entrance, because the first floor was where the family would've lived and the ground floor was where the animals were kept. In the winter, the body heat rising from the cattle supplied a primitive and odoriferous form of under-floor heating. In the countryside, it was still not unusual for the basement to be used for keeping small animals or for storage, but in renovated houses and holiday homes, like this one, they were more likely to have been converted into living space.

But the entrance, to the left of the double staircase, in which Jarret was standing was on the ground floor. Its heavy oak door had been propped open with a giant brass candlestick that must have once adorned the altar of a church or cathedral.

Once again, in different circumstances, the room behind him would have been impressive, its opulent interior a stark contrast to the rough, uneven courtyard he'd just left behind. Four or five leather armchairs and two settees were arranged around a pair of low walnut-wood coffee tables. The flag-stoned floor looked newly laid, as recent as the four abstract paintings in chrome frames adorning two of the whitewashed walls. A standard lamp stood in one corner and overhead a chandelier of coloured glass bathed the room in curious light.

A little way to the left of the open door stood the spiral staircase that Alicia had described to him that led to the bedrooms. It creaked expensively as he climbed.

The corridor upstairs was narrow and blocked off from the rest of the house by a locked door. He climbed beyond it to the one above, where two medium-sized windows admitted just enough light for him to be able to distinguish a row of bedroom doors. Thanks to Flo, Jarret knew there were no other guests staying in the *manoir*. He ducked past one of the windows and hurried to the third bedroom, and, not having to worry about disturbing anyone, walked straight inside.

Again, the interior of the room reeked of money and, as with the other rooms he'd visited, everything about it was neatly and precisely arranged – everything, that is, apart from Alicia's clothes and suitcase. It was as if they'd been scattered by an explosion. But the explosion had been a human one – one, Jarret could see, that contained a lot of anger.

Her suitcase lay on the floor at the foot of a wooden four-poster bed. Someone had obviously taken a knife to it. The black canvas outer material had been slashed open and the pale grey and blue patterned interior lining shredded into ribbons.

He examined it before laying it on the bed in the hope that he could still make use of it.

Alicia's clothes didn't seem to have been damaged, but had been scattered around the room, each garment occupying its own space, as if for examining. Quickly, he raked the clothes crudely together in piles and started to cram them into the slashed interior of the suitcase. The lock appeared to have been unbroken and, if he fastened his leather belt around it, he felt sure it'd hold together as far as the van.

The en suite bathroom was windowless. He switched on the light and a gentle hum told him he'd also activated an extractor fan. Which was fortunate, because the smell that enveloped him on entering brought him to an abrupt halt.

Alicia's cosmetic bag had been slashed open and dumped in the toilet bowl, empty, with its lining dangling into the water. The bottles, tubes, jars and whatever else it once contained had been piled like rubbish into the washbasin, their contents emptied, squeezed or shaken to create a chemical sludge – toothpaste, perfume, dusting powder and whatever else. Filling the air with a sickly sweet stink that clung to his lungs. Part laboratory, part perfumery. Only her toothbrush and comb had been left undamaged. He snatched them up, quickly shutting the door behind him.

A new urgency now impelled him. The damage he'd witnessed was petty, but crazed. Carrying the suitcase in both arms, to avoid it breaking open, he wound his way carefully down the spiral staircase and returned to the doorway leading into the courtyard. This time he delayed, allowing time for his eyes to grow accustomed to the light outside. Then, he sought out the wall on the far side of the main house that connected it to a weatherworn, adjoining barn, which comprised the third building surrounding the open-ended courtyard. Built into the middle of the connecting wall was an arched doorway that, according to Alicia, led to garages where he'd find the box of wine she'd hidden on the night she left.

For a moment, Jarret considered leaving the suitcase behind one of the settees and collecting it on his way back. There were advantages to travelling light, but having to retrace his footsteps might not be such a clever idea. If he took the suitcase with him, however, he'd have to look for a different route out of the *manoir*.

The contrast between the sun and the blackness of the shadows seemed no less acute. He fumbled one-handed for his sunglasses. The temperature was climbing and the courtyard still deserted. Hugging the shadow, he hurried towards the arched doorway and hoped that nobody had locked it. There was no sound of voices from the direction of the pool.

On opening the arched door, Jarret checked everything on the other side was safe before going through. This was a part of the *manoir* he'd not been before.

As he approached the garage block, he saw at once that Alicia's description of it as a barn was a bit far of the mark. Although it had been constructed in traditional grey granite and with a *lauze* roof to match the house, each garage unit had a separate up-and-over green painted metal door, which looked secure and indestructible. As if the countryside around was teeming with car thieves. The temptation to open one and take a look inside was great, but good sense warned him it wasn't worth the risk. They could be alarmed and connected to a different circuit to the rest of the house.

To the right of the garages, he found the rosemary bush Alicia had described. He pulled back the tangle of spiky foliage and the sweet musty smell instantly evoked thoughts of roast lamb and Italian cooking. The box of wine was stashed beneath the bush, leaning longwise against the garage wall. But instead of being in cardboard as he'd expected, it was in a box of natural pinewood with a nailed-down lid. A paper label saying 'Fragile' had been stuck to it. And on one of the sides, stained or burned into the wood, was a coat of arms with the name Château La Tour Saint Briac written underneath it in an archaic font.

With a suitcase and a box of wine under each arm, he made his way awkwardly towards the front of the house. Already sweating, he groaned inwardly at the thought of the walk ahead of him. Then, just as he had turned the corner and was heading for the main gate, he heard footsteps crunching across the gravel car park towards him. He returned to the garages and stashed the suitcase and box of wine in the hiding place behind the rosemary bush.

He was straightening himself up when a large bearded

man, carrying a toolbox and cordless electric drill, rounded the corner of the house. When he saw Jarret, a look of surprise spread across his face. Though he was large, he was not threatening. If this was Flo's odd-jobbing husband, then Jarret had been wrong to think he too was into dope. The circumference and overhang of his belly suggested he was a man who definitely took his pleasures elsewhere.

Jarret spoke first.

'Ah, Monsieur! Excellent.'

The fat man looked surprised. It was still lunchtime and he was obviously expecting to have the *manoir* all to himself. Jarret could see him paining to work out what a stranger might be doing there at that time of day.

'Er … bonjour.'

He had a strong English accent.

'Do you work here, Monsieur?'

Jarret continued to speak to him in French, using a strong local accent – too many syllables and a voice resembling the quacking of a duck. He didn't want the man to know he was British. And he was playing for time. He had no idea how he intended to resolve the situation, all he knew was he needed to keep talking and not allow the man to ask him any questions.

The man placed his tools carefully on the ground beside him, wheezing slightly. With a broad smile on his face, Jarret walked towards him.

As his previous question had gone unanswered, Jarret guessed that the man knew little French, so this time spoke to him in halting English.

'I have something important, er ... urgent for Monsieur Adams. If you work here, you would, maybe, take it to him for me? My name is Jean-Louis. I am pleased to meet you. Monsieur, er …?'

Jarret held out his hand to shake. He examined it, then limply enfolded it in a grime-smeared version of his own. It felt like putty. His smile revealed teeth ravaged by neglect.

His voice when he spoke was surprisingly high.

'Morgan.'

'Bonjour, Monsieur Morgan.'

'I didn't hear your car arrive.'

'No, I wasn't sure. I parked further down the track and walked. It is not easy to find your way around here.'

'It's a pretty big place. There's a lot to do here. You can give me whatever you're delivering. I'll make sure it gets to Mr Adams for you.'

If he'd thought it through, Jarret might've foreseen that that was the only direction the conversation could take. But he hadn't and began to panic. Reaching into his back pocket, he produced his dried out wallet, curled and discoloured by the pool water. He fumbled inside it, desperately searching for anything he might give to Morgan. Anything to deflect attention away from the fact he was a deliveryman with nothing tangible to deliver. At last, he selected a not-too-damaged business card, given to him several months before by a plumber who had mended a faulty boiler at Le Papillon. He held it in front of Morgan's face so that he could register it, but lowered it again before he had a chance to read it.

'Some time ago now, my boss's firm did some work here for Monsieur Adams and he has still not been paid for it. My boss asked me if I would call in on my way to another job and ask Monsieur Adams to telephone him this evening. Here is his business card. It has the number written on it. Perhaps, you could take it to Monsieur Adams now, so I can tell my boss that his message has been delivered. Perhaps you could also find out what time Monsieur Adams intends to telephone him. Thank you.'

Obediently, sag-faced with concentration, Morgan took the business card from him and examined it. Two lines immediately appeared in the lard above his nose, as if to emphasise the seriousness with which he took the errand. If he really was Flo's husband, her true amour and the mechanical wizard, then Jarret had severe doubts about the woman's taste.

'Okay. Give me five minutes.'

'I will wait here for you. Then you will be able to tell me what Monsieur Adams has said.'

'Mind these tools for me till I get back.' He indicated the cordless drill and toolbox on the gravel beside him.

'Of course, Monsieur.'

Jarret watched as he made his way slowly towards the arched doorway leading into the courtyard, his old T-shirt stained and sagging at the neck, his jeans cheap and ill-fitting. The door looked hardly wide enough, but once through, he closed it conscientiously behind him.

'Fuck.'

Springing into action, Jarret emptied the tools onto the gravel. Then, picking up the cordless drill and the empty toolbox, he threw them into the undergrowth at the back of the garages.

Anything to keep Morgan occupied while he got away.

7 (Friday pm)

Jarret halted about five metres from the front door and killed the engine. The Willie Nelson tape died with it – he wasn't sorry. It was either listening to the incessant throb of the Renault's diesel engine or Didier's Willie Nelson tape. As questionably more entertaining, he'd opted for the latter. Jarret had tried often, but could make no inroads into Didier's addiction to Country and Western music. Over the years, their only compromise had been a stand-off. He didn't play any when Jarret went round for dinner and Jarret didn't play any jazz or classical music when Didier and Yvette visited him.

There was no sign of Alicia. He was disappointed she wasn't there to greet him. Then she hadn't seen the white van before, so she was right to be careful. After all, it was what he had told her to do. But she must've been watching. Because no sooner had he opened the back doors of the van and reached inside for the battered suitcase than she appeared beside him.

She hugged him and kissed him on the cheek.

'You clever boy. And the wine as well?'

'Take a look in the van.'

'You're a genius. You've got back everything for me.'

This time she kissed him fully on the lips. Lingering just long enough to arouse his interest before pulling away. Then her mood became serious.

'You didn't have any problems?'

'Not really; it went more or less as I planned.'

'You didn't see Adams then?'

'Not Adams, no. A couple of people – but I doubt if they'd be able to recognise me again. Wait a minute.'

He reached in the van for his baseball cap, then pulled his dark glasses from the neck of his T-shirt where they'd been left to dangle. He put them both on and turned back to her. Though he wasn't wearing the glasses when he met Flo, he thought it would stop her worrying.

'*Voila*! Total disguise. I'm surprised you know who I am.'

'Who saw you?'

'I was like the invisible man. They won't remember a thing. I promise.'

Worry lines appeared on her brow and her mouth tightened. His inability to be serious seemed only to increase her anxiety.

'Don't mess around. Tell me who you saw.'

He told her briefly about his encounters with Morgan and Flo, describing them and telling her what he'd said and who he'd pretended to be. He was pleased with himself. But that didn't ease her concern.

Inside the house, he'd laid the mutilated suitcase on the kitchen table and removed his belt from around it, so that she could open it up and look inside. But she appeared reluctant to touch it. Instead, she reached towards the wine box and traced a line across the coarse grain. An absent gesture, but one so sensual that Jarret could almost feel it. As on the previous evening in bed together when her presence was exciting but her distance left him feeling alone.

'Adams isn't stupid, you know. It won't take him long to work out that it was you who took the suitcase. From now on, I think you ought to be careful.'

'I'm always careful. Adams has only got my office address and I can't see him wanting to cause trouble there.'

'It won't be long before he finds out where you live. And don't believe he won't come looking for you.'

'I'll deal with it, if it happens. Don't worry. You're quite safe for now.'

'I'm just telling you to be careful, that's all. You've got no way of knowing what he's capable of. Just be careful for my sake.'

Jarret wondered what suddenly made her an expert on Adams's behaviour. Why should he care about a suitcase containing nothing but women's clothes? Yet the shredded remains on the table in front of them said something different. And, given her mistreatment, of course, she'd be worried about him – because he'd want to make sure she kept her mouth shut.

'I'll take the case up to your room. You'll be able to check it through in private. Unfortunately, Adams has trashed all your cosmetics. So when you want, write me out a list and I'll see what they've got in the pharmacy in La Fouillade. Your wine I'll put in the cellar when I come down. Leaving it in the open the last couple of nights can't have done it any favours.'

'No. If you don't mind, I'd like to keep the wine … everything with me.'

'If your father likes good wine then it's best we keep it at an even temperature. I'll put it in the *cave* at the back of the house.'

'Losing it once was enough. I'd just like to keep it with me.'

'I'll carry it up for you as well.'

He retightened his belt around the lacerated suitcase and slid the box of wine off the table.

'I've got another suitcase you can have upstairs. It's not exactly a fashion item, but it'll do the job. I don't really have a use for it; I don't do that much travelling any more.'

She accepted his offer and thanked him, but he hoped she'd have no need of it for a while.

#

It was already mid-afternoon when Jarret arrived at Didier's farm to return the van. No-one seemed to be about. Yvette's car wasn't there and the big double doors to the barn were open and the tractor missing from inside. He left the keys in the ignition, knocked on the front door and when no-one answered began to walk back to Le Papillon.

After his lunchtime's activity, the cool shade of the woodland and sporadic bursts of birdsong were reviving. But he hadn't walked far before it hit him that he'd missed out on a meal and was really hungry. To pass the time he composed the supper menu – avocado with a vinaigrette dressing of fresh herbs, garlic, black olive oil made tangy with a little freshly squeezed lemon juice, followed by chicken breast in a tarragon cream sauce and baby steamed potatoes. Engaging for the palate without being too heavy. But what appealed more was the prospect of another evening with Alicia. What he was composing in his head was to be the feast before the real feast.

And for the cheese course, a little lightly grilled goat's milk *cabecou* with honey and toasted pine kernels and a green salad. And for dessert a ewe's milk yogurt with sliced *mirabelles* and chopped walnuts. The Aveyronais believed walnuts to be Nature's Viagra. What harm could a handful do?

Again his thoughts had returned to Alicia and he quickened his pace along the winding path to Le Papillon.

#

When Alicia came downstairs in the evening, she looked stunning. The dress she'd selected was ivory with a small repeated purple and scarlet pattern. Jarret remembered hastily cramming it into her suitcase at the *manoir*. The two thin, purple straps over her shoulders stood out darkly against the café latte of her suntan. The brevity and tightness of the garment left him tongue-tied.

'Well?'

'Well!'

She laughed, but he could see she was a little flattered. And this was the first time she'd laughed since the return of the mutilated suitcase. That pleased him.

'I think you approve.'

'Approve? I could eat it.'

'How about a drink first?'

'There's champagne already chilling in the fridge.'

Jarret felt scruffy in his barely ironed black shirt and faded jeans.

When they'd set the table in the courtyard, Alicia sat herself beneath a large green parasol while Jarret hurried to the kitchen to collect the glasses and champagne. He placed them on a tray beside a bowl of green Provençal olives and a plate of sesame seed breadsticks. He didn't want to waste a minute with her.

The pop of the champagne cork echoed off the wall of the house, momentarily silencing the chatter of nearby birds. He handed her an empty glass and stood beside her as he filled it. As soon as he'd finished, he bent down and kissed the exposed flesh of her shoulder.

'Down boy, concentrate on your drinking.'

The champagne bubbles danced nose-high as they drank. The courtyard was gradually shading, but the air that fanned them felt as if it could be blowing off a radiator. Looking into her eyes, he allowed himself to dream for a moment. He lifted his glass to her.

'To … to the future.'

'To the future.'

They sat back. The cool liquid danced on their tongues and the alcohol slowly infused their bodies. They were silent. Sparrows gathered in the honeysuckle, but tonight their incessant chirping, which normally annoyed him, went unnoticed, so too the martins darting and hoovering insects from the sky above them.

He refilled their glasses.

'Tell me, what are you actually doing here?'

'Ah, an existential question. What are any of us doing here? Give me a moment to think about it.'

'You know what I mean. Why are you living out here in the middle of nowhere?'

'You read my flyer yesterday morning. You know what I'm doing here.'

'I just don't see you as this sort of up-market Mr Fix-it. No more than I see myself as a chartered accountant.'

'Am I that unconvincing? I got your suitcase back for you, didn't I? And your box of wine – I managed that all right. So I really am a Mr Fix-it. That's my vocation.'

'You finished twittering?'

'I can continue, if you like.'

'Answer seriously. What are you really doing here?'

'Escaping, enjoying myself, working, loafing – take your pick. Where could you find a more perfect place than this?'

'Do you want me to list them? Cut the ex-pat gibberish. Who or what are you trying to get away from?'

'I'd prefer to leave that for now, if you don't mind.'

'But I do mind. We're about to go to bed together for the second time, so I think I deserve to know a little more about you. So answer me. What are you escaping from?'

'From a world that doesn't exist any more – a place I once believed in that turned inside out, did somersaults and ended up standing on its own head. Look upon me as a sort of refugee – one from another planet. Let's drink to alien life forms. More champagne?'

'Not good enough. Talk to me seriously. If we're sharing, it's everything or nothing.'

'Then you'll need a drink. Let me fill your glass for you, you'll need it.'

Jarret reflected for a few moments on fragments of a past he would shortly try to piece together. The mood was about to change, his story would see to that. He took a sip of champagne.

'It seems like a million years ago, but I used to run a small production company making documentary films for TV. It specialised exclusively in filming in conflict zones – you know, places like Kosovo, Sri Lanka, Sudan.'

'You mean war? There have to be better things to make programmes about than that?'

'Idealism. I was young when I started. I believed I could make a difference. I just didn't factor two things into the equation – the way television transforms images of violence into entertainment, and the fact that gradually I began to get a buzz out of it all. Over time I developed into what, on the outside, seemed like a successful, happy professional. While on the inside, I was a total fuck up – drink, women, cocaine, whatever I could get my hands on. I'd an attractive girlfriend, a good home, as much money as I needed. Everything. And I felt I was going nowhere and I was on fire. Sad, eh?'

'So what exactly went wrong?'

'Don't ask. This is sadism.'

'Too true it is. So tell me.'

Reluctantly, Jarret told her the story of Columbia – the drunkenness, the camerawoman, the deportation. His voice, though quiet, was deep and seemed to fill the room. Alicia sat still and listened to him without reaction, but when he'd finished her tone was gentle.

'It was a tragedy, but we all make mistakes. I know that from bitter experience. But that's not the end of the story. That still doesn't tell me how you ended up here.'

'Enough of me; for now, let's concentrate on some of your bitter experiences. They're bound to be more interesting to hear about than mine.'

'You don't wriggle out of it that easily. Tell me what happened after that.'

'You really are a sadist. It's sordid and it's not me any

longer.'

'Doesn't matter. We can try to change, but who we were is always part of us. I want to hear the rest.'

Jarret poured himself another drink. After what she'd said, he was afraid she might change towards him. But, so far, she'd offered no judgement. He would continue.

'After Columbia it all seemed to happen in a desperate sort of Peckinpah slow motion. Just like when you're suffering from shock or you're in a car crash and the final seconds before impact seem to last forever. Columbia didn't start it and, you're right, it wasn't to be the end either.'

'Don't be too hard on yourself. Look on the bright side: you didn't kill anyone.'

'There you're wrong. In effect I did. I killed Freddi, the camerawoman. But thanks for the attempt at consolation.'

'You can't stay in this dump and brood your life away forever. It's not over, so don't waste it.'

'There's a story I once heard about Celtic monks. Apparently, once they'd finished their training, they'd leave the monastery and enter the wide world in order to preach the word of big G. But they would have no idea of their eventual destination. Just wander through Britain and the Continent until they arrived at a place where they felt they belonged, which gave them a sort of spiritual buzz. And that's where they'd settle and do their preaching. As soon as I came to the Aveyron and saw this valley, I got the same kind of buzz. As if I'd always been heading towards this place. It's very strange, but I feel like I belong here. Hey, but don't worry, I'm not going to start preaching.'

'Sounds like you already are. How about topping up my champagne and finishing the real story? And no more Celtic monk crap.'

'I thought the Celtic monk crap answered your question perfectly.'

'I prefer to hear the real crap. Now go on.'

Once again Jarret was being forced to confront events

that he would rather have kept hidden.

'Okay, you want another little story. Here goes. Once upon a time – and a very long time ago it was – there was a crazy little man, who thought he was a big man, called, let's say, Jay. One day, after he'd managed to get one of his colleagues and best friends killed, a wicked witch somewhere inside his head cast a spell and his neat world went into tailspin. For a while everything seemed to be going fine: his small production company limped along, before gradually clawing its way back into some lucrative contracts. He'd a biggish semi-detached house on the Clifton Downs, an office and editing studios in Bristol and a dedicated workforce, who'd mostly become friends. On the surface, he was one of the princes of the universe. But that witch inside his head began to laugh and weave her spell. There was to be no escaping – Columbia had irrevocably changed his life.'

'Comparing this dump to what you left behind, you're not kidding.'

'Anyway, it came to the crunch one night after a party at a friend's country cottage, when our hero had offered to drive a princess back to her apartment in the city. He wasn't worried because Trixie, his long-time partner, had grown so used to him not coming home that she no longer bothered to ask him where he'd been. It was well beyond the witching hour and he was driving through a little Somerset village, not far from Bristol, when his wheel hit the kerb, bursting his front tyre. Now the bright thing for him to have done would have been to stop, but the prince of the universe was far too drunk to be able to change a wheel, and far too impatient to get the princess home, to be standing around waiting for the breakdown van to arrive. In fact, the only thing on his mind was to get to the princess's apartment and getting her into bed. So he drove on for about another five miles before the deflated tyre had completely worn away and sparks were leaping from the now-exposed aluminium rim. He'd just entered the city when a flashing blue light appeared in his mirror. Next thing, he'd been stopped, breathalysed and taken to the police station to be charged – with the sobering prospect of being locked away in the deepest, darkest dungeons of the evil wizard.'

'I've got to hand it to you, you really know how to mess it up in a big way. But there was no accident. This time you didn't kill anybody.'

'I could've killed myself, my passenger, anyone else who'd been unlucky enough to get in my way. But the point was, it was Columbia all over again. There followed the amateurish farce of the British Magistrates Court and I came out of it with a fine and a driving ban. I was lucky. But by that time I'd had enough. I wanted out. I sold the company to my colleagues for a song. I needed to free myself from the old lifestyle. I didn't intend to quit on life. I just needed to stop for a time and do some serious thinking.

'Crazy thing was, Trixie, my partner, stuck with me through all the crap – my lousy temper, the womanising, the alcohol. But as soon as I sold the business and told her I wanted us to leave the UK and come to live in our holiday home in France, she wanted to have nothing to do with me. Next thing I knew, she'd started legal proceedings for her share of everything and then managed to get me barred from entering the Clifton house by claiming I'd been violent towards her. So there I was, suddenly, wham, in the middle of yet another crisis. One that I eventually walked away from with a half-finished holiday home, a dwindling bank account and an unusable CV – while Trixie got the house in Clifton, the cars and a chunk of our bank account. And there you have it – the perfect credentials for a Celtic monk.'

'I can't feel sorry for you. And it's no good feeling sorry for yourself either. Worse things have happened.'

'Not to me they haven't, but you're probably right.'

'You won't find what you're looking for in this place. Why did you keep all those things belonging to Trixie? Why didn't you throw them away a long time ago? Are you hoping she'll come back to you?'

'Not any more. It's true, I was for a while. She'd always loved this house. I hoped she'd want to see it again, if only for old time's sake.'

'But she never has?'

'No. Too much poison, too many scars for that to happen.'

'Is she the reason your house isn't finished yet?'

'Trixie was the one with the ideas. But there's not much more still to do really, just what the French call the *grenier*, the roof area. And that doesn't require much either – some plasterboard walls, some new floor boarding and a little bit of wiring for lights; most of the plumbing's already been done. But now it's just me living here, I don't need the extra space any more. We had plans drawn up for developing the outbuildings. But unless business picks up, I can't see that getting done either.'

'What's that covered-up hole at the back of the house for?'

'Who's been doing some snooping around, then?'

'I went for a walk earlier. It's lovely countryside.'

'That hole was intended to be the swimming pool. It went the way of all the other plans. I lost interest in it anyway. I keep it covered over to stop water collecting, otherwise come springtime I'm kept awake by a chorus of love-sick frogs.'

'It's dangerous with all that long grass around it. I almost fell in.'

'Doubly so, because the idiot builders got the plan the wrong way round and put the deep end closest to the house. I should fence it off, but there's only me and I don't use the back that often. Maybe one day I'll keep ducks on it.'

'This is a good place for ducks, not for people.'

'You leave my house alone.'

'Okay, it's perfect for a holiday, but I wouldn't want to spend the rest of my life here.'

Jarret was disappointed. She'd made the place alive.

'There's still a little bit of champagne left, if you'd like to share it?'

'Why not? *Salut*!'

'*Salut*! That's enough about me. What about you?'

'I've told you all there is.'

'I know the sad parts. Now I want to hear about the good times and then maybe the ones in the middle.'

'Later. I think it's time we took our glasses inside. I don't feel hungry any more – not for food anyway.'

'And here's me been slaving in the kitchen.'

'It'll keep.'

She reached across the table and took Jarret's hand, then ran her fingers slowly across his palm. Thoughts of his past instantly dissolved, eradicating self-pity. As if she'd flicked that switch, her eyes became electric and inviting. Though a minute ago he was starving, food no longer interested him either. She slid her chair away and got to her feet, never once taking her eyes off his. Dusk was gathering and the sounds from the woods and fields around were becoming muted. He drew her to him and in the fallen light they became one silhouette.

'I'd still like to know more about you.'

'You will.'

8 (Saturday am/pm)

Once again, Jarret was up first and went to collect the croissants and bread from the *boulangerie*. The wind had turned to the west and small, puffy white clouds were moving swiftly across an otherwise clear blue sky. Although the early sunlight remained bright, the air was cool and refreshing.

At 10am, he had an appointment with a client in the nearby village of Monteils. The client's house had been burgled when he was away in England, and he was anxious about purchasing an alarm system. This was to be a preliminary meeting. As much as Jarret hated leaving Alicia on her own, his income wasn't such that he could turn down the opportunity of making some money. He was being hired at an hourly rate to do the translating.

He left the croissants and fresh bread on the table, then laid a place for Alicia. Beside it, he put a vase containing seven red and gold gladioli he'd just picked from the garden. He preferred them to be growing outside, but wanted her to think of him while he was away.

Jarret was convinced Adams would be unable to find Le Papillon that quickly and by lunchtime at the latest he'd be back. To be on the safe side, though, the previous evening he'd made her agree once again to keep herself hidden until he returned. And if the worst happened and Adams did call, he'd taken the precaution of telling her where she could find a path leading up to an old wooden hut in the woods. She could slip out of the back door and be there in no time. It may be fairly rough up there, but at least she would be safe, and he could come to find her again when he returned.

Like all drives in the Aveyron, it was never the distance that determined the time it took, but the bends, the hills and the narrowness of the roads. Monteils wasn't far from Solac, but the journey was never a swift one.

His client turned out to be an amiable man in his sixties, called Mr Phillips. And after their initial handshake, he let it be known that he was to be called Robert. His overweight wife came in and offered to make them tea, but Jarret declined. He wanted this to remain a strictly working visit. In normal circumstances, getting onto a personal level would be good for business. But today, unless her name was Alicia, being familiar with a client was not his priority.

To Jarret, Robert had the mannerisms of a retired engineer or accountant. His slender build was that of a man more accustomed to deskwork than to physical labour. His expensive house and relaxed assurance were evidence of his past success. He was a man who'd made plans and decisions that'd worked. Certainly, never rash or spontaneous, and now he was reaping the benefits – but right from the beginning Jarret had a suspicion there was something missing from his life.

Robert's questioning, though ponderous, was meticulous and considered. As soon as Jarret had sat down, Robert had handed him a pile of brochures he'd been collecting from companies who made or specialised in fitting burglar alarms. He'd been excruciatingly thorough. He had a pen and paper ready to make notes. Then, as Jarret translated for him, he weighed up and lingered over every piece of information, greeting each new detail with a tiny shrug of his stooping shoulders.

The slow rate at which they proceeded frustrated Jarret, but he didn't show it. He continued to translate with care and attention until they'd finished. He understood the terms and the technicalities because he'd done his homework. When he'd spoken to Robert on the phone the previous Monday, he'd a hunch that a little background preparation wouldn't go amiss. So when he'd finished translating the brochures, he got out his laptop and selected the first of the two demonstration videos he'd downloaded in English for Robert to watch. 'To give him a fuller picture.' Right away Jarret could tell he was impressed.

But it wasn't until almost two hours later, two hours of talking the subject this way and that, that he was able to leave. Robert still hadn't made up his mind. In the scheme of his retirement, two hours was nothing. He wanted more time to think it over, take another look through the brochures and maybe see if there were any alternatives available. At which point, Jarret knew he'd achieved what he could and it was time to back off. Robert was bound to be in contact with him again soon with a new list of questions. What he couldn't tell was whether this morning had been a diverting interlude or whether he did seriously want to buy an alarm system in the near future. But then it hardly mattered; he'd bill him either way.

They were engaged in a final handshake when Jarret became aware of the noise coming from inside the house. It was Robert's wife. She hadn't come to say goodbye because presumably she'd not forgiven him for the refused cup of tea. But she wouldn't permit him to leave without being aware of her.

He steered the Grand Cherokee carefully out through the imposing gateway and into the narrow lane. But it wasn't long before his desire to return to Alicia made him press down a little too urgently on the accelerator. Taking chances while driving was something he'd vowed to himself he'd never do again. But then again, there was little on the road and it was already well past midday, so any Frenchman with an appetite would have already been at home. Or so he reasoned.

It wasn't until he narrowly missed colliding with a small white Peugeot 205 on a tight bend that good sense once again prevailed. The Jeep had veered into the middle of the road, forcing the other driver to swerve sharply and narrowly miss going over the edge and into the hillside trees. The angry sound of the Peugeot's horn echoed in his ears as he drove away.

#

Ten minutes to one and the sky had taken a turn for the worse. The morning's fluffy white clouds had been replaced by larger, greyer, faster-moving ones. As he got out of the Jeep, he could feel the chill wind tug at his thin shirt and he knew it wouldn't be long before it rained.

Some weeks ago, he'd met an old farmer outside of Solac – a remarkable man, well into his nineties and the survivor of a labour camp in Nazi Germany. A man whose experience of life clearly dwarfed his own. As a topic of conversation, Jarret mentioned the awful weather they were having. By way of reply, the old man shook his head as if weighed down by a weary burden of knowledge. 'This,' he'd told Jarret, 'is a year of thirteen moons. Thirteen. Weather's always bad when there are thirteen full moons in a year. Very little that's good happens in a year like that.'

Having been brought up in a city, it'd never been an abiding preoccupation of his to count the number of full moons in a year. Beneath the neon and between tall buildings, he'd never paid them a lot of attention. It wouldn't have mattered to him if there were twelve or twenty-four of them. But that was then, and on the evidence of the awful summer weather in the Aveyron, the old boy had a point. Though it'd take more than that to convince him to revise his attitude towards black cats and the underside of ladders.

Despite the clouds overhead, Jarret approached the

farmhouse feeling good about life. As he pushed open the heavy front door, he half hoped he'd be greeted by a waft of cooking smells. Or the sight of an open bottle of wine standing ready for him on the table. But more than anything he wanted to see Alicia again. Experience the thrill of having her close to him, and to himself.

But the kitchen was once again deserted. He called out to her, to let her know it was now safe for her to come out of hiding. She didn't reply. So he went to the bottom of the stairs and called again. He stood still and listened to see if he could hear sounds of her moving round the house. There were none.

Thinking she might be asleep, he went upstairs and quietly opened the door to her bedroom, so as not to wake her. But not only was she not there, but the suitcase he'd given her and all her clothes were not there either. He checked the en suite bathroom. That too was abandoned. Tidy, as if she'd never used it.

A growing feeling of panic started to grip him – like a giant fist had hold of his stomach and was slowly squeezing it tighter. She can't have gone away. She can't have left him like that. Something must've happened to her.

He remembered the hut on top of the hill. Someone must've called while he was out and she'd hidden herself in the woods, like he'd told her to do. He'd told her to remain where she was until he came to find her. Momentarily, he felt a sense of relief. But then he became puzzled. If she'd been frightened by someone, why did she take the suitcase and the wine with her? They were unnecessary encumbrances.

The giant fist inside him squeezed tighter.

Had Adams found Le Papillon faster than Jarret had anticipated?

It was just beginning to drizzle as he started along the path that led up the hillside. Before he'd left the house, he'd had the presence of mind to check the back door. It was locked, with the key still in it. Also, he'd checked all the downstairs rooms for signs of a struggle, but there weren't any. If anything, they looked neater and cleaner than he'd remembered leaving them. He'd examined the courtyard and the track leading up to the road, but there were no footprints, no suspicious tyre tracks, nor signs to indicate that anyone had called at Le Papillon in his absence. Or had left.

Between Jarret's and Didier's properties were two small tree-covered hills. Didier had long ago christened them *Les Nichons*, because it amused him to think of them as a pair of female breasts. As one of the hills was larger than the other, he'd further distinguished them as *Le Grand Nichon* and *Le Petit Nichon*. The hut in the clearing, where Alicia was hiding, stood on the top of *Le Petit Nichon*. The narrow path leading to it wound tightly back and forth up a steep incline through the trees. By the time Jarret reached the clearing at the top, his clothes were already damp. Driven by a strengthening westerly wind, the trees offered little shelter against the drizzle.

Before he opened the door to the hut, he could feel the foreboding. The clearing was too undisturbed. There were no flattened tracks through the long grass. No disturbance of the weeds in front of the hut door. The frayed string that was used to tie it shut was still knotted. She'd never been there. He knew it. It was obvious. But he felt compelled to pull open the door and look inside.

The derelict, musty-smelling interior reminded him of graveyards. And that was enough. For the next thing he knew he was running like a madman back down the tightly winding path towards the house. And for no real reason, the words of a poem came to mind and echoed repeatedly as he ran.

And there she lulled me asleep
And there I dream'd – ah! woe betide!

The latest dream I ever dream'd
On the cold hill side.

He brushed away the overhanging branches of trees and at the tight corners crashed against the undergrowth in his clumsy attempts to turn quickly. Though he moved like a man with a purpose, he had no real idea what it was he intended to do next. He felt urgency of panic, but the only thing crossing his mind was the poem.

At one of the bends, his left foot caught in a tree root that had grown across the path and he fell heavily – scratching his face and twisting his knee as he hit the ground. The pain he felt was almost a welcome distraction. He checked to see if anything was broken and, deciding it wasn't, carried on slowly back to the house.

Once there, he changed from his wet clothes into dry ones and re-examined his knee, which he noticed had already begun to swell. In the kitchen, he poured a large glass of water, sat down at the table and tried to decide what to do next. Then he noticed something he'd missed when he first came home – that Alicia had eaten the croissant he'd left her for breakfast. Not only that, but half the baguette had gone as well. He looked for her dirty plate, but that had been washed up and put away with her knife, cup and spoon. The butter too was back in the fridge and the remainder of the baguette placed neatly on a cleaned work surface. He looked around hopefully for a note she might have left. That would explain to him why she was no longer in the house.

There wasn't one.

His anger welled. If Adams was responsible for any harm coming to Alicia, *he was a dead man*. Adams was an animal that needed to be put down. In his old line of work, Jarret had witnessed death in many of its random guises. At times, it had looked so casual, so easy. But that wasn't his way.

No, he had to calm down.

Over the past few days, Alicia had told him a little about herself. He went to the desk in his office and took out a pad and a ballpoint pen. By putting things on paper, he might make sense of them. He paced back and forth, stopping only to jot down details as they emerged from the confusion of his brain.

The family – perhaps she'd telephoned her family and they wanted her to go back home. Perhaps there was an illness or they'd somehow got to find out what happened at the *manoir*? But why hadn't she left him a note?

After writing the word 'left', he was seized by a sudden terror he tried to suppress. That that was what she'd done to him – left him.

After just those two nights they'd spent together.

He couldn't think what he'd done to upset or offend her. He paced up and down the room, the fear of abandonment haunting him.

But if she'd left, why no note? Not even a 'goodbye' or 'it'll never work out, so don't try to contact me'. Then it had to be Adams. Or she was scared to be left on her own? But that didn't explain the breakfast and the cleaning up afterwards. And where would she go? It didn't fit with her reason for staying with him in the first place. There was nowhere. Though maybe it made her feel safer having other people around. He'd never spoken to her about it. They'd never spoken about any of their fears.

His head was a jumble.

He picked up the phone and rang Didier. Jarret had told Alicia that he was a good friend. It was just possible she'd walked over to his farm. But when Didier answered he confirmed what Jarret already feared, that he'd not seen her either. But he quickly added that he'd very much like to. So why didn't they come over for dinner?

Jarret made a sound that wasn't really a word, and hung up. Didier's contentment had made his lack of it more intolerable.

Three reasons to discount Adams's involvement – firstly, the speed at which he'd have to find Le Papillon; secondly, that Alicia would have been on her guard and able to get away; and, thirdly, the house hadn't been trashed, which, knowing Adams and Fraze as he did, would've been an inevitable trademark of their visit. So he had to look elsewhere. But where? As far as he knew, she'd no other friends in France. So it had to be the family. She'd arrived in Rodez by plane. If she were returning to the UK, then that would be the airport she'd use.

He looked at his watch. There was only one direct flight a day, from Rodez to Stansted, and that didn't leave until shortly after four in the afternoon. He'd got just over three hours to get there. Even allowing for hold-ups, he had plenty of time.

Then he remembered the red Citroën hire car he'd hidden in the barn. In frustration, he chucked the pad and ballpoint onto the desk.

Why hadn't he thought about it before? She wouldn't be able to get to the airport without it. If it was still in there, then he was back to square one. But why had he seen no fresh tyre marks on the track?

He limped painfully across the courtyard. His knee hurt more than ever now. The encephalin his body produced wasn't enough to ease it. He needed a couple of Paracetamol.

The barn looked to be secure. On first glance there was no evidence that anyone had recently entered. Jarret heaved the two heavy wooden doors back as far as they would go to allow in the maximum amount of light. He took a couple of paces inside and squinted into the gloom. The corner where he'd hidden the car was empty. The old tarp he'd used to cover it had been bundled to one side. The old tools were scattered beside it. The wood and iron plough, he'd moved in front of it, had been tugged away.

He walked to the end of the barn as if he needed to verify what his eyes had already told him. Newly disturbed dust particles floated in the air around him, their mustiness nauseating. The car would have to have been driven by Alicia. Adams would have had no need of it. He turned and quickly began to retrace his steps.

He was halfway across the barn when he saw it – on the iron-rimmed front wheel of an old wooden cart. A scraping of red paint. He crouched in order to take a closer look. The wheel stuck out and the car had reversed into it, scraping the paintwork along the driver's side of the Citroën. Perhaps even denting the bodywork.

#

Old green anorak and mobile phone on the passenger seat beside him, he steered the Jeep along the track towards the road. Looking at his watch, he calculated that he'd two and a half hours before the Ryanair flight took off from Rodez-Marcillac for Stansted. That would give him about an hour and a half before boarding began and leave a minimum of half an hour to find Alicia. Which, given the size of the airport, shouldn't be difficult.

He slid David Grey's 'White Ladder' album into the CD player. A perfect album to be miserable to.

At Rieupeyroux, the fine drizzle that misted up the windscreen turned into rain. Once out of the small town, the dipping, winding roads behind him, he could accelerate. Although it was summer, there were few other vehicles on the road. And the ones that were he overtook.

It was still raining when he dropped down towards the by-pass around the *préfecture* town of Rodez. The big cathedral, on its hump-backed hill, sombre and leaden in the half-light, was as depressing as Jarret had ever seen it.

The passenger terminal at Rodez-Marcillac airport was fairly new but tiny: a couple of planeloads of passengers and it was bursting at the seams. On a sunny day people could sit on the grass outside. But today it was wet.

It was also a holiday season and a Saturday and the car park was already fairly full. But Jarret ignored it and instead parked illegally in front of the flying school. He didn't intend to be there long, so couldn't see it'd be a problem.

As he feared, the terminal was chaotic. He went straight to the Gents toilets. He looked a mess. The cut on his face had bled again and his hair had dried in strange tangles and stuck up at the back of his head. Splashing water liberally over his face and hair, he tried to neaten himself up. He didn't want to appear before Alicia like a madman. To flat his hair, he used his fingers as a comb.

The café-bar was noisy and full. A clamour of customers was at the counter, waiting to be served. A quick glance around the packed, litter-strewn tables sufficed to tell him that she wasn't there. At the check-in desk, a queue spilled raggedly across the concourse. Everywhere there was bustle and a hubbub of noise – but Alicia was nowhere.

He made his way outside, past the car rental desks and the brightly lit tourist information office. Under the covered area in front of the terminal building, a young couple inhaled their pre-flight cigarettes. Though their shorts were different colours, their legs were an identical pink in the raw wind. The space reserved for returned hire cars was at the rear of the control tower. Only three of the cars parked there were red – two Renault Cleos and a Citroën C3 – one the right make, but none the right model. And none with a scratch down its side.

Returning to the terminal building, he went directly to the Hertz rental desk. Once he would have gone straight to the passenger check-in, but following 9/11 all information was controlled. At the counter, a well-trained girl with shoulder-length red hair smiled at him and asked if she could help. He smiled back and launched into a half-prepared story. He told her he was a gîte owner from near

Najac and, when the cleaner had arrived at the property that morning, she'd discovered that a young lady who'd been staying there had left her laptop behind. Now, he knew the young lady in question had hired a car at the airport and he was wondering whether Hertz might be able to assist him to find her.

The girl looked concerned. She said she'd do what she could, but wasn't prepared to infringe any rules of client confidentiality. So Jarret gave her Alicia's full name and waited, as she scrolled through the information on the screen in front of her. But no-one by that name had rented a car from Hertz that week.

At the Europcar desk, the response was the same. A girl with dyed blonde hair listened politely to his questions and the story about the forgotten laptop. The little lozenge-lens glasses she wore made her look modern and efficient. He tried describing Alicia to her. Finally, she turned to a young man sitting at a table behind her and asked him if he'd seen anyone matching Alicia's description. He was surprisingly pale for a Frenchman, with a sprinkling of pink acne. When he spoke his voice was high-pitched and sounded as if it had only recently broken. No, they have a lot of clients at this time of year, but she definitely wasn't one of them. If she looked anything like the way Jarret described her, he'd certainly have remembered.

Jarret thanked them both politely for their help and turned to leave. But really he would have liked to have cleared the counter, taken the pale Frenchman by the front of his polo shirt and punched him in the face.

9 (Saturday pm/Sunday am)

The evening was buried in a cloudy twilight – a misty greyness obscured by a feathery drizzle. The houses and the trees beside the road had been reduced to dark outlines and the slash of the filtered sunset was red with rawness.

When the turning to the Manoir Ivant came into view, Jarret slowed. Shifting the engine out of gear, he allowed the Jeep to freewheel over the uneven track, the slight incline enabling it to roll thirty metres before inertia forced him to pull over and leave it. The remaining distance he travelled on foot.

Manoir Ivant was in darkness, a black slab against the shifting greyness of the clouds. He'd been back to Le Papillon to collect his shotgun and was carrying it broken open under one arm. He now snapped it shut. The time for safety was passed.

He went through the big gate leading into the garden at the front of the main house. It had been left ajar. No light shone from the two rows of windows to interrupt the gloom. He scanned the building for movement. He was nervous. He settled the shotgun stock under his arm and cupped his right hand beneath the fore-stock. He stopped still, listening for the sound of any activity. But there was only the wind in the trees and, in the direction of the garages, the slow dripping of water, amplified by his fear.

The garden in front of the *manoir* was neat and unexceptional. The lawns on either side of the paved pathway smelled as if they'd been recently cut. There were no steps, unlike the back of the house, as the ground reached the level of the first floor. The big front door looked seldom used; Jarret suspected the *manoir* had few visitors.

If anyone was home this evening, it appeared they were not in the main house. He pointed the barrels of the shotgun at the ground and pressed the bell. The front door was new and carpentered out of oak. Under a black metal door handle was an old-fashioned keyhole, above it a security deadlock.

Jarret listened as the bell sounded inside the house and in the courtyard at the back. And perhaps elsewhere in the complex. The sound was too modern, too strident for the antiquity of the place and for the agelessness of the countryside around. But there was no answer. He pressed the bell a second time and waited. The cemetery stillness inside the house returned.

He stepped back and examined the front of the house more closely. The shutters had been left open, which meant there was either someone in the house, which he doubted after the noise the bell had made, or they'd gone somewhere and would be back shortly. Jarret felt a twinge of unease at the thought of Adams coming back to find the Jeep parked beside the track. But dismissed it. He'd deal with Adams if the need arose. Right now, his priority was finding Alicia.

He walked down the slope at the side of the house that he was already familiar with from his last two visits. The converted barn he'd broken into the day before had become a looming dark mass. As he nervously rounded the corner at the end of the barn, he pointed the shotgun before him. On the circular table by the swimming pool, where Adams and Fraze had dined the day before, there were two stained, empty glasses and a half-finished bottle of red wine. Jarret picked it up by the neck and read the label – Saint Emilion Grand Cru. Adams certainly knew how to look after himself. One of the wooden chairs beside the table had been arranged at an angle, as if the drinker had been facing the swimming pool and looking at the countryside beyond. The other had been knocked over and lay on its side a few metres away, as if someone had been in a hurry to get out of it.

The area at the back of the complex was as silent and shadowed as the front. He made his way along the side of the swimming pool towards the courtyard. Everywhere seemed abandoned. He sifted the evening sounds for evidence of a human presence – music, TV, voices, footsteps, the sound of dishes. But there was nothing. Only the growing sensation of aloneness.

He stood there and listened on in the gathering darkness, undecided whether or not to continue with his search. He was almost certain he was there alone. There was something that didn't feel right. And he lacked the composure to work out what. A wind drove the drizzle into his face like a cold veil. His leather jacket needed zipping up, but he wouldn't let go of the shotgun to do it. He felt miserable.

He retraced his steps past the swimming pool and the circular picnic table and back towards the front of the house. As he passed alongside the converted barn, with its open windows and shutters, he looked nervously at the dark rectangles in case at any moment a face should appear. He was soaked through and cold. At the front of the house, he pressed himself against the cornerstones and scanned the lawns – then the car park and the black silhouette of the woodland beyond. The dripping of water and the wind that made the trees sound like surf, the way it moved the branches in the half-light, all kept him on edge. He felt exposed to the shadows.

Stooping suddenly, as if he were about to start running through a low tunnel, he set off in an arc across a lawn towards the entrance gate. Once on the gravel of the car park, he decreased his pace to a slow trot and began to zigzag in the direction of the track, and the ultimate safety of the Jeep. He was aware it wasn't the smartest thing he could do. If he tripped and fell he was more than likely to blow his own brains out. But he was already spooked and fatigued from a day that seemed never-ending. He needed rest.

He needed Alicia.

Head up, bent almost double, Jarret wove erratically across the completely empty car park, like an armed and dangerous Groucho Marx. At every pace, the gravel sounded like a rifle shot.

Running with his head close to the ground, a piece of white paper on the grey surface of the gravel caught his attention. Though the wind was still strong, it had been fixed to the rough surface of the stones by the drizzle. He hadn't noticed it when he arrived. It'd either been blown there or he'd crossed the car park by a different route. He rotated three hundred and sixty degrees before daring to peel it carefully from the ground. It was already beginning to pulp. He could see that some of the ink had started to run in pale grey rivers. He glanced at the printed section at the top of it. It was a receipt – from Lageste, a wine-seller from a nearby village. Raising the hem of his polo shirt, he placed the wet paper flat against his stomach and tucked his shirt carefully back into his jeans. The paper felt damp and unpleasantly cold against his skin, but it was the only way he could think of transporting it without destroying it completely. It was nothing much to show for his evening's visit, but it was all he had.

#

That night sleep wouldn't come. With no plan, no clear idea of what he should do next, he floundered. Only his anxiety remained constant. But he lay on in bed, kidding himself that he was getting the rest he needed, while all the time his mind was whirring like a gaming machine.

Then, just after 5 am, he erupted from beneath the

102

bedclothes and ran naked down the stairs to his office, only remembering the knee he'd twisted the day before when he tried to turn too sharply in the hallway. He gulped back the pain and continued to the office.

During the panic of the previous day, he'd not been thinking clearly. In his eagerness to be doing something, anything, he'd achieved nothing, forgetting the most basic and obvious things to check. At just after 5 am, lying there not even half asleep, those things came crashing into his consciousness. He was angry with himself. How could he have forgotten to check his emails and telephone answering service for messages? Alicia could've contacted him at any time, making all the driving and running around he'd been doing a waste of time. What a stupid fuck! Why did his emotions always get the better of him? Why did he find it so difficult to stay calm?

But the brief flood of hope he experienced swiftly evaporated. There was nothing in his email inbox, except the message he'd anticipated from Robert, his client near Monteils. Then he dialled his answering service, only to be assailed by Trixie's solicitor wanting Jarret to call him back about some shares that should've been declared at the time of the legal division of property. He was unaware he still had any shares. And if he did, they certainly wouldn't amount to much. He erased the message.

More miserable than ever, he returned upstairs to get dressed. His brain was racing – lying any longer in bed was not an option. Only the fresh air might help him think more clearly. But when he opened the front door and stepped outside, the pervading dampness felt heavy in his lungs, like he was drowning.

#

It was Sunday morning, just before eight o'clock. The roads were deserted. On the drive into Villefranche-de-

Rouergue he'd hardly passed a car. When he got there, the town was only just beginning to awaken. Beneath the large trees in front of the Café-Bar du Globe, market stalls were being erected. Flowers, fruit, vegetables and bread were being unloaded from the backs of vans and laid out for display on trestle tables beneath multi-coloured awnings. The sky was grey, but the previous night's drizzle had been carried away on the early-morning wind.

Jarret's office was in the rue de la Cannelle, near the centre of the old town. Villefranche de Rouergue had been built in the thirteenth century, on the north bank of the Aveyron River. At the time, it'd been a new type of town called a *bastide*, with a central square and grid-like streets that spread and interconnected from it. Tall buildings and narrow streets shaded it from the sun in summer; but in winter, when the wind blew from the north or east, it was colder than a refrigerator.

The Jeep rumbled across the cobbles of the main square, the Place Notre Dame, where Jarret found a parking place. In contrast to the narrow streets that led into it, the old square was light and spacious, despite being loomed over by the Collégiale – its thrusting entrance like the paws of a predatory beast.

Cutting through the lower arcade at the bottom end of the square, he made his way to the rue Marcellin Fabre and took the second turning left into the rue de la Cannelle. It was an even narrower street than most of the others in the old town, almost an alleyway, and darkened by the height of the terraced houses that formed it.

Until he'd heard the sound of the Solac church bells, he'd not realised it was a Sunday. Since Alicia's arrival, time had meant little. But he knew it wasn't going to be a day of rest. Though his landline answering service at home afforded nothing, the answering machine in his town office might – especially if she'd kept his flyer. His mobile had drawn a blank too.

Jarret stopped at an old, battered wooden door and removed a larger-than-life key from his pocket – no deadlocks, no security devices – and inserted it in an ancient lock. Above the door was a professionally produced sign – black lettering against pale green. It read in English 'R I P – Restoration Information Protection' (then in smaller lettering) 'Help and advice on life in France – Professional Consultancy & Translation Service'. In fact, any words he could think of that might attract English-speaking custom. Inside, the dust-scented air reminded him that he hadn't contacted his cleaner for a couple of weeks.

He went straight to his desk to check the answer machine. Nothing, not even a client. Then he rechecked his mobile for a text or a voice mail that might have come in since he left Le Papillon. After that, he didn't know what to do. Only that he wanted to break something.

The office interior had been painted white. An attempt to make it brighter and more modern – even the stone walls and beams. To appear efficient, the big desk, facing the door, was usually cleared of everything except for a telephone and his laptop. Behind the desk hung a large framed map of the department of Aveyron and overhead a lighting track containing eight halogen spots, which lit the room. But, despite his best efforts, it was impossible to disguise the office's age and decrepitude.

The only message to arrive was in the form of a fax. But it wasn't from Alicia, just a client wanting to know if Jarret had found him a mason yet to rebuild a wall of an outbuilding that had collapsed the previous winter. There was a hint of irritation in the tone and he felt like crumpling the paper into the bin. But he needed the business, so he folded it neatly and pushed it into the back pocket of his jeans.

So, the office was another dead end. And he had no idea what to do next. Worn down by the previous night's lack of sleep, he felt helpless. He needed some coffee to wake himself up. He'd go down to the café by the river and grab a cup of coffee.

Before he left, he took a last look around the office to see if there was anything he'd missed. There was nothing. Then, just as he was about to leave, the door imploded, striking the wall with such force that it bounced half-shut again. A large man with cropped hair and the bleary-eyed menace of a nightclub bouncer entered, blocking the light from outside. A rococo of dark tattoos covered his arms and more ran down the sides of his neck and disappeared beneath a black T-shirt. On the back of his dangling left hand, tattooed in black, were two upside-down single letters from a strange alphabet. They conjured thoughts of Alicia – but not in the same way.

The man looked at Jarret, then surveyed the office, before stepping aside to let an older man enter. A third smaller man with collar-length black hair remained outside, guarding the door.

As soon as he entered the office, the older man began speaking.

'Mr Jarret?'

Part question, part statement.

Jarret retreated behind his big wooden desk. The situation was already developing beyond his control. He wanted to put a barrier between himself and his visitors.

As he approached, Jarret was conscious that the older man's eyes were fixed on his own. He had on an expensive dark suit and shiny black leather shoes that drummed confidently on the tiled floor. His hair was steel grey, like wire, and cut short, but not so that it exposed the contours of his skull. A white scar intruded into the left side of his hairline, like a lopsided parting. Maybe he was fifty, maybe more, but with the cold eyes of a man you didn't argue with. Or so Jarret thought. A tiny bulge of flab overhung his waistband, but he looked like a man who took care of himself.

Jarret replied to his question.

'That's me. How can I help you?'

'I must admit I wasn't expecting to find you here this morning. But then we make our own luck, don't we, Mr Jarret?'

That all depended how you defined luck. He wondered what the man would have done if he hadn't found him there this morning. Worked out another way of getting into the office?

'You could say that, I suppose.'

'Indeed I could. But now I've got lucky, perhaps I can persuade you to help me in a small matter. You see I'm trying to locate a certain person and I believe you are in an ideal position to be of service to me. Professionally, that is.'

His speech was measured and his voice quiet, but each word was so clearly articulated he could've be shouting. And beneath them all lurked a hint of menace, encased in the harsh bite of a Northern Irish accent – Orangeman or Catholic, a man defined by the Troubles.

'If I can help you professionally in any way, I'd be delighted.'

'Good. Interesting office you have here, Mr Jarret. Decorate it yourself did you?'

'I paid a decorator to do it.'

'Not too much, I hope. But then again, they didn't have a lot to work with. Never mind, it could've been worse.'

'Thanks.'

'May I sit down?'

'I'm sorry, please do.'

'It's not conducive for us to talk with you standing up there like that. Why don't you make yourself comfortable too? Now that's much more cosy, is it not, Mr Jarret?'

'You said you were looking for someone.'

'In good time. How long have you been working here?'

'Two years.'

'And before that?'

'Making programmes for television.'

'Working for?'

'Myself. I ran my own production company.'

'I thought as much – an independent man. A man who likes to do things his own way. Am I right there, Mr Jarret?'

'Something like that.'

'Now, don't be diffident; we should all acknowledge the things we're good at. Take me, for instance. I'm extremely good at obtaining the things I want. Isn't that right, Sammy?'

The abrupt question clearly surprised the man standing by the doorway. Probably because he was unused to being consulted. But though struggling from the excesses of the night before, he reflexed a formula response.

'Yes, Mr McBryde.'

'Thank you, Sammy. Now go back to sleep while I talk to Mr Jarret. Alright then, let's get down to business – the small matter in hand that I mentioned. I believe you've been working for a certain person recently, a very attractive young blonde lady. Is that not the situation you've … how shall I put it … found yourself involved in, Mr Jarret?'

Jarret felt his temperature drop. An already complicated world was becoming more so. He fumbled for a suitable reply. If McBryde was playing a game here, it wasn't one he wanted to be involved in. He'd no idea what the stakes were.

'Now, now, Mr Jarret – no need to be so coy. I have my sources of information. And given the circumstances, I've no reason to believe they'd lie to me.'

From inside his jacket McBryde produced a business card. He held it up for Jarret to read. **J. Jarret, RIP, Consultancy and Translation Services**. He didn't hand them out to anybody. They were reserved strictly for his clients.

'Mr Adams and I had a little tête-à-tête yesterday. That

is what you call it in French, is it not? He mentioned that you paid him a most interesting visit a few days ago, though sadly it appears you didn't quite hit it off together. You got yourself into a little trouble, I hear – that was unfortunate. Mr Adams can be a very difficult person to get to know.'

Once again, Jarret didn't reply. Not out of bravado or toughness, or because he didn't think it was necessary, but because the muscles in his neck had become rigid. He wasn't sure he could speak.

'Well, Mr Jarret, I'm waiting.'

McBryde's eyes had never left Jarret's face. A fifty-year-old pugilist assessing an opponent's weakness, before he destroyed him. A man who only respected strength.

Jarret found it difficult to hold the stare – looking directly into the pinpoints of darkness that transfixed him. He nodded slowly several times to unlock the rigidity in his neck. Then, adopting the ghost of a smile, he spoke.

'You've my business card.'

'Mr Adams kindly let me have it – on permanent loan, shall we say. Are you feeling alright?'

Jarret didn't imagine Adams would have had much choice in the matter. Then he recalled the deserted *manoir* of the evening before – its eerie abandonment. The upturned chair by the swimming pool, the half-finished bottle of wine. He tried to lighten the mood.

'Adams and I didn't see eye to eye. But, then again, I did get some use out of his swimming pool.'

'So I'd heard. A very impressive pool it is too. Now let's get back to business – our business. The girl, Mr Jarret, where is she?'

'That's something I could be asking you.'

'Don't play games with me, please. I'm far too impatient for that. Do you want me to get Sammy to ask you the same question? He's not quite as subtle or articulate as I am.'

'She walked out on me yesterday morning. I haven't seen her since.'

'Well, go on. I'm listening.'

Not saying anything more clearly wasn't an option, but the less information Jarret divulged to McBryde the better. His relationship with Alicia had to be expressed as solely professional.

'She didn't tell me where she was going. I went to see another client and when I got back she'd left. No note, nothing. I've been running around ever since trying to find her. If you want to know the truth, I'm more than a bit pissed off with her. She didn't pay me my fee – and nobody can afford to work for nothing. I know I certainly can't.'

'Nice try. Where is she?'

'I told you. She left yesterday morning. She's probably miles away from here by now. I've checked out all the obvious places – Rodez airport, the next-door farm, Adams's house. Now, this morning, I've come in to the office to see if she's left a message for me. So far I've found nothing; she just seems to have vanished.'

At the mention of his visit to Adams's house, Jarret wasn't sure, but thought he noticed McBryde's jaw tighten. He placed Jarret's business card back into his suit jacket pocket and put his hands on the desk in front of him. His voice remained soft and measured.

'And what did you find on your visit to Mr Adams?'

'Not much. It was getting dark, but there were no lights on, and no-one answered the door when I rang. It looked like he must have gone somewhere.'

'Yes, he must have. He told me he was thinking he might take a little trip.'

'Listen, if you don't know where Alicia is either, then I'm afraid we're both stuck.'

'Alicia? Ah, Alicia, yes. … Yes, I might have been expecting …'

At the introduction of Alicia's name, there was an uncharacteristic hiccup in McBryde's fluency. The edges of his mouth explored a smile. It allowed Jarret to maintain the initiative.

'If you could clue me up on any background information you've got on her … I don't know how much you know … but anything you can tell me might help me find her. For both of us, that is.'

McBryde looked at him hard.

'I don't know why, but for the moment I'm thinking of believing you, Mr Jarret. Though I regret I am unable to give you any more information regarding … er, Alicia than you already possess. If you are telling me the truth, and I don't see any reason in the circumstances why you wouldn't be, your investigations, so far, would seem to have been reasonably thorough. Perhaps you are a man I can take seriously after all. Mr Adams failed to enlighten me on that point. He left me a bit in the dark, as it were, so I shall have to trust my instinct here. Now let me see, how does one do this? I have a proposition for you. I'd like to hire your professional services to find our missing friend, dear Alicia. Which would give you the double advantage of continuing your search for her while earning a little money for yourself on the side. A double whammy, Mr Jarret. You see, like I said, I need you to find her for me as well. You might say … yes, that's right … that I'm acting on behalf of her family. We're all very concerned about her and what she might get up to in her present state of mind. You see, she's been behaving quite strangely recently. I know this is not part of your advertised expertise, but how does that proposition strike you? I can assure you, I'll make it a very lucrative one. And that way you'd be helping Alicia as well.'

It struck Jarret as a nightmare. But he was not in any position to make choices. If he didn't accept, there was only guessing as to what the consequences would be. Though he was sure he wouldn't have long to wait to find out. In the short term, the offer presented him with a compromise that might buy him some more time.

'I never turn down work. But I must warn you that, so far, I've hit a bit of a brick wall.'

'Brick walls are there to be demolished, Mr Jarret. I have every faith in you. What say I offer you twice your usual hourly rate? Which means I want you to drop everything else and concentrate one hundred percent on finding the fair Alicia. Obviously, the boys and I will assist in every way we can. We'll organise a little race of it if you like. You find her first and you'll get a five thousand Euro bonus – we find her, and you just get your fee. A deal?'

'A very generous offer – I hope you won't be disappointed.'

'I seldom am. To indicate the faith I have in you, I'm going to give you a thousand Euros as a down payment. Call me twice a day to let me know what you've found out, where you are and exactly where you've been – I need you to keep me in the loop at all times. And I need always to be able to find you. Is that clear?'

'As crystal.'

'Here's my mobile number, I've written it down for you. Any problems getting through to it, contact the number I've written below it. Call me twice a day, midday and evening, or if you discover anything you'd think I should be interested in, and that's not a request. Understood? And the moment you locate her, call me immediately. I don't want any more cock-ups.'

'Cock-ups?'

'That doesn't concern you. Have you quite understood everything I've told you?'

'Yes, quite.'

'Good. Now I won't disturb you any longer. You have work to be getting on with.'

'I'll call you this evening.'

'Of course you will. Before, if it's necessary.'

With that, McBryde got abruptly to his feet, sending his swivel chair rolling backwards on its casters. He held out a large hand for Jarret to shake – to seal their contract. His grip was firm and his hands were rough, but Jarret was surprised by the coldness of the flesh. Sammy opened the door for him as he exited, and left it wide.

But Jarret didn't mind. The fresh air felt good. It would be a while before his pulse returned to normal.

Outside in the rue Cannelle, McBryde said something to the man with collar-length hair, who turned round and looked at Jarret as if he'd offended him.

10 (Sunday am/pm)

Jarret's brain was whirring. He didn't want to think about what he'd got himself into. Just the trio of different people – Alicia, Adams, McBryde – who somehow seemed to fit together. But their connection made no sense.

Yet of one thing he was sure – that McBryde's presence in the Aveyron meant trouble for somebody. And he'd do everything in his power to make sure it wasn't him.

But he couldn't cover up the fact that Alicia's disappearance had left him feeling abandoned. Though he'd no idea what had happened to her, he felt strangely hurt. She had been the promise of a new beginning. Now he felt worse than if she'd never entered his life. Nothing would please him more than if she walked into his office at that very moment, but he knew it wasn't going to happen.

Now he'd entered into a contract and, whichever way he looked at it, he was destined to be the loser. If Alicia was somewhere safe, then all well and good, let her stay that way. He'd take McBryde's money on the pretence of working for him – he had no choice. He'd already confronted the possible consequences of not doing so. But it put him in an awkward position. To be seen to be looking for Alicia while at the same time making sure she was never found.

He had no idea what he was involved in, but had to make up his mind about what to do next. He paced the office until a first step presented itself. Albeit an absurd one.   That he had somehow to detach himself from Alicia. To remain too emotionally involved would make it impossible for him to function. So he had to fix it in order that, from now on, he viewed her as just another person, another woman from his past. Then, and only then, would he be free to concentrate on an assignment that's only goal was its own failure.

From bitter experience, Jarret knew that the best way to get over one woman was by being with another. Getting over Trixie had taken him a long time. But after several messy entanglements with other women and a heap of recriminations, the scars eventually began to heal. As for now, all he could expect in the circumstances was a quick fix, a brief sexual overlay in which to submerge his emotions. And he knew a woman who could arrange it for him. Her name was Martine. She'd once been one of his clients, or rather he'd done her a favour. She'd never forgotten it.

#

It was not quite ten o'clock and Jarret knew the narrow, cobbled streets of the town on a Sunday morning would be all but deserted. The shortest way to Martine's apartment was to cut down the rue de la Republique and cross over the Pont des Consuls. But he wanted to know whether McBryde trusted him, or whether someone would be watching his every action. If the second was the case, then he could never allow himself to make a mistake.

Locking the heavy wooden office door, he began walking briskly in the direction of the square. Then, as if suddenly changing his mind, he turned a hundred and eighty degrees and backtracked down the slight incline towards the opposite end of the rue de la Cannelle.

Heading down the narrow street towards him was a young man with dark curly hair. If he'd witnessed Jarret's erratic change of direction, he showed no reaction. His first impression was of the man's immaculate presentation. His black jeans and short-sleeved grey shirt were adorned with crisply angled creases, though neither garment appeared to be brand new. As they passed, they acknowledged one another with polite *bonjours*. So nothing to get suspicious about – just a young man out walking on a Sunday morning. Nevertheless, at the corner of the street, Jarret stopped and watched until the man had exited the rue de la Cannelle and turned in the direction of the Place Notre Dame. He didn't once look back.

Following the rue Merciers north, past the Chapelle des Penitents Noir, Jarret left the narrow streets of the old town and entered the first of the wide boulevards that led to the river and Martine's apartment.

The boulevard Haute Guyenne was nearly empty as he entered it. It was already too late for church and too early for the Sunday diners to be out. There were a few cars. He crossed the two lanes of one-way traffic without difficulty and turned back to examine the streets and doorways on the opposite side of the boulevard. Again there was nothing suspicious – only two small boys careering over the pavement on miniature mountain bikes.

Keeping the old town to his left, he made his way towards the Place Jean Jaurès and then into the Boulevard Charles de Gaulle – west then due south. From time to time he checked behind him to see if he recognised anybody, or if the same face reoccurred. But the farther he walked, the more relaxed he became.

Martine's apartment was not far from the railway station. He knew his visit would surprise her, but decided against phoning ahead. Sunday morning she'd be lingering on in bed, prolonging the remnants of a beauty sleep that'd probably last until lunchtime. And though he knew she'd complain about being disturbed, she'd only be pretending.

He stopped to take a final look at the road behind him before turning into a street lined with two neat rows of terraced houses. Halfway along it on the first floor of one of the three-storey houses was Martine's apartment.

Jarret pressed the doorbell twice and settled himself for a long wait. After a short time, he pressed it again. Several more minutes elapsed before he heard a key turn in the door leading onto the balcony above him. A moment later, a sleepy-eyed, tousle-headed Martine leant out over the edge of the wrought iron railings. She squinted, straining to focus on the unwelcome caller in the street below. In her haste to get up, she'd forgotten to put on her spectacles.

'Martine, it's me – Jarret.'

'Jarret? What do you want at this time on a Sunday morning? You're ruining my beauty sleep. I'm not even dressed yet.'

'I'll wait.'

'You might have to wait a long time.'

'I can be patient.'

'Patience – is that a virtue or an affliction, I'm never quite sure? Give me five minutes and I'll make us some coffee.'

'No need – I'll take you to the Globe and buy you a cup. Hurry up and make yourself decent and I'll throw a croissant in as well.'

'Coffee'll do. What would I want with decent?'

'Thought you might like to give it a try some time.'

The croak of an ironic laugh and she was back inside in search of her clothes – and, hopefully, for a pair of spectacles. But he'd been standing at the front door for only a few minutes, when it was opened by a smiling Martine. She puckered in anticipation of their exchange of *bisous*. He was not easily embarrassed, but the loud pink quilted dressing gown, pair of fluffy, matching mules and the red dyed tangled mop of hair made him want to get her off the street as soon as possible. He kissed her and hurried her inside the house, but not before he'd checked over his shoulder to make sure that no-one had seen them.

"My god, what happened to your face?"

'Let's say I was outnumbered. You could've got yourself dressed first.'

'I couldn't leave a handsome young man like you standing out in the street. I've got my neighbours to consider. I don't want them to think I've got men queuing for me, especially on a Sunday morning. Come on in and wait upstairs. I'll try not to be long.'

Martine's first-floor apartment consisted of a good-sized lounge, reasonable bedroom, tiny guest room, small kitchen and even smaller bathroom. Her view from the balcony was of the street outside or, more accurately, the front of the terraced house opposite. Much of her furniture looked as if it'd been an inheritance or that she'd had it a long time. All she'd bought recently were the African carvings, the little china animals, the orange and black carpet and the yellow cushions that illuminated the old red sofa like moons in a Martian sky.

But Martine was one of the kindest people Jarret knew. The hole he'd once got her out of had been a deep one – in her terms, anyway. When she'd got in contact with him, she was desperate. He'd several times wondered what harm she'd have done herself, if he hadn't picked up his phone that day.

On a friend's recommendation, she'd contacted two young, unemployed men to decorate her apartment for her. It was a good arrangement because it meant she could pay for the work in cash and avoid tax and the men would be able to earn money without having their benefits stopped. The men agreed a price and she gave them a deposit to buy the necessary materials.

So far so good, and in little more than a week the work was finished. But unfortunately for Martine, when it came time to hand over the money, she was having a problem with her bank and couldn't withdraw the cash she needed to pay them. Though the problem was the result of an administrative error, her account had been temporarily frozen and there was nothing that could be done about it, until 'certain procedures had to be followed'. And that would take a little time.

But the two workmen thought she was trying to trick them and became angry. They demanded she paid them compensation for having to wait. Then, when the money was still not forthcoming, they demanded double. The problem was what she'd done was illegal and in employing the two men she'd actually committed a crime. She'd no contracts, no estimates to produce and there was no way she could tell anyone in authority what was happening to her. In fact, having no family, there was no-one she could turn to. She didn't want to involve close friends because she was ashamed. And all the time, the amount the two men demanded kept getting larger and larger. Until one day they threatened her.

At the time, Jarret didn't know what precisely she expected of him or why she'd chosen to call a foreigner rather than a Frenchman. Perhaps she just found it easier to explain the situation to an outsider. Or, perhaps, she imagined foreigners less likely to be governed by the law of the country and that somehow they could literally eliminate her problems for her. But more than likely, she just didn't want judging. And maybe the judgement of a foreigner counted for less in her eyes than the judgement of a fellow countryman. And in that respect he was a good choice, because he was in no position to judge anybody. He listened to her, just asked how much money was involved and then went about seeking a solution.

The two young men were opportunists. Comfortable threatening a single middle-aged woman; but when Jarret confronted them, they quickly backed off. He never let on who he was or in what way he was connected with Martine. He just led them to believe that he and his 'friends' weren't particular how they solved Martine's problem for her.

But these weren't really tough guys – just a couple of hyenas scavenging around for whatever scraps they could find. And in Martine they'd thought they'd found a meal. But once a small element of coercion was applied, with no argument, they backed off. He told them that if they ever bothered Martine again he would find them, but next time he wouldn't be so nice. And hoped they'd believe it. Then he paid them what they were owed, no more, and they were extremely grateful to get it. Which meant they were happy and Martine could regain her peace of mind. Afterwards, she always acted as if she owed him.

The door to the bedroom opened with a shriek of un-oiled hinges and Martine emerged on her way to the bathroom. Under her arm, she carried a large cosmetics case. Still barely awake, she looked all of her fifty-odd years. Her dyed red hair, which had broken free from its night-time ribbon, required a hairbrush and lacquer to tame it.

'What've you called for? Don't look at me like that. I know this is not a social visit.'

'I need one of your favours.'

'British! Why don't you just come out and say it – you're looking for a little female company. That's not a difficult thing for a Frenchman to say.'

'I'd appreciate it if you could find someone for me for tonight. Is that possible?'

'I can probably arrange it. Tell me what time? Where?'

'Eight o'clock? At Le Papillon?'

'Easier if it was in town, but I'm sure I can find somebody willing to travel to that rundown farmyard of yours. Let me write it all down before I forget … your place, eight o'clock this evening. I'll phone around for you later. A good-looking young man like you, you must have them queuing up. Me, I'd eat you alive and come back for seconds. Why won't I do for tonight?'

'You know very well why. Can you imagine our friendship surviving us being in bed together? But thanks for the offer anyway.'

'What's friendship got to do with sex? Alright, I was only teasing.'

'Well don't. Go and get ready or it'll be lunchtime before you get breakfast.'

'Sounds better and better. Breakfast and lunch.'

'Sorry, I've got work to do this afternoon.'

'On a Sunday? But you're not going to be too busy to be bedding someone this evening, are you? Perhaps one day I'll be able to twist your arm and make you take me to a restaurant.'

'You're on. We'll make it a date.'

'Aren't I just the lucky girl. And when's that going to be?'

'Soon.'

'I won't hold my breath then.'

Having noted Jarret's evening assignation, she shut her appointments' diary and shuffled in her mules to the bathroom. To do battle with her make-up and eliminate whatever blemishes she didn't want the world to see. Jarret smiled at the thought of her trying to apply lipstick and mascara while still half asleep.

The apartment was dusty and unaired, with the clinging aroma of a cut-price air freshener. The door to the balcony had been left open. The sun had now climbed above the rooftops opposite, but was little more than a watery disc. Its feeble rays barely penetrated the living room.

Jarret moved onto the balcony to clear his lungs. The air he inhaled tasted damp in his mouth, as if it'd drifted off the nearby river. It was one of those mornings when there would be no respite. He leaned out over the wrought-iron balcony railings, apropos of nothing, to see how much of an all-round view of the street he was able to get. And a voice inside his head, his mother's, screamed at him to be careful or he was going to hurt himself. But, as he'd learnt when young, there was no point in fate, if you couldn't tempt it.

That was when Jay caught sight of a movement out of the corner of his eye – the fleeting figure of a man crossing the junction at the far end of the street. For a brief second their eyes connected and they shared a knowledge. Then he was gone. But Jarret had recognised him – the curly hair, the pressed grey shirt, the black jeans. The image seared into his psyche and left him feeling hollow and afraid. This was the same young man who'd passed by him in the rue de la Cannelle. Not a coincidence. The man had quickly turned his head away and crossed the junction. And to anyone but Jarret, he could have been innocently checking for traffic. But to Jarret the message knew differently.

So McBryde didn't trust him after all.

Re-entering the apartment, Jarret crossed quickly into the hallway and began hammering on it with his fist on the bathroom door.

'Okay. Okay. I'm hurrying.'

'I've got to go. Something's come up. I'll speak to you about it later. I'm sorry.'

Instantly, he heard the click of a key turning in the lock and the partially made-up face of Martine appeared round the door.

'So now you're not even taking me to breakfast. What's wrong?'

'It's nothing serious. It's that I've just remembered I'd promised to meet a client at the office this morning. I'm sorry. I've got to hurry. Next time, eh?'

'Next time give me more warning. And, next time, it'll be lunch or nothing. And I mean nothing. Okay?'

'It's a deal. I promise.'

'I don't want a deal. I want a lunch date. Do you still need the girl for tonight?'

'Yes. I'd better.'

'Better? It's not obligatory, you know.'

'No, I'd appreciate it if you could.'

'So, Martine's good enough to arrange that for you, but

not good enough to take out for breakfast? You're looking anxious. What's the matter?'

'I've an important client to meet, that's all.'

'Tell me why I don't believe you? Now get out of here. I'm going back to bed. And hey! Give me a kiss before you go. You're not in that much of a hurry for that, are you?'

As he closed the front door of the apartments behind him, he rubbed an imagined red lipstick smear from his cheek. Outside, he checked both ends of the street. The curly headed man had crossed the junction to his left. So Jarret turned right and headed towards the river. Whichever direction he went in now, he knew it was a gamble. McBryde had been too good for him.

The pale sky was tinged with a deepening grey. The morning air had never warmed, but Jarret didn't notice. He was sweating – underarms already damp and shirt sticky against his skin. At the end of Martine's street, he checked nervously behind him and then along the riverbank, in both directions. Turning right, he hurried back towards the Place de la Republique, where the street market would now be in full swing. Though there'd never be a big enough crowd in which to lose himself, the thought of being among people was a spurious comfort.

He crossed the Place de la Republique to the Café-bar du Globe, where he found an empty table overlooking the river. Overhead, a tree spread its huge branches and blocked out the sky – welcome in the sunshine, but sombre and irrelevant on such a day. In order to get a better view of the square, Jarret angled his plastic chair away from the low stone wall beside which he sat. But not so far that he wasn't able to keep half an eye on the bridge to his right. The market stalls were now doing a steady trade. And from the café tables around him came the comforting murmur of relaxed Sunday voices.

After a short wait, a bored waitress appeared and he ordered an espresso. But his eyes remained fixed ahead of him, searching for the curly haired man in the pressed grey shirt. On the Pont des Consuls to his right, a young woman in a loose blue cotton jacket was bent over the parapet of the bridge, gazing innocently into the water below. From the movements of her head, Jarret could see she was following the dark silhouettes of fish as they glided beneath the arches.

His coffee arrived and he paid the waitress. He gave her a roughly counted handful of coins and told her to keep the change. She was unimpressed. The first hot strong sip of the coffee failed to satisfy him, so he stirred in two of the sugar cubes that rested in the saucer beside it. If not for his eyes, darting back and forth over the scene in front of him, he could have been any other customer whiling away a Sunday morning.

It took him a while before he realised that what he was doing was stupid. He drained the remainder of his coffee in one gulp, till all that was left was the dark sediment. The man who was following him was a professional, Premier League. If at that moment he had Jarret under surveillance, then he wouldn't even know it. The growing awareness of his vulnerability made him feel impotent and angry. Thrusting his chair back, it collided heavily with the one behind it. A startled middle-aged man holding a glass of milky coloured *pastis* cried out and turned in protest.

The time for decision-making had arrived – whether he passively accepted his situation and acknowledged that, no matter what, the curly headed man would always be following him, or to do something about it. He stopped in the centre of the bridge and looked down into the water. Dark shadows of fish still wove beneath the arches. He watched them for a minute or two, as if mesmerised. Then made up his mind. He would act – return as quickly as possible to the Jeep and get the hell out of Villefranche.

The young woman in the blue jacket had moved to the far side of the bridge. Her shoulders were slightly hunched and her right hand held up to her ear. Jarret thought she must be talking into a mobile phone, but her palm and the curl of her long fingers hid the tiny instrument from view. Her hair was dark brown and short, and from the back could have been mistaken for a boy. Not seeming to move, she somehow kept her body and face turned away from him.

Once across the Pont des Consuls, he turned right down the Quai de la Sénéchaussée and continued walking beside the river, close to the old town. Too agitated to think of anything more sophisticated, he'd come up with a simple plan, one that depended for its success on knowledge of the intersecting streets. He'd decided to continue along the quay for a short distance, until he came to the theatre, where he'd cross the road, then, cutting between it and the École Maternelle, head towards the Place du Présidial and then back into the old town. Eventually ending up at the Place Notre Dame, where the Jeep was parked. If the person following him was unfamiliar with the grid-like arrangement of streets, then he'd quickly get lost. If he knew them, then Jarret could either resign himself to being followed or lie in wait for a confrontation.

As he passed behind the neat little Baroque-ish theatre and beyond the École Maternelle, he took care not to hurry. For his plan to work, he had to lure his follower into the grid of streets. At the Place du Présidial, he turned right and penetrated deeper into the old town, where increasingly the high buildings crowded out the watery light. When the time came to make a move, he knew it had to count. If he mistimed it, he'd be easily followed. Time it right and he had every chance of getting away.

When he reached a tiny square surrounded by grey houses, he erupted into a sprint. His running feet resounded on the paving stones, as he took a diagonal course from one corner to the other. Without looking behind him, he left the tiny square and turned into the Rue Guillame de

Garrigue. The pain from his injured knee sparked through his thigh like an electric current. In the quiet of Sunday, his clattering feet resounded like a sacrilege.

At the rear of the Collegiale Notre Dame, he stopped and listened for the giveaway sound of running feet. The dark stone of the church loomed over him like a precipice. Nothing. The streets that surrounded him remained silent.

But he wasn't convinced. To be doubly certain, he set off on a final helter-skelter towards the arcades at the north side of the Place Notre Dame – a position that afforded him a wide view of the square. Despite the aggregating pain in his knee, a mixture of fear and panic propelled him there in little over a minute. He was not in good condition. His chest heaved as his breathing struggled to return to normal.

When as satisfied as he could be that he hadn't been followed, he moved quickly across the cobbles to where the Jeep was parked. Several metres away, he pressed the car key and saw the lights flash and heard the reassuring click of the driver's door as it unlocked. Without bothering to buckle his seat belt or wait for the engine coil properly to warm up, he turned on the ignition and accelerated off in the direction of the church and the road out of town. All the time checking in his rear-view mirror that he wasn't being followed.

Leaving the town behind, Jarret drove south along the valley road, beside the river. Though Solac lay some distance away, it was a route with which he was familiar and would ultimately take him back to Le Papillon. At the tiny village of Floirac, he turned left across a narrow river bridge which led to an equally narrow road that wound steeply from the valley to the top of the ridge.

After crossing a railway track, he accelerated until he reached the first of a number of hairpin bends, tightly folded into the contours of the hillside. After the second of them, he halted, checked the road both ways, then made a three-point-turn, until facing the direction he'd come. He pulled into a tight space beside the road partly obscured by the trunks of trees and turned off the engine. He was gambling that anyone trying to follow him would be so preoccupied with the meanderings of the road that the Jeep, partially hidden by the foliage, would go unnoticed – until too late. Jarret, on the other hand, had a clear view of the hairpin below him and a broken one of the hillside as it fell away to his right.

He kept his hand on the ignition key and pressed the button to open the electric side window and listened. If there was a vehicle following, he'd hear it as it laboured out of the valley below. Kilometres back, he'd resolved that if the driver turned out to be a curly haired man in a grey shirt then he'd use the Jeep as a battering ram and run it off the road – and to hell with the repair bill.

A point would have been made.

11 (Sunday pm)

Jarret struggled out of the Jeep and bent down to rub his knee. It required an ice pack to reduce the swelling. He knew he'd be crazy to think about doing anything else today. Anyway, he'd had enough. He was no longer worried about Alicia. And if McBryde had a problem with that, then too bad – he'd already been in his face enough for one day. And if he wanted to know what Jarret had been doing to earn his money, he'd tell him he'd been making phone calls to set up a series of interviews. Door-to-door business couldn't begin until Monday because nothing opened before then. And as this was rural South-West France, Tuesday would be a more realistic timetable. But McBryde was bound to get agitated before then.

Inside the house, he emptied all the freezer trays into a clean tea towel and made himself a makeshift ice pack. He'd been thinking about the evening and trying to eliminate most of the excess fluid from around his knee joint. His face and body were in bad enough a state, but when Martine's woman arrived, he didn't want her thinking he was deformed as well.

Though he'd earlier convinced himself that the purpose of the brief rendezvous was to overlay any of the feelings he had for Alicia, he now found himself looking forward to it. The idea of spending the evening with a mystery woman began to arouse more that his curiosity. Especially one he'd never get to know personally – not even for the first time.

Stripped, he examined his battered body. At the front and

left side of his torso were the two large, ugly contusions. They looked as if a yellow-brown liquid had been spilt across his stomach and side. How would tonight's mystery woman react to them? Not be repulsed, he hoped. He'd have to keep the lights turned low.

So far as he knew, Martine's 'girls' were unique in the Aveyron. Though they were not exactly girls and neither did they belong to her. They were not strictly 'working girls' either – in so far as they didn't make their living from sex. Not full-time anyway. What Martine offered was a simple service, operating as a paid go-between – for women who needed or wanted to make some extra cash, no questions asked, and for punters chasing a fleeting moment of pleasure. Most of the 'girls' contacted her for two or three tricks and then, for whatever reason, got on with their lives. Others became more regular. Driven by who knew what – money, danger, the excitement? But of those there weren't many.

The liaisons Martine sent her 'girls' on she called her 'little favours'. 'Favours' because that's what she believed was the outcome for everyone involved – the guys, because they got the pleasure; and the 'girls' the cash. Anyway, that was the way she justified her not quite moral, not quite legal activities. After ruining her back as a nurse, she saw it as a harmless way of supplementing her disability pension. Other advantages were that it paid cash on the nail and the taxman was never the wiser.

As all sex for money was a dangerous game, Martine not only selected the 'girls' but was also choosy about which men she accepted as their clients. If she ever came across anyone she felt uncomfortable with, client or 'girl', then she'd exclude them from her lists. Perhaps promising to do them a 'favour' in the future, but she never would. Her vetting system was crude and cost her money, but it was important to her that no-one should be harmed. Occasionally, she'd place an ad in the personal column of the free paper, but the bulk of her business was carried out by discrete word of mouth.

And Martine always tried to avoid her 'girls' making a rematch. What she managed was strictly-for-sex encounters – not a pairing-for-life dating agency or a marriage-wrecking bureau. The last things she was looking to create were complications.

Jarret shivered as he rubbed himself down with a freshly laundered bath towel. After the ice pack had finally begun to lessen the swelling around his knee, he'd chosen to take a cold shower to prevent it stiffening again and to keep alert for the evening. He'd hardly slept the previous night and didn't want to start feeling drowsy.

He'd not touched any of the mess he'd made in the kitchen the day before, after Alicia had walked out. Plates, cups and a half-finished jug of coffee lay abandoned on the work surface and table. Not enough for the dishwasher, so he piled everything into a bowl in the sink and opened the cupboard beneath it in search of washing-up liquid. The next thing he knew he'd caused an avalanche, as assorted coloured objects tumbled in hollow-sounding chaos onto the tiles around him. Not for several seconds was he able to absorb what was happening. Then, as the commotion subsided, he recognised the confusion of shapes as Didier's gourds. He'd forgotten he'd stashed them under there.

It took him four trips, an armful at a time, to remove the gourds from the kitchen to the garden outside. Gently, though not without a twinge of guilt, he placed them on the concrete apron jutting from the back door. There they stood or lay on their sides, a prehistoric array of contortions and colours, science fiction in their oddity. Beyond them, the cover of the unfinished swimming pool had begun to sag in the middle from the weight of the previous day's rainwater. He considered tossing a gourd onto it to see how well it'd float. But time was pressing. Instead, he lifted one side of the cover and ran as much water as he could onto the earth at the far side. He didn't want the weight of the water causing the cover to fall into the empty pool. It'd be difficult to remove it again on his own.

#

Having to wait made him apprehensive. He'd done the washing-up, the bedroom was tidied and there was a bottle of champagne chilling in the fridge. So much for him having quit drinking: the events of the past few days had already put paid to that. It'd been one thing after another – Alicia, Adams, McBryde, the man with curly hair, and now him standing around waiting there like a nervous teenager for the arrival of a woman he'd never before met.

Sometimes Martine's 'girls' enjoyed being pampered in a way they weren't always at home – while other times they wanted to get down to business and be away. Not that he was by any means an expert. The only previous experience he'd had was when he'd been looking for a fix to help him get over Trixie. Martine, at the time, had suggested that meeting one of her 'girls' might help. And she was right.

Whatever direction the evening might take, he was prepared for it. He'd put a plate of white asparagus rolled in slivers of smoked trout in the lounge, with another of pate de foie gras spread on *petit gateaux* and a bowl of freshly roasted hazel nuts lightly dusted with Fleur de Sel Guérande and coated with the merest dribble of walnut oil. His philosophy being always to present food that he himself wanted to eat. Otherwise, why bother?

On the CD player a recording of Handel's recorder sonatas was already playing softly, left on repeat. However good the musicians were, it was hard for them to inject significance into what amounted to eighteenth century muzak. But he knew it was the perfect soundtrack for a romantic tryst. It could play on and on, be talked over or listened to and would never offend or entertain very much.

He listened agitatedly as the punctuated drifts of music reached him from the lounge – the jangling purr of the harpsichord penetrated by the piping of the recorder. Notes that would never possess a sufficient density to drown out other sounds – such as an approaching vehicle, or footsteps. He began to pace the kitchen, his eyes returning again and again to the window, checking the track above the house for the tell-tale movement of a vehicle through the trees.

It was midway through the CD that he detected the slow sound of tyres grinding towards the house. He went to the window and watched until he saw the lights and the dark silhouette of a vehicle through the trunks of the trees. But at the second curve of the zed zigzag, the car pulled to a halt in a small parking space he'd created when he and Trixie had first moved into Le Papillon. A flat area between the trees that he always kept cleared of undergrowth so that local huntsmen could use it. Many times on weekends during the season, they'd leave their vans and four-wheeled drives and go off along the public footpath into the woods beyond. No matter what he thought about hunting, he'd been advised that keeping *la chasse* sweet was good local politics.

No further sound or movement followed. He pressed his face against the window, but was unable to see as far as the clearing. He thought about going outside to find out what the problem was, but didn't want to appear too anxious. He was still hesitating over what to do next when a car door slammed. Then his ears attuned to the sound of footsteps, female footsteps, as they descended the slope towards the house. He moved quickly away from the window. Outside, shadows had lengthened, but it was still daylight. Her footwear, Jarret knew, dictated the speed at which she moved towards the house. By the uneven rhythm of her footfall and her hesitations, he could tell she was having problems. High-heel problems. He knew he should go outside and help her. Then again, why hadn't she driven down in the car?

The footsteps continued shakily past the window and up to the front door. A short pause followed, in which he wondered whether she might've decided to leave – then came an explosion on the brass doorknocker that shattered both the evening calm and his equilibrium. It'd made him jump, and without giving him time to move, exploded for a second time. It irritated him. So before answering it, he counted to five, took a deep breath and tried hard to smile.

And there she stood, smiling back at him, the entire shock of her. Mouth moving. Sounds emerging. But Jarret found himself unable to understand what she was saying. She wasn't speaking to him in a language he didn't understand, but she might have been. He just held onto the door and looked at her, frozen. And though he knew he should respond in some way, to offer her some kind of greeting, he could no longer decipher language. He was dumb.

If she wasn't standing in front of him, he might have invented her.

'Aren't you going to invite me in? I've had a mother of a job finding this place. I know I'm late, but it's your fault living in an out-of-the-way dump like this. Why are you smiling at me like a clown? Nervous? Don't worry, we'll soon loosen things up.'

She talked her way inside the house and he closed the door behind her. Although he was still doing his best to respond, he found it hard to concentrate, to believe the person in front of him was to be taken seriously and that someone wasn't making fun of him.

The black wig she wore had a thick fringe, which tumbled towards her perfectly plucked dark eyebrows. It was too thick to pass as real and had a glossy, bluish sheen and a curl crossing each cheek that pointed toward the corners of her lipstick-scarlet mouth. Large earrings bobbed from pierced lobes in pendulous clusters of black and red wooden beads. Her neck was hidden beneath a wide multi-coloured bead choker from which emerged two silver chains and a coloured wooden pendant suspended on a corded black string that reached to her cleavage. Her shape was emphasised by a clinging, ribbed cotton dress that swelled over her hips and buttocks and down to her black stockinged calves. The line of its fall was interrupted at the waist by twists of coloured strand fastened by a woven black buckled belt. To complete the costume, she carried a shoulder bag, which glowed with Rastafarian orange, red, green and yellow like a hashish sun. Goth with a style idiosyncratically her own – or rather with a style she'd idiosyncratically copied.

She was straight from 'Something Wild' – a film that shifted effortlessly between seduction and love, comedy and thriller. Its characters, script and choice of music – everything about it Jarret had fallen in love with a long time ago. He couldn't remember how many times he'd watched it. It was his 'Casablanca'.

But he didn't know why this woman had dressed up as the movie's heroine. He'd been preparing himself for sex, not a parody. And who had told her he'd had fantasies about Lulu? Someone was making fun of him. It definitely wasn't Martine, but neither was this woman's costume a coincidence.

But at the very least, the evening would be a performance and take his mind off Alicia.

'No, no, I'm sorry. That wasn't any sort of welcome. It's just I'm a bit … a bit … Yeah. You're not exactly what … what I was expecting.'

'You're disappointed. You don't like the way I look, is that it? You want me to leave? But let me tell you, I've got a lot better things to do this evening than waste my time in this backwater. And you don't look so great yourself, if it comes to that. You don't stand up straight. You're sort of lopsided and your face is a mess. The house looks nice

134

though. How about calling a truce for the moment and you getting me a little drink before I go?'

'Yes. No … I mean … I'm not disappointed at all. You look … well, you look … just fine.'

'Wow. You certainly know how to hand out the compliments. If I wasn't so underwhelmed, I'd be flattered. You're obviously not the smooth, sweet-talking type, but I'm sure you've got a heart of gold. What about that drink then?'

'Sorry. I'm not thinking. Sit down. No. Not here, I've put out some food in the lounge. You don't have to eat it if you don't want to. Champagne be alright?'

'Now that's more like it. Nothing like a nice mouthful of bubbles to relax things.'

But nothing was further from Jarret's mind than relaxing. In fact, it was racing. A look-a-like fantasy had just walked into the house and he'd welcomed her like an idiot. Melanie Griffiths straight out of the opening scenes of the movie 'Something Wild' was almost standing there before him – in all her alluring craziness. And offering him a charade, he knew, he couldn't resist playing.

Once in the lounge, he popped the cork and filled two flutes with chilled champagne. But she didn't relax. She was too curious about her surroundings to remain stationary. Instead, she was set on examining everything in the room: the ornaments, books, the CDs. Picking up an object here and an object there, scrutinising it, then more often than not absent-mindedly placing it somewhere different. She even managed to rummage through a table drawer, almost as if she didn't realise what she was doing, then leave it open after her. And all the time she continued talking, talking and asking questions. An unsubduable, desirable whirlwind that successfully and seductively had gatecrashed his life.

Then it crossed Jarret's mind that if the scene was going to be successfully acted out he was going to have to play the role of the movie's hero, Charlie – a blond, fey and unco-ordinated businessman played by Jeff Daniels. Jarret's behaviour might've so far come across as gauche and diffident, but he was still going to have trouble being him. In fact, he thought he more closely resembled the psycho, ex-con husband, played by Ray Liotta – muscled, dark eyed, wiry. And, like him, ultimately disposable. But then, if he examined this stand-in heroine more closely, as she strode about in front of him, talking endlessly, she didn't exactly fit the part either. She was taller and sharper featured than Melanie Griffiths and her voice was lacking a certain element of warmth, though she was no less shapely or attractive for all that. And the costume was not entirely right either, but it was near enough for his lust to forgive the discrepancies.

It still gnawed at him how she could have found out. If Martine had said nothing, how was it possible this woman could have talked to his friends or ex-colleagues in England? There was no way for her to connect with them. Then again, he was not prepared to ruin the evening ahead by worrying about it.

All of a sudden, Lulu became bored with examining his property. She crossed to the low coffee table and took a piece of smoked trout and asparagus. Jarret watched as she took the asparagus spear into her mouth and began to chew. It was the first time she'd been silent since she'd arrived. Still chewing away, she held out her champagne flute for him to refill. As she reached towards him to retake it, her bracelets slid down her arm and rattled like cheap percussion. She took a long, slow sip of the champagne. From between the curls of her false lashes, she raised her dark brown eyes to his. For several seconds, she peered at him, almost aggressively. Then she pouted, her scarlet lips parting in an almost perfect white smile.

'What have you got for us to drink after this?'

'Whatever you like; name it.'

'What are you, some sort of alcoholic? I'd like whisky;

got any?'

'Malt, blended, Irish or Scotch?'

'If you're trying to be impressive, skip it. Just whisky'll do me fine.'

'Just whisky it is then.'

'It's only to get drunk on. Like sex, it always goes to the same place in the end. But you've not said anything about my English. I hope my accent's not bothering you.'

Rather than bothering him, he'd been too mesmerised by her to notice what language she'd been speaking. Just as he hadn't noticed the absurdity of the dark glasses she was wearing pushed to the top of her head. But now she mentioned it, he was only too aware of this new aspect of her outrageous persona. Her syntax was good but her accent, sometimes barely detectable, was at other times a caricature of itself. Her near-perfect English pronunciation was often swept away by the mockery of a heavy nasal twang. Now he was conscious of it, it was bizarre. But then so was everything else about her. He was only sad her absurd accent wasn't American.

When Martine spoke to her 'girls', she always clued them up on the type of person she'd arranged for them to meet – excluding intimate details, names, etc. On the few previous occasions he'd felt the need for somebody, he'd noticed that the women she'd paired him with, with tonight's exception, had been of a fairly similar type – middle class, polite and neatly, though not expensively or seductively dressed. The other thing they had in common was that they'd wanted to try out their not very good English on him. Tonight, the woman he'd been paired with had so much confidence in her own ability it didn't even sound like she was practising.

'Where did you learn to speak English?'

'Martine's rule – no personal questions.'

'You're good and you certainly don't seem to need the practice. *Si vous préférez, nous pouvons parler français?*'

'Ah, but always practice makes perfect – so I refuse to speak to you in French. Now, if we're to become just good friends, we must have names. What shall we call each other?'

'What about Martine's rule.'

'Not real names, stupid, made-up ones.'

'Choose one for yourself first.'

'Let me think ... um. For me – I'm going to call myself Lou. How do you like that?'

'What's that short for – Lulu or Louise?'

'Naughty – no questions. Maybe it's sexier for you if I call myself Lulu. What are you going to be called?'

'I'd find it more interesting if you decided for me. I'm not great at things like this.'

'Indulge me. It's only meant to be a bit of fun. Okay, let's see ... Let me have a proper look at you. Ah, so good-looking – I think I'm going to call you Charlie. You don't really look like a Charlie, but that's how I'm going to start to see you from now on.'

'I don't think that's how I see myself either. Change it.'

'Not permissible – just one choice each and you let me do the choosing for you. That means, from now on, you're a Charlie.'

He was watching her closely. She was good. Those were the names of the two main characters from 'Something Wild' – Lou (short for Lulu?) and Charlie. Her performance had seemed spontaneous, her selection of the names random. Was it a massive coincidence that she enjoyed the opening of the movie as much as he did? But if someone was enjoying a harmless joke at his expense, what was the point in taking it too personally? And from the point of view of an antidote to Alicia, what she'd got on offer was just about perfect.

'What's eating you?'

'Nothing, I was just thinking.'

'Well don't. Go and get the whisky bottle and a couple

of glasses, then we can go upstairs to your bedroom and get down to the evening's business. By the way, your food was okay ... I've certainly had worse. Those little things, I bet you even made them yourself. One day you're going to make some girl very happy. Though on second thoughts, taking a closer look at you, probably not.'

Jarret took two tumblers and a bottle of Glenfiddich from the cabinet, then led Lulu up the stairs to the bedroom. She'd terminated the pleasantries and now she appeared eager for things to get physical – no doubt because she wanted to get her money and leave.

As soon as they entered the bedroom, she whooped and leapt on the king-sized bed and began to bounce up and down, without removing her high heels.

'This'll do – big and soft and bouncy. If you get my meaning? Go on then, get your kit off. What's the matter, you the shy type? This has got to go, though.'

With that, she wrestled the duvet off the bed and to the side of the room where she abandoned it in a heap beside the window.

Jarret did what she said – took his clothes off and draped them untidily over the back of an armchair. He felt suddenly vulnerable. He wanted her to undress too. But all she did was remove the bag from her shoulder. She placed it on the bedside table, but within reach. She half-filled a glass with Glenfiddich and gave it to him. Now he was naked, he began to wonder whether she was about to produce a pair of handcuffs from a transparent plastic make-up bag, just like her movie namesake. But she didn't. She left her shoulder bag where it lay.

'Drink up, Charlie. You look like you've never done this before. Go on, get on the bed and lie down. Don't you want to see what little surprises Lulu's got in store for you? I promise not to beat you up like the last woman seems to have done. What happened?'

He didn't reply, but lay naked on the bed, as she'd

instructed. Still fully clothed, but this time without her shoes, she climbed on the bed and stood astride him, like a female Colossus. For some moments, she remained quite still and studied him, erect and supine beneath her. Once more, she was establishing the rules. He was the client, he was the one who should be in control, but that was not how it felt.

Slowly, she lowered herself onto him until he could feel her weight pressing against his stiffness. The simultaneity of pleasure and pain caused him to wince, but that only made her laugh. Crossing one arm over the other, she gripped the sides of her dress and pulled it expertly over her head, revealing a black high-waisted g-string and matching strapless bra. Amused at Jarret's reaction, she leant forward, transferring her weight to her arms and planted a long, smearing scarlet kiss on his lips that made his mouth look as if it might be melting. But when he tried to kiss her in return, she pushed him back onto the bed.

'Now, now, Charlie. Not in the rules. Just lie back, take a drink and watch me closely.'

She unclipped her brassiere, brandished it above her head like a trophy before swirling it round and tossing it across the room. Then, teasingly, seductively, she began to lower her g-string over the smooth pale skin of her stomach and hips. Stopping only when she revealed the top of a patch of pinker skin where pubic hairs had been. Stretching back to her full kneeling height, she placed a fist on each hip, as if challenging him. Allowing him to take in the full implication of what she was and to enjoy it – the small breasts with jutting pink nipples, the flat stomach, the thrusting hips, the whole heady cocktail of her potency.

'What do you think, Charlie? Do you like it?'

'Lulu, at moments like this I don't think.'

'Hey, I can probably use that one. Write it down for me, will you? But do you like what you see, Charlie?'

'Like it! I don't know whether to eat it or consecrate it.'

140

'A poet! Flattery will get you everywhere, Charlie. Finish your drink.'

With that she was back on her feet and straddling him. She slid the g-string over her thighs and kicked into the corner of the bedroom. The skin around her pudenda was freshly shaved and glowed like a pink fig leaf against the white flesh of her thighs. If Lulu had prepared herself like this especially for an evening with him, he was flattered.

'Here, put this on before we start.'

She tore the top off a condom packet and handed it to him. She watched as he self-consciously rolled it over his erection. Alicia hadn't demanded he used a condom.

Slowly, tantalisingly, she lowered herself onto him.

Jarret knew that sex was for anyone, but the afterglow was exclusively for lovers. It felt like Alicia and he had been lovers. The sex they shared had been good, but the afterglow had been precious. But Lulu was about sex and for her a silent afterglow was a waste of time.

'Well, big boy, what do you think of that?'

'I told you at times like this I don't think. Though I'd like to know how you got to be this good.'

'Flattery again, Charlie. Try getting your head around the word "practice". I'd be embarrassed to say more. Even if I were allowed to.'

'Your rules this time, or Martine's?'

'Always mine, Charlie. But I also believe that rules are only there to be broken. Don't you agree with me? If, for instance, two people were getting on as well as you and I this evening, then what possible harm would it do to deviate a little from that little rulebook of hers? After all, who can it hurt? And who'd get to know about it? How about you and I make a little trade? Question for question. I ask you something. You ask me something. You tell me something and I tell you something in return.'

'It'll be your funeral if she finds out about it.'

'Are you going to snitch on me?'

'Certainly not.'

'Well, there you are then.'

'So, tell me how you came to work with Martine.'

'No, no, Charlie. New rules. I go first. Anyway, that wasn't a question, that was an imperative. For my first question, what I want to know is … Who are you trying to forget? I think it would make it easier for you if you told me all about her.'

'What do you mean "her"?'

'Call it female intuition, Charlie. We girls just have a way of knowing these things. And don't try and deny it, it's written all over you. Do you want to do this trade or not? Tell me about her.'

'I'm not sure I can.'

'Come on, Charlie. It's not good to keep things bottled up.

'Okay, you'll never get to meet her. I'll not tell you her name but, in short, she was blonde, beautiful. I'd done a little job for her – sorted something out. We slept together. I was with her for two beautiful days and nights. Now she's gone, probably left me – end of story. I don't feel good about it, but life goes on. You're supposed to help me get over her, anyway, not talk about her. Now it's my turn.'

'Too brief, Charlie. New rules – if your answer is too brief, I get to ask another question. You told me a bit about what she looks like and the time you spent together, now fill me in on a few of the details. I like to be able to imagine things. Like where did you meet her?'

'She contacted me – she was a client. Like I said, she needed me to do something for her.'

'Screwing your clients, Charlie, that's not very ethical. If there's a register for what you do, maybe you should be struck off it. What did she need so badly that she had to go to bed with you to get it?'

'No. You got it wrong. It wasn't like that. It was personal. Anyway, client confidentiality prevents me answering the first part of your question. As for having to go to bed with me – I can't think of anything she asked me to do for her that money wouldn't have covered.'

'Now you're beginning to intrigue me, Charlie. Women hate secrets – other people's, that is. They just don't like giving away their own, that's all. You want me to tell you a few of mine, then you'll have to loosen up a bit and start being honest with me. So far you've just succeeded in whetting my appetite. What did she want you to do for her?'

'Okay, it's no big deal. She wanted me to collect some personal possessions she'd left at a someone's house. She didn't want to go back for them herself, that's all, so she hired me to retrieve them for her. Nothing more exciting than that.'

'Why wouldn't she go back herself, Charlie?'

'Because of the guy who owned the house where she'd been staying – not really a friend, more a total shit. And the mutant he lived with – perhaps they bent both ways – also a shit first class.'

'I still don't understand why.'

'Because of what they tried to do to her.'

With that she climbed on top of him.

'Ooo, that's good, Charlie. That makes me horny. Tell me more. Tell me the details.'

With Lulu sitting astride and looking down on him, any integrity he professed ebbed away. It was more effective than torture.

'Come on, Charlie. Spit it out.'

Compliantly, Jarret described what had happened to Alicia at the *manoir* and all he knew about Adams and Fraze. As he spoke, she writhed with obvious pleasure. But the moment he was finished she was ready with more questions. He couldn't see what the turn-on was, though as long as it was working he continued. He did, however, omit telling her about what happened at the swimming pool or about the gun.

143

When he finally stopped talking, she looked content.

'Thank you, Charlie. Now, let's see what we can do for you. What d'you want to ask me? Something a little *risqué*, perhaps?

And then the reciprocal stories began, probably not truthful ones, just stories that revealed to him nothing about her life and that were so overlaid with obscenity that it wasn't very long before Jarret didn't care about the answers and they began to have sex again.

For a short while afterwards, the evening drifted in a cocoon of alcohol until their breathing returned to its normal tempo. Then, with no prior word, or gesture, she was out of bed and getting dressed. He propped his head on the pillow and watched as she groped in a corner of the room for her underwear, before passing the un-shuttered window in search of her dress. The jewellery adorning her arms and neck jangled to the busy tune of her movements. As she entered a pool of lamplight, the black hold-up stockings she'd all the time been wearing made her flesh look even paler. He wanted to enjoy her again, for her to come back to bed one last time. But something in her manner prevented him from asking.

Moving round to his side of the bed, she turned and hesitated for a moment, seeming to be trying to decide whether she'd take the time to freshen up in the en suite or get dressed immediately and go. But she stood there for almost too long, her body made even more desirable and mysterious in the chiaroscuro of the lamp-lit room. The faint shadow between her shoulder blades, the darker hollow of the small of her back and the swell of her buttocks like a moon and its eclipse.

Because the sex between them had been a face-to-face encounter, it seemed he'd failed to notice a dark shape blemishing the right side of her lower back. She'd kept it hidden from him. But as she stood there now, almost in a pose, he couldn't possibly miss it. Her right buttock turned slightly towards the light, and above it a dark tattoo. Or two, to be precise. Two inscrutable symbols.

'Come here. Let me see your tattoo.'

'What do you mean? This?'

She pointed a long false nail to roughly indicate the tattoo.

'What's with women and these strange symbols? What is it, some occult sign, some sort of sexy graffiti? I don't understand.'

'This one is sort of personal. Why, have you ever seen something like it before?'

'My client had one.'

'What did she say about it?'

'Not much.'

'Tell me what she said it meant to her.'

Pouting again meltingly, Lulu moved back towards the bed. She fixed him with her eyes as if suddenly he'd re-interested her. Sitting beside him, she let the clothes she'd been holding drop onto the floor. Then, leaning over him, she gently stroked his thigh.

Alicia had never told him what her tattoo meant – he'd never asked her. In fact, neither of them had ever talked about it. But he thought he might be able use it as a way to lure Lulu back into bed with him. And have more sex.

'She didn't tell me exactly what it meant.'

'What do you mean "exactly"?'

'Well, like I said, "exactly". Come back to bed and then we can discuss the semantics of "exactly" like two uncivilised adults.'

'Tell me what she told you. Then I might consider it.'

'She didn't tell me very much. Tell me what yours means. Maybe hers means the same. Can't we discuss this later?'

'No. What did she tell you?'

'Nothing. She didn't tell me anything. I didn't ask her.'

There was an instant eructation of breath and the hand

that'd been gently stroking his thigh slapped it loudly in exasperation.

'You stupid waste of time.'

Instantly, she was back on her feet and re-gathering her clothes from the floor where she'd dropped them. She slipped the black dress over her head and tugged it towards her ankles in a gesture that seemed almost prudish. Jarret noticed that something was different about her. Something about her movements had changed. She was still desirable, but she was no longer the same Lulu. And when she'd spoken to him last something there had changed too. She'd been different. There were no more "Charlies". No more sounding like a fuck-everything-or-anything-good-lifer. She was serious, as if her focus had shifted from between her thighs to between her ears.

'Hey, if she didn't tell me, she didn't tell me. So what's the meaning of your tattoo?'

She turned and looked at him, but with a dismissive and angry expression. Despite the mask of her make-up, he felt the full frost of her heavy dark eyes upon him.

'Do you seriously want to know? You're not just wasting more of my time?'

Her French accent had disappeared and been replaced by a southern English one.

For a fleeting instant he had a vision of her as a dominatrix – a nanny or a nurse with a whip; maybe a stern headmistress. He blinked to dispel it, then nodded and tried to look serious.

'I'm interested.'

'If you're not bullshitting again, I'll tell you. You're right, they are symbols. The first one translates as 'dragon', the second 'lady'. Dragon Lady. Do you know who the Dragon Lady was?'

'Haven't a clue. Tell me.'

'The Whore of Babylon from the Book of Revelations – where she's described as sitting astride a dragon. She's the controller of kings, the mistress of manipulation, the ruler of rulers. The madman who wrote Revelations despised her because he was a man, writing a man's old morality. Now that old morality is being rewritten. Because every day there are more and more of us sitting astride the dragon and making it move in whatever direction we want it to. This is not all too deep for you, is it, Charlie? My tattoo is an expression of that power. It's neither sexy nor as submissive as you'd no doubt like it to be. Just a mark of the way things are changing.'

'Wow. And for my next question.'

'Don't be pathetic. You only reinforce the stereotype. Goodbye, Charlie. I wish I could say it was good to know you.'

'Whoa, not so fast! Was that a freebie or do you want paying for this evening?'

Her arm had stretched out towards the door handle. She paused abruptly. The question appeared to have surprised her and it looked as if she was mulling it over. Jarret observed the moments it took for her to reach a decision. Why the hell was she there in the first place, if it wasn't for the money? The Whore of Babylon would've reached a conclusion in no time.

'Why not?'

'That's too surreal for me. My wallet's in the back pocket of my jeans on the chair over there. Chuck it over and tell me what I owe you.'

She moved purposefully back into the bedroom, but her high heels mocked her tight-lipped determination. She squeezed the pockets of his jeans in turn until she found the one containing his wallet. Ignoring Jarret's request to throw it to him, she opened it herself and extracted five one hundred Euro notes before throwing the open wallet and jeans back onto the chair. By local rates 500 Euros was an enormous rip-off for an evening's pleasure, but he said nothing. He'd not experienced too many or any other evenings like this one and he certainly wasn't going to ruin it by haggling. Thanks to McBryde, he was able to afford it.

'Fuck it!'

Lulu was on her way back to the door when she stopped and bent down to undo the straps of her too-high high heels. She removed them with difficulty and held them dangling from her left hand, like soiled undergarments. Shorter and with a change of posture, her transformation into a new persona was now complete. She was no longer Lulu.

'Fuck it again.'

And once more she was back in the room striding towards him.

'Here, Charlie, it's charity night. Have the last one on me.'

And two one hundred Euro notes fluttered onto the bed beside him – leaving him unsure whether to feel patronised or flattered.

12 (Monday am)

It was just before dawn the next day, when Jarret was roused from his sleep by a freezing sensation in the pit of his stomach. An instant later, he was sparked into stark wakefulness. His limbs still clumsy from sleep and the previous night's alcohol, he climbed unsteadily out of bed. He swore loudly at himself. Fuck. He'd forgotten to phone McBryde. Forgotten that he'd promised to call him the previous evening to keep him clued-up on the search for Alicia. Lulu's visit had so completely preoccupied him that everything else had been erased from his mind. And when she'd left, he'd finished the whisky and passed out like a light.

He swayed downstairs in his crumpled, un-matching shorts and T-shirt. It was just after six, almost an hour before the church clock in the village was primed to strike, but he'd made up his mind to phone anyway, without delay. If McBryde considered him incompetent for not calling before, this would prove he was about to make an early-morning start. But he was praying McBryde was asleep, with his phone turned off, because leaving a voicemail would be easier.

Through the mists of the Glenfiddich, he took a moment or two to construct a plausible story. He removed from his wallet the piece of paper McBryde had given him the day before. Two telephone numbers were written in large, confident numerals – McBryde's mobile and the back-up.

Jarret took a deep breath and awaited the automated

response. He wondered whether it would be the voice supplied by the phone company or whether McBryde had recorded a message himself. The phone rang once, twice, then a voice he didn't want to hear answered it.

'Speak.'

'It's Mr Jarret.'

'I know who it is. Speak.'

'You asked me to keep you up to speed on what I'm doing.'

'Late, but I'm listening.'

'So far I've had to do everything by phone. I made a number of calls yesterday afternoon and last night and I think I may have come up with a couple of leads. The strongest one I'm going to follow up this morning. Contacting you before I'd come up with a firm strategy, I'd thought would be a waste of your time.'

'Don't think, Mr Jarret. Call me twice a day, morning and evening, like we arranged. Don't deviate, or you'll have me thinking I'm spending my money unwisely. I'm sure you don't want me to have to come and see you for a reimbursement. Okay, Mr Jarret, you've made a bad start, now impress me.'

'This morning, I'm driving into Villefranche. From the information I collected from the phone calls yesterday, I think it's got to be worth me checking out the car rental companies. There are five of them. I think the vehicle she hired was probably from nearby and not Rodez airport, as I previously thought. As soon as I can establish where, there's going to be a trail to follow.'

'Sounds plausible, but I don't want you wasting your time. No stabs in the dark, no hunches – I like facts. Understand? You get me facts, ones I can use, and I can foresee our friendship being a brief, but happy one.'

'Car rental companies is a logical first step, believe me. I'll get back to you as soon as I know anything concrete.'

'And, Mr Jarret, never lie to me. I don't like being lied

to. I always have a way of finding out the truth. Like I hope, when you weren't busy making phone calls yesterday evening, you had sufficient time to enjoy the charms of your little visitor. By all accounts, she was a bit of a stunner. I'm impressed you're out of bed so early. Goodbye, Mr Jarret. Keep in touch. And keep in the front of your mind what I've just said to you.'

With that, McBryde terminated the call, which was fortunate, because a moment longer and Jarret's language skills would have deserted him. As he walked back into the kitchen, his hands were shaking. His mouth had gone dry. He took a mug from the mug tree and filled it with water.

How did McBryde know about Lulu? Had he been watching? Did Lulu work for him? No, that can't be credible – because Martine had sent her. Or had that curly haired bastard from yesterday managed to get something else over him? The ambush on the hill had come to nothing. And there'd been nothing suspicious in his rear-view mirror all the way back to Le Papillon. Nevertheless, it seems he'd managed to follow him anyway.

But what had panicked Jarret most was that during their three-minute phone call he'd done precisely what McBryde had warned him not to – lie. About everything. Right down to the number of car rental companies there were in Villefranche. In fact, he'd no idea how many there were. For some reason he'd imagined it would sound efficient and convincing if he offered up a number. To survive, even for another day, he'd have to start telling the truth.

#

As Jarret dressed, he once again checked his damaged body. It was healing well. The contusions were more lurid but less painful and the swelling in his knee joint had all but gone. He buttoned his shirt and examined his reflection in the bathroom mirror. A vivid love bite discoloured the base of his neck, near the left shoulder. Shit, he mumbled, but couldn't help smiling: he'd not had one of those since he was a teenager. He had no recollection of Lulu biting him there, but then her visit had been sufficiently distracting for his mind to have been elsewhere anyway. He tugged at the collar of his shirt to make sure it covered the blemish. After all, when he started asking questions, looking respectable was about the only asset he would have. If that didn't work, then he'd little or nothing to fall back on.

To match the carefully ironed sky blue cotton button-down, he selected khaki chinos and a pair of slightly worn but highly polished black leather shoes. Then, to make himself look a little more dynamic and well-to-do, he rolled his shirt sleeves up two turns and snapped on a Tag Hauer watch with a silver strap – a left-over vanity from his TV days. He was unsure whether to take a Filofax and mobile phone or a laptop. In a world of superficialities, looking right was important. He decided on the black leather Filofax: the laptop was too cumbersome. He slipped a silver Parker ballpoint into the little loop underneath the clip.

From the desk drawer in the office he removed a telephone directory and opened it at the yellow pages index. He'd lied to McBryde about the number of car rental companies in Villefranche. Now, he'd need to know the correct answer. He turned to the section headed *Location d'Automobiles* and, with a feeling of trepidation, began counting. He did it carefully, running his finger along the lines of addresses, then checking them against any box adverts. He double-checked and checked again. This was his first piece of luck of the day. An omen? There was no way McBryde would be able to catch him out on that one. He'd counted five. Villefranche actually had five car hire companies. He copied their addresses and phone numbers into his Filofax.

On the desk, next to the Filofax, lay a crumpled piece of paper Jarret had forgotten about. The now-dried-out receipt from the wine merchant, Lageste, he'd found in the car park of the Manoir Ivant. He examined it for several seconds before screwing it up and throwing it into the waste-paper basket. It was another irrelevance.

How McBryde knew about his meeting with Lulu was still praying on his mind. But it wasn't until he was about to leave the house that the full flood of paranoia washed over him and stopped him dead. What if this curly headed man was not as good as Jarret thought he was? What if he, or someone else, had attached a tracking device to the Jeep, so that his every movement could be monitored from a safe distance? No wonder he'd seen no-one.

He went back upstairs, stripped to his shorts and put on a pair of worn blue overalls and beaten-up trainers. In the barn, he located two dusty metal ramps and placed them parallel to each other in the courtyard. Carefully, he drove the Jeep up onto them, so that its bonnet and front wheels were raised off the ground. Taking a torch and a screwdriver from the glove compartment, he slid underneath the car to inspect it. With the screwdriver, he scraped away the mud and animal dung that'd got there from his driving along country roads.

He worked slowly and methodically, easing his way carefully over every square centimetre. It took him twenty minutes. Then he checked beneath the bonnet, searched in the luggage area, between, under and down the back of the seats, under the rubber mats and beneath any loose pieces of carpet, and finally, in the glove compartment. As an afterthought, he went back and removed the covers from the interior lights and carefully checked each of the bulbs. Almost three-quarters of an hour had gone by. He found nothing. But he still wasn't certain.

The feeling that something was wrong persisted. In the dirty washing basket he found the clothes he'd worn to the office on Sunday morning. He tossed them into the washing machine and set the programme for long wash. He thought about going upstairs to check his shoes and belt, but even his paranoia didn't stretch that far. But he took the piece of paper McBryde had written the mobile phone numbers on and copied them into his Filofax. He then tore up the piece of paper, dropped it down the toilet and flushed it.

Thoughts of good omens and the smugness he'd felt at guessing the correct number of car rental companies had disappeared. He nosed the Grand Cherokee along the pot-holed track towards the main road, alert for any movement ahead of him. Above, grey cloud blanketed the sky. Once again it looked like rain.

#

Jarret arrived in Villefranche a little after ten to find it practically deserted. Still sleeping off its weekend hangover. He negotiated the one-way streets round the edge of the old town, heading in the direction of Farrou and Figeac. A progress which was halted, briefly, by one set of traffic lights and a solitary car crawling round the roundabout on the edge of the town. After the roundabout, he turned into the Avenue Croates, where Hertz car rental was located. He checked his mirror one last time, but the road behind him seemed empty.

Not far along the Avenue Croates, off to the right, was an empty field surrounded by a clutter of houses and small businesses. At the far end of this field stood a simple memorial to honour a group of men who'd been executed and buried there.

When Jarret first learned about the revolt of the Croats, he'd tell his friends that Villefranche-de-Rouergue had been the first place in mainland France to be liberated from the Nazis in World War II. The sad memorial was a remembrance of its failure – yet another one of history's almost-forgotten gestures.

Jarret had searched the horror of the story for a moral

but, no matter how long he thought about it, it eluded him.

Distracted by the story of the Croats, he realised too late that he'd missed the turning to the Hertz Rent-a-car office. A glance in his mirror quickly convinced him that an abrupt stop and U-turn was out of the question, as from out of nowhere a Renault Clio had driven up behind him while he was lost in thought. Instead, he decided to drive on towards the second establishment on his list. To avoid making a second error and missing it, he slowed down to under the 70kph limit and focused his attention on the hotchpotch of commercial premises ahead of him on the right. The motorist in the Renault Clio immediately tailgated him.

The business premises he was looking for were tucked away between a sports store and an outlet for artisan furniture. An ugly sign bearing the name Automoberia in black lettering against a pink background had been affixed to the front of a single-storey, square, metal-clad building. The forecourt and parking area were set back from the road and the entrance to it was narrow and abruptly angled. Large stones had been strategically placed to prevent anyone cutting the corner by driving on the grass. With the result that Jarret was forced to swing out almost into the middle of the road in order to make the slow turn into it; a manoeuvre provoking a long angry horn blast from the Clio behind.

The cheaply tarmac-ed forecourt in front of the building was pitted and the lines indicating the parking spaces were already faded and worn. Selecting one, across from the office entrance, Jarret reversed into it, ensuring that the Jeep's neat grille, its only surviving worthwhile feature, would be clearly visible. No other cars occupied the visitors' spaces. He collected his mobile phone and Filofax from the seat beside him and once again flipped through the details of the bogus story he was about to tell. He'd tried it out once before at the airport at Rodez, but today, without the distraction of a busy terminal to assist him, it had to be flawless.

Jarret was halfway across the forecourt when he changed direction in mid-stride. The rear of a little red Citroën C1, at the end of a short row of cars to the left of the entrance, attracted his attention. He walked quickly to it and round to the driver's side. Maybe the omens were with him after all. A scratch beginning halfway down the door and ending just above the rear wheel was clearly visible. He could barely believe it. It was neither deep, nor requiring anything much more drastic than a repaint job, but was as incriminating as DNA.

Entering the rectangular box of an office, he was immediately struck by the trademark stench of stale cigarette smoke and photocopier spirit. Little money or imagination had been expended on furniture – just four blue plastic chairs and a small circular low table, its synthetic surface strewn with well-thumbed car magazines. Facing the door was a counter, which may have once been cleaned – but not recently. The other side of it, a middle-aged man sat slouched behind a veneer desk, studying a sheet of paper. When Jarret entered, he didn't look up, though he must have seen him as soon as he arrived in the car park. Nor did he take any notice of him as he stood at the counter, engrossed as he was in his sheet of paper. Or at least that was the desired impression. In normal circumstances, Jarret would have become angry; but, today, given the nature of his visit, he remained outwardly calm. Upsetting anyone at this point would get him nowhere.

At length, the man behind the desk scribbled something across the bottom of his piece of paper and nodded towards Jarret, as if to let him know that he now existed.

When Jarret spoke, his cheery '*bonjour, monsieur*' was met with a nod.

'Sorry to bother you on a busy morning like this, but I was wondering whether you'd be kind enough to help me with a little problem I've got. Over the past week a young lady's been renting a cottage off me. When she left on Saturday morning everything seemed fine. But when I went around to do my final check yesterday, I found her expensive laptop computer. She'd left it inside one of the wardrobes. She must've missed it when she came to pack. Now comes the problem – because she only rented the cottage at the last minute, I'm afraid I don't have any forwarding address for her. So I came here to see if you'd be kind enough to help me locate her?'

'How d'you know she rented a car from us?'

'She'd mentioned the name of your company to me, said you were very good, and just before I came in I noticed the car she'd rented parked outside.'

'What was her name?'

'Taylor, Alicia Jennifer Taylor.'

'I'll see what I've got, but I'm not promising."

Now that he was no longer sitting down, Jarret could see that he was overweight and that, close up, complementing his florid complexion was a pair of bloodshot eyes. Strands of black greasy hair had been pulled across his scalp. And his drinker's nose was underlined by a neatly trimmed moustache.

Jarret watched as he ambled to a grey iron filing cabinet in the corner. His car rental service was obviously too small to warrant a computer system. The top drawer slid open with a harsh grating sound and he rummaged amongst the files. Nothing looked as if it was that efficient. A brief silence followed as the man scanned several documents, before trying to re-cram the files back into the over-filled drawer. He returned to the desk empty handed and supplied Jarret with the information he expected but didn't want to hear.

'Nobody by that name.'

'She was blonde, attractive. She rented the red Citroën C1 off you. The one with the scratch down the driver's side.'

157

'That wasn't her name.'

'That's the name she gave me when she rented the cottage. Perhaps she was called that before she got married. Maybe she just wanted a quiet week away from it all with nobody bothering her.'

'Perhaps.'

'Look, I'm not doing this for my benefit. I just want to return the lady's property to her, that's all. There's nothing in this for me, you understand.'

'That wasn't her name. Anyway, I can't divulge it, it's confidential.'

'What about an address?'

'I've only got a local one.'

'She's going to be worried. Anything. I'd – we'd both be grateful.'

Once again he searched through the top drawer of the filing cabinet. The document he returned with was flimsy and almost transparent. Back at the counter, he brandished it in front of Jarret's face to affirm its veracity.

'The only address I've got for her is the Manoir Ivant. Is that your place?'

'Yes.'

'Not exactly a cottage, is it?'

'No, the cottage is in the grounds.'

'I see. Then that's no help to you.'

'Some. Is there anything else you can tell me, Monsieur ...?'

'Malvy. Like you said, she's a very attractive young lady and a very generous one too. You were right, she had a little accident with the car, but insisted on paying me a thousand Euros for the inconvenience. I mean, she'd already paid for fully comprehensive insurance, so it's not as if I'm going to be out of pocket over it. Still, I'm not complaining. Like I said, she's a very generous lady.'

'Can you remember what day she picked the car up from you?'

'Thursday morning – early, very early. She was waiting at the office when I arrived.'

'What time was that?'

'Eight-thirty. Eight-thirty to nine.'

'Did she have anything with her – suitcases, carrier bags?'

'No – nothing that I noticed. I'd say she'd been walking for some time though. She looked sort of hot and tired to me. But it was possible something had upset her, a boyfriend or something. Difficult to say really, I'm no expert on women. Though when she moved inside the office, I'd say her feet might've been troubling her.'

'How did she pay you?'

'Paid in cash, cash for everything. The only thing I remember her carrying with her was her handbag.'

In response to Monsieur Malvy's obvious liking for cash, Jarret extracted a fifty Euro note from his wallet and held it on top of the counter.

'I don't suppose, if I put this into the staff collection box for next Christmas, you might by any chance remember what the young lady told you her name was?'

Jarret assumed Malvy was also the owner of the business. He acknowledged the note on the counter in front of him with the faintest of smiles. His eyes scanned the car park to make sure no-one was about to enter the office. Then, giving Jarret a brief nod of compliance, he re-examined the document he was holding between his nicotine-stained fingers.

'She's called Roberts, first name Julia.'

'Julia Roberts! Are you sure?'

'As I'm standing here. Take a look for yourself.'

Sure enough, clearly printed in small precise letters was Roberts, Julia, followed by a fairly indecipherable signature. He'd just wasted fifty Euros. Name – a film star; address – the Manoir Ivant. After the brief surge of expectancy, he realised he'd once again got nowhere.

Either Malvy had never heard of Julia Roberts or he was treating him like an idiot. He handed over the fifty Euro note.

'Here, give this to your favourite charity.'

'I will, sir, you can count on that. Glad to have been of help. But, please, this must be a secret between the two of us. But none of us mind breaking a few rules to help a lady, do we now?'

'Keeping secrets has always been a bit of a problem with me. I suppose I'm one of those unfortunate people who doesn't know when to keep his mouth shut. But, then, in this instance I've got nothing to lose. I'm not the person taking the risks here, am I?'

Jarret felt better after the outburst. If it made Malvy worry, then he was happy. Returning to the Jeep, he slammed the door and settled back in the driver's seat. He stared through the dirty windscreen, allowing time for everything to sink in. Julia Roberts was a Hollywood actress. He'd seen her a couple of times in movies that he hadn't thought much of. It was a strange choice of name. Alicia had never mentioned she liked the cinema. Yet it was unlikely to be her real name. So he must assume she was intent on covering her tracks. But from whom? Adams, he assumed. Or McBryde. But there was no mileage in guesswork.

Then there was the time she booked out the hire car – early Thursday morning, Malvy had said – a couple of hours before she'd phoned him in the Hyper U car park. So what was she doing during those couple of hours? And what had Malvy said – that it was likely she'd walked some distance before arriving at his office? Walked from where? The Manoir Ivant and then waited for the car hire office to open? That was a long hike for anyone who had the proper gear and knew the road. Had she been that desperate?

And why Automoberia Car Rentals? But the answer to that question was easy. First, it was privately owned and, secondly, when cash was involved, it was unlikely Malvy would have been over-scrupulous in his double-checking. If she'd handed him a bundle of notes, carefully checking her credit card or ID might've just slipped his mind. She was a smart woman. She'd chosen wisely. Few questions had been asked and no truths given. If it hadn't been for that scratch down the side of the car, Malvy would certainly have mislaid her records and pocketed the money.

It was now clear to Jarret that only two certainties had emerged from his visit to Automoberia. That, though it was the last thing he wanted to do, he was going to have to return to the Manoir Ivant to question Adams. Regrettably, all paths led back there. The second certainty, and one which gave him a little more pleasure, was that if McBryde had had him followed and sent someone to question Malvy, then he'd be no closer to finding Alicia than he was.

A third certainty was that Alicia's story about the drive from Rodez and her escape from the Manoir Ivant had not been true. And for that he was sorry.

A sudden rapping on the side window of the Jeep jolted Jarret from his thoughts. He looked up and there was Malvy, still holding onto the fifty Euro note, a thin sheen of perspiration covering his forehead.

'I think you better take this back. It's much too early for Christmas.'

Jay lowered the window, took the note and dropped it on to the passenger seat. He didn't want to return it to his wallet. It felt soiled.

'I thought about what you just said. But if you've given me nothing and I've given you nothing, then there's nothing for you to blab about? Anyway, I was only trying to …'

Jarret had had enough. He turned the key in the ignition and the engine, coughing into life, drowned out Malvy's final words. He turned to him as he drove off.

'And a very Happy New Year to you too.'

13 (Monday am)

It'd be the fourth time in five days Jarret had paid a visit to the Manoir Ivant – a habit that was definitely lacking in highs. He negotiated the roads around the outskirts of Villefranche on autopilot, lost in thought and to the world around him. Adams would not be happy to see him. Briefly, he played with the idea of stopping at Le Papillon for the shotgun.

It wasn't until he was driving along the river valley towards Monteils that he noticed the deterioration in the weather. Clouds, which were high when he set off that morning, had dropped to the tops of the ridges, devouring them detail-by-detail. It was not yet raining, but through the open window of the Grand Cherokee he could smell the approaching damp, that metallic aroma of pure water, being blown in by a north-west breeze. The earlier heaviness was dissipating and the season was once again in slow retreat. At the first shiver, Jarret pressed the switch to close the electric window.

The Jeep once again rumbled over the track leading to the *manoir*, dipping and lurching until it reached the car park in front of the arched entrance with the big wooden gates. He, for no reason, locked the Jeep and crossed the loosely spread gravel, then followed the neat path to the front door. When he pressed the bell, its too loud electric note pierced the tranquillity and shattered whatever vestiges of assurance he still clung on to. The house resounded and the courtyard behind it echoed in mimicry.

He waited, before ringing again.

Nothing.

He moved back to get a better view of the house. Everything looked still and serene. Only when he walked towards the left corner did he notice what in the gloom and drizzle of his last visit he'd missed – that the garage doors, instead of resting horizontally in their runners, were buckled and at different angles to the ground. Each door had been fitted with a remote control sensor. Though from the evidence of the long silver scratches and dented metal, they'd not been used to gain entry. The one garage Jarret could see clearly inside was just a clutter of emptied-out boxes, their contents strewn across the grey surface of the concrete. Everything concerning the *manoir* so far had been fastidious. He didn't believe this could have been Adams' doing.

The discovery caused a new surge of alarm. He returned to the front door and for a third time pressed the doorbell. The shrill electronic note seemed to scream even louder in the tomb-like house. Still there was no answer. No footsteps, no voices, no movement. Nothing.

He tried the handle, but the front door was so firmly locked that it didn't budge a millimetre in its frame. The shutters covering the front windows were still open and pegged back, as they had been two nights before. But, apart from the garages, nothing else about the *manoir* appeared out of the ordinary. Nothing had been smashed, nothing broken and there was no evidence of a forced entry.

Drawing on his resolve, he moved along the front of the house and looked through each of the ground-floor windows in turn. The rooms inside were neat, ordered – again, with nothing out of place, nothing to suggest there'd been a problem. The orderliness reminded Jarret of a museum – the same precision, the same lifelessness. It was pure Adams.

The sensible thing to do now, he knew, would be to

leave, return to the Jeep and get the hell out of there. But two reasons prevented him from doing so – one, the chance of discovering a clue to the whereabouts of Alicia; and, two, being able to impress McBryde by adding the visit to his busy morning's worksheet.

The side of the house that led towards the swimming pool remained precisely as before. Perhaps the grass had grown a bit longer, but it couldn't be called untidy – certainly it wouldn't have made him reach for the lawnmower at Le Papillon. A fine drizzle was now being driven in on the chill breeze. Once again, he'd forgotten to bring a coat with him.

Even though it was no longer hot, the four windows in the barn conversion were still ajar. But this time they were not Jarret's preferred means of entry. He wanted his visit to be out in the open and legitimate. He'd got nothing to hide and he was quite prepared, now he had McBryde lurking in the background, to face whatever music Adams could conduct. Nevertheless, he filed away the fact that, if a break-in did prove necessary, open windows indicated that the alarm system was once again likely to have been disengaged.

It was approaching lunchtime and there was something odd about the place. Flo and Morgan should have been in their little cottage at the back of the pool. It was inconceivable they'd not heard the doorbell. Although he had some answering to do to Morgan, he half hoped they were around. Someone to talk to would prove reassuring – someone to talk to. The continual silence was unsettling.

Jarret rounded the corner of the barn conversion. On the circular table beside the pool were the two empty wine glasses, now part-filled with rainwater. And the half-finished bottle of red Bordeaux – its Grand Cru label damp and darkened. The wooden chair, with its tied-on blue cushion, lay on its side like before. But apart from the addition of Saturday night's rain, nothing appeared different.

He walked on to beside the pool, his eyes straining through the drizzle for a view of the cottage. The front door had been left wide open. Evidence of life or ... abandonment? He wasn't sure. In the gloom of Saturday night, he'd have been unable to see it. Once again, he resisted a strong urge to leave and return to Le Papillon.

But he owed it to Alicia. If anything bad had happened to her because of Adams, then ... Momentary anger filled him with a flimsy courage and he strode away from the pool and into the wide courtyard – alert for sound or movement. But the vast space between the buildings was deserted.

He scanned the buildings, then the twin ascent of the stone steps to the second level back door. A dark, thick shadow down the vertical of the right jamb suggested it too might have been left ajar. But the distance made it impossible to be sure. His eyes dug into the darkness of the far corners and into the depths of the dead-eyed windows. All remained still and silent. And except for the rooftops and the granite walls, which were darkening in the drizzle, everything was as undisturbed as he'd remembered it.

#

To Jarret's right, as he stood facing the main house, was a large barn opposite the one which had already been converted. Its junction with a high stone wall completed the *manoir*'s angled U-shape perfectly. So far, the barn had not been touched, but in all probability was in Adams' plans for the next stage of development. The high stone wall which adjoined it to the house contained the arched door leading to the garages. The entrance to this unrenovated barn was through another larger arched doorway with two heavy ancient wooden doors, both of which were firmly shut.

It wasn't until Jarret's first hesitant steps towards the

main house that he noticed a dark irregular shape, laying on the cobbles the far side of the courtyard. He moved closer to get a better look and, as he did so, more shapes began to emerge, spread beyond and around the first. But in the poor light it was difficult to make out what they were.

In all probability, they were old rags left out by a workman that the wind was blowing around, because the barn was where building materials were being stored for the renovation work on the cottage. Something Jarret himself was only too familiar with. His barn at Le Papillon was stacked with usable remnants left over from projects completed years ago, and that he could never quite bring himself to throw away. Everyone who owned an old house knew it went with the territory.

But there was something about the colour of the rags that wasn't right. He walked slowly towards them. There were more of them than he first thought, strewn across the cobbles beyond the shelter of the outbuilding's overhanging roof. Already the drizzle had reshaped them, flattened them, making them difficult to make out. He stopped and scanned the length of the barns, searching once again for signs of life – someone watching him, an electric light, anything. But the only sound that reached him was of water dripping from the un-guttered roofs onto the courtyard.

Once again, he walked slowly towards the barn. Ten metres away from the arched doorway, he distinguished a pair of black boxer shorts – manufacturer's name emblazoned across the grey waistband. A further few paces and he identified the dull shape of a sock, and beyond that the green, red, black vertical stripes of an expensive shirt, its front torn, ivory coloured buttons scattered on the cobbles around it.

Shit.

A pair of white trousers and a number of other garments lay scattered to his left, nearer the house. But he didn't move to examine them.

166

Whatever was inside the barn, Jarret didn't want to see it. Common sense screamed at him to leave whatever was in there to the gendarmes. Entering the barn was the last thing in the world he wanted to do. But if Alicia was in there, if anything had happened to her, she shouldn't be found by a stranger. His picked up the boxer shorts by their elaborate waistband and examined them as if they and they alone held the key to whatever had been happening there.

The next instant, he reacted with revulsion, suddenly aware of the saturated object he was holding. Disgusted, he hurled the boxer shorts as far away as he could into the courtyard, where they landed with an audible smack. He wiped his hand clean on his damp chinos.

The ancient latch lifted effortlessly, but the door it was attached to was stubborn. Only by tugging on it using his full weight did he get it to slowly yield. Though wormholes and weather had taken their toll on the wood, the rough hand-forged nails, protruding from the contours of grain, held it firmly together. As the door inched open, Jarret fought to prevent his imagination reaching into overdrive.

A pale light entered the interior and he followed it inside. The first thing he saw made him retch. His stomach muscles buckled and his throat gagged. He narrowed his eyes until they became wrinkled slits, as if peering through partially closed lids diminished the horror which was confronting him. After several more contractions, his mouth tasted bitter and dry. This was a horror like none he'd seen in a war zone. He'd heard stories of atrocities happening in Kosovo and Macedonia when he was there, but he'd never known whether to believe them or not. They were always recounted to him by gruesome bastards who seemed to revel in the disgust they evoked. In Africa, he'd heard stories too, but he'd eyewitnessed none of them. Now his virginity was broken.

In the middle of the barn, hands strapped to a crossbeam above his head, was Fraze – or what used to be Fraze.

His back had been forced against a crude wooden pillar, used to support one of the crossbeams, and his hands tied behind him. His legs had been tied, one either side of the pillar, securing them and forcing them slightly apart. A grey funereal light seeped from the door and from the two horizontal rectangular windows high up in the wall.

Ignoring the screams coming from inside him, Jarret moved closer.

Fraze's nose had been removed and one of his eyes gouged to look like a devil's – weeping bloody tears. The other eye was lifeless, and for the first time Jarret noticed the delicate fair eyelashes that framed it. One of his ears had been completely severed. A heavy object had been used against the jaw and mouth, blood discoloured his chin, and from the concavity of his cheek, it was clear not many of his teeth had remained intact. The bastard, who'd made a fool of him, now appeared gentle and transcendent. An image came into Jarret's mind of a martyred saint, his skin marked by stigmata. On his left side a floating rib had been fractured and bent inwards by the force of a blow, probably from the same heavy object used on his jaw. But, compared to what Jarret discovered next, all that must've seemed like a game.

Around his feet the earth floor of the barn was dark with blood and flies, and the inside of his thighs and shins and both feet were discoloured from the gush that must have emanated from his severed genitals. If it wasn't for the crudeness with which they'd been removed and the blood and the stench and the buzz and darting of the small black insects, Fraze could have been modelling for the statue of a wingless angel.

Summoning the courage, Jarret took Fraze's head in his right hand and gently lifted it. The flesh was quite cold, but the head moved easily, meaning the body had processed beyond rigor mortis. Death, therefore, must have occurred more than thirty-six hours before. Time enough for the flies to discover it, but probably insufficient for the first maggots to hatch. Then Jarret shuddered. At the thought he might still have been alive when he called there on Saturday evening.

A smell, other than the barn and of death, began to seep into Jarret's nostrils – a familiar one that seemed out of place in the dank interior of the barn. A smell which possessed two surfaces – both of them identifiable, overlapping but not complementary. One was the smell of burning – the other of cooked meat. The nausea rose again and he retched – a heave of contracting muscles terminating in the same dull ache.

He examined Fraze's body for signs of burning. There were no blackened marks, only the blood from the torn genitals congealed against his now ghostly tan. Screwing up his eyes, he looked into the darker recesses of the barn for the origin of the smell. But there were no other bodies strapped to beams, no figures sprawled in a death pose on the cold earth.

Then he became aware of the tell-tale sound coming from behind him. Over the first swarm of flies, there was the unmistakeable sound of another. Another with another focus, with a host other than Fraze to concentrate on – another mess to eradicate. Jarret knew that flies could locate death perhaps faster than any other creature. Within days they'd have a body crawling with maggots and, in time, strip it to the chalk of its bones. They functioned as Nature's cleaning company – corpses, food, excrement – no job too messy.

Jarret prayed. Unbeliever, rationalist that he was. A man suddenly wracked by a new nausea. He prayed – to an unspecified deity – his pulse accelerating and his imagination filling with images of new horror. *O please don't let it be her ... not like this ... not in this filthy, stinking, cess hole of a barn.* But whether he recited the prayer on his behalf or Alicia's was uncertain.

The light coming through the opened side of the double door made identification difficult. But he'd seen enough to make him realise his terror had been justified. Swaying unsteadily for a moment, it was as much as he could do to remain upright. Behind the unopened half of the door, slumped forward but not on the ground, hung the shape of a second body, smaller than Fraze's, more fragile. Jarret knew it had to be her. His stomach frosted over and his legs became columns of useless ice. That bastard Adams had finally done it. Tears exploded down his cheeks and a choking sound, like a cough, escaped from his throat. She was dead. Jarret vowed that he'd find him and kill him. That he'd hunt him down, if it took up the rest of his life. And when he found him, he'd make sure Adams knew who it was who was going to kill him and why. Because he'd be looking right into his eyes when he did it.

In the shadow of the crudely finished door, the dead shape hung strangely. Jarret moved ever closer to it, then stopped, because what he saw made him want to scream. Open his lungs and let his vocal chords rip apart the afternoon. But it wasn't fear or grief that possessed him now, but the music of destruction – because of what had been done to her.

The desecration of the flies burned in his ears. He wondered why they kept on moving when what they were settling on was dead. She was no threat to them now.

Another step closer and he recoiled, as if an invisible hand had pushed him hard in the middle of his chest. The figure behind the door had remained in an upright position because it had been crucified. The fresh horror of this discovery reactivated in a chaos of revulsion and loathing. The body in the shadows was slumped forward. Its weight held by whatever cruelty has been hammered through the palms of its hands. Its right foot has been nailed to the door, leaving it to support itself on the left one alone. The foot nailed to the barn door had forced the legs apart to reveal the genitalia. There were none, just a dark discolouration.

Enough!

The next moment he was outside and gagging on the fresh, damp air. The shock had stripped him of volition. It was time to leave, but his task was incomplete. He couldn't let anyone else find her like that. He had to cover her.

He re-entered the barn, and as he did so he unbuttoned the front of his shirt. There was nothing else he could use to drape over her tortured body. But it wasn't necessary. The corpse behind the door was not Alicia, but male. Was male. A face he recognised. Suspended by two ugly nails smashed through his claw-like palms – his chin resting on his chest, his hair lolling in rats' tails over the bony contours of his forehead. It was Adams. Acridity emanated from the ugly marks that covered his body. His arms and chest and both nipples had been horribly burned. His navel had been obscured and both thighs criss-crossed with torment.

Beside Adams's body on the ground, tilted on its side, was a blowtorch, its pale blue gas canister inappropriately colourful against the dark earth of the floor. Now it was apparent why he mistook him for a woman – because whoever had tortured him like this had completely erased his manhood. Burnt it away. This had not been the work of seconds or minutes. The torture Adams and Fraze had been subjected to had been slow and methodical.

Like a man in a trance, he found himself once again inhaling the clean, damp air of the courtyard. He needed to think. Because if Adams hadn't done this, there was only one other person he could think of who might have. And it scared him.

He tugged the big double door from its position against the wall and dragged it, groaning in protest, across the cobbles. Enclosing the darkness – like the lid on a coffin.

14 (Monday am)

The air outside was no drier or warmer than before, but after the stench of the barn it smelled pure. Jarret stumbled to the centre of the courtyard, numb and confused. His anger had ebbed and been replaced by a sense of foreboding. He'd hated Adams and Fraze and everything they stood for and for what they'd done to Alicia; but, even in his profoundest thoughts of revenge, he would never have wished that fate on them.

The very stillness of the Manoir Ivant was tomb-like. The grey light and the drizzle enfolded the buildings like a watery shroud. So far, he had found two bodies. There were possibly more. And Alicia's could be one of them. Like it or not – he'd no option but to continue with his search.

Then a sudden sound behind him sent him spinning in reflex – weight on the balls of his feet, body hunched over, fists clenched. With difficulty he sought the source of the danger, his mind still reeling from the violent obscenity he'd just witnessed. The sound was like a machine gun. Or rather someone imitating a burst of machine gun fire. But amplified by the buildings and the silence of the courtyard.

His eyes flashed from building to building and into the countryside that lay beyond the pool and the little stone cottage. Searching for the danger before it destroyed him. Then a black dot ripped across his sight, *Chack, chack, chack, chack, chack.* A warning. A call beating in his temples and threatening to rip out his heart. *Chack, chack, chack, chack.* Then it took to the air. And he saw that the black dot had a yellow beak and feathers, and was as startled as he was. Heart pounding, he watched as the blackbird flew in the direction of the cottage.

Tucked away as it was, snug at the bottom of a slight incline, the cottage might once have seemed cosy. Now it seemed to be sinking in the drizzle. Though built at a distance from the main house, it was still close enough to allow Flo and her handyman hubby to be on permanent call. Jarret hoped they'd had the sense to run away.

The small picket gate, in front of the cottage, opened onto a narrow path. Left ajar, it moved almost imperceptibly, a parody of motion in the drizzle-laden breeze. Jarret crossed the tiny garden to the open front door. He knocked. Then he knocked again. There was no answer. He went inside.

The front door entered directly into a lounge-cum-dining room, though beneath the disorder and clutter, it was difficult to distinguish which was which. The best that could be said about it was it fulfilled a purpose. Intermingling smells of marijuana, patchouli oil, sweat and stale beer permeated the gloom.

From the lounge, Jarret climbed the open-plan wooden staircase to the bedrooms. They relieved nothing other than a repeat of the squalor and clutter that attended Flo and Morgan's everyday lives. No bodies, no evidence of violence – only light and a welcome breath of air from the half-open windows.

It was not until he'd returned downstairs and crossed what passed as a dining area towards the back of the cottage that he became conscious of the smell. Not strong – but distinguishable above the others. A smell that was as sweet as it was unpleasant.

The space between the dining area and the kitchen was littered with parts from a dismantled motorbike. The cheap floral wallpaper had become spattered with grease. Unlike all the other inside doors, the door to the kitchen was shut. As he opened it, the black iron handle felt cold against his palm, colder even than Fraze's dead flesh. The door, lighter than it looked, clattered against the wall. Instantly, a swarm of flies rose from a dark object, spread in the centre of an old wooden table, too small to be human. A large black-handled kitchen knife protruded from it at right angles.

Peasant cottages in the Aveyron rarely admitted much light, but of all the rooms in this one, the kitchen was the darkest.

He flapped at the resettling flies with his hand. The kitchen knife pinioned a dead cat to the surface of the table. The scratch marks on the wood indicated its death wasn't immediate. Or painless. But the stench in the room didn't emanate from the dead cat, but elsewhere. He lifted the lid of a pan, on a filthy gas stove, and found the stew inside was already rotting.

He escaped back into the fresh air.

On the far side of the courtyard were the renovated barns. When he looked inside, they were as he remembered from his previous visit – as neat and tidy as Adams would've wanted them to be. After what he'd witnessed, their orderliness came as a strange relief.

Only as he crossed the courtyard towards the main house did he become aware of the strengthening wind, as it pulled at his shirt and drove the drizzle against the side of his face. He made up his mind to enter the main house by way of the lower floor, a way he knew from his previous visit.

The giant brass candlestick still propped open the heavy wooden door. As he climbed to the top of the house, the spiral staircase once again creaked, but no longer with that same reassuring sense of affluence. He felt his way down the badly illuminated corridor until he came to the room where he'd found Alicia's slashed suitcase and its scattered contents, and nervously opened the door. But there was nothing this time to be found. The room had been cleaned and tidied and looked so different from his previous visit and might even have been the wrong one. But all the other bedrooms he looked in were the same – ready for future visitors who'd never arrive.

Jarret retraced his steps down the spiral staircase and into the courtyard. His earlier impression had been right. The door at the top of the stone double staircase leading to the main house had been left ajar. Given the weight and thickness of the wood, it would have taken a very strong wind to open it. There hadn't been one. He felt his heart staccato. He'd already witnessed more than enough without having to go any further. But he still hadn't found Alicia.

Wearily, he climbed the worn stone steps.

The door was open just wide enough for Jarret to be able to glimpse the white plasterboard wall. He pushed on it and it swung three-quarters open. The grey exterior light feebly penetrated a corridor that ran from the front of the house to the back. Again, he heard the noise of flies, but he was no longer surprised by it. Numbness had taken its place. He felt like sleeping. But Flo had already beaten him to it: curled as she was like a child on the polished wood floor. Flo, Florence – what did it matter what she was called now? What did it ever matter? Foetus-like, she was peacefully asleep. Only she was not asleep. There was a dark pool haloing her head like a pillow, though not as soft or as comforting. Her throat had been cut and the blood had gushed and ribboned down the wall on the right-hand side of the corridor.

Jarret searched inside himself for the appropriate emotion. What he stared at, what had happened to Flo, was as hideous as anything he'd so far encountered. But his feelings had become obscure. He could no longer connect with them. As he walked past, he was careful to avoid Flo's congealed dark halo, as if stepping on it might wake her. But the revulsion he might earlier have felt had been repressed.

175

He checked inside the two large rooms that led off the corridor. Only the thought that he might find Alicia – another victim of this carnage – propelled him. He struggled to concentrate. But the rooms were empty. There were no more bodies.

At the bottom of the stone staircase was a door identical to the one at the other side of the building. Like the other, it was heavy and made of oak, but was not held open with a giant brass candlestick. Apart from the garages, this was the final place Jarret had to look. He tried the handle, expecting the door to be locked. It wasn't. He pushed it wide and looked around for a light switch. There were no windows and whatever light there was came through the open door. The switch, halfway up the wall to the right, was modern and had been recently fitted.

Wearily, Jarret looked around him. And if he could have still felt surprised, he might have been. The space in front of him was totally different to anywhere else in the *manoir*. The modernisation was crude and the decoration rough and unfinished. None of the beams had been sandblasted, the floor was basic cement and the walls had been only crudely white-washed. And, unlike anywhere else, it was dusty. But all Jarret registered at first was that there were no bodies. Only after that the space had been divided into two open-sided utility rooms – one equipped as a washroom and the other as a kitchen store with deep freezes and a fridge almost large enough to enter. That it was where Flo had worked. Where she must have been coming from when he first saw her.

In the shadow of a recess stood another entrance, running, he supposed, beneath the centre part of the main house. As he approached it, he right away saw there was something wrong. The old wooden door hung askew on its hinges. And where the lock fitted into the frame, was newly splintered wood.

Inside, there was pitch darkness. He ran his hand over

the cold stone wall until he found a light switch. It felt curiously round. It was only after he pressed it, with a loud click, that he realised that it was old and made of china, and must have been there when Adams had bought the house. Strange that he should have kept it.

The single fluorescent light blinked into life, revealing a very large *cave*. Eight rows of recently constructed wooden racks stood on the newly concreted floor – each with its neat rows of bottles. Jarret stopped and examined those nearest to him. They were vintage and expensive. Like elsewhere in the *manoir*, money seemed no object.

Despite the dirtiness of the stone walls and the beams overhead, the bottles were free from dust. They'd not been there long. Then Jarret remembered finding the receipt for wine stuck to the gravel of the car park. It had been from Monsieur Lageste, the local wine merchant. Though the racks had largely been filled, the empty boxes in the corner indicated that Adams was still in the process of building his impressive selection when he was killed.

Venturing deeper into the musty interior, Jarret passed racks crammed with Bordeaux, Burgundy, Rhône, Alsace and Champagne wines. In pleasanter times, he would have enjoyed himself – just looking. The rack farthest away from the door had been reserved for local wines – from Marcillac, Gaillac, Entraygues and Millau, wines that were unlikely to age beyond eight to ten years.

Lying on its side in the shadow between the rack of local wines and the stone wall was a wooden wine box. Its lid had been levered off and nails protruded from it like sparse, silver teeth. The box itself was empty, but beside it was the broken neck end of a wine bottle, with three-quarters of the label still adhering to it. He was surprised he couldn't smell the stale wine. Out of a drinker's curiosity, he picked up the bottle by the neck and held it towards the light. As he did so a little white powder dropped down the front of his shirt and stuck to it.

He moved to beneath the fluorescent light at the centre of the *cave*. The powder had a consistency that looked very familiar – something that reminded him of his past. Before everything had imploded. He sniffed at it. Then wet his finger, slid it around in the neck of the bottle and rubbed it against his gum. Cocaine. Pure cocaine. Superior to anything that had ever come his way. The bottle must have once been full of it?

He now understood why Adams carried a gun. And maybe explained what had happened. He'd been tortured to reveal where his drugs were hidden? But that had not been enough to stop him being killed.

Jarret felt the fear return. He looked down at his hand holding the bottle. It was shaking. He'd had enough. He was about to discard the bottle on top of one of the racks when the flapping label caught his attention. The words printed on it screamed at him. He held them to the light and re-read them carefully – almost letter by letter. As if by doing so he could alter them. But they remained the same – Château La Tour Saint Briac. The wine Alicia had bought for her father.

Jarret went to where he'd earlier found the bottle and collected the empty wooden wine box, which had lain on the ground beside it. Once again, he returned to the light in the middle of the cellar to examine it. He held it up so he could clearly see the words and logo carved into the side of it. The ground under his feet seemed to be giving way. The implication was stark. The box he held in his hand corresponded exactly to the one Alicia had asked him to retrieve for her.

Wanting to disprove his own evidence, he went round each of the racks and shook a number of bottles. But they contained only what they were supposed to – wine. He wished desperately it were otherwise. But it was clear that it was the La Tour Saint Briac consignment that had contained the cocaine. And Alicia had six bottles of it,

178

which explained Adams's anger towards her. And towards him, who'd come stumbling like an idiot between them.

Now he understood that if Alicia wasn't dead, she was in serious trouble.

Outside, the light seemed even less real. The heavy drizzle driven into his face by the wind was refreshing. He made a final visual check of the courtyard, then headed for the arched door in the stone wall, which joined the barn where the bodies of Adams and Fraze were to the main house. It was the quickest route back to the car park.

As he passed the garages, he saw that his earlier suspicion had been correct. Each one had been violently broken into. The tool used to wrench them open had buckled the sides and bottoms of the metal doors. To the right of the garages was the rosemary bush where Alicia had stashed away the wine box for him to pick up. Now a dead man was lying in the middle of it, crushing it in two like a centre parting. By the size of the stomach, there was no doubting who he was. One of his oil-stained hands lay stretched against the red-brown earth, the other was across his chest, as if he'd tried to protect himself.

Jarret walked quickly past. He didn't care how they'd killed him. He'd already travelled too far down that particular road to wish to find out. That Morgan was dead was indisputable. That Alicia wasn't one of the persons lying among the dead was also indisputable. For now that would do him.

15 (Monday pm)

Jarret stripped and crammed his wet, corpse-reeking clothes into the washing machine and started it rotating. In the shower, he scrubbed at his skin until it was pink and almost raw, to liberate himself from the impregnation of death. But neither the shower gel nor the shampoo had the power to overlay the stench that lingered as much in his mind as in his nostrils. It felt as if it was oozing from his body like sweat.

After leaving the *manoir*, Jarret had driven straight to the river village of Laguépie where, from a pay phone near the railway station, he telephoned the gendarmerie. He'd chosen Laguépie partly because he knew it, but mainly because it was situated in the neighbouring departement of Tarn et Garonne, the same as the Manoir Ivant. After pointing the local gendarmes in the direction of the murders, he then intended returning the short distance back across the border to Le Papillon, and away from the ensuing investigation. If the call was ever traced, it could never be traced back to him. He wanted the repercussions from the slaughter at the *manoir* to remain exactly where they were. He'd already enough to worry about without gendarmes knocking on his front door.

The gendarme on the other end of the telephone exhibited an audible lack of interest. Being contacted during the two-hour lunch break was plainly something he wasn't keen to encourage. But as Jarret continued to describe to him the magnitude of the crime at the *manoir*, his excitement mounted. Until, finally, shaking off his lunch-time torpor, he fired off a number of questions, none of which Jarret had the slightest intention of answering. Neither his location, address, name or contact number. So he hung up.

After Laguépie, he drove in the direction the Jeep was facing, towards St Antonin and along the river valley. An indirect route home, but it made sense – in case anyone in the village had noticed him. If so, and the gendarmes asked questions, he wanted them looking in the wrong direction.

#

By the time he'd dressed after his shower, the afternoon was already too advanced to think about returning to Villefranche. Anyway, after the *manoir*, he just didn't have it in him to do any more. A strange lethargy had descended. Tracing Alicia's movements after she'd returned the hire car would have to wait until morning. For a moment he thought about phoning Automoberia, but convinced himself another personal visit in the morning would be more persuasive. It may or may not be important, but he'd like to know what had happened and where she'd headed after dropping off the hire car – whether she'd walked away or whether someone had come to pick her up. He was annoyed with himself for not having asked the questions earlier.

But, right now, all that could wait. He just wanted to sleep. He lay back in the chair and closed his eyes. The fatigue he felt was palpable. But his brain resisted.

Since the discovery of the cocaine, the stakes had become undeniably higher. And even if he managed to locate Alicia, he was doubtful he'd be able to help her. She was in too deep.

Outside the window, a sudden burst of sunlight illuminated the courtyard. Jarret got up from his chair and, almost instinctively, headed straight for it. His need

181

for warmth and light was greater than his need for sleep. The cloud was beginning to break up, patches of blue punctuating the dull grey curtain. But in the bluster of a north-west wind, it remained too chill for comfort.

Turning his face towards the sun, he shut his eyes and tried to relax, allowing the moment to drift as if it were the only reality – or, at least, the only one that mattered. That all the other things were in a dream he hadn't really woken from – a nightmare that the sunlight would finally dissolve.

How long he remained in that trance-like state, he couldn't say. But quite suddenly he opened his eyes and shuddered – a shudder not caused by the chill wind. He'd promised to phone McBryde. And, all at once, images of what had happened at the *manoir* returned.

Feeling a mixture of fear and obligation, he went inside.

'It's Mr Jarret. I'm keeping you updated, as requested.'

'Where are you?'

'At home.'

'It's rather early to be there, is it not? I trust you've got something important to tell me.'

'I've been following a very strong line of inquiry. Once I've finalised a list of names and addresses, I'll be able to get on to it again first thing in the morning.'

'Okay, so let's have it. I hope it's good.'

'I think you'll be pleased.'

As Jarret spoke, he carried the portable telephone back into the sunshine. If he was to endure this conversation with McBryde, at least he could breathe fresh air while doing so. Above him, a handful of swifts trawled the sky for insects. Step by step, he recounted details of his visit to the car hire company – his ingenuity in locating the office and discovering the car and some spiced-up details of his interview with the owner.

To avoid interruption, he talked rapidly. He didn't want McBryde asking questions. Especially ones he didn't want to answer. His account lasted for more than five minutes before he ran out of things to say. But McBryde seemed satisfied and told him that he could now start looking somewhere else – a suggestion that filled him with panic. He had no other line of enquiry and no idea where to look for one. For the moment car rental was the one string to his one bow. To stay healthy he had to be of use to McBryde, and to be of use he had to have something to sell.

He tried convincing McBryde that it was imperative he returned to interview the owner of the car hire company. That something had come up since the morning that required further sensitive inquiry, if it was to bear fruit. That everything was at a delicate stage. He used the words 'sensitive' and 'delicate' optimistically, because sensitive and delicate McBryde was not. And further, he'd need the information he got from the telephone calls that afternoon to formulate further questions.

When he'd finished, there was a chilling silence.

'I'll give you until tomorrow evening, Mr Jarret. After that, we'll talk to the gentleman ourselves. There may be something that's slipped his mind. I'm certain he'll find me a little more persuasive than you.'

'I'm certain he will.'

'And tomorrow I'll expect you to work harder for your money, otherwise you'll start making me very unhappy. And that wouldn't be a good thing to do.'

'You won't be disappointed.'

'I trust not. Tell me, is there anything I can help you with?'

'No, no, everything's going along fine for the moment, thanks.'

'So what else have you done? It's been a long and weather-wise not very pleasant day, so I'd like to think you've been using my money profitably. Perhaps you visited somewhere else that might be of interest to me? Some other inquiries, maybe, you'd like to tell me about?'

If McBryde didn't already know about the bloodbath at

the *manoir*, it would soon be splashed across the media. And neither circumstance nor discretion dictated that Jarret should be the principal source of such information. He'd already taken elaborate precautions to avoid being in any way connected.

Almost on cue, a cloud obscured the sun, throwing a dark shadow over the courtyard and the trees beyond. A blackcap from somewhere near the house repeated its insistent, monotonous call.

Then Jarret felt the dark stab of paranoia. McBryde had known about Lulu's visit to Le Papillon. So what did he know about his visit to the *manoir* this morning? Had he had somebody watching him? The curly haired man? Nothing could be trusted any more. Maybe McBryde already knew about everything. Maybe, he …

'Are you still there, Mr Jarret? Did I ask you something that was too difficult for you to understand? I don't appreciate not being kept fully in the picture. I'm sure you can understand that. So what else have you got to tell me? Where I'm concerned, there's no such thing as irrelevant information. So spill.'

But Jarret was unable to reply. His thumb depressed the red telephone icon and the call terminated. He knew he should redial immediately – claim he'd been cut off and attempt to put things straight. He could then go on to describe what he'd seen at the *manoir*. But he also knew he was never going to, that it was already too late. His silence had revealed everything. Phoning back and coming clean might be enough to save his skin in the short term, but that was all. If McBryde had had him followed, he must also know that Jarret had made a telephone call. And it wouldn't be long before he realised it was to the gendarmerie. Was that, in fact, what he'd been anxious to learn – just how much of a liability Jarret had become? Terminating the telephone call like that had supplied him with the answer.

Though he'd not anticipated it happening so soon, his

choices had just run out. Before long, McBryde would pay him a visit – and he didn't want to be around when he arrived. And he couldn't run to the police. Because, like Alicia, they could never guarantee his complete protection either. But run he would have to. Abandon Le Papillon and the new life he was building. Then images of his curly haired shadow sprang to mind and he felt more helpless and vulnerable than ever.

For the moment everything at Le Papillon was peaceful – no movement other than the birds and the wind in the trees. Jarret had parked the Jeep beside the barn under the protective cover of the walnut tree. It had nearly a full tank of diesel. Before the day was through, he was going to need it. He checked the single track that led from the house up to the beginning of the zed bend. In the summer, it was largely obscured by weeds and the overhang of foliage. The wind now and then parted the leaves, allowing a partial view of what lay beyond. As the sun broke through, the shadow of a cloud retreated across the line of his vision.

It was then that he saw it – something shiny at the lower bend of the track. An intermittent glint coming from the parking space he'd cleared for huntsmen. The adrenaline rush he felt was almost audible. He waited for the wind to move once more amongst the trees. And then he saw it, a car's chrome grille and headlight briefly visible through the shifting foliage. Partial and fleeting, but unmistakeable.

Everything was now happening faster than he'd anticipated.

McBryde had already penned him in.

With the telephone in one hand and a bottle of calvados in the other, he took the stairs to his bedroom two at a time. The room was still a mess from Lulu's visit. From the window he could see nearly the entire vehicle – the logo, the two staring headlights and chrome grille surround stark against the black bonnet. It was an Audi. Its design lines disappeared beneath the shadow of the trees. Jarret guessed it was a new model A4 or A6 – low-slung, fast. He'd have no chance of losing it in the Grand Cherokee, even on the roads around Solac.

The day had already taken a toll. He pulled the cork from the bottle of calvados and took two long draughts. So much for him having quit drinking. Almost at once he felt the alcohol circulate through his system. It made him light-headed, but began to calm his fears. He took a long last draught for luck.

Keeping a cautious eye on the car in the trees, Jarret fetched a small rucksack and packed it with clothes and a bag of toiletries from the bathroom. Any larger piece of luggage was bound to attract suspicion. One mobile phone call or a vehicle blocking his exit and it would all be over. He wanted everything he did to appear quite normal. If he could leave Le Papillon with the Audi following him like a well-trained sheepdog, he'd have achieved his goal.

Downstairs, he took his passport from the desk drawer in the office and slid it into one of the side pockets of the rucksack. Then he collected a raincoat and his leather jacket and left them, together with the rucksack, by the front door, which he locked securely. As he left the kitchen, he switched on all the electric spotlights, so if anyone came near, it'd appear he was still in the house. Next, he pulled his toolbox from under the stairs and searched through until he found his Swiss Army knife. From a nail above the back door he took a bunch of keys and returned to the hallway. There he unlocked a cupboard and took out a shotgun. Next to it was a camouflage jacket that he'd bought during his brief flirtation with the French hunting scene. He'd lost quite a bit of weight since his heavy drinking days and the jacket hung loosely from his shoulders.

Checking first to make sure that the Audi hadn't moved, he returned through the house, turning on the hall lights as he went and those on the landing above. After exiting through the back door, he locked it behind him, turning the key twice in the heavy-duty lock. Straightaway he made for the shelter of Trixie's buddleia hedge. There he stopped to check out the area between the farmhouse and the edge of the valley to make sure there was no-one lying in wait for him. He took his time. He couldn't afford to get it wrong. When at last he quit the dense, purple-flowered foliage, he crossed over to the edge of the valley and began to pick his way carefully down the steep incline. At the bottom of the shadowed valley, a stream was gurgling.

The sunlight had already dissipated and a perceptible chill descended on the thickly grassed, undulating slope. Moisture from the previous day's drizzle quickly made the bottom of his trouser legs damp and heavy, and filled his trainers with a clammy cold. The going was slow – his ankles angled and strained over the uneven ground. Every so often he stopped to check the edge of the valley above him. If McBryde or any of his men looked over and found him there, he was in trouble. An image of what'd happened to Adams passed before his mind. He would have nowhere to run.

Once at the bottom, Jarret followed the clatter of the stream for about seventy metres until a line of trees towered above him. There he started his steep ascent back to the top. Breathless, he arrived at the trees and began to search for the arcing footpath, which would lead him through the woodland. A dampness and mustiness hung in the air.

As soon as he found it, he followed it along the contour of the hill to the centre of a tiny clearing. From there, he took an even narrower footpath that wound between the trees towards the area where the Audi was parked. To avoid being seen in the car's wing mirrors, he made a final detour before crawling towards the vehicle on his stomach. He moved slowly and carefully, trying to disguise his movements in those of the wind in the foliage and trees.

One of the Audi's two occupants was talking on a mobile phone. Jarret could hear the rumble of his voice, followed by intervals of silence. The voice was deep and monotonous and sounded heavy with the boredom. After ringing off, he put the phone in the top pocket of his shirt and turned to his companion in the driver's seat. An incomprehensible discussion followed before the man with the mobile in his shirt pocket swung round and reached out for something on the rear seat of the car. For a few moments it seemed out of his reach and looked like he'd have to get out of the car to get it, but then he swung back holding a small white bag in his left hand. Taking a triangular packet from the bag, he opened it along its longest side and offered the contents to the other man. There was another brief rumble of conversation, then the man took a sandwich from the packet he was being offered and they began to eat.

Crawling the final few yards was made more difficult by the fact that Jarret was holding the shotgun. But leaving it behind him in the trees wasn't an option he was prepared to consider. If there was an emergency, he wanted it beside him. To prevent it scraping along the ground and attracting attention, he held it in front of his face in both hands, and wriggled forward, using his elbows and his legs to propel himself.

As soon as he reached the rear of the car, he slid beneath it like a clumsy mechanic. Laying down the shotgun, he felt in his jacket pocket for the Swiss Army knife. With the gun within easy reach next to him, he worked one of the knife's short blades into the wall of the left rear tyre. On more modern cars like this one, the tyre walls tended to be shallower, with a much smaller ratio of height to width, which meant their metal wheel rims ran much closer to the road than was the case with older vehicles. For what Jarret had in mind, that made them perfect.

Trying to avoid hitting one of the steel cord belts that reinforced the tyre, he jiggled the blade in an exploratory fashion into the dark sidewall. To prevent the air escaping in one noisy rush, he worked slowly and precisely, stopping every now and then to listen. When he detected a first hiss of air, he pulled himself to the other side of the vehicle and repeated the delicate operation until he was satisfied that both tyres were slowly deflating.

Because it entailed turning round, it took him even longer to crawl back into the trees. Once there, he settled back on his haunches and surveyed the scene in front on him. The car he now recognised as a 3.2 Audi Quattro. Another time, another circumstance, he'd have liked to drive it. The two men in the front seats were still eating. From time to time, they exchanged a word or looked across at the house, but never for long.

Every time a cloud obscured the sun, the lights in the windows of Le Papillon glowed brighter.

When Jarret was satisfied that nothing had aroused their suspicions, he left.

#

Returning to the house, he changed into dry clothes and abandoned the wet ones in a heap on the bedroom floor. It didn't matter any more. On the bed, where he'd thrown it, was the bottle of calvados. It was all he could do not to take another drink. But what he was about to do next required concentration, not courage.

Downstairs, he checked for phone messages a final time and then his e-mail to see if there was anything from Alicia. But there was only another message from Trixie's solicitor and two pieces of work-related correspondence. He deleted them – they were all irrelevant now. He folded his laptop into its black canvas carrying case, which he placed on his shoulder.

What a screw-up! He selected an unopened bottle of Penderyn whisky and rammed it into his already full rucksack, then he chose a bottle of his oldest, most prized calvados. No point in depriving himself. It was going to be a long evening. Or, at least, that was what he hoped.

Placing the rucksack in a black bin bag, he carried it along with another bag of kitchen waste to the Jeep. Pressing his key to open the back, he placed them both ostentatiously inside. The laptop on his shoulder was unlikely to cause the men watching him any alarm. He slipped it off and slid it between the bin bags.

Overall, it had never been a bright day and dusk was beginning to fall early. With the lights left on, his old house looked cosy and inviting against the gloom. He was sorry to be leaving it.

Returning inside, he put on his leather jacket and then broke the shotgun and hung it over his left arm. Over that, to disguise the shape, he hung his raincoat. Given the weather, it was not unreasonable he should be carrying a raincoat. From the table he took an old biscuit tin – the underneath was rusty and on the lid was a picture of a Scottish Highland scene. The tin contained every high-velocity cartridge he possessed. He'd never cared much about the shotgun before, but for the present it gave him confidence.

He took off his jacket and climbed inside the Jeep. Each of his actions was measured; choreographed at an exact pace, so as not to arouse suspicion. If it looked like he was trying to escape, then the men watching him would prevent it.

He turned the ignition key part way and waited for the diesel engine's coil to warm up. He watched as the panel lights in front of him blacked out one by one. Still taking his time, he depressed the clutch, before giving the key a final quarter turn. At once, the engine rumbled into life, then settled into an easy purr. He smoothly pulled away.

Slowly, he drove along the track, headlights dipped. The men in the Audi were now watching him with renewed attention. Only when he'd nearly reached them did he switch the headlights onto full beam. The smooth lines of the Audi looked out of place, too symmetrical, too designer, against the backdrop of the ancient woodland. In its front seat, two figures shielded their eyes against the sudden glare and attempted to slide down out of sight, so that he wasn't to notice them. Stupid. The car had all the time been positioned where he couldn't miss it.

So why so coy?

And, suddenly, he knew the answer – and tensed. Because in the full brief wash of the headlights, as the men were ducking, he was almost certain he caught a glimpse of curly hair. Involuntarily, he changed into third and accelerated, only braking just in time to negotiate the tight bend. But not to miss a deep muddy puddle that emptied itself along the side of the Jeep and across the neat black bonnet and windscreen of the Audi. An infinitesimal revenge, which made him feel no better.

By the time the driver of the Audi had turned on the engine and cleared the windscreen of mud, Jarret was already a quarter of the way down the track leading to the road. But at that point he slowed. Curiosity got the better of him and he concentrated his attention on the rear-view mirror.

In his anxiety to maintain visual contact with the Jeep, the driver of the Audi attempted to take the second corner of the zed bend out of Le Papillon a little too fast. Jarret watched as the rear of the Audi skidded across the track and angled helplessly into a line of brambles. The driver's attempt to rectify the skid only resulted in it now sliding uncontrollably to the other side of the track and coming to rest in a shallow gully. With two flat rear tyres, there'd been little chance of him keeping control.

As Jarret continued to watch, two doors of the now leaning and immobilised Audi opened immediately and the two men got out. One rushed to the rear of the vehicle to see what the problem was, and on locating it kicked at the useless tyre in frustration. The other, who'd had to climb out of the gully side of the car, had already begun to talk into his mobile phone. His body language was agitated and his curly head bobbed up and down as he spoke.

When he came to the road junction, Jarret employed a bluff that he hoped would buy sufficient time for him to disappear in. Instead of heading directly towards Solac, his ultimate destination, he turned left, away from it, and drove instead towards the village of La Fouillade. He made the turn slowly, allowing enough time for his two pursuers to digest the manoeuvre and for the curly haired man to relay it to the person with whom he was speaking.

For the next half an hour, to doubly cover his tracks, Jarret zigzagged through the countryside down a succession of narrow, winding lanes, until he finally arrived at the tiny village of La Capelle-Bleys. At the church, he turned right into the narrow entrance which separated the church from the restaurant, and entered an almost empty parking area. There he reversed the Jeep into a parking space in the farthest corner, switched off the lights and settled back for a long wait.

15 (Tuesday pm/Wednesday am)

Like other villages in the area, Solac after eleven o'clock in the evening was deserted. Jarret negotiated the Jeep along the tight lane beside the church and then turned abruptly and descended into a medieval street of old stone houses. The orange glow from the overhead lanterns made everything look cosy – a warm world of soft-edged shadows.

The house he was looking for was tucked into a corner at the bottom of the road. It was terraced and once formed part of the village's fortifications. It had a large stone staircase, which jutted way beyond its front wall and led to a heavily shuttered front door on the first floor. But Jarret ignored these steps and, taking a bunch of heavy keys from his jacket pocket, unlocked instead the folding wooden shutters to a door on the ground floor, slightly below the level of the road. The door opened into a large, cool, musty smelling interior that not long before had been converted from a pigsty into a kitchen/dining room.

Wasting no time, he unloaded the shotgun and the rest of his possessions and placed them inside the room. From a small cupboard in the corner near the cooking hob he took another set of keys and crossed from the house to an old barn that stood across from it, slightly off to the right. Unlocking the double doors, he opened them as silently as he could and steered the Jeep inside, careful not to collide with the doorframe of the diminutive entrance.

Once back inside the house, he locked the folding shutters and door behind him, but without switching on a light. Taking a pen-sized Maglite from his rucksack, he followed its beam out of the kitchen and up a creaking wooden staircase that led from the back room to the landing above. Before he entered the lounge, he removed a bath towel from the pine chest of drawers that stood outside the bathroom and used it to cover the small lounge window, preventing the possibility of light spillage being detected from the road outside. Although a heavy wooden shutter already encased the window, he didn't risk switching on the standard lamp in the corner until it was done. The lamp had a feeble forty-watt bulb. As long as he remained in the house, that was as much light as he could risk, and as much as he was going to have to get used to. His safety depended on the house seeming unoccupied.

Partly to celebrate everything so far having gone to plan and partly to calm his nerves, he took a tumbler from the cabinet against the wall and poured himself a too-large vintage calvados. His prolonged period of abstinence now seemed years away, a mere blip in his alcoholic lifestyle. He knocked it back and poured himself a second, bigger drink, before sinking into a large green leather settee. Suddenly, being by himself in the semi-darkness seemed sublime.

The owner of the house was a client of Jarret's, called Mark Jansen. When he wasn't staying there, he paid Jarret a monthly retainer to check the house for weather damage, insect infestations, break-ins and the like. A job that Jarret did more or less regularly and carried out more or less conscientiously. Over the two years he'd been engaged to do it, he'd come to know the house well. It'd seemed a happy place and Jansen had spent many agreeable months there away from his job in the States. He called it his 'hideaway', which, at that moment, was exactly what Jarret required.

After the disastrous phone call to McBryde, it was the first place Jarret thought of coming. Being so close to Le Papillon, he wagered McBryde wouldn't think of looking for him there. But if the worst happened and he was discovered, he knew the house had three exits – four if he fancied climbing through the Velux windows and scrambling over the rooftops. And as the house was in a village with neighbours, any commotion or any shooting taking place would result in someone contacting the gendarmerie. And though Jarret didn't exactly welcome the involvement of gendarmes, it was preferable to a meeting with McBryde.

But for the present, wrapped in his accumulating alcoholic haze, he settled back. The stone walls surrounding him were a metre thick. An ordinary bullet wouldn't penetrate them. After so much insanity, he gratefully embraced the descent into the first of what he hoped would be a succession of long quiet, if lonely, evenings. Outside, the silence seemed palpable. He listened till he could almost hear it. Then an owl hooted and in the distance he heard a dog begin to bark. And he listened to them instead.

After an hour, he began to drop off to sleep. The thought of looking for sheets and duvet covers and making himself up a bed was too much – even trying to make it as far as the bedroom. Curling his arms around the bottle of calvados, he settled into the warmth of the leather-scented settee. And in less than a minute he had drifted into an alcoholic slumber.

He'd barely been asleep for half an hour, when he was awakened by the penetrating ring tone of his mobile phone. For a moment, he had no idea where he was or what was causing the noise. Before reality invaded his alcoholic slumber. The horror that it was McBryde calling to invite him to a late-night tête-à-tête caused him to hesitate. But fearing the noise might be heard outside, he flipped open the phone. Didier's name appeared on the screen, and he relaxed.

'Hi, Didier. You're normally tucked up by now. What's wrong?'

'Listen, Jarret, I've got a bit of a problem here. I was wondering whether you'd come over and give me a bit of help.'

'Why? What's happening?'

'There're men prowling about outside. I don't know what they want, but it doesn't look good. I think they've got guns.'

'Then lock the doors and phone the gendarmerie right away.'

'You're my neighbour. You can get over here quickly. Anyway, there only seem to be two of them. We'll just need to frighten them off. And you know I don't want gendarmes on the farm, they've a habit of sticking their noses into things that are of no concern to them.'

'Okay, I'm on my way.'

'I'll be waiting. And bring that fancy gun of yours with you, if you still have it. Just in case they might need a little persuading.'

'I'll be ten minutes.'

'I've been trying to get you on your house telephone. Where are you?'

'I'll tell you later.'

'Yvette's calling me. Take care. And be as quick as you can.'

#

Jarret steered the Jeep off the track that led to Didier's farm and into a field beside it. He'd driven the last part on sidelights. Until he'd taken time to assess the situation, he didn't want to alert the men of his presence. With the Jeep out of sight, he killed the engine and took the shotgun from the seat behind him, and loaded it. Then from the old biscuit tin he took six more cartridges and divided them between the side pockets of his leather jacket. Overhead, the cloud cover was dense and so low that the sky appeared a shade lighter.

He set off at a trot, but the running made him nauseous. After twenty paces, he slowed down. He tried keeping in a straight line, but the calvados caused him to feel dizzy. Then he stopped abruptly and threw up into the gully beside the track. After that he felt a little better. But by the time he reached the gateway to the farm, he needed to stop again to get his breath back. He paused and listened for any sounds coming from the dark buildings around the *basse cour* of Didier's farm. For a moment all seemed quiet; then came the sound of raised angry voices. One he recognised as belonging to Didier. The other was a stranger's. Then a woman's voice cried out – Yvette's.

This was not going to be as straightforward as he'd been led to believe on the telephone. He wished he'd not been drinking. He needed a plan of action. The direct approach would be to walk in the front way and force a confrontation; but given his sobriety and level of competence, that would endanger everyone. Instead, he headed for the darkness of the trees that flanked the eastern slope of the *Grand Nichon*.

In the utter darkness, the woodland floor proved difficult to negotiate. Maybe it wasn't such a good idea. The going would be slow, but it was all he could think of doing. He lurched between the tree trunks towards a halo of light showing above the farm buildings. Not making a noise or tripping over was difficult. Occasionally, stray branches swept into his face and eyes. There had to have been a better way.

When he drew closer to the farm buildings, he made out a sizeable gap between two of them and detoured towards it. The voices reaching him were loud and angry. As he'd moved through the woodland, he'd tried to block out the noises coming from the farm. He could no longer do it. He felt scared. Scared that he wouldn't be able to do anything

197

to help. Didier and Yvette were his neighbours and his good friends, and what was it he'd offered them in return – this? They were contented and settled in their world and now, because of his stupidity, he'd blown it for them. He had no doubt that what was happening to them was his fault.

He manoeuvred clumsily into a position where he could see. In the *basse cour* in front of him he counted four people – three upright and one face down, arms out stretched, bent across a heavy wooden table. He rechecked the shotgun to make sure it was loaded. If it came to the crunch – and he prayed it never would – he'd have two shots, just two opportunities to find a target. If he managed to miss with either, then whichever of the men remained alive down there would probably kill them all.

The male voices in the yard below him sounded even more agitated, though they were no longer actually shouting. He was still too far away to make out what was being said. So he began to edge closer – but even more circumspectly now, taking care that no-one could hear or see him. Though the ground was still uneven, it had started to slope downhill and, as he approached closer, the trees were becoming less numerous.

There were fewer than twenty metres before he'd have an uninterrupted view of the farmyard. But, even at that distance, the scene before him looked ugly. Didier was tied with his hands above his head and the rope attached to a large rusty hook protruding from the wall of one of his piggeries. Yvette had been tied face down to a heavy wooden picnic table, which had been positioned parallel to the piggery and directly in front of Didier. The two men in the yard Jarret had never seen before. One, dressed in a dark T-shirt and jeans, was aggressively thrusting his crutch against Yvette's buttocks. The other, dressed in a suit, was standing next to Didier holding an automatic pistol, which he gestured with as he spoke.

With ten metres still to crawl before he could get a

reasonable shot, the stakes suddenly ratcheted higher. The man in the T-shirt and jeans had taken a knife from his pocket and flicked it open. A glint of light angled abruptly off the stark steel blade. Jarret froze.

Then, all at once, the voices became more animated and Didier started to rant. Jarret watched as the man in the suit threatened him with the gun to keep him quiet. But it didn't work. So he smashed him across the mouth with his fist. If Didier's jaw had been relaxed when the fist made contact, it would have probably broken it.

With renewed urgency, Jarret edged closer to the hideousness unfolding before him. At his present distance, a shot was not impossible; it would be possible, but erratic. He could hit any of them.

The blow to the jaw hadn't knocked Didier out cold, but had stunned him sufficiently to shut him up. All Jarret could hear now was Yvette cursing – her strong local accent intensifying the spit of her anger. Then the man in jeans angled his body over hers and whispered something into her ear. The response was immediate. She pulled frantically at the ropes that secured her to the table. But as the side of the knife ran lengthwise against the vulnerable flesh of her neck and the volley of curses died away, she became still. Only the laughter of the man in jeans was audible. He turned the blade over and repeated the action on the other side of her neck. Only this time, he moved the knife more slowly.

For a moment, the whole of the yard was hushed – time suspended. Didier was frozen and powerless to do anything but hang there and watch. When the knife blade accidentally cut through Yvette's skin, she briefly cried out. Both men turned towards Didier, who shook his head at them – his eyes pleading. Then he audibly pleaded that he knew nothing – that they had to believe him, because that was the truth.

Jarret crawled the final few metres in a dream-like slow

motion. To make the two shots was difficult enough; to do it without hitting either Didier or Yvette was a nightmare. He manoeuvred himself between the trees, looking for an angle from which he could miss them both.

The barrel of the shotgun had been fitted with a full choke designed to limit the spread of the shot and to concentrate its kill potential – if the shot expanded over a wider radius, it would scatter and be less lethal to a large mammal, like a wild boar. Nevertheless, despite the limitation of its deadly radius, there could be no margin for error.

The man in the suit walked slowly across to Didier, smiling and talking in a low, threatening voice. Without warning, he pummelled a fist into Didier's stomach that jolted his head forward against his chest and pumped the air from his lungs. Groaning and defenceless, he sagged suspended from his hook. At a nod from the man in the suit, the man in the T-shirt and jeans slid the knife blade under the belt of Yvette's three-quarter-length blue slacks and began to cut through it. She writhed in terror, but when the knife blade was withdrawn from the belt and run again across the soft skin of her neck, she became still.

The knife cut through the belt and then through the waistband of the slacks, leaving it free to run unimpaired through the rest of the lightweight material. When the cut was wide enough, the slacks were roughly pulled from around her waist and allowed to fall around her ankles. The man tugged her left leg from the impeding garment; then, with an unwarranted violence, he kicked at both her legs with his heavy boot until they were spread apart. Yvette whimpered, but offered no other response.

The blade was then inserted beneath the elastic of her panties, which fell to the ground like flayed skin. To excite himself – or terrorise Yvette – he drew the flat, cold side of the knife across her well-fed buttocks, while with his other hand the man tore at the thin material of her summer shirt. Immediately, Jarret saw her body close against him, stiffening against the indignity, the violation of his touch. As if she were no longer present, in an instant she became dead to him. Sensing this detachment, the man kicked her ankle, this time with enough force to have broken it. She choked back a sob – but it was the sob of a woman who despised being helpless.

Using the gnarled trunk of an oak tree to steady himself, Jarret raised the over-ornate Franchi shotgun to his shoulder and took aim. He was aware of the blood pumping loudly in his ears. As he prepared to fire, he tried to obliterate all thought of the consequences of his action, seeking justification in something Kierkegaard once wrote: that there were certain occasions when it was right for human beings to act outside the law.

To be lawless in a lawless situation.

Didier struggled against his ropes. The man stared across at him, taunting him – while Yvette remained silent, her body shuddering from the violence of the rape. It was possible for Jarret to end it with one shot, but he couldn't. He had a clear view. He could take out the rapist with the first barrel. But he couldn't make the second shot because the man in the suit was standing right next to Didier. If he aimed the shotgun wrongly, he'd eliminate them both.

From Yvette's expressionless face, Jarret could see that she'd once again quit the scene – her body was being violated, but mentally she was refusing to let him touch her.

But Didier could tolerate it no longer and once again started to rave. The man in the suit pointed the automatic at him, though to no effect. He lifted the gun as if he were going to hit Didier across the face with it. As he did so, Didier swayed sideways, allowing his full weight to be taken by the hook above his head, and lunged at him with a ferocious kick. It was off target and easily avoided. But the fury behind it forced the man to step backwards and sideways.

201

At once, the sound of an explosion rocked the farmyard – a lethal discharge that removed the side of the suited man's head, which coloured red as he crumpled. Jarret had held the gun wrongly and fired it inexpertly, but accurately. The recoil absorbed into his shoulder. He fumbled for the second trigger. In his haste, an age seemed to go by. Then, with the report from the first blast still echoing round the farmyard, he took aim for a second time. Another explosion. And a slightly comic figure, jeans unzipped, suspended, frozen in mid-thrust, slowly fell back and away from Yvette – tumescent for a final time.

A silence enfolded the courtyard. Indeed, it was as if the whole farm and countryside had been shocked into stillness. All movement and commotion was erased. As if around them a whole universe had come to a halt and was listening. Yvette too remained still. Didier just stared at the figure bleeding on the ground beside him. Jarret felt fatigue overcome him and sat on the ground, slumped against the gnarled trunk of the oak tree. The only thing that he was aware of was the dull ache the recoil had set off in his shoulder. He must have held the gun too loosely. He'd never managed to get it right. Then he'd never needed to. If it wasn't for the ache, he could have been forgiven for wondering whether the events of the evening actually happened. But the dull ache reminded him that once again his life was in pieces. He wanted to curl into a ball and sleep.

'Where were you? You said you'd be here in ten minutes, not ten hours.'

Didier's voice cut through the silence and his descent into self-pity.

'And you said you could handle things.'

'If you'd shown up on time, I might've done. Are you going to do something or are you going to leave us like this all night?'

The rapist's knife was lying on the ground next to

Yvette. Jay cut her free with it and wrapped her in his leather jacket. She looked into his face as if she didn't recognise him. Then she simply nodded. He helped her across the farmyard to one of the two plastic chairs that had been placed beside the kitchen door for sitting outside on in warm evenings. She was shaking, but there was no sign of tears. As he sat her down, her tight grip on his arm relaxed and she tried to smile.

'I'll be okay now. Go'n help Didi.'

Didier was hanging there like a meat carcase – though the burning in his eyes indicated he was still full of living. Living – but he was also angry and hurting. His body had been pounded, but what had happened to Yvette, Jarret knew, had hurt him more. In time, both would heal – his body the faster than the pain that seared his mind. Jarret helped him to the chair beside Yvette. He sat, rubbing his jaw, which was swelling but didn't look broken. She reached a hand out to him. And he took it. And together they stared motionless into space – a space that lay somewhere between the courtyard and infinity. There could be no cure for what happened tonight, but Jarret could see hand-in-hand they would move beyond it.

For the moment invisible to either of them, Jarret crossed towards the piggery where Didier had been tied up. He moved like a sleepwalker, as if drowsiness was the only way to protect himself from the reality. For one day, he'd already seen too many dead bodies and too much blood. If it wasn't for the alcohol still in his bloodstream and the injection of courage it gave him, it was doubtful he'd have moved at all. He stood first alongside the suited man. The automatic pistol lay on the ground beside him. He couldn't bring himself to touch it, so propelled it with his foot into the yard. He moved across to where the rapist lay beside the table. His wound looked as if it had been pumping blood for several minutes, though now it had stopped. Two strangers frozen in ungainly deaths – one with half his face shot away, the other missing the back of his head.

Jarret had witnessed wounds like that before. He'd seen them on the corpses of wild boar while out hunting with Didier. Pellets fired from a shotgun didn't travel in a straight line, like an ordinary rifle – but spread as soon as they'd left the barrel. So the greater the distance between target and shotgun, the greater the spread, which was still the case even after impact.

The two men's heads were evidence of that – and the high velocity cartridges he'd used. The pulped flesh and blown-away bone and brain. But Jarret didn't feel the revulsion he'd expected – that would come later. Though, through the fatigue, two other emotions had started to emerge: anger at what the men had done and guilt for a situation he blamed himself for having caused. He prodded the body of the rapist with the barrel of the shotgun to check for signs of life he could see quite plainly weren't there. He felt embarrassed at the sight of the man's still-exposed penis. He turned wearily back towards the farmhouse.

'This is a complete screw-up. You'd better let me call the gendarmes.'

Didier snapped out of his trance in an instant, and looked alarmed.

'No. I said no gendarme. I want no policemen on my farm. We can deal with this problem by ourselves. By the time tonight's over, no-one'll be able to prove these shits ever existed.'

'The gendarmes are going to come anyway. People will have heard the shots. We'll only get into bigger trouble if we try to cover it up. And if they don't find the bodies first off – they'll come back with dogs. You can't make these guys disappear.'

'No-one's going to find anything, trust me. Because when I finish there won't be anything to find.'

'Terrific, suddenly you've become a magician!'

'Not a magician, a pig farmer. And pigs, if you didn't

already know it, will eat anything. Once we get these boys sliced up, they'll be gone in no time. Be like a second supper to them. Any bones they don't eat, I'll get rid of later.'

'You can't do that.'

'Leave it to Yvette and me. You get their car out of here and lose it somewhere. We'll go through their pockets and remove anything that the pigs can't eat or that won't burn. Clothes can go on the bonfire – but any mobile phones, watches, keys and weapons, you take away in the car with you and get rid of.'

'This isn't going to work. It just isn't right.'

'Relax.'

'Anyway, how am I going to get back? I'm drunk, tired and all I want to do now is go to bed.'

'Wherever you dump the car, I'll come and get you. Okay?'

'The shots. What about the shots.'

'There were only two. Don't worry about it.'

'But someone will have heard.'

'Where will you take the car?'

'You're not listening to me, are you? I don't have a good feeling about doing it this way.'

'Jarret, there isn't another way. I'm not going to stand by and watch my neighbour arrested by the police, especially after he just saved my life. Where will you take the car?'

'Okay, you win. Let me think. What about Najac? Tourist village, probably a week or two before anyone will get suspicious about an abandoned car. And it's close, but it's far enough away to be safe. If I leave now, I can make it back on foot by the morning.'

'Give us a couple of hours to clean up here and I'll come and get you. Make your way down to the St Blaise bridge at the bottom of the town and stay there hidden in the trees until you see the van.'

Yvette had just risen to her feet, holding the leather jacket tightly around the lower part of her body. Gingerly, she placed her full weight on her left ankle, testing it. Jarret could see that the bruised flesh and the open cut just above the ankle bone on the inside. It was already beginning to swell. Tentatively, she explored several paces, before Didier went to her and offered his arm in support. Impatiently, she waved him away.

'Don't fuss me. I'll be all right – I'm going to live. We've got work to do. But first things first, I need to get clean.'

'Take it easy for a while. I can clear up here. Jarret can give me a hand to drag the bodies over to the sties.'

'Didier, I'm fine. Cutting up those bastards'll give me a real pleasure. And by the look on Jarret's face, I don't think he's going to be a lot of help to you.'

'Then I'll do it by myself.'

'Didier, shut up and get the bodies moved. I'll be back to help you in five minutes.'

Didier walked with Yvette into the house and returned several minutes later with a plastic carrier bag. Crossing the yard, he started searching the dead men for any objects and adornments that wouldn't burn. He removed watches, tiepin, neck chain with a gold crucifix, keys, mobile phones, guns and a knife, and dropped them in the bag. Loose change and paper money he stuffed into his own pockets. Only the rapist carried any identity, in a wallet in his back pocket – a driver's licence with an address in Seine-St-Denis, Paris. But it was of no concern to Didier: he was not about to hand it over to the gendarmes. When he was satisfied that all uneatable, un-burnable items had been removed, he handed the bag, together with the keys to the car that the two men had come in, to Jarret. As an added precaution, he removed the two spent cartridges from Jarret's shotgun and threw them in with the other items.

'Now get out of here.'

'You'll not be able to stay on the farm after this. It won't be safe. The person who sent these animals is sooner or later bound to come looking for them. They didn't just turn up here out of nowhere. I'm staying at the Jansen house in Solac. Pack some things and come and join me there. We can talk and it'll give you a chance to think things over. You know you've got to get Yvette out of here?'

'We'll see about it. Now get out of here – some of us have got work to do. I'll be a couple of hours. And remember, when you've finished, get yourself down to the bridge and wait there for me. Don't try walking back, in case anyone sees you. I'll be there as quickly as I can.'

Although Jarret was reluctant to leave Didier and Yvette to clear up the mess he'd created, he was at the same time relieved not to be staying. He'd never killed anybody before. Realisation of the consequences had yet to catch up with him. He eased himself into the leather front seat of the men's brand new Mercedes saloon. The engine stirred into life with barely a sound – a butterfly to the Jeep's bullfrog. The car glided across the farmyard's undulating surface. The automatic gearbox and the comfort of the seats made Jarret feel like a passenger.

As he drove along the track towards the farm gate, he looked in his rear-view mirror. Yvette, now dressed in working overalls, had re-joined Didier in the yard. Her hair was still wet from the shower. As she limped towards him, her mouth was moving and she was pointing as if she were giving instructions. Every inch of her looked as if she meant business. Didier was dragging the body of the man in the suit across the cobbles towards the nearest piggery. He stopped, said something to her and she held up the knife she was holding.

16 (Wednesday am)

It was after three in the morning when they eventually entered Solac. The clatter of their engines reverberated against the silent grey stones, shattering the stillness of the old square. But no lights flipped on, no shutters were thrown open – if anyone had been wakened, they'd merely cursed them and rolled over. Jarret led the way in the Jeep. Didier and Yvette followed in their Peugeot. It had been recently washed and polished and inside smelt a lot cleaner than the van. Yvette must've insisted.

As soon as the two vehicles had negotiated the narrow entrance and were parked alongside each other in the barn, they entered the house and right away Jarret began preparing a cafetière of strong coffee. It was going to be a long night and they needed to talk.

Upstairs in the lounge, the calvados bottle was still lying on its side by the settee where Jarret had dropped it. From the cabinet, he selected the three biggest tumblers, then took the bottle of Penderyn whisky from his rucksack and half-filled each of them. For a time, no-one spoke, just remained inside their own thoughts and drank.

The spell was finally broken by Didier.

'It's you they were after, you know. They wanted to know where you were.'

'Fuck. I didn't mean to get you into this. I don't even understand how I got involved myself.'

'Didier didn't mean anything by it. He just thought you ought to know. It's not your fault. They were bad men.'

'If only it wasn't. I never for a moment thought you'd get tangled up in this.'

'Well, we are, so we need to talk. I've got a farm to run and no *fils de putain* is going to drive me off it.'

'It won't be safe for either of you to go back for some time.'

'You have a choice, I don't. Yvette's going to stay at her sister's in Montauban. I've got to get back to the farm. I've got my rifle, my dog and no-one knows the place better than I do. Next time anyone calls to have a little chat with me, I'll be waiting for them.'

'It's too dangerous. These men are professionals. If there is a next time, there won't be any messing around. They'll just kill you.'

'In the countryside, Jarret, on my own farm, I'm the professional.'

'It's still crazy. Just give it a couple of days, then see how things look. It's me they're after. If they can't find me, they'll assume I've got away. Maybe they'll leave you alone after that.'

'It's no use arguing with him. He's already made up his mind. We talked about it earlier and if that's what he's decided, that's what he's going to do.'

Yvette moved closer and put her arm around Didier's shoulder. She kissed his stubbly cheek. Sitting there together on the settee, they were an item. He looked pleased, yet embarrassed at this outward show of emotion. In return, he gently squeezed her leg just above the knee. Jarret suddenly had an absurd picture of them at home in the evening, snuggled up together, with the irritating strains of 'Stand By Your Man' playing in the background.

'Okay, what's your plan?'

'Tomorrow morning, or rather this morning, I'm driving Yvette to the railway station; after that I'm returning to the farm – but I'm going on foot. If anyone's there, waiting for me, they'll no doubt be watching the track. I'll go through the wood and the fields and come in the back way. The animals are going to need feeding. There's no way I can afford to abandon them for one day, let alone a few. I can't just sit on my arse in this place trying to sort my life out while the world goes to hell around me. That's a luxury I don't have.'

'I'll come with you then. That's the least I owe you.'

Didier and Yvette snuggled up even closer. Jarret offered them both a refill of whisky, but only Didier accepted. They drank again in silence. Talk about the future had created a different anxiety in each of them. Yvette kissed Didier lightly on the cheek and laid her head on his shoulder.

But Jarret remained concerned.

'What about the bodies? Is there anything we still need to do?'

'Stay calm, my friend; everything's taken care of. Just be happy that the pigs are enjoying themselves. In a couple of days nothing'll remain. The clothes we've already burned, but I'll light another bonfire on the same spot today to make sure there's nothing left. If anyone asks about the shots, I'll tell them I was out shooting foxes last night. There's nothing to worry about. You threw away what they had in their pockets?'

'They're in a black plastic sack at the bottom of one of Najac commune's wheelie bins. I doubt if anyone'll rummage through it. But what about you, Yvette? You must get yourself to the doctor – the sooner, the better. You need an HIV check, but not round here. I can drive you to Montauban, if you like?'

'You stay and look after Didier. I'll see a doctor soon enough in Montauban. And stop mothering me – what happened tonight was humiliating and disgusting, but I'm not a cripple. I'll get over it. But thanks for thinking of me.'

'What about your ankle?'

'No bones broken. Like I said, I'll get over it.'

'Yvette's already talked to me about it and I respect

210

her decision. Believe me, Jarret, she'll see a doctor soon enough. I think the fewer people we get involved in this the better. So let's leave it at that.'

#

It was the same shrill noise, but this time it seemed to be coming from much farther away. Devoid of lamplight, the darkness in the room was impenetrable. Reluctantly, he shook himself from the cosy sleep that enfolded him. His mouth tasted bitter and dry and the pain in his neck, caused by sleeping with his head up against the arm of the settee, was excruciating. The temptation to close his eyes again was immense, but the sound in his ears was too insistent to be ignored. He crawled across the wooden floorboards, feeling in front of him, trying to locate its source. Somewhere through his hangover, its shrill call tone screamed urgent.

Jarret pressed the receive button and grunted a greeting.

'I assume that's you, Mr Jarret. We're going to have to meet.'

He froze. Then suddenly he was awake. The words were McBryde's, but it was a woman's voice that was speaking. She spoke seriously in a voice tinged with aggression – and, like McBryde, was not expecting to be argued with. Then, adding nothing to her opening remarks, she awaited a reply. Comfortable with the obvious confusion she was causing him.

He felt his way to the lamp in the corner and switched it on. As if illuminating his surroundings would help him think.

'Who's that? Who's calling?'

'Let's just say a friend, someone who has your interests at heart. Now listen to me, Mr Jarret, if you want to survive this mess you've got yourself into, I suggest we arrange to meet one another as soon as possible.'

'I don't know who you are. Why would I want to meet you?'

'I told you, trust me. It's the only way you'll survive. We've got to meet. You name the place, the time and bring with you whoever you want. But when we get down to the serious talking, it's just you and me. What I've got to say is for your ears alone.'

'I don't know.'

'McBryde and his friends are getting closer, believe me. I'm on your side. That's all you need to know for now. When can we meet?'

'I'm not sure.'

'You don't have much time left.'

'My mobile will have automatically stored your number. I'll call you back when I've thought about it.'

'Lucky I haven't blocked it then. Don't wait too long, Mr Jarret. You've been warned. You won't be again. Do the clever thing.'

As Jarret rang off, a wildly stubbled, half-dressed Didier appeared in the bedroom door. His eyes, sunken and barely visible in their sockets, struggled, like his brain, to focus. His voice had lowered a pitch and sounded thick and slurred.

'What's going on? Who was that? What time is it?'

Three questions fired off in rapid succession that Jarret didn't have an answer to. He hadn't a clue what was going on. No idea who the phone call was from. And was completely in the dark as to what the time was. Didier staggered towards him and settled heavily in a leather armchair – despite his unshaven and weathered appearance, he looked like a lost little boy. Jarret tried telling him about the woman on the phone, but he didn't seem to take it in. Just sat there with closed eyes until Jarret had finished speaking.

'Wonderful. So what time is it?'

Jarret's watch was on the floor beside the settee. He took

it over to the lamplight in the corner so that he could see it. The hands made no sense to him. The shadowy nature of the room, which should have made him feel safe and secure, instead made him feel incarcerated and depressed. He squinted again at the face of the watch.

'God, it looks like it's nearly ten o'clock.'

'*Merde*, that's not good! I'm supposed to be driving Yvette to the station this morning and the animals haven't been fed since yesterday. I can't take her to the farm with me.'

'You concentrate on your farm; I'll drive Yvette to the station. We can get back in touch again later. My mobile'll be switched on, if you need to make contact.'

'I'll tell Yvette to hurry and get herself ready.'

'When she's ready, that's fine. But I'll have to take her in your car. The Jeep's too conspicuous.'

'Not a problem. Like I said, I'm going to walk to the farm from here anyway.'

'What about Yvette? Is she alright to travel after last night?'

'If she says she is, yes. She knows her own mind and, if she's made it up, there'll be no arguing with her.'

Didier returned to the bedroom to tell Yvette to get dressed. Alone again, Jarret took his mobile from his pocket and searched the display for the number of his last caller. It wasn't one he recognised. He scrolled through the directory of 'recents' anyway on the off chance it might match one he'd already stored. It didn't. He hesitated over what to do next. That he was in trouble was obvious. That he didn't have the slightest idea what to do next, except hide, was beginning to dawn on him. It was not the way to solve anything.

Without further consideration of the wisdom or craziness of his decision, he pressed the call-back button and listened as it automatically dialled. Like all wagers, this one was irrational. But the moment to gamble had come – if he won, he won; and if he lost, well, he'd already lost anyway.

'Hello, Mr Jarret, good to hear back from you. Glad you didn't take too long about it either.'

'You know Saint Antonin Noble Val?'

'I can find it. I'm listening.'

'The cafe near the covered market at three o'clock this afternoon. Come alone or there's no meeting.'

'Understood.'

'How will I recognise you?'

'I'll do the recognising. Three o'clock, café by the covered market, St Antonin. Goodbye.'

Jarret rang off and right away went downstairs. In Jansen's office, he searched through the drawers of the desk until he discovered what he was looking for. At the back of the right-hand side middle drawer, lying on its side and looking like a child's grotesque toy, was an up-and-over handgun with two forty-four millimetre barrels. But its murderous appearance was misleading, because it was not in fact a deadly weapon – just Jansen's idea of protection against the non-existent dangers he faced during his infrequent visits to Solac. More to do with his own ignorance than from any threat from French rural village life.

Jarret removed it from the drawer and went into the kitchen, looking for a plastic carrier bag.

Manufactured by Verney-Carron, the maker of sporting guns, the two forty-four millimetre barrels fired nothing more destructive than soft rubber balls. Though its name might have sounded like something from an action comic – Flash-ball – it was not a toy, because the velocity of its discharge was such that the effect of the impact on anyone unlucky enough to get in its way was equivalent to a technical knockout in boxing. Firing it once at a target in Jansen's garden convinced Jarret that if the size of the barrels didn't compel surrender, then the force of its impact certainly would. But, as Jansen once said to him – having it just stops you worrying.

#

As soon as she was ready, Jarret drove Yvette to Villefranche-de-Rouergue to catch the late morning train to Montauban. She'd left Didier behind with mixed feelings. She knew she had to go; but, at the same time, knew it'd be a struggle for him without her. More than that, she was worried something might happen to him. When they unclenched after a long, final parting embrace, it was clear from the expressions on their faces the respect and affection they had for each other. But beneath it all she was afraid.

In case any of McBryde's men were on the look-out for him, Jarret set Yvette down in a car park a short distance from the railway station. He knew she'd be forced to drag her suitcase the last couple of hundred metres, but there was no point in taking unnecessary risks. Him they knew. No-one apart from the two dead men would've seen her before, so there was no reason to believe that she wouldn't be safe. Hurting – but safe.

Before she got out of the car, she took Jarret's head in both hands and planted a warm, wet kiss on his cheek, leaving a red smudge, which he wiped away as soon as she was out of sight.

'Please don't leave him by himself. And you, Jarret, you be careful too.'

He watched as she limped towards the station, dragging her suitcase over the uneven surface of the pavement.

17 (Wednesday am/pm)

It'd developed into a cloudy-sunny, hide-and-seek sort of day. Just dropping down from the high land of the Aveyron into the river valley meant that the temperature rose by two degrees. But the damp patches on the grey surface of the road testified that it wasn't a game that the sun was always winning.

The road running alongside the river was straight by local standards and therefore fairly fast. Keeping most of the time within the speed limit, Jarret was able to maintain a level 90 kilometres an hour. Approaching Feneyrols, he slowed and turned right over the blue-painted river bridge into the little village. He followed the narrow streets until he found the road that would take him in the direction he wanted to go, only now on the opposite side of the river. The quickest way would have been to take the main road to Saint Antonin, but that would mean having to enter the town by its only river bridge. If anyone was watching out for him, that was the way they'd expect him to come. The road from Feneyrols, in contrast, was little used and unlikely to warrant the same attention.

But Jarret had already made up his mind that if anyone was going to be watching the town, that person would be him. Before his meeting with the woman on the phone, he would acquaint himself with every detail of the town. He didn't know who he was looking for, but watching for anyone or anything suspicious gave him an advantage. And, more than that, a chance to survive.

It was just after eleven forty-five when Didier's Peugeot bumped up over the kerb and pulled into one of the parking spaces that'd been marked out on the pavement. It was just beyond the gendarmerie. Perhaps the same gendarmerie he'd spoken to on the phone when he reported the murders of Adams and the others at the Manoir Ivant. He turned the engine off, but remained in the car, his seat belt still buckled. He examined the street around him, unwilling to leave the vehicle until he was convinced it was safe to do so. And convinced he wasn't being watched. His fingers fidgeted with the ignition key, ready to re-engage the engine at the slightest indication that anything was wrong.

But, as it moved towards lunchtime, so did the tranquil little town. Shops started to close, cars pulled away and people began to make their way to cafés or homes to eat. Hard as he looked, nothing about any of the activity appeared suspicious. Nevertheless, he waited.

At twelve thirty precisely, he made a move. After collecting the plastic carrier bag off the back seat, he locked the car and disappeared down one of the side alleys leading to the covered market in the centre of the town.

There were still two and a half hours to go before the meeting. Two and a half hours to inspect every street, every alley and every person he came across in the little town – several times over, if necessary. And then, only when satisfied with what he'd seen, would he be prepared to step into the café for his rendezvous. Any person, any suspicious activity, anything at all that looked threatening, and he'd leave. Although the woman had been persuasive over the phone, he couldn't eliminate the possibility that it was a set-up arranged by McBryde. And if he missed something or made a mistake, he was a dead man. But, for the time being, he was gambling that he was already ahead of the game.

The supermarket carrier bag in his left hand contained a number of items – bananas, dried sausage and a slab of Cantal cheese. He'd bought them in the village shop in Solac before he left. These were not items specially selected for his lunch, but had been chosen to disguise the shape of the Verney-Carron Flash-Ball gun that it also contained. Tucking a gun that size into his waistband or one of his pockets wasn't an option.

#

So much had happened in only a short space of time. He'd been too busy to think. As he checked the interconnecting streets and alleyways of the little town, a realisation slowly dawned that he bore on his shoulders the weight of two dead men. In his work, he'd witnessed death – the dead and sometimes the dying – but he was never the one who'd been responsible for it. If he hadn't acted, Didier and Yvette would almost certainly have been killed. There was consolation in that – but only some. Now he was a different person, with another lost virginity, but a loss that brought no pride or elation. As he trudged through the streets, it was almost as if he felt the weight bearing down on him. It wasn't just the guilt of having done something wrong. He'd coped with having done wrong things for most of his life. Nor that he'd committed a crime. It was the knowledge of what he was capable of that oppressed him. A dark knowledge from which there was no escape, because it was inside him. And would always be there.

The day felt humid. In the time remaining before the rendezvous, he circled and intersected the town so many times that his calf muscles began to ache and his clothes stuck to him with sweat. Every one of the damp-smelling alleyways and almost deserted streets was becoming as familiar to him as the landscape surrounding Le Papillon. With just half an hour to go, he focused his attention on the main square, which, like everywhere else he'd encountered so far, looked benign and unthreatening.

Once lunchtime was over, the square gradually became busier. The weather was improving and the sun, having slipped from beneath a covering of cloud, had begun to shine brightly. Using the side streets, he circled around the square until he found a vantage at the entrance of a shadowy alleyway. It was about as far away from the café as he could get and still have a clear view of what was going on there. Half-hidden in the recess of a doorway, he composed himself, as best he could, and settled to wait. Ever alert to the minutiae of events that unfolded before him. In his left hand, he gripped the plastic carrier bag. It contained the only guarantee of security he had – but like the memory of the dead men, it had begun to weigh heavy.

Three o'clock came slowly. Tourists had filled the tables outside the little café – but a solitary woman occupied none of them. A large waitress in her middle thirties moved systematically among the customers, taking orders and serving drinks. From a street beside the café, a coach party of elderly French emerged onto the square. They wore the expressions of an attentive kindergarten class and looked vaguely lost. Their guide said something to them and they gazed in unison at one of the buildings. When she spoke again, they obediently followed her and were gone.

All was quiet for a while – then the first hint of trouble. Jarret reached his right hand into the carrier bag and fumbled amongst the groceries for the comforting presence of the gun. A man in his early twenties, carrying a newspaper instead of a guidebook, had just sat down at one of the tables. Before sitting, he'd examined the faces of the people around him and then the square. But he'd not found who he was looking for. The waitress came to his table and he ordered. Then, after looking about him again, he opened his newspaper and began to read – but he was turning the pages too quickly to be paying them proper attention. From time to time he lowered his paper and gazed across the square. When his beer arrived, he took a long draught, finishing almost half of it. He was nervous.

Several more minutes elapsed before Jarret caught sight of her – a woman wearing black-framed wrap-around sunglasses. She appeared to be in a hurry, her gaze fixed upon the café as she strode confidently past the covered market. At the café, she went straight to the remaining empty table and stood with one hand on the back of a chair, the other on her hip. With barely disguised hostility, she examined the faces of the people chatting around her.

As with the young man, the person she was seeking wasn't there. She tapped her foot impatiently. Then, with a degree of irritation, she wove her way between the tables towards the dark empty interior of the café. The young man reading the newspaper must've registered her arrival, but they never once exchanged glances. They were too professional. Jarret felt his composure ebb. But as long as he could see them and they couldn't see him, he was in control. The square was becoming an unhealthy place; but, for the moment, he was too curious to leave it.

The woman re-emerged squinting into the outside light and quickly replaced her dark glasses. She seemed a little less confident now. Perhaps flirting with the outlines of the thought that what she'd planned might conceivably have gone wrong. Another slow look around the square, before she returned to the one empty table, pulled out a chair and sat with her back to the café. She had a clear view of everything going on in front of her.

From his hiding place, Jarret watched her, memorised her. If he ever came across her again, he wanted to be able to recognise her right away. He examined her closely. She wore a khaki jacket and jeans, mid-blue T-shirt and a pair of white trainers. She was dressed for efficiency, not looks. The only jewellery she had on was a watch. She wore no make-up, though she was certainly not unattractive. And there was something about her which, despite himself and the situation he was mired in, he found intriguing. If this were the woman who'd phoned him, then he regretted not meeting her. It would have been interesting. Unfortunately, the presence of the young man with the newspaper made that impossible.

He quickly checked over his shoulder to make sure that his escape route back to the car remained clear. The narrow street was quiet and, as far as he could see, empty. He turned back to the woman in the café and was just preparing to leave when something happened to stop him. The young man with the newspaper suddenly got to his feet and waved to an attractive girl in a summer dress hurrying across the square towards him. His smile was broad and white and his eyes seemed suddenly to have come alive. When the girl reached him, they embraced – too long for the comfort of customers at the nearby tables. As they finally unclenched, he spoke and gestured towards his drink. She shook her head in refusal, so the young man placed some money on the table, knocked back his beer and they straightaway left. As they walked across the square, smiling and talking, he put his arm around her waist and pulled her to him. His newspaper remained folded on the table behind him.

The woman stood up to acknowledge Jarret well before he'd got to the café. There was a hint of relief in her expression. But by the time he reached her, the mask of assuredness had slipped back into place. She smiled broadly with her lips, but she offered no greeting. Behind her dark glasses, he suspected her eyes remained cold and business-like. And, as far as he could see, too serious a woman to mix work with informality. Neither was she about to make him feel comfortable.

As soon as he arrived at the table, she sat down and indicated that he should do the same. She pointed to a chair opposite her. She wanted him in her direct line of vision.

'Well, you finally condescended to make it. I thought I was the one that was going to be late. Why are there no proper roads round here? You can spend the whole day going nowhere. Let's get to business.'

Her voice had a stern authority that made him instinctively want to sit up straighter. He felt like a small boy being told to behave. The world she came from was ordered and free from doubt. Which, given the confusion and darkness of his own mind, he found strangely attractive.

But he still didn't know whether he could trust her. He felt inside the carrier bag for the gun and the comforting bend of a trigger. He pointed it at her beneath the table.

'What do you want?'

'I'll have a Perrier.'

'No, what do you want with me?'

'I'd still like a Perrier. Ice and lemon.'

Jarret summoned the waitress and ordered Perrier waters for both of them, though his preference would've been for something much stronger.

When the waitress had gone, he found himself staring, once again, into the blank lenses of her wrap-around sunglasses. They added to her inscrutability and to Jarret's discomfort. She sat still and upright, and studied him – as if his exterior contained a clue as to the person he was. He too tried to sit still.

'What do I want with you? It's not so much what I want with you, but what I can do for you. Don't flatter yourself you've got anything to offer me. The bottom line here is – get lucky and we might be able to help you save your life. But I'm not making any promises.'

'Jesus! What d'you want? And don't say Perrier. What's happening? Who are you?'

'That's not important for now. Tell me what you know.'

'About?'

'About what's going on here.'

'I don't understand.'

'Let me give you a name – Adams. Start by telling me about Adams.'

'What?'

'Everything you know. Don't keep anything from me or I can't help.'

'You want me to tell you in a street café?'

'You chose the place. I thought it was because you felt safe here. And anyway, we're running out of time. So tell me what you know.'

'Safe, maybe, but not private. Okay. How it began? In summary, I suppose it goes something like this – that I had a client, sort of girlfriend, who disappeared, then some primal thug came along and employed me to find her for him; now he's probably coming after me too, but I don't know why. Because I don't know what's happening.'

The waitress arrived and placed two glasses, containing ice and a slice of lemon, and two bottles of Perrier beside them. Jarret poured his right away and took a long drink. Partly because he was thirsty, but mainly because he wanted time to think. He wouldn't tell her about the cocaine adhering to the inside of the broken bottle in Adams's cellar. Or about the link between the broken bottle and the case of wine Alicia claimed to have bought for her father – Château La Tour Saint Briac. That drugs were at the back of what was happening he had no doubt. But as long as the woman refused to divulge her identity, he'd not say much. Just enough to hold her interest.

'Tell me about your girlfriend.'

'First it's Adams, now it's my girlfriend. Tell me who you are. Then tell me why I'm sitting here listening to you. If I walked away right now, what difference would that make to you?'

'I'd be exactly where I was before and you'd be completely screwed. Not a brilliant strategy. Always remember this, Mr Jarret – you feature in this game as a disposable entity. You're a pawn that no-one really could give a fuck about. Here one minute, gone the next, and nobody would've noticed. I'm prepared to help you because you might be some sort of use to me. There's no other reason for this meeting today.'

'Who are you?'

'Who I am is for me to know and for you not even to guess at. But because I don't think you're in a position to tell anyone else, I'll give you a little something to get your head around. Have you ever heard of SOCA … the Serious Organised Crime Agency? The UK's recently set-up answer to the CIA/FBI? You're not on the ball any more, since you came out here, are you? It's all started going a bit soft up top, isn't it? So if I said SOCA to you – then it's up to you to find out what I'm talking about. For now, that's all I'm prepared to give you.'

'Give me some proof.'

'No.'

'Okay, if you won't tell me who you are, tell me what you're doing here.'

'Our current interest revolves around the activities of a certain Mr McBryde, whom I believe you know. An unpleasant bastard – but only a small defecation in a very much larger pile of shit, which it has become our business to try to flush away.'

'Why am I mixed up in all this?'

'Good question. There's a theory … but all we can be certain of, at the moment, is that your blonde friend's arrival here in France has been responsible for causing a considerable amount of disruption to the shit pile. We don't know how she's done this, but we're grateful to her. It's even meant some serious head-cases being sent down here from London. If you really want to know why you're involved in all this, you'll have to ask your girlfriend. Because, apart from the shit pile, she's the only one who knows the answer.'

'I can't believe all this was her fault. As far as I know, all she ever wanted was to recover a suitcase and get her life back in order.'

'Then you're more naïve than I thought you were. Or a bigger liar.'

'I don't see how she fits in. She was the victim in all this.'

'You've no idea of the scope and the power of the people she's upset, have you? I called you this morning because I thought you might try to make a run for it. So listen to me carefully; it's very important you understand what you've got yourself into. These people, the organisation we're dealing with here, are first division. They make money, more than a lot of countries in the world, and in order to do that they control – activities, people and places everywhere. And they're hard-cases. And those who come in contact with them are either too afraid to talk about it, or they're dead. And that's the reason we've come to this armpit of civilisation – because, for one moment, in this one place, thanks to your blonde girlfriend, they seem to have lost a little of that control. And, for the brief moment that's happening, they're vulnerable.'

'I don't know anything about what's happening. I've told you that.'

'We'll go into that later. For the moment just listen to what I'm telling you. Afterwards you're completely free to make up your own mind – but if you turn us down, don't make any plans for your future – because you won't have one.'

'Okay, I'm listening.'

'Then listen carefully. The organisation these people work for is run by a ruthless bastard called Lazar Zharkoski, a very clever, very psychopathic Kosovan, whose origins go back to somewhere in Macedonia. No-one's very certain where he started life – but that he grew up and cut his teeth during the conflict in the region is undisputed. A conflict you had some experience of, I believe. He began life as a small-time crook manipulating the black market and any other scams he could get his filthy fingers into. Over time he gathered a group of thugs around him who specialised in using violence and terror to achieve their ends. Sometimes those ends were nakedly criminal, others were hidden beneath the political banner of regional nationalism. Before hostilities were brought to an end in Kosovo, Lazar had already laid the foundations of the network that would grow to become the criminal organisation he now controls. He's an intelligent man with a university degree, but utterly ruthless and, now, extremely powerful. So much so that his interests have grown to cover any lucrative enterprise he can force his way into, bent or legitimate. His operation is now spread across the globe and has become a monster with many heads – as law enforcement agencies cut off one, another grows to take its place. The organisation itself has no one name, and all the enterprises it operates, straight and otherwise, are independent of each other. The only thing they have in common is that Lazar Zharkoski directly or indirectly controls them. Sometimes they interact – but always invisibly and always through offshore accounts – with enormous fiscal sleight of hand. But that's for the various governments and the forensic accountants to take care of, not us. Our focus is on overt criminality, and with Lazar Zharkoski you get the lot – drugs, kidnapping, extortion, illegal disposal of waste, money laundering, people smuggling, prostitution, gambling. You name it – he runs it. There's even been talk recently about him being in league with Somali pirates.'

'I thought you said it was McBryde you were after?'

'You're right. We followed him out here. But he's not the entire purpose. Like so many others, he's just a small piece of the puzzle. Sure, our operation has limited focus, but it's wider than just McBryde and his interest in your girlfriend. Zharkoski has drug-smuggling routes across Europe and as far as we can tell the rest of the world, including China and Iran. And France is no exception. They run through the country like rivers, which flow in every direction. Our objective is to block up the river that uses the Aveyron as a conduit. Why? Because drugs from this one, particularly, are most likely to end up in the UK. We share our information with other European agencies and maintain close collaboration; that's the reason we can continue our surveillance work in France. But if any arrests are to be made, that honour will fall to the French alone. Though we've trailed the drug route from South and Central America to various Francophone countries in West Africa and then via sea traffic into France, we've not worked out yet how the drugs get to the Aveyron and from there into the UK. But the information we've gathered so far indicates that they do. And the recent flurry of activity in the area involving Zharkoski's men seems to confirm it. Also, there's another one of them living semi-permanently not far from here who goes by the name of David Trevor, who we believe is at the epicentre of it all. But he's a slippery bastard and we can never manage to get close enough to him to nail him down.

'Where did Adams feature in all this?'

'He was merely a bit player who flitted in and out when required. The Manoir Ivant was his base in the region, but he also had others dotted around elsewhere. He was primarily a back-up. But it's not him we're interested in – it's Trevor. He's the one that makes everything function smoothly; without him the conduit becomes blocked. So now you have it, that's the overall picture – so be grateful. That's everything I'm going to tell you. A while ago, you asked me what I wanted from you. It's quite simple – if you can keep McBryde running around chasing his own shadow for a few days, it'll make it easier for us to get on and do our job. The man's like a bull in a china shop – he's got everyone jittered, including Trevor. And that suits us just fine. If you can keep him occupied while we continue to probe, you'll help us a lot. Right now, he seems to be very keen to find you. But you must understand, you mustn't leave the area. We want McBryde to believe that you and your girlfriend are still in the Aveyron and within his reach.

227

Keep him looking, but keep him guessing. What's perfect at present is that you've got him completely agitated and, like all men, the more angry he is, the more likely he's going to do something stupid. As I said, normally Zharkoski has everything running like clockwork. His drug routes take PhDs to understand, but they function smoothly – as did this one, until now. Now cracks are starting to appear and we need them to get bigger. Questions?'

'The more you tell me, the more I want to get the hell out of here. I can see that from your point of view this might sound like a good idea. To me, it seems like I'm the only one here with everything to lose. How exactly do you expect me to keep McBryde angry and continue to stay alive? The only stupid thing I can see him doing is kill me.'

'Was it you who phoned the gendarmes about Adams? Don't answer. Someone, they thought, with an English accent called them about the murders. We're assuming it was you. When you spoke of him just now you did so in the past tense; also, you didn't correct me when I did. So, if we're right, then you're already well aware of what McBryde's capable of doing, and that those poor bastards will have been only too grateful to die. And you also know that could just as easily happen to you. So work with us and we'll try and look after you.'

'You've not answered my question. What do you expect me to do?'

'In good time. Adams was a small cog; he messed up and now he's gone. He was probably the one responsible for cracks beginning to appear in the operation; but, thanks to you, the French police are now all over it and we can't get a look in. Which brings us to your recently departed girlfriend. What was her name? What did she call herself?'

'Alicia.'

'Through the looking glass. I wonder where she got that name from? Did she have any other names?'

'At the car hire, she filled in a form calling herself Julia

Roberts. She told me her real name was Alicia Jennifer Taylor.'

'You're kidding! Jennifer Taylor? And you're that stupid that you believed her?

'If that's what her parents christened her, why wouldn't I?'

'Don't be naïve. Jennifer Taylor … Jenny Taylor … genitalia. One of Zharkoski's lucrative rackets is prostitution. He controls tens of thousands of working girls throughout the world – from the lowest ten-pounds-a-hand-job hooker to the minimum thousand-pound-a-night class act. But there's one thing he insists on with every girl who works for him, and that is she carries his personal trademark, tattooed on her, so that everyone can recognise whose property she is. Just two marks, tattooed above the right buttocks. Letters from the Serbian alphabet – his own two initials. An egotistical, pathetic act by this brutal, ignorant male tyrant that probably amuses him. Have you ever seen a tattoo like that? Your lady friend didn't have one, by any chance?'

'Not that I can recall. No.'

'I know you're not telling me the truth. We've got to start trusting each other or this is not going to work. Have you seen a tattoo like that before?'

'Who's not being trusting now? The answer's no – so let's move on. Now, why won't you answer my question?'

'Being circumspect is one thing, but playing games is something else. Now don't fuck with me.'

She removed her dark glasses and looked at Jarret closely. Her eyes were a warm chocolate brown, but their expression was cold.

'Why don't you just answer my question?'

'I know you've seen these tattoos on Alicia because you told me … Charlie. And you've seen them before on me. Haven't you? Though mine was only hennaed on, just to see what you might make of them … Charlie. So your answer's actually fucking 'yes'. So I know you're not telling me the fucking truth.'

The café, the chattering tourists at the tables, the square, everything around Jarret went into a spin, like his mind. A vortex. He resisted the momentary urge to hold on to the sides of his chair in order to remain upright. He let the gun fall back into the bag resting on his lap. He was aware his cheeks had become flushed with embarrassment and that his forehead was so hot he could only imagine he'd broken into a sweat. The loose khaki jacket she wore had covered up her shape. In broad daylight before him, with no make-up, no wig, no jewellery, no phoney French accent, how could this serious, metamorphosed female be his fantasy Lulu? Had he been that drunk? That stupid?

Now her whole face was smiling at him. Mocking him.

'Don't worry, Charlie, my experience of men has taught me that when they've got other things to look at, they rarely remember a face. Don't feel bad about it; your gender's not the most gifted.'

'Lulu, or whatever your name is, I didn't … C'mon, how could I recognise you? This is a joke.'

'The other night was the joke. This is serious. This is what it's always been about. Everything I've just told you is absolutely true. Believe me or you won't survive very long.'

'You think Alicia was once one of Zharkoski's women?'

'Not once, still is. Is that so difficult for your male ego to take? Though, if it's a consolation to you, I'm sure she's one of those at the top end of the market.'

'You think Adams was her client then, not a friend at all?'

'Adams was nobody's friend. What exactly did your girlfriend want you to do for her at Adams's house?'

'That's what you were pumping me for the other night. It wasn't just a stupid game. How did you find out about 'Something Wild'? About Lulu and everything?

230

'It's our job. My colleagues in the UK told me it was surprisingly easy to get your friends there to talk about you.'

'And how did you persuade Martine to agree to the switch?'

'Pressure. She just didn't like the alternative to not agreeing with us. That's all the questions I'm going to answer. Now you answer mine. What did Alicia ask you to do for her at Adams's place?'

'Like I told you the other night, collect some possessions for her, a suitcase with some clothes in.'

'Nothing else? Were there other things in the suitcase beside clothes?'

'No. I packed it myself. She did ask me to pick up half a dozen bottles of wine she'd bought as a present for her father, but that was all.'

'Wine. Were they full bottles?'

'Judging by the weight, yes.'

'And they were definitely bottles. Did you look at them?'

'No, but I could hear them chinking together when I carried them.'

'So, why the turmoil? Tell me that. It can't be because some high-class hooker has walked out on a client. Or trying to break away from Zharkoski. No. Either she knows something that can incriminate one or more of them, or she's walked off with something that doesn't belong to her. There's no other explanation for all this sudden activity. Let's hope we get to her before McBryde does, that's all. So tell us where she is.'

'I've told you already. I don't know where she is. Now, for one last time – what exactly d'you expect from me?'

'Like I said, we want you to keep McBryde chasing his own tail – nothing more than that. He's your client, he'll listen to you. He's come all the way out here to sort out the little problem with Alicia. You're connected with her, so he's suspicious of you, but he hasn't made a move against you yet because he's unsure how you fit in to all this. If he knew for certain, he'd have killed you by now. In the meantime, he believes you might be of use to him – that you might lead him to Alicia. For the moment, you have his full attention … and that is something we'd like you to maintain. Keep in telephone contact with him. Tell him you're in Rodez, Villefranche, Millau. Tell him anything you like. Keep him off balance. Keep him moving in the wrong direction. Tell him you've found her, arrange to meet with him and don't show. Keep him angry, keep him confused and, above all, try not to let him catch up with you. That's got to be a simple enough task, hasn't it? As an ex-media man, I'm sure you'll come up with a lot of ideas of your own. What do you say? Will you help us?'

'If you're asking someone like me for help, you've got to be desperate. I'll think about it.'

'Don't take too long, Charlie. Time is not on any of our sides.'

Now the clouds were winning the game of hide and seek. A grey light pervaded the summer afternoon, and depressed it like a frown on a beautiful face. The square that was, half an hour ago, bright and bustling with tourists, was now beginning to empty. The shadow beneath the covered market, cool on a hot day, looked chill and uninviting. Around them, the tables were one by one being abandoned – cups, glasses, paper from sugar cubes littering their shiny but stained surfaces.

'I've got your number. I'll ring you.'

'When?'

Jarret was about to reply when his attention was drawn to a figure striding across the square towards them. The man coming towards them, looking full of determination, was all too familiar to him. All at once a flood of adrenaline rose inside him – his neck muscles tightened and eyes narrowed as if he was about to be hit. In reflex, his hand reached back into the carrier bag on his lap for the cold comfort of the pistol grip. He tested the tension of the trigger – felt its reassurance. After killing two people, this was going to be easy. He shut his eyes briefly to block out the thought that this time it would be public.

Then, with a spring, he was on his feet, shouting at the top of his voice like one of those homeless, paranoid alcoholics he'd passed a hundred times on city streets throughout the Western world. Lulu's eyes grew wide and bug-like in surprise and her jaw tightened, distorting her not unattractive face. She crouched in her chair, as if preparing for action, and let the glass of Perrier water she was holding fall from her grasp as she turned. The man with curly hair had stopped in his tracks about ten metres away from them.

'That's far enough, fucker! One more step and it'll be the last you'll ever take. Get your hands up and keep them away from your body. Do it now!'

Having turned right round, Lulu reached for the inside of her jacket. She sought out the target of Jarret's sudden outburst of insanity. The curly headed man had half raised his hands and, uncertain what to do next, taken half a step backwards. The few people remaining at the tables outside the café had ceased their conversations and were staring about uneasily. The sense of shock was palpable, with Jarret frozen in a manic half-crouch, pointing a plastic carrier bag at the surrendered man's chest.

For a moment everything stopped, as if waiting to see what would happen next. And Jarret likewise, for, apart from shooting the man, he had no idea what he was going to do.

'Calm down, Charlie, he's on our side.'

'That bastard's been following me. He's one of McBryde's.'

'We've been following you – it's our job. Now come on, Charlie, relax. I don't know what you've got in that carrier bag, but it's beginning to freak people out. Put it away. You're making us all look like complete wankers.'

The curly headed man in jeans slowly lowered his arms and continued uncertainly towards the table. He was fuming. As he reached for a chair, Jarret produced a cellophane-wrapped dried sausage and pointed it at his chest.

'One false move buddy and you're a goner. Fancy a slice?'

'Get this prat to shut up or I'm going to do something he'll regret.'

'You won't be so brave when I show you my banana.'

'Shut the fuck up, both of you. Steve, what do you want?'

'Sorry to butt in, boss, we've got to talk urgently. Like now. Away from here and away from this jerk.'

'We're just finishing. I'll be where we arranged to meet in five minutes. Now go.'

Obediently, he started to leave when a thought prompted him to turn back to the table. His eyes were burning with a barely suppressed fury. As Jarret learned from his soccer days – always get your retaliation in first.

'We must do this again some time. But I warn you, I've still got a wedge of cheese in this bag.'

'You almost killed us the other night, pissing around making holes in our tyres. Pull anything like that again and you're the one that's going to need repairing. Understand?'

'I promise I won't tell anyone that you and your partner were cuddled up in the back seat together when I did it. You looked so cosy. It would've been a shame to disturb you.'

That did it. Unable to keep a rein on himself any longer, he was round Jarret's side of the table, ready to throw a punch, when he found himself staring into the forty-four-millimetre barrel of the Verney-Carron Flash-ball. He froze, staring disbelievingly at a weapon which, for all he

herself to six full ones from Adams's cellar. He couldn't. It was better that she … they didn't know about it. Even, perhaps, were made to think of her as a victim. That way she might ultimately survive. Gloomily, he considered his future. The grim certainty that tomorrow was likely to be no more promising than today. Assuming, that is, he had a tomorrow.

His sat slumped in the driving seat, shoulders hunched with the increasing feeling that, as the hours passed, everything was becoming more hopeless. Lulu's offer of protection was little more than a plea for his help. He had to face it, depressing though it was: he was all on his own. There was no-one he could turn to, no-one he could really rely on. But that wasn't quite true. He could rely on Didier. But that wasn't an option he was prepared to consider. He couldn't involve him any further – that would be unfair to him and to Yvette.

He drove, like an automaton, through the village of Espinas, conscious of nothing other than the mire of his own thoughts, and on towards Pradinas. From his experiences in Iraq and elsewhere, he knew that one of the first rules of security was to vary your route. Otherwise you laid yourself open to ambush or kidnap. Though his actions were without thought, that was in fact what he was doing. At Pradinas, he took the turning towards Najac, a different route from the one he'd come on. Only as he approached the track that led to the Manoir Ivant did the familiar landscape trigger a reaction and cause him to realise too late what he'd done. A stupid lapse and he knew it, but he'd come too far to turn round. He'd have to bluff it out. But what did he have to bluff out? Nothing. His reason seemed to be deserting him. On a drizzly summer evening, what was so special about a green Peugeot travelling down a quiet country road? What was suspicious about it?

Passing the entrance to the *manoir*, there was no roadblock, no police vehicles, no automatic weapons aimed at the windscreen of his car. Just Jarret and his paranoiac imagination. As he drove on through the summer countryside and the flanking woodland, heavy with its dark-leafed trees, he felt almost disappointed at the lack of police presence.

At Najac, he stopped to phone Didier. He'd pulled into one of the spaces in the nearly deserted car park in the Faubourg. From there, he could watch the traffic in both directions. Insistent drizzle misted the windows of the car – but instead of worrying about it obscuring his visibility, it made him feel strangely secure.

'Didier, this is Jarret. How's it going there?'

'Two strangers came snooping around this morning, but when they saw their friends weren't here they left. Since then, it's been quiet and I've managed to get on with a little work. I've had to be pretty careful though. Your place, on the other hand, is an entirely different matter. I took a stroll over there after lunch to see if everything was okay, and the answer is – it's not, not by a long way. There are probably about five men there, maybe more – I didn't get that close to have a proper look. Some were in the house, some outside – at least a couple in the space at the top of the track with what looked like automatic rifles. I don't think I'd go back there for a while, if I were you.'

'I'm coming to see you.'

'Don't bring the car with you. If you're coming, come on foot across the fields. They may or may not be watching the road, but I haven't got the time to find out. I have to feed the animals before the light goes. Where are you now?'

'Najac. I'll get to you as soon as I can. Where will you be?'

'Go into the main barn. Make a noise as you open the door, so I know it's you. Don't go creeping around and don't call out. Once you get there just sit inside and wait. I'll come to you as soon as I can. Set your mobile phone to vibrate – if there's a problem, I'll contact you. If I haven't heard you arrive, wait for a while, then call me.'

'Right. I'm on my way.'

'I'd leave the car by the old bridge if I were you, and make my way from there.'

Although Jarret was fairly certain he wasn't being followed, he didn't risk taking the direct route. Instead, he detoured through the little village of Les Mazières. Despite his earlier lapse of concentration, he knew as the risks multiplied that the margin for error diminished. The call to Didier had focused his mind.

Just before crossing the narrow bridge over the Sérène, he pulled into a rough lay-by-cum-dumping-place for road-mending materials. Then he edged the Peugeot, as far as possible, into the shadow beneath the spreading green foliage of a hazel, where it was also partly hidden by a large mound of grey gravel. On the other side of the bridge was the Solac/La Fouillade road that passed the turning to Le Papillon and Didier's farm. Taking his still-damp anorak from the boot, he zipped it up to the neck and pulled the hood over his head and tied it in place. To anyone passing, he'd look like just another farmer crossing a field on a damp evening. Next to where the anorak had been was a tartan blanket. He unfolded it to reveal the broken-open shotgun and the old tin containing high-velocity cartridges. He lifted out the shotgun, selected a cartridge for each barrel, then snapped the gun shut, ready for firing. The rest of the cartridges he placed in his two side pockets. For an instant, he considered taking the Flash-Ball pistol with him too, but it was too much of a toy. If he had to go for the knock-out, then a technical one would no longer be good enough.

He crossed the bridge, with its battered and bent iron railings, and turned right along the road. He jogged the short distance to the gate that opened into the first of Didier's fields. No-one was about. Or at least he saw no-one. The entrance to the track was visible from the gate. If he took that option it would have been easier; instead, he heeded Didier's warning. Before opening the gate, he scanned the hedgerows for signs of movement. Everything looked quiet. Underfoot, the field had been churned up by the hooves of cattle. After only a few paces, he realised he was wearing the wrong shoes. Water and mud seeped inside them and the lack of tread meant that the progress he made over the uneven ground was slow. Hunched inside his anorak, head down into the wind, he felt like a mobile green sack with a shotgun, and about as terrifying.

The farmyard, when he finally got there, was empty. The only sound coming from it was the dripping of water from the un-guttered outbuildings. And from behind the house, the barking of Didier's hunting dog in its metal enclosure. Jarret stopped at the corner of the gable-end of the stone barn. A gourd plant had been trained along it and water from its leaves trickled onto his face and hood. For a minute or two, he watched and listened, attentive to any unusual movements or sounds coming from the yard – but in truth hoping to catch a glimpse of Didier. Through the muffle of his hood, the dripping water reminded him of the sound of high-heel shoes on a pavement.

With his back against the wall, he rounded the corner and moved slowly towards the barn door, all the time keeping the yard covered with a nervous side-to-side sweep of the shotgun. Having heard and seen nothing suspicious, he leant the gun against the wall and unlatched the door. As it opened, it scraped heavily across the ground, creating enough noise to alert Didier of his arrival.

Only Didier didn't appear.

Inside, the barn was in semi-darkness and smelt damp and slightly mouldy, a smell Jarret recognised as coming from the earth floor. Scraping the door shut behind him only succeeded in plunging the barn into a deeper twilight. He hesitated, uncertain what to do next. Call Didier or remain there quietly and wait for him? The silhouette of Didier's old tractor stood out against the dim light. It was battered, old and orange, and had once belonged to Didier's father – part of a past and a foreseeable future. If only the same could be said for himself.

He crossed, climbed up onto its single seat and settled down to wait. Fumes rose unpleasantly from the ancient engine and cocktailed with the damp, mouldy smell pervading from the floor. He unzipped his anorak and pulled down the hood. Though the barn was cool, he was beginning to sweat. At any moment, he expected the door to burst open and McBryde to be standing there ready to crucify him. The thought of it made him shudder. He fingered the trigger of the shotgun nervously.

After what felt like a very long time but was no longer than a few minutes, his mobile phone began to vibrate against his thigh. It startled him. And in his panic to answer it, it became tangled up in the material of his pocket. He twisted it to free it and flipped it open. It was Didier.

'I heard something. Was that you?'

'I'm in the barn.'

'Stay where you are, I'll be right across.'

Thirty seconds later and the barn door opened, just far enough to admit one person and one dog. Then it scraped shut again. Right away, the dog ran across to the tractor and flattened himself to the ground, eyes fixed on Jarret, as if by an invisible wire. An alert Didier – rifle in both hands, finger on the trigger, ready – followed him. When he was close enough to confirm that the person on the tractor was Jarret, he called the dog to heel. It lay on the ground behind him, eyes still firmly fixed on Jarret.

'I've just finished feeding the animals. Come with me.'

Lying on its side, against the wall, was a heavy home-made ladder with flat-sided, nailed-on pieces of wood as rungs. Didier propped it against the mezzanine floor at the far end of the barn. As soon as it was positioned, the dog shot straight up it. Jarret could hear it snuffling and scurrying about on the bare wooden floor above them. Not

241

wishing to risk his luck alone with the dog, he let Didier go first. When they were all together, Didier drew the ladder up onto the mezzanine after them: a primitive drawbridge allowing them one way in and, more worryingly, only one way out.

The mezzanine was Didier's new home. It was a crude space, and not exactly homely, but with the addition of a few household items, he'd done his best to make it so. He'd brought a mattress, a folding table and, from outside the kitchen door, one of the off-white plastic chairs that he and Yvette had sat on the other evening after Jarret had killed the two intruders. In the corner, he'd placed an old-fashioned food store with a dull grey mesh and, beside it, an open suitcase containing an untidy tangle of clean clothes. This was the place where he intended to remain until the trouble had disappeared. Or, stubborn as he was, until he'd been killed. The grubby mezzanine also served him as a lookout post. Beneath the apex of the gable, a small window allowed an unobstructed view towards the gateway into the farm.

To Didier, this was his Alamo. But Jarret was by no means certain about it. If anyone managed to get inside the barn with a high-powered rifle, then the wooden floor would give them as much protection as a piece of cardboard. The solid, un-sanded chestnut wood boards were certainly a testament to enduring rural carpentry, but were no defence against a high-velocity bullet. Remaining at ground level and using the stone walls for protection would not only increase their options, both in attack and defence, but also make their lives much easier. But Jarret had been friends with Didier long enough to know that he'd have his reasons for choosing the mezzanine, so arguing with him would be a waste of time.

Didier shooed the dog into a corner and put his rifle down on the mattress. After rummaging under some dusty sacking piled against the gable wall, he emerged with a red plastic bottle crate. He placed it on the floor beside Jarret and indicated that he should sit down.

'Coffee?'

He filled a saucepan with water from a bottle and placed on the tiny Campingaz stove. From the food store he removed two tumblers and a jar of instant coffee.

'Or would you prefer something stronger?'

'Both.'

Didier half-filled two more tumblers with cheap whisky. Jarret normally detested his lack of taste in whisky but, for once, he was uncritical. Such was his need of alcohol that he'd drink the diesel from the tractor if he thought he could get a hit from it. They sat there together in silence and watched the water warming in the saucepan until it emitted the first strands of steam. Then, without waiting for it to boil, Didier removed it from the stove and mixed in the coffee granules. By the time he filled the two glass tumblers and handed one to Jarret, it had already stopped steaming. And though it tasted foul, Jarret found it strangely comforting. In fact, being with Didier was strangely comforting. His total lack of taste was the only thing constant in a day of utter turmoil.

He finished the coffee with difficulty, then drank what was left of the whisky in two large gulps – to take the taste away.

'When it begins to get dark, I'm going over to take a look at Le Papillon.'

'I'll come with you.'

'No, stay here and take care of the farm. I'll be right back. I have to see if those men are still there.'

What was happening at Le Papillon could never be his problem. Already Jarret felt mortified that he'd managed to get both Didier and Yvette tangled up in a mess, if not of his own creation, then one that belonged exclusively to him. If anything bad were to happen to Didier, there was no way Yvette could run the farm alone – and Jarret could never sanction the thought that through him she'd lost everything. No, he was adamant nothing like that could ever be permitted to happen. Before that, he'd sacrifice himself.

Didier poured another half-tumbler of whisky and they sat, each immersed in his own thoughts, half an ear cocked to the noises of the approaching evening for anything that might indicate a threat. The drips off the roofs had become more numerous now – a ripple of watery applause across the empty courtyard. Somewhere across the valley, a buzzard shrilled and, in a tree nearby, two crows argued noisily. Then, except for the water from the roofs, the sounds around them gradually faded with the light.

At half-past nine exactly, Jarret rose to leave. From the tiny window overlooking the gate, all seemed tranquil, if more sodden and darkened by the rain. *Only an idiot would be out on a night like this.* He hoped it were true. That when he got to Le Papillon, he'd find it deserted. The dog's eyes followed him, as he made his way to the edge of the mezzanine, but its body remained quite still. Didier was deep in some inner recess, head bowed, shoulders sagged, as if an invisible weight was pressing down on him from above. After locating the ladder, Jarret slid it noiselessly towards the blackness of the uneven floor below.

Shotgun in one hand, he descended warily. The rickety rungs creaked beneath his weight, like arthritic joints. At last, Didier stirred.

'I'll come with you.'

'Stay here. I'll phone if I need you.'

For one of the few times since Jarret had known him, he didn't argue. Just collected his rifle from the mattress and crossed to the filthy window, where he rubbed on the glass with his sleeve.

Jarret was apprehensive about leaving the security of the barn. He opened the door just wide enough to squeeze through and peered into the gloom that greeted him on the other side. A sound in the darkness behind him made him start, until he realised it was just the ladder being withdrawn onto the mezzanine. A sudden feeling of abandonment again overwhelmed him. But that was how things were. How they had to be.

He tried doing up his anorak but, in his haste, the zip became stuck halfway, jammed by a piece of loose material. Fuck. Pulling on it harder only made it worse. A couple more tugs in the opposite direction failed to release it and, in the gloom, he was unable to see what needed to be done.

He crossed the yard towards the main entrance to the farm.

A short distance beyond it was the well-trodden path that linked Didier's property to his own. Underfoot, the conditions were damp and slightly slippery, but beneath the surface the ground had remained fairly firm. The path followed an arc through the woodland at the foot of *Le Grand Nichon* and emerged onto the track that wound its way down to Le Papillon. It was a back route and he was unlikely to meet anyone, but, every so often, Jarret would halt, hold his breath and listen intently for the noise of other humans. But all he could hear was the sound of the woodland around him.

When he finally reached the track, that too was deserted. Nevertheless, he settled himself on the damp ground, behind a chestnut tree, and began to keep watch. To go any further meant crossing the space that lay in front of him. Any attempt to do so, without first making sure it was safe, would be suicidal. He'd no idea what was out there. He had Didier's evidence – but what Didier had witnessed was a long time ago. For now, he'd no intention of going any farther.

He peered into the fading light.

#

245

For what seemed like an age, the scene in front of Jarret remained unchanged. He began to psyche himself into making the short journey across the track and entering the woodland on the other side. He didn't have far to go. Ten or eleven paces, at the most. And, anyway, he thought, who the hell would want to be out on such a night? And if there were anyone still around, they'd surely be sheltering in his house.

From his position, behind the chestnut tree, he'd seen and heard nothing suspicious. Earlier, when Didier had visited Le Papillon, it had been daylight and the weather had been fine. Now, it was dark and miserable. He'd almost convinced himself that the time was right to make a move, when he sensed more than heard a sound coming from the other side of the trees, a distance to his left.

As he rose to his feet, he failed to notice his grip tighten on the trigger of the shotgun. Only an accidental collision of the weapon's barrel with the trunk of the tree brought him to his senses. A soft thud of metal on bark that, to his ears, seemed to echo through the night. Only then did he release his pressure on the trigger and avoid sending a volley of shot into the darkness.

The footsteps ceased. He listened on, but there was nothing. Then a dim light flickered at the very edge of the isthmus of trees, which protruded into the bend of the track to his left. A small red light, which shone brightly for barely a second, then dulled – a nicotine glowworm that intensified and faded as it came towards him, until tossed into the air and rolled away, sparking by the wind.

The man who'd discarded the cigarette was big. A neck as wide as his head, broad shoulders and thick arms – the sort of upper body physique acquired by spending hours in the gym. But the cigarette smoking suggested that he'd not got bulked up for playing sport, nor did his overweight midriff. Nor the rifle he was carrying. When the man came within range, Jarret lifted the shotgun and aimed it at his head. Only the man stopped, stared briefly into the darkness of the track and, seeing nothing, turned and slowly retraced his steps – before rounding the isthmus of the tree and descending towards the house. Jarret watched him until he disappeared.

After checking to make sure everything was clear, he crossed the track and entered the woodland on the far side. His thought was to shadow the direction of the large man in the hope of discovering how many others were with him. He moved circumspectly between the trees, creating as little noise as was possible. If the man on the track was on the lookout for anything tonight, it would be a vehicle, not a person on foot.

Halfway across the isthmus of trees, he was halted by the sound of a car door slamming. The man had beaten him to the other side. A brief conversation followed, a susurration of lowered voices, but Jarret was unable to distinguish the words. Then the car door slammed a second time. Followed by the shuffle of uncertain footsteps. There were at least two men. Once more, he crept slowly forward, only now in the direction of the car sounds.

He'd almost emerged at the other side of the trees when he saw the silhouette of the second man moving along the track, away from him. He moved forward and crouched behind the foliage of a young hazel. The edge of the woodland came to a halt at the top of a steep bank, giving Jarret a view of both the man and the outline of the car he'd just left.

This second figure was slimmer and more fearful of his surroundings than the first. His movements were jerky and he looked uncomfortable. The clatter of the water falling from the leaves of the trees clearly unsettled him. He looked like a city boy spooked by the lack of street lights. But his erratic behaviour made him that more dangerous. Nervously, his rifle pointed everywhere – arcing the track in the direction of the house and then sweeping the line of trees on the bank above him. At the first suspicious sound or movement, he was likely to empty the rifle's magazine in its direction.

Jarret had arrived at the point of no return – the last chance to change his mind. But even before he'd left the barn, he foresaw only one course of action. The only way to remedy the suffering he'd already caused Didier and Yvette, two lives he was on the verge of destroying – two innocent victims of his stupidity and cowardice. It wasn't them McBryde was looking for. In point of fact, it wasn't even him – but Alicia. But the responsibility lay with him. He could give himself up, right there and then, and end it. But the consequences didn't bear thinking about. No way did he want parts of his body amputated and left to rot, the way that Adams's and Fraze's were. Sure, with Alicia he shared a couple of ecstatic nights, but she'd left him – so he owed her little. But he'd no intention of putting her in the firing line or quitting on her, either.

So there were no further decisions. The answer was in front of him – not even the choice any more between fight and flight.

He edged a little closer to the parking space and the men's car. The interior light was turned on and slumped in the passenger seat was the large man with muscles. In the dim light, Jarret recognised him from the visit he'd paid on Sunday to his office in Villefranche with McBryde. From a box on his lap, he pulled a succession of tissues and dabbed with them at his hair and beard, which were still wet from the rain. His action was gentle and methodical and, for some reason, Jarret felt touched by it.

Finally in position, he watched until the second man had rounded the corner of the isthmus, before levelling his shotgun at the windscreen of the car. The bearded man lowered his window and discarded a handful of wet tissues onto the damp earth outside. After raising the window again, he settled back in his seat and closed his eyes. No doubt warmer and drier than he'd felt five minutes before.

The single-barrel discharge cracked open the night and shattered the windscreen of the car with the same high velocity that it shattered the man's skull, jolting him backwards before slumping him sideways against the blood-spattered passenger door of the Silver Grey Mercedes.

The report was quickly reabsorbed into the landscape. Jarret stood, for a moment transfixed, listening to the car's sound system – the voice of Norah Jones. The dead man and her, two universes that just didn't fit. The incongruity held him. Then he remembered the second man and moved quickly back into the trees.

He took cover behind the gnarled trunk of a mature oak, from where he had clear sightlines along the twin forks of the zed – to the house and back up the slope towards the road. The occasional drift of music merged with the rainwater from the trees; everything else seemed to have paused, as if waiting. There were no human sounds. In Le Papillon, the upstairs and downstairs lights had been on when he abandoned it; now he could see only the downstairs ones.

For a moment, Jarret panicked at the thought that the man with the rifle might sneak up on him through the trees. Then he recalled the city boy, the man he'd seen walking nervously up the track. He doubted he'd have the ability to creep noiselessly through the woodland. He removed the spent cartridge from the barrel of the shotgun and reloaded.

He listened. The noise of the water from the trees and, from the darkness beyond the house, came the mournful hoot of an owl – then another, a distance away across the valley, echoing it.

In the inactivity, another thought occurred to him. What if someone in the house, at that very moment, was scanning the woodland with a night-sight attached to his rifle? He'd be an easy target – though preferable to a tête-à-tête with McBryde.

A movement close to the bank attracted his attention and he focused on a patch of darkness to his left. The movement in itself was neither dramatic nor threatening, as a shimmer of light reflected briefly off a shiny surface. Light which originated from the house. As a light off the surface of a trembling leaf – or he was imaging it?

Then came another movement. A shimmer of light this time, close to the bank, followed by a sudden dash forward. Then a jittery hesitation, followed by another short dash. As the man moved towards him, he swung his rifle in a wide arc in an attempt to cover the track and the woodland above him. Then, before risking a few more paces forward, he spun around to check behind him. As he drew closer, Jarret could hear his hurried, irregular breathing. He called softly to the dead man in the Mercedes, a single syllable name that sounded like Siv or Ziv. McBryde had called him Sammy, but then McBryde could do what he liked. He was not going to get a reply – only the voice of Norah Jones reached his ears, making everything seem romantic and cosy. He hesitated, uncertain what to do next, before edging closer.

Jarret squinted down the barrel of the shotgun to where the wet blond hair was stuck with rainwater to the side of the man's skull. And fired. Just one shot, at a two-metre range. The impact tossed him sideways and he made a sound that seemed like a sigh – as if what had happened to him was inevitable. Instantly, he was transformed into a rag doll twitching in the dull water of a muddy puddle.

This time, Jarret didn't wait for a response from the house, but crashed down the bank towards the back of the parking area and the safety of the woodland beyond. If anyone had been watching from the house, the percussion flash from the second cartridge would've given his position away. The first shot he might've got away with; the second they'd have been watching for. He ran through the wood until he collided with a sapling and fell, dropping the shotgun and attempting to roll sideways away from it. He lay where he was, quite still, expecting at any moment to be sheltering from a hail of bullets.

But still no reaction from the house.

He'd been making enough noise for a family of wild boar. He lay where he was for several more minutes before feeling confident enough to move again. He picked up the shotgun and went in search of the narrow footpath that would take him through the woodland towards the valley. He'd used it only two evenings ago when he'd punctured the Audi's tyres. As soon as he found it, he followed it downhill a short distance before turning back into the woodland and picking his way towards the lights of the house. When he'd reached the edge of the trees, he stopped. He now had an uninterrupted view of the buildings below – the courtyard, the barn, the house and, more importantly, its two exits, front and back.

As he'd advanced through the trees, the shotgun shells, weighing his anorak pockets, had bounced against his sides with a barely audible rattle, reminding him of the need to reload. But, once stationary, he couldn't risk the noise it would make, so settled back on his haunches to observe. When it was all over and his soul was frying on some metaphorical hotplate, there'd be time enough to consider the accruing repercussions of his insanity. But, for the moment, it was his body, not his soul, which he had to worry about. That, after all, was the purpose of the game.

All of a sudden, the house was plunged into total darkness, as if the current had been switched off at the mains. The electric yellow light, which had spilled across the courtyard and faded against the trees, was replaced by a filtered, watery moonlight. The house was transformed into a solid black silhouette against the milky grey sky. Jarret's focus on the silhouette was total. Minutes passed. No activity or sound issued from the blackened interior.

Whoever was in there was hesitant. They'd been taken by surprise. And, like Jarret, were waiting and watching, uncertain as to what to do next.

But Jarret had all night. And was gambling that whoever was inside the house hadn't. He settled himself more comfortably on the damp ground, water seeping through the back of his jeans. And, once again, waited.

#

Between the edge of the woodland and the house was a grassy incline. Soon after they bought Le Papillon as a holiday home, he and Trixie employed a local landscape gardener to clear and seed it for them. But all that remained now was an unkempt wasteland with as many, if not more, weeds and wild flowers as original grass. To make it easier to look after, they'd decided against planting trees or shrubs or creating any flowerbeds. Even without detours, running the sit-on lawnmower up and down the bank was precarious enough.

This thirty-metre expanse of unkempt open ground separated the woodland and the entrance to the courtyard. Anyone looking to leave the house safely, therefore, was left with two realistic choices. Go through the front door, cross the courtyard and enter the woodland on *Le Grand Nichon*, at the back of the barn. Or leave through the back door and either cross the open expanse towards the woodland or climb down into the valley and use the sparse undergrowth of the hillside as cover.

Jarret remained motionless, keeping watch on the house, until gradually his legs began to stiffen. Rainwater had already seeped through the material of his anorak. His shirt and T-shirt stuck to his body with a clammy chill. The luminous dial on his watch moved in slow motion. The tedium numbed his concentration. His lids were heavy with the weight of nothingness and the inexorable lullaby of the rainwater falling from the trees. Only physical discomfort prevented him from sleeping.

A click of the lock of a door amplified above a whisper by the sound box of the courtyard suddenly aroused him. It had come from the front of the house. Then, from the back, came the creaking of an un-oiled hinge. His heartbeat quickened.

In the murky light, a crouching figure darted towards the cover of the barn and the trees beyond it – too distant for Jarret to get in a shot. The back of the house remained quite still. But it was the direction which caused him the most concern. The man who'd run off into the woodland would have trouble enough finding his way in the dark. And, anyway, was heading away from Jarret. But anyone emerging from the back of the house would inevitably be coming through the valley towards him. The fact that he hadn't seen anyone didn't mean they weren't already on their way.

Though seriously light on firepower, Jarret knew the terrain. He didn't move until the feeling had returned to his legs. Then he picked his way through the trees towards the valley – not daring to quit cover until he reached the shrub and bramble of the steep meadow that sloped down to the stream. His progress was slow – any false movement or sound would make him a target.

He was about to quit the cover of the trees when he remembered that he hadn't reloaded the shotgun. Now only one of the barrels contained a dischargeable cartridge. If more than one person confronted him in the valley, he was heading for trouble – dead trouble. But once again he couldn't risk attracting attention.

A few metres below the edge of the steep meadow, he settled back on his haunches and scoured the valley below. His ears were attuned for the slightest sound, his eyes sweeping the semi-darkness for movement. The rain had just about completely stopped and a damp breeze blew against his cheek. His earlier discomfort was all but forgotten. Now what concerned him was to find out whether someone had exited the back of the house. Or if he was in the valley alone. The answer was not long in coming. Someone was advancing towards him. He heard the rustling of long grass and the muffled curses of someone stumbling on the steep slope of the valley.

No other voices accompanied the first, and no-one told him to shut up – just a lone figure struggling to find his footing on the uneven slope. If Jarret moved close enough to him, one loaded barrel would be enough. But first he had to intercept him. He guessed there were no more than thirty metres between them. If the man maintained a parallel course along the side of the valley, it would be fine. But if he started heading downwards, he'd be difficult to track.

But the man making his way towards him wasn't used to such terrain. After only another minute, there was a scrambling noise and another muffled curse as he again lost his footing – the same voice, followed by the same nervous silence. Jarret tried unsuccessfully to calculate the man's distance, but the route he was following appeared to be leading him directly towards him. He crouched on one knee, shotgun pressed against his shoulder. He tracked the man's slow progress with growing impatience.

Before long came the sound of laboured breathing, punctuated by occasional brief mutterings as the man toiled through the long grass of the uneven terrain. On a city street, Jarret would have steered well clear of the person he saw emerging out of the darkness in front of him. But, tonight, in the countryside, he was no more than vermin to be eliminated.

He held the shotgun tightly, the breach close to his chin, and waited. The silhouette of the large wheezing man approached closer – an overweight silhouette armed with an automatic rifle. Without him knowing a thing, a couple more paces and Jarret would put an end to his misery. But he stopped and wiped his brow with the palm of his right hand. Whether it was sweat or rainwater that had fallen on him from the trees, as he'd left the house, Jarret was unable to see. He felt another stab of impatience at the delay. He wanted the man to move. Right away. To become unmissable.

But before anything could happen, another voice whispered loudly from the top of the bank.

'Jerry … Jerry … Are you all right? Can you see anything?'

The voice was heavy with an eastern European accent. There was a pause as the man, Jerry, tried to recover enough breath to speak.

'Nothing at all. There's no-one down here. This is fucking killing me.'

Unaware of the irony, Jarret checked his aim and unleashed the contents of a single cartridge into the torso of breathless, heavy-bodied silhouette that stared up out of the valley in front of him. A headshot would have been too risky. He listened to the groan as the impact staggered the fat man backwards, causing him to lose his balance and tumble, backwards, head first down the slope. Then hell broke loose above him – but he'd already had the presence of mind to throw himself sideways and use the slope to roll downwards and away from where he'd fired the shot.

Bullets flew everywhere. And, for an instance, the world became unreal. As if Jarret were in a film in which violent actions have no consequences – and death only a solution to the storyline. The gunman above him had no notion of a target. He stood at the edge of the valley spraying bullets at random. If he hit anything, it would be by luck.

Sliding further down the slope to behind the flimsy cover of a bramble, Jarret took advantage of the chaos above him to replace the two spent shotgun cartridges. No-one would hear him above the noise of the gunshots as he broke open the shotgun and reloaded. It was instinct that positioned him behind the bramble's flimsy cover; though it offered a partial hiding place, it gave no protection from the flying bullets. To his right, he could hear the dying man moaning from somewhere in the damp long grass – crying out to his friend for help.

Once he'd reloaded, he moved quickly to a new position – to put as wide an angle as possible between himself and the spray of the bullets. Climbing as quickly as the terrain allowed him, he made his way in an arcing line towards the top of the bank – careful not to slip and end up blowing his own head off. His eyes were all the time on the gunman above him. Again, the dying man called out to his friend, who for the moment had ceased firing.

'Shut the fuck up! I'm trying to listen. I think I may have got the bastard.'

But there was no way the man in the valley was going to 'shut the fuck up'. For him, the world had contracted to encompass no more than pain, misery and his own physical salvation. Jarret watched as the gunman on the edge of the valley levelled his rifle at his wounded partner as if he were about to shoot him – then appeared to change his mind. From the darkness of the slope, the groans and pleas of the dying man continued.

Jarret lay in the long grass at the top of the valley. The gunman had not been shot at – only his partner. In the quiet that followed, his confidence grew. He stared into the darkness for confirmation that Jarret was dead. His head cocked slightly so that his right ear was angled to detect any sound coming from below – from another wounded man. With the passing seconds, he grew more confident still. He took a few tentative paces downwards into the valley. Then he hesitated, climbed back up and began moving sideways along it, an action which brought him closer to Jarret. He took another pace downwards, then again hesitated. He was unable to make up his mind, uncertain whether to descend further into the valley and take a proper look or to remain where he was. But uncertainty was a fatal error.

On the soccer pitch, Jarret had been taught to make decisions and back them with everything he'd got. The man in front of him was backing uncertainty.

Realistically, the target was still too far away. A shot at that distance was optimistic. But Jarret fired anyway. A blast that, once again, ripped through the night and echoed in his eardrums, causing them to throb.

It was as if the gunman had had his legs whipped from under him. As if an invisible rope had pulled them sideways. He held on to his rifle, but in doing so fell heavily on his shoulder – his body at an oblique angle to the slope, head tilted in the direction of the dying fat man.

Though there'd been no hesitation – he'd made his decision and acted – the execution had not been accurate. Too late, Jarret regretted what he'd done. The man lay in a painful heap on the ground, with his legs mangled, but the rest of him was uninjured. Which meant he remained dangerous. The shock as yet had not kicked in, nor the pain begun to accumulate. The man struggled to roll on to his stomach and raised his rifle to a firing position. His shoulder seemed to hamper him. He fired defensively and at no real target. Nevertheless, bullets hit the earth close to where Jarret was lying, forcing him to, once again, roll down the slope into the valley.

Then nothing – just a click and a silence.

The man on the ground was struggling. He had his hand in his jacket pocket and he was pulling at something. Jarret could see that the movement was painful to him and that there was an urgency to it. He was puzzled. He raised himself off the ground to look. He couldn't work out what was causing this strange behaviour. But as soon as he did – he realised he'd won. The man's gun was out of ammunition. He was panicking, pulling at his pocket, trying to retrieve another magazine, which in his haste had become stuck there. His jacket had been hanging loose and, as he pulled the magazine towards him, the side of the jacket came with it. He tried freeing the magazine by twisting it, but the jacket twisted too and the pocket only tightened around his hand. His growing panic restricted his thinking. The more he pulled at the magazine in his pocket, the more desperate he got and the more difficult it became to free it. He needed to use two hands, but wouldn't let go of his rifle.

Jarret walked towards him. By the man's staccato breathing, he could tell that the pain in his legs was augmenting. Not out of pity or, indeed, registering very much at all, other than he'd won, Jarret levelled the shotgun and with the remaining cartridge ended his struggle. There was no joy in victory. He watched as the man's rifle slid sideways and his head sank slowly onto the grass, as if suddenly overwhelmed by an enormous fatigue. A fatigue Jarret realised he shared.

Once again he reloaded. The pockets of his anorak were becoming lighter. The three dead men and one dying inhabited the darkness around him like the ghosts of a dream. Though his senses remained alert, he felt deflated and numb. It was too soon to think about what he'd done or its consequences. Or of the life he he'd been trying to build for himself in France. All he knew was that once again everything had gone wrong for him.

The shotgun's recoil had been absorbed by the muscle and bone in his shoulder. He could tell that the joint was already stiffening and beginning to lose its flexibility, as if someone had hit it several times with a mallet. He'd never learnt to fire a shotgun properly and wouldn't be able to carry on much longer.

19 (Wednesday pm)

The solid shadow of the house loomed over him. The moaning from the valley continued, but more quietly now – the man was near death. In the distance, a dog barked, probably one of Didier's. No other sounds impinged on the silence – there'd been too much noise and too many deaths for anything to dare.

Jarret paused a moment. He'd killed four men. Two guarding the track and the two from the house – that made all of them. Enough to have captured or killed him if Didier hadn't warned him of their presence. He'd have got in, but never got out again. And if they'd let him live, it'd only be so they could take him to McBryde for questioning – a prospect that made death preferable.

He didn't know if there were any other gunmen, nevertheless, he felt a sense of relief, of optimism taking hold. He walked slowly towards the rear of the house. There was more cover there and not so many windows. Every few paces, he halted and listened – his eyes searching the shadows for movement. The drizzle had all but cleared and the moon slipped from cloud to cloud like a passing headlight. The dripping water from the trees in the woodland and the large walnut that shaded the back of the house had eased. And the sound of moaning from the valley had all but died away.

At the corner of the house, he leant with his back against the wall and surveyed the area of open ground he'd just crossed. For several seconds, the moon emerged from behind a cloud. The dead man lay still just beyond the edge of the valley, sprawled, dark stains discolouring his shirt and faded jeans. Beyond him, the woodland formed a solid wall, punctuated only at its perimeter by the dark verticals of trees. Above, the sky had grown higher and the cold light of stars was embedded between the shifting clouds. The breeze, which moved the dark foliage around the house, was gentler.

Once he was reassured that everything was quiet, he slipped around the corner of the house, in the direction of the back door. He took cover behind the buddleia hedge, and waited – watching the windows for any sign of movement from inside the house.

When at last satisfied all was clear, he followed the line of the hedge until it ended about five metres from the trunk of an ancient walnut tree. In a good summer, its overarching branches shaded the house from the furnace of the afternoon sun. With the moon behind it and the rain on its leaves, it drooped like a laden shadow. From his new position, he could see that the back door had been left half open. Probably by the fat man he'd shot in the valley. The small entrance area-cum-cloakroom, on the other side of the door, was in darkness. Which even in the fleeting moonlight was impenetrable. For several moments, he thought about entering. Plucking up the courage. But there was always the thought of what the darkness might hide.

He left the shelter of the hedge undecided whether to enter the house or circle it first to make certain there was no-one still inside – so he neither quite moved towards the door, nor past it. With the result that his attention, focused on the need to make a decision, became briefly internalised.

The voice, when he attuned to it, seemed from far away. Not in terms of distance, but in terms of time. He registered it, but with its temporal proximity removed. It neither spoke loudly nor quickly. It didn't have to. Within its tone, there was the presumption of obedience, the clear and calm understanding that it was not to be messed with or disobeyed. Worst of all, there was the dawning realisation of the purpose of its presence there. It'd frozen him once before; now it did so again. Game over. His neck muscles locked and the pain in his shoulder irrelevantly intensified.

Suddenly, he wanted to scream. But fear kept him silent.

'No quick movements, Mr Jarret; remain exactly where you are. Now, very slowly place your gun onto the ground beside you. Keeping it so I can see it. Then step away. Thank you.'

The voice came out of the darkness a little distance behind him. But he could sense it moving closer. After he'd placed the shotgun on the ground and stepped away from it, a shadowy figure crossed the periphery of his vision, from the direction of the back door. The close-cropped hair, the silhouetted head, the firm broad-shouldered body were as disquietingly recognisable as the voice – and too lethal to ignore. The automatic pistol in McBryde's right hand was almost unnecessary.

'Well, Mr Jarret, it seems we're never going to get to have our little cosy tête-à-tête after all. That's disappointing. I'm sure you've got a few stories you would have liked to share with me. But what will be will be. Though I suppose it was inevitable it had to come to this in the end, whether you had found … what did you call her? Alice? Alicia? … or not. But you are not an unintelligent man, Mr Jarret. I'm sure you'd already worked that out for yourself. Just try to find some consolation in the fact that you didn't really have any choice – if you'd refused to help me, you were dead; and if you agreed, which you did for a while, then you were still going to end up dead. What choice did you have? Life can be very cruel. But if it makes things any easier for you, I want to tell you that you impressed me here tonight. I really didn't think you had it in you. You seemed such a nervy person. I assume you've killed them all. Yes. I'm sure you have, or we wouldn't be here now. Would we?'

Under no threat, McBryde was savouring his moment before the kill. The fate he had in store for Jarret had already been determined, predetermined even. But astute as McBryde was, he was sadistic. And before him stood his victim and he was savouring it and what might pass in his sick world as wit. It wasn't that he was guilty of being indecisive. He was enjoying the kill. The cat toying with a mouse, aware of the game's only outcome. But just as much as being in control, he enjoyed the sound of his own words.

Jarret tried backing off a little – trusting to the darkness. For, however long McBryde continued to speak, and to toy with him, was the only time left for Jarret to act. But even as he did, he was resigned to the fact that he'd never escape. McBryde was too professional to let that happen. And Jarret had no plan – no real idea what edging backwards into the night was going to achieve. Other than he had to do something rather than just stand there meekly and wait to be killed.

Though Jarret concentrated on McBryde intently, his words flowed over him. He hated losing, but bad winners he hated more. It made him irrationally angry. Tonight, he was being subjected to both. He may have missed the meanings, but not the sneer in the sound of the words.

The seconds ticked by and McBryde continued speaking.

'It's a shame I'm not recruiting, Mr Jarret. I might have had a use for you. But then again, I could never have trusted you. Not like those bastards out there – totally stupid, but dependable. To the very end.'

There followed a sound, mid-way between a cough and a choke, which Jarret interpreted as McBryde's attempt at laughter. It ended as abruptly as it began.

McBryde raised his pistol to fire. But, as he did so, he noticed for the first time that the distance between him and his target had perceptibly increased. To rectify it, he took a pace forward. But Jarret retreated further and a little faster. McBryde walked quickly towards him – pistol at arm's length, pointing directly at Jarret's chest. But then something happened. Something … an object … exploded beneath his foot with a loud crack. He lurched sideways and, as a reflex, he fired. The bullet flew past Jarret's head, close enough for him to feel the displaced air against his cheek. Then another loud crack, this time beneath McBryde's other foot, and he again lurched sideways, but in the opposite direction, cursing as he did so beneath his breath. He took another pace forward and more objects began to rattle and clatter around his feet like skittles. He kicked out – and something hollow spun into the darkness, its weight easily absorbed by the too-long grass.

'What the fuck …?'

Aware that this was probably the only opportunity he'd have, Jarret hunched forward and ran towards the corner of the house and the darkness beyond. Not so much ran as scurried, like a rat towards its hole. But McBryde reacted quickly. Holding the pistol at arm's length, in both hands, he brought it level with his right eye. Jarret sidestepped, as if that simple action alone could save his life; to avoid the inevitable bullet that was about to come hurtling towards him. He knew it was fanciful – but he could hope.

McBryde fired. And Jarret fell.

All of a sudden, it was like a dream – something soft seemed to be wrapping itself around him like a shroud, preparing him for burial. And he sank gently into a ground that appeared to offer no resistance to his slaughtered body. Ghostlike, he could feel himself passing right through it.

The moment of his death and he was exhilarated, released. Free from fear and pain, as if he were floating. Then a hard surface rose to meet him, crashing across his back and shoulders and bouncing his skull so hard that when he opened his eyes they were watering and what was left of his world swam in a distorted haze. He never guessed that the ground could be that hard.

Then there was a whisper as something settled beside him. He was in too much pain to try and make out what it was, but he didn't fear it. From now on, nothing could hurt him. There was no more fear.

But it wasn't his body that brought him screaming back to life. It was the sight of McBryde standing at the edge of the half-built swimming pool, smiling down at him. His too-white teeth reflected in a burst of moonlight. Around Jarret and covering his legs, like a giant's body bag, was the green plastic tarpaulin he'd used to cover the pool to prevent it from collecting rainwater. It had broken his fall, only to keep him conscious enough to witness being killed for a second time. He wished it hadn't. There was no escape. McBryde raised his gun and pointed it at him for the third time. And Jarret closed his eyes.

When the sound of the shot snapped against the side of the house and reverberated round the confines of the empty pool like a ricochet, he was in darkness. It wasn't that he was scared any more – he'd gone beyond that. It was just that he'd suddenly tired, tired of everything – the killing, the confusion, the unhappiness, the self-destructive urge that seemed to haunt and follow him from place to place. Now it was over. He'd no treasured belief in an afterlife. It had ended.

The sound of a second shot swirled round the empty space. The empty space that was no longer inside the swimming pool, but inside his own head. The shot was loud but not deafening. But no engulfing anaesthetic blackness followed it. Only the persistent dull aching in his back and skull and the pounding throb of his right shoulder, where he'd held the shotgun.

A third shot – and it happened, like a dead crushing weight. No burning inner sensation, no sharp punch like he'd been stabbed, just an all-over blow, which took his breath away, followed by a remorseless downward pressure as if his very life was being squeezed out of him. He didn't expect it to be like that. He didn't expect it to feel like he was being suffocated. And when the hurt happened, it hurt – not in one place, but over his entire body.

'Intimate, Mr Jarret. Do you not agree?'

Hot stale breath burnt against his cheek. Beside his right ear, a weak voice was speaking to him that he wished he'd never have to listen to again. Jarret's eyes opened wide with renewed terror. Lying on top of him like an exhausted lover was McBryde, blood trickling from the corner of his mouth. He was trying to smile, but his eyes were beginning to dull – as if something inside had been unplugged.

'Never say I go down without a fight.'

Jarret pushed upwards and sideways in order to try to free himself from the oppressive dead weight crushing his torso. But McBryde was struggling too. He seemed to be trying to fight with him. And just as Jarret had almost managed to ease himself free, he felt an acute pain above the elbow of his right arm. He looked down and was appalled. McBryde, teeth clamped, was biting insanely into the loose flesh on the inside of his bicep. In a sudden burst of panic, Jarret heaved himself free – frantically ripping off his anorak as if it was on fire. It felt as if a part of his upper arm has been removed with it and left between the scald of McBryde's deranged jaws. Like a monster in a horror movie, he was refusing to die. But once Jarret had rolled away, it was clear McBryde was mortal after all – a man, albeit a tough one, who was already fading, and fading fast.

'Are you alright?'

Another voice removed in time – but not in place. A voice so familiar, so welcome and yet so impossible, that he couldn't believe it didn't originate in his own head. The evening had not been kind to him. If this were delusion, it was insupportable. Almost too afraid to do so – he looked up towards the edge of the swimming pool. The person standing above him, pistol in hand, was totally dishevelled. The blow to his head was playing tricks with him. He screwed his eyelids tightly shut, as if to dispel a mirage. But when he re-opened them, nothing could have been more real.

In the entire world, the person he most wanted to see was standing above him. He started to cry.

'O God! You're hurt.'

'Alicia? Jesus, I thought …'

Tears rolled down his cheeks. He was sitting next to a dying man and crying like a baby, his chest and shoulders heaving with joy and misery. At the bottom of the empty swimming pool, his sobs sounded like laughter.

20 (Wednesday pm/Thursday am)

The rest of the night went by in a daze. Clutching the pistol, as if there were more demons lurking in the darkness, Alicia steered Jarret like a blind man back to the house. As soon as she'd sat him at the kitchen table, she went to the cupboard and took out a fresh pack of ground coffee. She spooned three heaped measures into the filter machine, then sat at the table opposite him. She looked scruffy and unkempt. Her hair had lost its sheen and hung lifelessly around her shoulders. But when he looked at her, she was still beautiful. Only now her beauty was natural, simple, with no make-up, no touches of artificiality.

Since the swimming pool, neither of them had spoken. He'd been crying, whether with joy or relief or because he was having a breakdown, he didn't know. But now he was back inside the house, his eyes were dry again. He looked around him like a person who'd lost something. The kitchen was the same, only now there seemed to be a detail missing. The old reassuring domesticity had gone. This was where he carried out the most mundane of tasks. Where he'd felt most at home. Among the food and the cooking pots. Now it was as if he no longer belonged in his own home any more. He hurried from the room in search of a whisky bottle. When he returned, he was carrying two tumblers. He put one in front of each of them. He held the bottle of whisky towards Alicia, who nodded, and he filled them.

His hands shaking, Jarret gulped down his whisky in

one. It almost made him choke. But by the time the coffee arrived, he was on his third. He was afraid to approach the only subject that consumed him – afraid of being disappointed. He searched out Alicia's eyes, hoping to discover in them the lingering intimacy he so desperately sought. Something, an electricity, that might continue to exist between them. Alicia was staring down into her coffee and it was impossible for him to see into them. He willed her to look up. More than anything in the world, he craved her intimacy.

He was confusing intimacy with permanence. His world had fallen apart and he was silently pleading with a woman who had already once abandoned him. A woman who he wanted to be the rock upon which to rebuild the rest of his life. He felt he was going crazy. After all, he hadn't got a life. And, in all probability, neither had she.

A sudden rap on the window startled them both. Jarret sprang to his feet and Alicia's hand had reached towards the gun that she'd placed on the table beside her. They'd both been miles away. Didier, stubble pressed against the window glass, was pointing with a large forefinger at the front door. He was checking to see if he might be intruding. Jarret signalled to him to come in. When he joined them, he was still carrying his rifle. His dark eyes flowed from Jarret to Alicia to the pistol lying on the table beneath her hand. He clearly didn't understand what was going on. He was on guard and looked uncomfortable. He placed his rifle against the wall and for the first time since Jarret had known him, he appeared lost for words.

Jarret helped him out.

'What kept you?'

'You said not to come. Anyway, I didn't want you blowing my head off. Are you alright?'

'I've been better.'

'It sounded like World War Three over here. There's going to be trouble if we don't get this mess sorted out –

and quickly. From what I can see, you've left bodies all over the place. This is going to be a tricky one to deal with.'

'The only way of dealing with this is to tell the truth. It's gone too far this time.'

'For the present, it's nowhere but here. I'm going back to the farm for the van, then I'll drive down to the road. Hopefully, none of the neighbours will know where the shooting came from. If any gendarmes turn up, I'll talk them into looking somewhere else. Meanwhile, you – and the lady, if she's willing – get the bodies and the cars out of sight. We'll think about getting rid of them later. Clear out their pockets, like the other night. And work quickly – there isn't much time.'

'Didier, you're not listening.'

'Just shut up and do what I say. I'll be back soon.'

By way of a farewell, he raised his rifle and was gone. Jarret and Alicia stared at the door that he'd slammed shut behind him. His visit had been breathless, but also decisive. In a world without volition, it had filled the vacuum. Though Jarret had choices, the luxury of clear thought was no longer his. He could act, but he couldn't think – not positively, not decisively, only lose himself in what had happened. Didier had done the thinking for him. He looked at Alicia. She seemed rooted. More lost than he was. The evening had been too much for both of them.

'Stay in the house, turn all the lights out and keep out of sight. If the police come, use the back door and get the hell out of here. Think about yourself, that's all.'

'I will. Thanks.'

Jarret collected the Mercedes from its parking place in the woods, the keys still in the ignition, and loaded the body of the blond-haired man onto the back seat. With the other dead man slumped in the passenger seat beside him, his head still leaning against the door, he drove down the slope towards the house. The Norah Jones CD had mercifully finished. The body of McBryde he'd leave in the pool and cover over later with the green plastic tarp. And the fat man's body could stay where it was in the valley – he'd need help to move it. But in the darkness and the long grass, it shouldn't be obvious. The other one, the man with his hand still in his pocket holding a magazine of bullets, he dragged to the car and manoeuvred onto the floor in front of the back seat.

Though the fall into the empty swimming pool had hurt him, it was the dizziness caused by the bang to his head that was the problem. The pain he could endure, but there were moments when it felt like he was about to fall over. And the alcohol hadn't helped.

He drove the Mercedes across the courtyard and parked it deep in the undergrowth behind the barn. It wasn't the proximity of the dead men that made him uneasy, but their silence. As he drove, he had the sensation that something was crawling up the back of his neck. He returned and collected the other car, the BMW, from the courtyard – presumably McBryde's – and drove it carefully into the undergrowth, next to the Mercedes. For the time being they were out of sight. If the gendarmes arrived and carried out anything like a careful search of Le Papillon, he'd not a hell's chance of keeping them undiscovered. But to a cursory glance, everything looked normal.

For a little over half an hour, Jarret had dragged bodies, driven two luxury cars, each one costing more than it would take to buy a small house in Solac, and searched through the pockets of dead men. If it hadn't been for the shock – the feeling of distance, that none of what was happening was real – then he'd have been capable of carrying out none of those things. When he returned to the kitchen, the lights had been turned out and there was no-one there. Alicia had done what he'd suggested and hidden herself away. He switched on the wall lights and turned one of the chairs around to face the door. He flopped limply into it, like one of the corpses he'd loaded into the Mercedes. Only he was actually in pain and his body was exhausted. But the pain kept him alert. He went to the table and poured himself a whisky to numb it. It didn't.

He hadn't sat there long when his mind started to wander – to embrace a world of possibility. He mapped a future for Alicia and himself that stretched before them like an endless sunlit beach, full of pleasure and happiness. Until, finally, the shadows of the dead men and of the wine bottles containing cocaine and of Lazar Zharkoski eclipsed everything. And there were the shadows too of the police and the curly haired man and Lulu and another criminal, who she'd said lived locally. So many shadows, so many obstacles in the way of the future. He turned back to the table to look for Alicia's gun, but she'd taken it with her.

He forced himself to his feet and dragged himself to the back door. He felt old. In a short time, his body had stiffened to the extent that all movement was becoming painful. A cold shower would ease it. But first, he needed a firearm and the reassurance that would give him. The shotgun was still outside, in the long grass, where McBryde had made him place it.

He stood on the concrete apron outside the back door and looked around him. The walnut tree cast a dark shadow in the now almost-unbroken moonlight, which highlighted the contours of the stone house. He leant back inside the back door and illuminated the panel light above it, making the walnut tree and the surrounding scene more intricate in detail. He couldn't remember where he'd put the shotgun. He was being threatened by McBryde at the time.

As he moved to the edge of the concrete apron, something strange caught his attention – a shape or shapes he didn't recognise. He hesitated. And smiled. Didier's gourds. Some were shattered, some were in hemispheres, others had survived intact – objects that preserved his life, long enough for Alicia to come along and save it. In the darkness, McBryde had walked right into the middle of them and they'd ambushed him, exploding beneath his feet and destroying both his balance and aim so that his bullets never hit their target. Jarret had been lucky – he'd only placed them there because he didn't know what else to do with them. Their remains now littered the grass around him. Civilisations had survived because of them; now so had he.

The shotgun had imprinted itself into the grass. The shape remained after he'd picked it up and tried to dry the breech against his still-damp jeans. The ammunition for it was in his anorak pockets at the bottom of the swimming pool. The thought of McBryde lying there, teeth deadlocked to his anorak sleeve, repulsed him. But his fear of the living and the threat they posed was greater. Without looking directly at the dead man, he retrieved a handful of shells from one of the pockets and retreated.

Armed with the shotgun, he settled once again into one of the kitchen chairs and awaited the unfolding of events. A gourd he'd scooped from the grass lay in the centre of the table behind him. One day soon he'd make that nesting box.

After an hour, he boiled a kettle for coffee. But the liquid tasted dull. He poured himself a whisky. That was better.

Another slow hour passed before he heard the distant chug of a diesel engine approaching along the track. It grew slowly louder. Taking the shotgun with him, he went outside. He listened again to make certain that the vehicle was not, in fact, heading to Didier's farm; then crossed the courtyard and headed for the shadow of the foliage behind the barn. From there, he could make his way up to the top of the *Le Grand Nichon*. Too late he remembered that Alicia was still inside the house. There was no time to return and warn her. The vehicle was bumping over the cobbles towards him.

He raised his shotgun.

An old white van pulled up with a squeak next to where

he was hiding and Didier climbed wearily out of the driver's seat, his joints stiff with fatigue. He seemed to have grown older since Jarret last saw him. His dog occupied the passenger seat, but made no attempt to abandon it. Didier looked around him, then began to make his way towards the house.

Jarret called out to him.

'Didier. Thank God it's you.'

'What are you doing over there?'

'Having a pee. Tell me what's been happening.'

'What's wrong with your toilet?'

'Nothing. What's happening?'

'An hour or so ago the gendarmes showed up ... someone must have telephoned them. There've been quite a few people wandering about ... neighbours from nearby farms and some people from the village. But it was like I told you, none of them could pinpoint where the shooting had come from. And I just tried to confuse things by sowing seeds of doubt in everybody's mind ... suggesting to them that it was probably someone celebrating by letting off a few fireworks or out hunting or maybe they'd been woken by a thunderstorm. But it was difficult to get them to change their minds. They may be simple country folk, but most of them can tell the difference between a gunshot and a firecracker. Anyway, eventually I persuaded the gendarme to take a look in the direction of Les Mazières. They were already pissed off at being called out in the middle of the night. By the time they'd finished trying to get some sense from a bunch of half-awake yokels like us ... with me saying the opposite to what everyone else was saying ... you could see they were pleased to get away. That we'd be unable to tell the difference between a car backfiring and a fart. Though they might come back in the morning and ask a few questions. So, tonight, we've got work to do ... while it's still dark. But, I'll tell you one thing, I'm going to do absolutely nothing until you've given me some of your whisky.'

'There's a bottle on the table. Let's go inside. And thanks.'

They sat down at the kitchen table and Jarret poured them both two large whiskies.

'*Santé*! I've earned this tonight.'

'I don't know whether or not I've earned it, but I need it. *Santé*.'

'A thought occurred to me while I was waiting for the gendarmes to show up – that no-one's ever likely to report these men missing, are they? It's probable they wouldn't have told anybody where they were going or what they were going to do when they got there. And if there are no bodies and no-one's reported them missing, then there's not been a crime, has there? It's really that simple. And if we can get everything cleared up here tonight, then there'll be nothing to find, even if the gendarmes do pay us a call. A little bit of noise isn't going to worry them.'

'They're not going to give up that easily?'

'Give up what? After tonight, I think they'll be only too pleased to give up. Once we've got things cleaned up here, it's just a question of acting normal and carrying on with things.'

'I don't know.'

'I do. How about another whisky?'

Two large whiskies later and Didier had rejuvenated. He ran through his plan – of how to get rid of the cars and the bodies before dawn. His speech was slurred, but his eyes had a renewed sparkle. Jarret didn't join him in another drink, but sat with his hand masking an empty glass. Though another drink would have inoculated him against the tasks ahead, there was a need to conserve the little concentration he had left. And hiding somewhere in the house was Alicia and, whether she wanted to or not, they needed to talk.

In succession, Jarret drove the two cars from their hiding places behind the barn and parked them near the entrance to the courtyard. Didier helped him retrieve the body of McBryde from the swimming pool and, with difficulty, the obese dead man from the side of the valley. They packed them both onto the back seat of the BMW and Jarret drove them to Didier's farm. Didier followed in the van, then drove him back to collect the Mercedes. In less than an hour, the incriminating evidence, except for blood and spent cartridge cases, had been transferred from Le Papillon to Didier's farm.

When the bodies had been stripped, Didier instructed Jarret to steer the cars onto a patch of unfarmed land at the foot of *Le Grand Nichon* that served as a cemetery for old farm machinery. He weaved his way to the centre of fifty years of corroding metal and flaking paint, two generations of technological discard, consisting of a tractor, thresher, a couple of ploughs and three old cars.

By the time the cars were in place, Didier had dragged three of the naked bodies into the dingy interior stink of one of the piggeries. Jarret helped with the final two, which they dragged into the piggery adjoining it. The surrounding stench and the obscenity of it reminded him of Adams's and Fraze's mutilated bodies. He watched as Didier went to a small metal cupboard next to the door and took out a rolled piece of sacking from which he extracted a butcher's knife.

He held it for Jarret to inspect. And received his answer.

'Okay, I understand. In the barn beside the tractor, you'll find two plastic cans of fuel. Take them and empty them around inside each of the cars. After you've done that, check the fuel tanks to make sure there's enough inside each of them to give us a big enough blaze. When you've finished, don't come back in here; wait for me in the kitchen. Make yourself some coffee and I'll come and get you. We'll burn the cars just before dawn and everyone's still asleep. You can pay me for the fuel later. Now get going; I've got work to do.'

Jarret poured a can of petrol around the interior of each of the cars. The smell it gave off made him blink away tears. On the back seat of the BMW, with all the other clothes ready for burning and stained dark by the fuel, was his old green anorak. It bore the imprint of McBryde and no longer felt like his.

The heat from the cars when they blew was intense. Each fuel tank burst with a muffled explosion and for a moment it looked like there was a danger that some of the trees in the nearby woodland were going to catch fire. But as soon as the flames reached their highest, they began to subside – like a firework display that disappoints because it ends too abruptly. Though the greying light of the near-dawn made the inferno less obvious, they were pleased when the flames and smoke died down. By the time they left, glistening with sweat from the heat, all that remained of the once-luxury cars were two charred skeletons.

'I'll get the sledgehammer and smash them around when they've cooled and I can get near them. Couple of days they'll be rusting along with the rest of the junk out there. A drink? I think we've earned it.'

'No, thanks, I need to get back.'

'Ah, the young lady ... Jarret's little secret. Who is she? Tell me.'

'Some other time, not now.'

'Afraid I'll steal her from you?'

'Thanks, Didier. For everything.'

'And, Jarret, remember.'

'What?'

'Give her one for me. A kiss, I'm talking about. That mind of yours!'

21 (Thursday am/pm)

The dawn was coming up as Jarret followed the winding track from Didier's back to Le Papillon. Along the ridgeline, a crack had appeared in the sky through which a deep pink stain was beginning to seep. As he watched through the trees, it spread, softened round the edges and transformed into a transparent golden yellow light. He hurt and he was dog-tired, but the erosion of darkness uplifted him. The morning's freshness on his skin felt clean, like the promise of new hope.

He pushed open the front door into the kitchen and turned on the light. His chair was where he left it, facing the door. His shotgun was on the table behind it. He went round the bottom floor of the house to make sure all the doors and shutters were secure. A small but futile attempt to keep the outside world at bay – if all went wrong and Didier's plan didn't work, tomorrow he could be in prison. But in the meantime every moment was his.

He was tired, too tired to think. Without sleep, time seemed like one long continuum. He should sleep, go straight to bed, grab a couple of hours and freshen up. But thinking of Alicia again had sent his emotions into turmoil – he was exhausted and at the same time felt wired. Here was the opportunity to relax for the first time in God knows when, and he couldn't. He calculated how big a whisky it would take to knock himself out.

Before picking up his glass, he unscrewed the top from the whisky bottle.

'You need to go to bed.'

How long she'd been there watching, he didn't know.

'I need a drink.'

'No you don't.'

Though it felt like he'd been caught in the act of doing something he shouldn't, he poured himself a drink anyway. But before he could take a sip, Alicia had taken the glass from his hand and was gently pulling him in the direction of the stairs. Like a child, he obeyed.

She was so fragile, so beautiful. The fatigue and the feeling of hopelessness left him: he shed them with his clothes. In the shower, he washed away the blood clot that was matting the back of his hair and examined his newly battered body. How come, recently, he hadn't gone to bed with anyone without the marks of a beating? When he returned, she was lying in the middle of the bed waiting for him.

No words were exchanged – instead, they made long, slow, gentle love. Her hair had been freshly washed and smelled, once again, perfumed and sweet, and her flesh was soft and smoothly perfect in contrast to his hard, bruised body. To him, being with her was like being in the waves of a warm sea and he luxuriated in the curves and troughs of her gentle motion.

And afterwards – as he lay there, the world beyond the shutters diminished – he was certain ... knew without a doubt that he wanted to remain with her forever. And wondered if it could ever be possible.

Her past he'd already put out of his mind. Who or what Alicia might once have been no longer concerned him. If someone had coerced her into doing something for their own profit, that was hardly her fault, and in the past. What she was right now was all he cared about. The person lying there in the crook of his arm was the person he wanted – just as she was. No judgements. No inquiries. Everyone deserved a second chance. He of all people understood that. His hands shook, but his body felt relaxed. And, in that moment, he almost believed.

But one question taunted him and wouldn't go away –

Where had she been since last he saw her? He didn't even want to ask her why she thought she had to leave – just where she'd been. She hadn't trusted him. But in her previous line of work, trusting someone would have been a luxury.

His mind spiralled as a new and delicious fatigue began to envelop him. With every steadying heartbeat, he sensed that sleep was drifting closer. When he spoke, it didn't even sound like his voice any more – and his words sounded slurred.

'Where did you go?'

'What do you mean?'

'When you left here, you went to Villefranche. Where did you go after that?'

'I took the hire car back to Villefranche, yes ... I was scared – with Adams around and you not there, anything could've happened.'

'I'm sorry. I shouldn't have left you, but you knew I'd be coming back.'

'Like I told you, I was scared. I wasn't thinking straight. Once I'd returned the hire car, I didn't know what to do next. I didn't want to risk the railway station or the airport in case someone was there looking out for me. I could've gone off in the hire car, but I thought that could be easily traced. So I took a taxi and came back here, praying it was still safe, and that Adams hadn't found it yet. As soon as I arrived, I tidied everything up, so you'd think that I'd left. Then I took some food and hid in that half-finished roof space of yours. Even when I thought there was no-one here, I'd hardly dare make a sound. It's been awful, but until tonight it's been safe.'

'You've been here all the time. But why didn't you let me know? I could've helped you. Even got you away from here, if that's what you wanted.'

'I like you ... I love you a lot, but I didn't know you well enough to be sure. I don't ... didn't really know how you'd cope. Maybe I wasn't thinking. There were a lot of bad people out there and you didn't seem to be the person who was capable of keeping them away from me. It seemed to me you were too nice. I didn't think you'd kill anybody.'

His reflex was to be hurt – that she'd had no faith in him. No trust. But she was right – he wouldn't have been any use to her. After all, it was her who had to rescue him. Without her, he'd have been dead. He'd have missed this moment with her forever.

'I suppose it turned out for the best. But you could at least try trusting me now. Everything's going to be okay, I promise. You saved my life, so I can hardly say what you did was the wrong thing. What I can't understand though is why, after hiding away for so long, you came downstairs when the shooting started. I'd have thought that'd be the last thing you want to do.'

'Believe me, when I heard that man come into the house, I was terrified. I listened to him talking and realised he was intending to kill you. Then all the shooting began and for a long time I didn't know what was happening. Eventually, when everything went quiet, I thought they'd killed you. Either way, no-one was moving around any more. Then I heard that man's voice again and I realised it was you he was speaking to. So I took the gun out of my bag and came downstairs. I got you into this. I thought the least I could do was to try and keep you alive. I figured I owed you that much.'

'Now I'm the one who owes you. Have you ever used that gun before?'

'Not exactly. I've never had to kill anyone with it – before tonight, that is. But I was taught how to use it a long time ago. It was the only thing near me I could trust. But let's leave that for the moment.'

'Whatever you say.'

He rolled over and pulled her close to him. He didn't want her to leave him again. Not ever. He wanted to protect her, to try to make her feel that from now on she'd be safe with him. That he would always be there for her. She stroked his hair, like she was soothing a child. His shoulder hurt and his hands still shook a little. She kissed him softly on the forehead.

But he was already asleep.

#

Jarret was dreaming deeply when he heard the sound. It entered his dream like a roaring angry beast. He sat upright in a panic. Something had hold of him. His eyes fixed on the blank bedroom wall. His arm was being pulled. The beast was inside. It gripped him tightly and was now shaking him by the shoulder, frantically. He turned to find Alicia, holding on to his shoulder, looking terrified.

'Who's that?'

Half asleep, he attuned again to the sound of roaring. Only it wasn't roaring, it was someone hammering on the front door. There was no time. He didn't bother to dress. The shotgun in his right hand, he fumbled the latch on the bedroom shutters with his left to release them. He shoved them outwards. A blast of transparent light filled the room. Immediately, he ducked beneath the stone windowsill and waited for a hail of bullets to shower him with splinters of wood and glass from the shattered window frames.

'Great life for some people! Thought you might be able to make it by lunchtime, though. Have you got a friend up there with you?'

His pulse quickened, as his body relaxed. He recognised the voice and supposed she'd not come to shoot him. If she had, she probably wouldn't have knocked on the door. Holding the shotgun out of sight, he leant part way out of the window. Lulu and two men accompanying her looked up at him.

'What d'you want?'

'Now that's not a very friendly welcome. Put some clothes on; I want to talk to you. And be quick.'

'Give me five minutes.'

From a drawer, he took out a clean pair of jeans and a T-shirt. Alicia too had started to dress. Even as it disappeared, he couldn't help marvelling at her nakedness. But her actions were urgent and although she seemed in control, she was nervous. Her handbag lay open on the bedside table and what looked like the smooth metal of a handgun was visible inside it.

'Who is it?'

'Spooks, police … that's what they say. They claim to work for some UK agency or other. I don't know if I believe them. But it's all right, it's me they want to talk to. They think you're miles away.'

'God! Not now.'

'Don't worry. I can handle it. Trust me … I think I know what they're after.'

'Will they search the house?'

'No, I won't let them. If you're worried, take everything and get yourself back up in the roof space. I'll call you when it's all clear.'

His body felt heavy, as he walked along the landing to the stairs. Given the amount of sleep he'd managed in the last forty-eight hours, it was an effort to be moving at all. And it was too early for his brain to be working properly. As he descended the stairs, the previous night's events replayed in his mind. In all probability, sooner or later, he was going to have to face up to the consequences. Why the fuck couldn't he have just up and left as he'd planned? But then he'd never have seen Alicia again.

'At last, lover boy! Your beauty sleep doesn't seem to have done you much good. You look awful.'

'I'm here on my own. I forgot to set the alarm, that's all. Want some coffee?'

'Why not? You two stay out here; I want to talk in private. I'll call you for some coffee when it's ready.'

Curly and a shorter-than-average, neat-looking man in his mid-twenties nodded in turn and wandered off in the direction of the picnic table, under the walnut in the courtyard. Presumably, as soon as the door was shut, they'd use the time he spent with Lulu to take a quick look around. For the moment, he wasn't worried because, with everything securely locked up from last night, there was no way they could get inside. They'd have no chance of finding Alicia.

'I'm going to make it strong and caffeinated. If you want decaf, there's instant in the cupboard. Help yourself.'

'Right now, I can use something strong. Why didn't you contact me back after our meeting, yesterday? I thought I made myself quite clear. We need to co-operate. Or rather, you do. You're staying alive by luck at the moment. Without us around to protect you, you're going to be dead meat.'

'I'm thinking about it. Hot milk or cold?'

'Neither. You've no time to continue to piss around. In fact, we thought you might already be dead. That's why we came here. You don't answer your telephone, you don't read texts and you're not replying to any of the messages I left for you. Why did you come back here?'

'It's as safe as anywhere.'

'I thought you'd already left this dump for good. We only came here because we were curious. But it doesn't matter. Because now we've got another problem – we've lost McBryde. There've been people out looking for him all over the place – we've even alerted the French – but somehow he's managed to have vanished. He gave one of our men the slip early yesterday morning. Now we haven't a clue where he is.'

'Good. I mean good … clever of him to have lost you. Sounds pretty careless to me.'

'We can't be everywhere and he wasn't exactly in hiding. Maybe we weren't paying enough attention, but we didn't expect him to up and give us the slip like this. You've got his number. We're counting on you to bring him back on our radar. Do that and I promise we'll look after you.'

'I spoke to him last night.'

'And what did you talk about?'

'I told him the girl he was looking for was already abroad. That she'd flown out of Toulouse Airport two days ago. He's probably gone off after her.'

'Where was she flying to?'

'I told him I thought she might be heading for the Far East – Thailand, Malaysia, the Philippines. Somewhere like that. She'd talked about it several times. I think she had some sort of bolthole already fixed up out there.'

'We can check passenger lists. Did she fly from Toulouse or somewhere else?'

'I'm not sure, but, anyway, you'll need to look for connections – London, Paris, Amsterdam, Frankfurt. McBryde's probably already done that. But if she's trying to cover her trail, she won't be travelling under her own name.'

'You reckon he believed you?'

'Why not? It's the truth. You know what he'd do to me if I lied. One cup of black coffee coming up. Sugar?'

'Just the coffee. I know what'll happen if you lied to him: he's going to be back here looking for you before you blink.'

'Lie to my employer? That would be unethical. Like I said, she was attracted to something in the Far East.'

'I've already checked you for ethics, remember. You seem to have a very short memory. '

'Bitchy. But you did ask me to keep him running round

for you.'

'I wanted him running round Aveyron, not the world. This is another fuck-up. Though it was strange he never went back to the hotel to collect any of his things. And why didn't you inform me of what you were doing. This little solo effort of yours is going to cause us extra grief. We're going to have to find him quickly. I need to get on the phone.'

'Tell 'Curly' and his little friend their coffee's ready – that is, if they haven't got themselves lost snooping about. This place is bigger than it looks.'

Before she moved through the front door into the courtyard, she'd already pressed speed dial on her mobile phone. Seeing her from behind, Jarret was reminded of the young woman talking into her telephone on the bridge in Villefranche-de-Rouergue. But no matter who this woman was play acting at being, she was above all a hard, in-your-face professional, doing whatever was needed to get the job done. She was a woman competing in a man's world and more than holding her own, and determined, if required, to be the hardest bastard around. And he harboured no illusions. He knew that if she got orders to arrest him and send him to Guantanamo, she would.

But with McBryde dead, Jarret could play a new game with her and play it as creatively as he liked. The immediate danger was over and, for whatever short a period of time, he was the one writing the rules. Lulu and company could court him for all they were worth, and he could create as many shadows for them to chase as he liked.

But there was a reason Jarret wanted to co-operate with Lulu. He needed her as insurance policy – a double indemnity. Because if the worst happened, he would need her help much more than she needed his. If the shit of the previous night's killings hit whatever judicial fan the French legal system put in its way, then it was going to require someone with more power and influence than

285

Didier's pigs to clean it up for him. And if Lulu and her pals really were spooks, or whatever she said they were, and they were on his side, then that was as perfect as it would ever get for him.

Yet, for the present, perfect seemed to be a long way away.

'That's sorted. There's no point in us continuing looking for McBryde here if he's gone jetting off around the world. Someone else can deal with that for now. Anyway, the person I spoke to seemed pleased with what you'd done. Even though, personally, I think it's a fuck-up.'

'Was that a compliment?'

'Not even close. I've just been given clearance from a superior to put something to you. What if I asked you to do something for me? What would you say?'

'That I'm listening.'

'This is serious. I need more commitment from you than that. This is a chance, for once in your life, to do something that's of some use.'

'Then it depends. What're you offering in return? For me being of some use to you.'

'Money *and* your life. I can package them both for you with a pink ribbon on.'

'Tempting. I'm still listening.'

'If our operation here's successful, it's unlikely you'll ever see McBryde again.'

'Explain how you're going to make that happen.'

'Only after you agree to sign a document. And, after that, only if you do exactly what I tell you to do. No more fuck-ups. Clear?'

'Clear. You want me to sign something without reading it first? I'll have to run that past my *advocat*.'

'No, on both counts. You can read it, but if you agree to work with us, then everything becomes deadly serious. This is not one of the wishy-washy liberal documentaries you used to make. You'll be operating under and limited by Section 4 of the '89 Act. Any disclosure and you'll find yourself in fucking prison. Do you understand?'

'The Official Secrets Act?'

'What else? There'll be no going back. And understand this: none of us here has a sense of humour, so we're not looking for a comedian to be working with us.'

'You want me to sign the Official Secrets Act?'

'If you're prepared to be useful, yes. If you're not, this conversation never took place. And who knows, open your mouth and your quiet life in France might no longer be in place either. A word or two with the authorities here and you'll find yourself back in the UK. I'll give you the document to sign later. For now, this is a verbal agreement. In front of witnesses.'

'I don't see any.'

'I'd like to see you try to argue that in court. There are three of us present. You're just unable to see the other two. So what do you say?'

'Okay. But I don't see how I can be much use to you.'

'Then fucking listen. I've already told you that this area is being used as a conduit for hard drugs, and that we've been following a route here from Africa. But there's a double bonus in cracking this operation, because we know, or suspect at least, that another route comes through here, one that operates from the East via the Balkans. So, as a conduit, this place represents a very important nut for us to crack. Yesterday, I mentioned that there was a house not too far away from here owned by a sleaze ball called Trevor. Do you remember?'

'Vaguely.'

'Well, we know he's implicated in this business – right up to his neck. The properties he owns stretch from the Seychelles, Morocco, Spain, Italy and in cities of the UK – some, we suspect, maybe most, play a part in the drug-smuggling operation. Initially, we'd suspicions it operated through his wife, who runs an antique business.

We thought the drugs were being smuggled packed inside the merchandise – furniture, figurines, whatever. But every time we intercepted a consignment bound for her, we found nothing. We even arranged for raids to take place on her warehouses in Italy and Spain. Again, we found nothing – the cupboards were bare.'

'I don't see how I fit into this.'

'He's here now, Trevor, stuck in the middle of this turmoil and wondering what the fuck's going on. But we're still struggling to find anything to incriminate him. You know the little village of Saint-Gaitan, not far from Laguèpie? That's where Trevor's is. A massive place, like Adams's, only bigger. The rich bastard had it renovated and rebuilt for close on a million euros. No middle-class squalor for him. If he owned this run-down place of yours, he'd rip it apart and start again. His legitimate front is that he runs several offshore businesses. Though we've never actually discovered where all the money that finances his lavish lifestyle comes from. But one thing we do know is he's one of Zharkoski's main men and, as such, knows about and has access to the totality of his crime network, or rather the way finances move about within that network. We've been trying for a long time to get agents close to him. None of them has managed it. His radar spots them a mile away and he clams. Electronic surveillance has failed us as well. If we're sophisticated, then he's always been one step ahead of us. He now makes his business phone calls using pre-paid disposable mobiles.'

'What is it exactly you want me to do for you? I still don't see how I fit in.'

'For the moment, we'd just like you to get him talking, get to know him. When the time's right, we'll feed you some questions. You're not an agent, but you know the area, so it just might be you have one or two things in common. And like you, he likes to drink. Each lunchtime, before he eats, he's in the habit of going to the café-bar in Gaitan for a pint of English beer. The bar's run by an Irishman who keeps it specially stocked for the ex-pats that live in the area. Quite a few other Brits use it, though usually lunchtimes it's quiet – which is why he chooses to go there at that time of day. What do you say about trying to talk to him, trying to get to know him for us? The advantage you've got is that you look nothing like an agent. Harmless, laid back, with one or two muscles – but nothing like an agent. You've got nothing to lose by it. So, can I count on you? What do you say?'

'Okay, so you'll protect me from McBryde; but what about the money you mentioned?'

'Successful or not, there'll be a plain brown paper package delivered to you. The closer you get to Trevor, the fatter you'll find that package could become. And from the taxman's point of view, it'll never have existed. Let's say we're prepared to begin at the bottom end of five figures.'

'What guarantee?'

'My word.'

'You're asking a lot.'

'I always do.'

'And no other guarantee.'

'Only my word, but it's every bit as good as my body. What do you say?'

'In that case, my answer has to be "yes".'

'Good. You'll make your initial contact today, while McBryde's out of the picture. I don't suppose you're going to complain about a lunchtime drink. Throughout this, you'll be answerable directly to me and only to me. Understood? I'm your contact, so you must never talk about this to anyone else.'

'Just the two of us – very cosy. When do I get to sign the document?'

'Don't get your hopes up; once was enough. Let's see how close you get first. If you find out nothing, you can say nothing. Where've you left your car? It doesn't seem to be about anywhere.'

'In Solac.'

'I'll run you there now. Do you have everything you need?'

'My wallet, jacket and car keys are upstairs. Give me a minute to collect them and I'll meet you outside. One thing before we start: I don't want Curly or any of his friends following me. I'll do this my way or not at all. If I'm going to be meeting this Trevor for the first time, I want it to be clear that I want no-one shadowing me, no people sitting round in cars with binoculars and no-one pointing electronic devices at me. Our meeting has to seem accidental and as natural as possible. If he's as good as you say he is, he's going to have his wits about him. Anything suspicious and he'll shut down or, worse, shut me down.'

'You'll be on your own, I promise. Now hurry up.'

It took no more than a minute to inform Alicia that he was going to have to leave for a while, but that she'd be safe. Although she'd returned to her hiding place upstairs in the *grenier*, Jarret could see she was on edge. He'd not seen her like that since the supermarket car park in Villefranche-de-Rouergue. As she stood listening to him, she held one hand behind her back. There was something in it she didn't want him to see, but he was in too much of a hurry to care. He kissed her once on the cheek and told her he'd be back some time in the afternoon. This time she made no move to kiss him back.

Outside, Curly and the neat young man were seated at the picnic table. Innocently, as if the last thing on their minds had been to give Le Papillon the once-over. Instead, they seemed engrossed in a map that was spread out in front of them. But when Jarret slammed the front door shut, they turned and watched as he double-locked it after him. Although Jarret had not yet signed any document, technically they were all now on the same side. Or rather, he was on theirs. He thought about going over and talking to them, until he read the hostility in Curly's eyes and thought better of it.

Jarret climbed into the front seat of the Audi, next to Lulu. He was about to speak. But before he'd had the chance even to close the door or put on his seat belt, she'd accelerated off – leaving two black parallels on the cobbles. He slid down in his seat, feet pressed against the floor. She was approaching the first corner of the zed much too fast. He grabbed the loose seat belt with both hands and prepared himself for the impact, following the inevitable skid. But it didn't come. As with everything else in her life, she was in complete control. She braked, let the back of the car slide out and guided it effortlessly around the corner. Then accelerated towards the next.

The corners of Lulu's mouth were turned up in a smile that remained in place until she was forced to stop at the end of the track, where it joined the road. After quickly checking in both directions, she turned right and accelerated towards Solac. Though Jarret had finally managed to attach his seat belt, he was pleased he'd not had breakfast that morning.

22 (Thursday am/pm)

On the same side of the road and a little before the *Maison de Retraite*, they passed a lay-by. Parked there, shaded and partly hidden by a line of young weeping willow trees, was a silver Porsche. In Paris or Toulouse, such a sighting would go un-remarked, but in west Aveyron it was like the visitation of a rare bird. Porsches just didn't drive by every day, or week, or month, or even every year for that matter. It took money to buy and run one and the Aveyron was one of the poorest departements in France. Not only that, but they were completely impractical on most of the rutted country lanes, and far too low to see anything coming in the other direction until too late. All it would take was a lorry cutting a corner or filling an entire country lane and it was curtains. So the presence of such a sports car immediately caught Jarret's attention.

Seated behind the steering wheel was a man, but, at the speed at which Lulu was driving, that was all he managed to take in. Apart from the fact that it was a Porsche and it was silver. And he'd not seen it around before.

They came to a halt in the village square and, as Jarret was opening the door, Lulu put her hand on his shoulder to stop him getting out. In a firm voice, she instructed him that, for the encounter to work, he had to behave naturally and be himself, and not try to put on any act or make up a cover story. And, as far as possible, he was to be honest. Because Jarret's main task was to make contact with Trevor, to build trust and try to get to know him a little, and that'd be easier if he were natural about it. But of equal importance – he was on no account to ask any questions, as questions would only create suspicion. Then she finished by reminding him of what Trevor was capable. She was precise and brief and wished him good luck, before looking away.

As soon as Jarret slammed the car door, Lulu executed one of the fastest three-point turns he'd ever seen. He walked the short distance from the square to the barn opposite Jansen's house and retrieved the Jeep. A woman watched him from one of the neighbouring houses, but nobody challenged him. After the breakneck of Lulu's helter-skelter, the lazy chug of the diesel engine along the narrow street beside the church was relaxing.

He drove past the chateau and the war memorial on his left and descended the steep slope to the main road. There, he turned right towards La Fouillade and followed the road until it reached the lay-by. Although he didn't have much time to spare to get to Saint Gaitan before Trevor had finished his beer and gone home for lunch, he wanted a closer look at the silver Porsche. He was curious – at the same time disconcerted by it.

He came to a halt five metres behind the Porsche and turned off his engine. Far enough away not to cause any alarm, but close enough to be able to see the driver. The Porsche's metallic paintwork gleamed, as if the car had come straight from the showroom. And the seventy-five suffix on the brand-new number plate confirmed what Jarret already suspected: that the vehicle had been registered outside of the departement, in Paris.

He'd fumbled in the glove compartment for a pen and a scrap of paper and was about to copy down the number plate when the driver of the Porsche repositioned himself in order to see who was behind him. At once, their eyes made contact and Jarret hastily looked away. He didn't want to arouse suspicion by seeming to have any interest in the vehicle or its driver. To deflect suspicion, he opened the door of the Jeep, climbed out and stood beside the offside front wheel. Looking concerned, he crouched down and ran his fingers over the tyre wall, as if feeling for tell-tale signs of damage. Then he stood and tapped the tyre rim with his foot. He sensed the driver of the Porsche was following his every movement. Jarret walked round to the other side of the Jeep and repeated his actions.

In return, he'd only received a mosaic of impressions, making it difficult for him to piece together a coherent picture. For a moment, he considered driving off and getting on with what he was supposed to do: contacting Trevor. Instead, he crossed to the Porsche and rapped on the side window with his knuckles, leaning over as he did so in order to get closer to the driver.

'Sorry to bother you, *monsieur*; you haven't got a tyre pressure gauge in your tool kit by any chance, have you?'

'No.'

And that was it.

The two men stared at each other for several moments before Jarret nodded his thanks, as the window slid closed. The driver, who'd obviously resented being disturbed, had already turned away. But Jarret had what he wanted.

Returning to the Jeep, Jarret stopped beside the front tyre again and kicked it. Then, shaking his head, as if despairing of solving the problem, he climbed inside and turned the key in the ignition.

The man in the Porsche was in his early thirties, handsome, too handsome, with dark eyes that were almost exactly matched by the sheen of his black hair. He was as immaculate as his car. His skin was perfect and his tan exact. His haircut was expensive and his shirt, like the Porsche, was brand-new. Just visible beneath the cuff of his shirt was a gold Rolex watch. He was pampered and could afford the best.

On his way to Saint Gaitan, Jarret mulled over the

details. The man in the Porsche didn't even seem to come from the same species as McBryde. If he was a killer, then he'd stepped right out of Hollywood. He was too perfect to be true. And he didn't have that blank, cold look he'd seen in other men's eyes, of those that'd killed. He got the distinct impression that he was in fact waiting for someone or something. But as his face betrayed no signs of recognition, Jarret assumed it wasn't him. And he looked too affluent to be a spook – and not bored enough.

Then, as he wound his way along the road towards La Fouillade, from whatever oceanic depths it arose, Jarret was overwhelmed with doubt. He wanted to return to Le Papillon right away. But he couldn't, because Lulu and the other two were probably still there. He'd never snatch enough time alone with Alicia to be able to talk. What a mess! What a complete fuck-up! And he'd left her sitting in the house with drugs worth in the region of six figures, while his house was probably being taken apart at that very moment by a group of spooks, or whatever they were.

But she knew where the back door was. She'd be stupid not to have used it.

And stupid was one of the things she was not.

\#

The bell that sounded as he entered the Bar Gaitan reminded Jarret of an old-fashioned grocer's shop. The interior was unlit. The only light that penetrated the gloom came through two windows situated at either far end of the long, narrow room and one by the door. After the brightness outside, it took a moment for his pupils to dilate sufficiently before he could see the furniture and the line of the wooden bar in front of him. Someone had smoked a cigarette in there recently, but mainly the air smelt of beer – draught beer. It made him thirsty. It came as a relief to notice that there were no other lunchtime customers.

What with everything that had happened and McBryde clomping around with all the delicacy of an elephant on thin ice, it would've been unlikely for Trevor to have remained in Aveyron. After all, if what Lulu had told him was true, he'd enough houses elsewhere to choose from.

But surely, if they'd been keeping him under surveillance, Lulu would've known if he'd gone?

A woman entered from the back and stood in the shadow behind the bar, so that part of her face was obscured. Jarret recognised her from his only previous visit. During the course of the evening she'd come up to him, put her hand on his shoulder and whispered her name. He hadn't known what she meant by it, but he could infer. He remembered her name. It was Francine. She was the owner's wife.

Arranged in front of her was a row of taps, each bearing a distinctive logo – Heineken, Guinness, Bombardier and Leffe. Jarret ordered a small glass of Bombardier and seated himself on one of the high barstools. If it tasted like crap, he could leave it and just sit there until the end of lunchtime, when he could return to Le Papillon. His instructions were simply to make contact with Trevor and to get to know him. If he wasn't there, he couldn't. He'd have fulfilled his assignment, so Lulu could have no complaint. It was important she remained on his side. Because if the gendarmes or the police uncovered even one of the killings, he'd need her.

Jarret let the warm flavour of the beer run across his tongue. It was good – and that surprised him. He raised his glass in a gesture of approval. Francine was seated at the far end of the bar and clearly bored. Mistaking his acknowledgement as a signal that he wanted to talk, she came over and leaned both elbows on the dark wood counter in front of him. From her eyes, he saw right away that this was a woman with needs that life so far had left unfulfilled. There was intensity in the way she looked at him, but also something defensive. She had her arms folded, perhaps expecting rejection. She was not unattractive and he was never one to turn down an offer; but at the moment she was an unwanted distraction. He leaned back on his stool in order to put a little distance between them.

'You've been here before. I remember your face.'

'One time, some years ago.'

'You never came back.'

'No. But I probably will after this.'

#

When Jarret re-entered the house, it came as no surprise that Alicia was not there. Straight away, he began to search for her. Or rather, for any sign that she might not have left again – wine box, suitcase, clothing, anything. But they were all gone – everything belonging to her had been removed. A brief pencilled note left in the indent of a pillow on his unmade bed was the only proof that she had ever been there. Written in confident handwriting, it betrayed no regret, divulged no deep emotion, and gave no idea of where she might have gone.

It read simply – 'Thanks for everything. Got to leave. I'm sure you'll understand. A. XXX'.

XXX … was that all it'd amounted to?

He'd never seen her writing before. Its lack of feminine grace surprised him.

Of course, Jarret understood her having to leave. Given all the things she'd caused to happen since she first arrived at Adams's, she'd be insane to stay. And, in the cold light of day, what was it that Jarret had to offer her? Apart from himself and a roof over her head? She had bigger ambitions – and he'd been convenient. In the short time they'd spent together, she'd come to know more about him than he had about her. Had there ever been a dead sister? He'd no proof of that. Or a Frenchwoman for a mother? Now he came to think about it, that faint accent of hers could've been

297

anything – Russian, Eastern European, Scandinavian. Had she ever told him the truth, even once? She'd lied to him about the suitcase and the carton of wine. And the rape? And who was the man in the Porsche? Was he connected to her? Her escape route to a better life? She'd merely been grateful to him, not loved, as the note and the XXX made clear.

But why should she care for him? Last evening, when McBryde and his thugs were there, Alicia had told him that she'd overheard everything that was being said. She could even overhear McBryde talking to him outside. So what chance was there she hadn't eavesdropped on Lulu's visit? Overheard every detail of the evening they spent together. And he'd dared to ask her to … even *told* her to trust him. Jesus!

He wanted to stop thinking. He'd had enough. But his mind was racing out of control.

If she was able to sell the cocaine, she was on the verge of becoming a rich girl. Which was presumably what had driven her. But a rich girl who was condemned to spend the rest of her life looking over her shoulder. McBryde might be dead, but Zivkovic would never give up trying to find her. Ever.

But what if she had someone to look out for her? Like the man in the silver Porsche, perhaps? Had that present on the front seat been for Alicia? Or had it been intended for someone else? The pink wrapping paper suggested it was for a woman. He was flashy and, as a man of wealth, could certainly afford to protect her. Or was he at that very moment embracing someone else – while Alicia was making her way across the fields in another futile bid for freedom?

And what about Lulu? If her goons had sealed off the exits from the house as soon as the Audi had gone, then they'd have Alicia trapped inside it. No, she would've been far too smart for that. Wouldn't she? The handwriting on the note had looked masculine. He felt a surge of anger. He wouldn't put it past Curly – the small-minded bastard – leaving it there for him as a joke.

Had that been what Lulu intended all along? To get him away from Le Papillon on the pretext of meeting someone, who probably didn't even exist? Getting him out of the way just long enough to enable them to locate Alicia, find the drugs and bundle her off in the car with them. Was that talk about signing the Official Secrets Act just crap to massage his ego and let his guard drop? She'd given him nothing to sign. And probably never would. And what proof did he have, anyway, that Lulu was who she said she was? Or the two men with her, come to that? Zilch, *rien* – he'd just had her word for it. She been confident and he'd bought it. Once again, he'd been taken in.

Suddenly, whatever matrix of sense Jarret had constructed to explain what'd been happening over the last week began to dissolve. Disappearing like an ice cube in water, until all that he was left with was transparent and refracting.

So who the fuck was Lulu? That wasn't even her proper name. And if she had taken Alicia, what did she intend to do with her? And who the fuck was this Zivkovic? And who was it mentioned him in the first place? Lulu! The bitch had screwed him, rubbished him, told him a storybook full of lies and even given him a lecture about the Whore of Babylon. It had all been so much crap.

The acid of paranoia burned through him again. His imagination turned toxic.

He took his mobile from his jeans pocket, unfolded it and speed-dialled Lulu's number. He didn't even have to wait for its ring to be answered. An automated Vodafone voicemail kicked in immediately and instructed him to leave a message. Its suddenness took him by surprise. Either her phone was turned off, or she was already talking to someone. He left a brief message. He requested her to get back to him about Trevor – that there was something urgent they needed to discuss. If she was the real thing, and only if, she'd get back to him right away.

All of a sudden, there was nothing else he could do but wait.

He returned to the lounge, poured a large glass of whisky and sank into the big leather settee where he and Alicia had made love on their first night together. An isolating silence settled around him. Jarret was used to being solitary, but the thought he'd never again see Alicia made him feel hollow. He closed his eyes and a jumble of images from the past week swam across his mind, images of the dead and the living. Killing brought consequences, which he'd have to survive or go under. The moral recriminations could wait. There was the important task of putting his life back together first – and that'd never been easy since Columbia. But Aveyron had been a new start and he was determined not to abandon it.

He went into the office in search of his Filofax. After finding the number he wanted, he picked up the portable house phone and punched it in, and before long was listening to the monotonous electronic ring tone of a French telephone. A slow, careful voice on the other end welcomed him to mundane reality.

'Hello. *Bonjour.*'

'Mr Phillips? This is Mr Jarret. You contacted me about translating further information on new alarm systems.'

'That's right. About a week ago. I thought you'd forgotten.'

'I've been very busy. When'd be a good time for me to call on you?'

'You've quite caught me by surprise. Let me have a think … let me see now. I've got the doctor on Friday. Getting new tyres for the car tomorrow afternoon. What about tomorrow morning? Would that suit you?'

'Fine. What time?'

'Ten o'clock.'

'I look forward to meeting with you again. We've a lot to go through.'

Paid by the hour, did Jarret care how much he had to go through? With Alicia gone, he was no longer in any hurry.

Hardly had he put the phone down and begun noting the time of the appointment in his Filofax than it began to ring. Lulu had certainly wasted no time in getting back to him – probably automatic redial. She'd probably called while he was talking to Phillips.

'Jarret, this is Didier.'

'What's wrong?'

'Does there have to be anything wrong for me to call you?'

'No, I thought the gendarmes might have called on you.'

'So far, so good – everything quiet.'

'So why you calling me?'

'Yvette's coming back tomorrow morning. She wants you to come over and eat with us in the evening. Anyway, we need to get together some time to make sure we've all got our stories straight. Don't see why we can't do it over a civilised meal.'

'Fine by me. What's on the menu?'

'Don't worry, it'll be chicken.'

'I don't think it's going to be possible for me to face pork again for a while.'

'Seven okay with you? And while you're about it, bring that attractive friend of yours.'

'If only.'

'You and women. No luck, eh?'

'No luck.'

'One day.'

Jay hung up and sipped slowly on his whisky. Another milestone on the road to restoring normality – he was pleased. He noticed that his hands had stopped shaking.

And he no longer cared whether Lulu phoned him back or not.

#

Around midnight, he began to doze. A CD of Tomasz Stanko's trumpet music was playing softly on the stereo. He hadn't eaten since the day before, but, strangely for him, he didn't feel hungry. Tomorrow heralded a return to work – a ten o'clock visit to Phillips's house to talk alarm systems. The sheer banality of it would go a step closer to putting his life back in order. He wasn't exactly content. How could he be? But even without Alicia, it was the best he'd been feeling for days. His mind was delightfully blank, the whisky having numbed any lingering qualms of conscience.

The phone rang at just after one in the morning. Stiff from lying on the settee, brain relaxed and furry with whisky, he struggled to the office to answer it.

'Jarret. This is Lulu. I need you to do something else … or perhaps I should say a friend of yours does.'

'I did what you asked. It's over. I'm finished. Trevor wasn't in the bar today.'

'I know.'

'What do you mean you know? How?'

'Just shut up and listen to me. I've got a friend of yours here. You'll never guess where we found her hiding this morning. And you told me you were there sleeping all alone. Tut, tut, Jarret. And you expected me to trust you? Anyway, your little friend's been good for business. She hasn't kept her mouth shut since she accompanied us this morning. She's a bright girl. Bright enough to understand that talking to us is the only way she's likely to escape prison. Now, let's get back to our little agreement. I …'

'I told you, I'm finished.'

'You might feel finished, but I assure you, you're not

302

finished with.'

'Alicia … You haven't done anything to her, have you? Because if you have …'

'Careful. Like I said, she can't stop herself talking – about everything. And I mean everything. Which is more than that handsome bastard driving the silver Porsche is doing. The one you looked at so closely in the lay-by this morning. All he keeps doing, according to our French friends, is bleat for his solicitor. But they assure me that, given a little persuasion, he'll come round to seeing the righteous way. Now to us.'

'I want to see her.'

'You can't. But if you want to help her, I'll tell you how.'

'I want to see her first.'

'Don't be stupid. She's been asking about you, though. But in time, do what you're told, and who knows what might be possible?'

'What are you going to do with her?'

'Oh, very touching. When she heard I was going to speak to you, she asked me to say she was sorry. How does that make you feel? Bit ambiguous, I imagine.'

'Cut the crap! What do you want?'

'Alicia is in a mess, yes? Since finding her *chez toi*, she's told us a lot of things – some we can verify and others that we can't. You see, we have a problem with her – she talks a lot and appears to be helpful; only we don't know whether everything she tells us is true or not. And we need to know. Soon. As much for her sake as ours. Will you help? '

'Don't you listen? I just said I fucking would.'

'No you didn't. You just asked me to cut the crap and tell you what I wanted.'

'Alright then – yes, I'll help.'

'Good. Now we're making progress. If you haven't already worked it out, this little local mess got started when Alicia stole the drugs from Adams and got him killed for it. Since then, we've learned a lot. We've gathered intelligence on how this operation works – but not everything. Because there's a missing piece to it and that missing piece is Trevor. And, as you yourself know, we're no nearer making contact with him now than we were before. Which is the single reason I'm talking to you, because you not only *parlez* the lingo, you can talk ex-pat as well. So help us and, at the same time, you'll be giving your little friend a helping hand by corroborating her story for her. No big deal; we just need you to make contact with him. There's nothing complex to it – just two Englishmen having a chat together in a bar. What could be more innocent?'

'Tell me when and where.'

'Lunchtime today, same place as before: the Bar in Saint Gaitan.'

'On one condition – and I mean it this time – that I do it on my own, with no-one following me. Or I'm not going to go through with it. Is that clear to you?'

'Perfectly. I'll be back in touch with you again in the evening. And try not to get more pissed than you already are.'

Jarret was about to reply when he heard the line go dead. She'd hung up on him.

His morning appointment with Robert would have to be cancelled. He wondered whether Alicia had really said sorry. Or had that been Lulu's little joke.

He returned to the lounge and poured himself another whisky. He knew he'd had all the sleep he was going to get for one night. The bottle neck rattled against the side of the glass. He sighed, sat back on the settee and stared ahead of him. The music had stopped, but there was no longer anything he wanted to listen to.

23 (Friday am/pm)

Jarret had never been one to frequent Brit watering holes. For him, living in France meant enjoying what was French. Neither did he go out of his way to have those facile conversations so many ex-pats indulged in about how useless and undependable the French were and how much better and efficient life was back in Blighty. It made him wonder what the fuck they were doing in France in the first place. It was the fault of too many English writers who churned out romantic, simplistic nonsense about the French way of life.

Francine recognised him as soon as he walked in, a broad smile spreading across her face. At once, she roused herself and came towards him. But she wasn't alone today. There was someone else at the other end of the bar with a large glass of beer in front of him. In the pervading gloom, it was difficult to make out more. Before speaking, Francine fluffed at the sides of her long, black-dyed hair.

'So you came back. Just couldn't stay away.'

It was a little after eleven-thirty. Jarret could only guess that the man at the far end of the bar was Trevor. To avoid suspicion, it would be necessary to talk to Francine, whether he wanted to or not. It would help if he sounded like a regular, even though Trevor may never have seen him there before.

'I thought you might be serving again today. Paddy's not much of a morning person, is he?'

'Or afternoon. Not great at any time really. Do you want

a beer?'

'A small one.'

'Bombardier?'

'You remembered.'

'There aren't that many people come in here.'

'Will you join me for a drink?'

'I don't seem to be doing anything else. White wine …
how about making that a large one?'

It was apparent the other customer had been doing little
to distract her. Bored, she was pleased to have someone
to talk to. When she returned with the glasses, both were
close to overflowing. The measures on the sides had been
ignored – a little gift to him, and to herself. He paid what he
owed. Then – unlike the time before, when he'd moved his
stool to put a distance between them – he inclined towards
her. Right away she lifted her glass to her lips and drank.

'Cheers. To whatever happens next.'

'Right. The future.'

They both drank.

'Good beer.'

'So what made you come back this time? Last time it
was more than a year. You getting to like the place?'

'I'm unattached. Last time, I told you, my partner didn't
like it. Now that she's an ex-partner, I'm free to do as I
like.'

'So I might see more of you?'

Trevor was watching them. Jarret daren't look directly
at him, but he could sense it. Although they'd spoken little,
they were attracting his attention. He leant closer still to
Francine and told her that his ex-partner, Trixie, hated bars
because she disliked the smell of stale beer. That it made
her clothes feel dirty. Also, she hated being in places where
people were too near to her. Which was why she'd refused
to go to Morocco with him, because in Arab countries the
men always stood too close. She was strange like that:
more like a manikin than a person.

It was bullshit. He made it up as he went along. But it held her attention.

He continued that, now that his ex-partner had gone, he was free to make his own choices once again. And though he missed the sex, he was not unhappy. At the mention of sex, Francine's eyes brightened and she finished her wine. If Jarret wasn't careful, the situation could get out of hand. Another day he'd have been flattered – interested even. But not today.

'Do you live far away?'

'No, not far ...'

Truthfully, he told her he lived in the commune of Solac, but lied about where. Jarret gave directions to a house with a white tower, which was in reality two doors away from Jansen's house, where he'd been hiding out. It was easier to sound convincing if the lie had a grain of truth in it. In places, he raised his voice in the hope that fragments of what he was saying about Solac would carry across the bar.

His attention throughout had been focused on the man at the far end of the bar, whom he assumed to be Trevor. And who, apart from taking the occasional sip of beer, had hardly moved a muscle. But now he was readjusting his position on his bar stool, perhaps to get a better look.

In contrast, Francine's curiosity was intimate and endless. She asked Jarret why he'd come to France and what he was doing in the Aveyron. So he told her, untruthfully, about his occupation. How it involved a lot of travelling. He dropped the names of places and businesses in London. Then he reeled off a list of towns and cities in the UK and Europe where his invented expertise, as a Script Consultant specialising in translation work, took him during the course of each year. He didn't even know if the specifications for such a job existed, but doubted anyone present would know enough to contradict him.

As he proceeded, Trevor's interest in him was intensifying. He raised his voice and emphasised his

307

pronunciation and accent, in an attempt to exaggerate his Britishness. But the man at the other end of the bar remained steadfast in his silence.

Staring failure in the face for a second day, Jarret stopped talking and began asking Francine about herself. Lulu would not be pleased with him. He quickly regretted asking Francine anything about her personal life because, one by one, emerged a litany of hard-luck stories: stories purely designed to elicit his sympathy and concern. As she proceeded, her face drew closer to his and her voice grew softer. As if the confidences she was sharing with him were meant only for an intimate.

Suddenly the spell was shattered.

'You English?'

The tone was gruff. Jarret recognised at once the type he was dealing with; on any other occasion he'd have found the interruption offensive. Today, he welcomed it. Francine, on the other hand, was furious. She glowered at the man at the other end of the bar with undisguised hostility. But she'd become too down-trodden to voice it. Without wishing to be unkind, he turned away and faced his interrogator. The conversation with Francine had served its purpose.

'British. And you?'

First mistake. Lulu had warned him against asking any questions. It had been a harmless one, but had still been a question. Had it been that easy to blow it?

'English through and through. Where you hail from?'

'Bristol, originally; now I spend most of my time commuting between London and here.'

To avoid the error of asking another question, Jarret quickly turned the spotlight on himself. That way he could monopolise the conversation, revealing himself as a person of little threat. He started by repeating what he had already told Francine – that he was a Script Consultant, specialising in translation work. But he added that the company he worked for was his own. Jarret made a quick assessment and doubly gambled that the man at the other end of the bar would be impressed by him being a businessman, but uninterested in him being something that was arty and vague.

Jarret told him that, because of the Internet, it really didn't matter where he lived. Apart from the meetings he had to attend in London and other European capitals, he could live and work almost anywhere he chose. Providing there was a reliable airport nearby. And Toulouse-Blagnac fitted the bill perfectly, and was only an hour and three-quarters drive away.

The man Jarret hoped was Trevor sipped his beer and gave the impression he was listening. Occasionally, he halted Jarret's monologue in order to ask him a question. He appeared comfortable with the situation – none of his questions was profound or sounded like cross-examination. Though the gruffness in his voice never diminished, he seemed relaxed enough. And his sentences, though clipped and interrogatory, became gradually longer.

Apart from what he'd learned from his appearance and manner, Jarret had so far got nothing from the other man, except that he was English. Five minutes passed and he found himself still talking nervously. Soon a new topic of conversation would have to be found, or else there'd be a lull; a lull, he knew, that Francine would be waiting to fill.

Pinned to the wall behind the bar, amongst the other soccer memorabilia, were two red jerseys with white sleeves – in the centre of each was a white O_2 logo and on the right-hand breast the familiar Nike tick; on the left-hand breast was a badge displaying a cannon and the word 'Arsenal' in white above it. Although replica kits could be easily obtained, there was something about these two jerseys that suggested they were special – positioned as they were at the centre of the display, like trophies, with everything else carefully arranged around them.

309

Jarret concluded what he was saying and nodded towards them.

'Do you reckon those are real?'

As a general truth of bar-room conversations, men who've had a drink or two tend not to notice an abrupt change of subject. This was the case with the man opposite, because, rather than arousing suspicion, he seemed to welcome it. Raising himself flabbily upright on his bar stool, he angled his body a little more towards Jarret. His lips parted in a wide smile and Jarret noticed that his teeth were disturbingly white, even in the gloom of the bar. And he found himself staring at the most precise and impressively unreal set of implants he'd ever seen.

'Both completely authentic. The jersey on the right belonged to Thierry Henry and the one on the left, Patrick Vieira. If such a thing as a great Frenchman exists – two of the greatest to have ever walked the earth. Been an Arsenal fan ever since I was a boy. Can't help myself. Thick and thin, good times and bad. Loyalty's one of the most important things in life – shows a reliable character. Got them as a present for Paddy. You know, the Mick that owns this place. He bet I couldn't get Thierry Henry's shirt for him, so I got him Vieira's as well. Only a question of knowing the right people. Hardly paid for a drink in this place ever since. Only sulky over there ever charges me.'

It wasn't much, but this was the first personal information he'd divulged. The security zone had been breached. Not that Jarret gave a damn about what he was learning. He'd made a deal with Lulu to find out what he could and it was a deal he'd stick to. He could certainly use that money she'd offered to pay him, concealed in the brown envelope and free from the taxman.

'Managed to get hold of the two jerseys after a home match right at the beginning of the two thousand and two, two thousand and three season. Do you know, by that time Henry had already scored a total of eighty-six goals in only a hundred and forty matches. Quite incredible. Both men came to us on transfer from Italian clubs – Henry from Juventus, Vieira from Milan. Can't help myself. My head is full of the stuff. Always regret not being around for the following season when Arsenal Football Club didn't lose a single game in the Premiership – the only team ever to have done so. Saw them play a few times on TV and got hold of the odd video recording; but, otherwise, too many things on my plate. First time I can remember having missed out on an entire football season. Perennial problem with working abroad – too many clashes of schedules. Europe's not bad; difficulty's when you're on another continent.'

He finished speaking and shut up. He'd been a football fan in search of an audience. His sentences were still clipped, but he'd spoken with a boy's enthusiasm. Perhaps he felt he'd revealed too much – about himself and his activity abroad.

Jarret felt uncomfortable. After the avalanche of words, the man's abrupt silence had surprised him. He didn't know how to continue. But not Francine; her antennae were alert to the end of the conversation. Smiling, she moved once again towards him. Leaning against the bar, thrusting out her chest, she was about to speak when Jarret pushed his glass towards her and ordered another beer. He didn't want to be rude, but contact with the other man was at too delicate a stage to interrupt.

Francine filled the glass precisely to the measure. No more freebies were on offer without the promise of something in return. Before taking a drink, Jarret turned back towards the other man.

'Cheers. To the Arsenal.'

'I can drink to that. Which team do you support?'

'Manchester United ... I suppose.'

Jarret didn't, but it was the only team he could remember the names of any of the players – Beckham, Giggs and, if pushed, maybe one or two of the others. He'd always preferred playing soccer to watching it. Watching people play sport bored him.

'… But not in the way you support Arsenal. I've only seen them occasionally on television. Never actually been to a match.'

'Don't know what you missed. Though with Manchester United probably not very much – group of overpaid glamour boys …'

And with that he was once again off, talking about his favourite subject. One he had endless opinions on. Which pleased Jarret, because it enabled him to sit back and do nothing other than feign an interest. Although in many ways he was a blinkered, one-teamer, Jarret found himself being impressed by the man's knowledge of his team's tactics and his ability to analyse the strengths and weaknesses of different players' abilities, the majority of whom Jarret had never heard of. It might have been bullshit, but it was impressive bullshit.

Then suddenly, as before, just as he seemed in full flow, he stopped and looked intently at Jarret, his face inscrutable.

But this time Jarret was ready – the subject of football presented endless possibilities.

'You certainly know the game inside out. Impressive.'

He was flattered.

'Wouldn't go that far. Just a matter of where you're born really and what you're born into. Me, it was London and football.'

'Where were you born?'

'Cardiff.'

'You're not Welsh, are you?'

Once again, Jarret was angry with himself. Although the British Isles was small in size, its prejudices could never be taken lightly. He should have lied. It was stupid to say anything that emphasised their difference.

'You don't sound Welsh. What happened to your accent.'

'I've lived for a long time in England.'

'I thought all Taffies were rugby men. The only thing that interested them, apart from drinking piss-weak beer and chasing sheep.'

'Not all, though I must admit that some sheep can be damned attractive.'

At that, the man laughed. A brief, gruff noise that he right away choked back.

'Well, you don't sound Welsh, I'll give you that. What can I get you to drink?'

Though Jarret was pleased, he could hardly believe it. Just when he'd once again thought he'd blown it, he'd made a breakthrough. He quickly emptied his glass.

'I'd like another beer, a small one.'

So he was no threat. Perhaps no-one Welsh and as incurious as he was could be that. What he'd thought of as his weakness in the other man's eyes, his nationality, had inadvertently become a strength.

Though Jarret had asked for a small glass of beer, two half-litres were ordered and duly arrived. He couldn't complain. Each man lifted his glass by way of a silent toast and took a long draught of the cold beer. Jarret's hands shook slightly as he drank, from nerves or the previous night's whisky.

Behind the bar, lack of attention had driven Francine back into her bored shell.

'Why don't you come over here? There's no point in us shouting at each other.'

So much for the confidence of status – there was no way the unknown man would ever be prepared to move and come over and sit beside Jarret. He was too comfortable and secure just where he was.

Obediently, Jarret picked up his beer and carried it to the dark end of the bar. As he approached, a stool was pushed forwards for him to sit on. He caught it and turned it back towards the bar, so that he could sit beside the man, not face-to-face like opponents. But side by side, like co-conspirators. Nothing he did or said must be construed as a threat. Without trust there could never be further progress.

As soon as the two men were seated together, Francine turned on her heels and left the bar through a door at the back, marked *Privé*. Jarret wondered whether it was to see if Paddy was awake and sobered up yet, or just to give him hell for being his usual hung-over self. The chance of anything more exciting happening had clearly disappeared.

'Trevor, James Trevor – and who are you?'

'Jack Trelawney.'

'Not a Taff name, anyway. Probably some English in you from somewhere.'

'On my father's grandfather's side.'

'Not all bad then. Down the hatch.'

There was no offer of a handshake. Instead, Trevor raised his glass to his lips and drained what was left of it. Reluctantly, Jarret felt impelled to do likewise. In one week, he'd transformed from a sober, if not clean-living individual, back into his old drunken self. Having to down the beer that quickly made his head spin. To lose control of himself now would be a disaster. If it were ever discovered that Jarret wasn't whom he pretended to be, he was sure there were more McBrydes in the shadows waiting to deal with him. His defence was to bring the conversation back to the man's favourite topic: football. Because, as long as Trevor was talking, he wouldn't be drinking.

'So, what do you make of the current England football team? Always seem to promise a lot, but don't seem to deliver.'

It worked a treat. Barely had he finished speaking, before Trevor started opinionating on the strengths and weaknesses of the national squad. Which was lucky, because Jarret knew little about the subject, though he was quite prepared to sit there and patiently listen, nodding in agreement at appropriate moments. Trevor ranged at will over the quality of the current coaches, team formations and the players' lack of national pride – that they were paid so much by their clubs that, at the end of the day, they only cared about themselves. But, perhaps, the main problems affecting the national squad, as far as he could see, were a congested fixture list and too many foreigners playing in the Premiership. Though, as an Arsenal fan, he admitted he was not really in any position to complain – when the team had a foreign manager and hardly an Englishman in the side.

The only flaw in Jarret's strategy in getting Trevor back on the subject of football was, rather than slowing down his drinking, it actually appeared to increase it. So, by the time he'd more or less exhausted his thoughts on the England football team, Jarret and he had consumed two more half-litres of beer and were about to start on their fourth, Francine having to be summoned from the back room on each occasion by means of a bell on the bar. Trevor wasn't yet slurring his words, but they'd begun to slip awkwardly from his tongue.

'Tell you one thing though. Come next season, I'm going to hire me a box at the new Emirates stadium and get myself back for all Arsenal's home games. And I won't let anything stop me this time. Got everything organised like clockwork. Tell you what – if you're still around, I mean if you're here in France, I'll take you along with me some time. A real treat for you – no atmosphere like it. Until you've experienced it, you just don't know what you've been missing.'

'I'd appreciate that a lot.'

'Maybe I can sort something out for the Manchester United game, or failing that …'

Trevor suddenly stopped talking, causing Jarret to turn to look at him. Though it was difficult to tell by the light of the bar, his complexion seemed to have become paler. His sagging jowls were motionless and he was staring at the big old school clock above the door marked *Privé*. For a moment, he appeared frozen in a cataleptic trance.

Then Trevor became alarmed.

'Fuck. She's going to kill me!'

'What?'

'My wife! She was expecting me back for lunch over an hour ago.'

'I had no idea. I'm sorry.'

'Not your fault – soccer talk.'

'Tell me if I'm wrong, but wasn't it Bill Shankly, the old Liverpool manager, who once said that football was not just a matter of life and death, but more important?'

'And he wasn't wrong, either. Mind you, he wasn't married to my wife. Tell you what, why don't you come back with me and lend me a bit of moral support? Do you know anything about wine?'

'A little.'

'I'll tell her you're a member of the wine club I belong to in Rodez. And we just happened to bump into each other by accident in the bar here. Lost all track of time. You up for it?'

'If it gets you off the hook.'

'Probably won't, but she'll be much calmer if you're there.'

Why this palpably affluent, powerful man with a criminal lifestyle should be in awe of his wife was a mystery. Given the money he had, he could afford to update the old model whenever he chose. A trophy wife on the receiving end of a hefty alimony pay-out wasn't going to do very much complaining. If, on the other hand, he decided to take the cheaper route, then he'd the necessary contacts to arrange a tragic and entirely foreseeable accident. McBryde for one would've obliged him. And Trevor didn't seem the sort who'd be prepared to take criticism from anybody.

Jarret was perplexed by his behaviour.

#

Outside, Trevor walked unsteadily in the direction of a shiny new Range Rover. He fumbled through the pockets of a pair of expensive slacks, trying to find his keys. In the bright afternoon light, Jarret could see, with the exception of his flabby, out-of-condition body, that everything about him looked expensive and tasteful. His leather-soled casual shoes, Breitling watch and fresh-out-of-the-packet Ralph Lauren blue polo shirt exuded an odour of the cash register. He guessed that he was in his middle fifties – but age-guessing wasn't something Jarret excelled at.

'How far have you got to drive?'

''Bout half a click.'

'I'll drive you home in the Jeep. You can come back and pick up your Range Rover later. No point in us both losing our licences for being over the limit.'

'Ah, the good old Jeep. Never any police around here … but you're probably right. Come back and collect it later. Anyway, can't find my damned keys.'

24 (Friday pm)

The *corps de ferme* where Trevor lived made the Manoir Ivant look like a slum. It was entered through a stone archway, either side of which hung large heavy iron gates. The courtyard was completely gravelled and immaculate. The pointing round the stonework of the house had been newly and expertly done – each piece of irregular granite cleaned and in perfect proportion to the sand-coloured cement surrounding it. The chestnut window frames and doors were expensive and new. And, off to the right, between one of the outbuildings and the main house, sparkled the water of a swimming pool – its white marble surround dazzling in the bright sunlight.

Standing in front of the *porte-fenêtre*, hands on hips, was a petite, olive-skinned woman, perhaps in her mid-forties. Like the building and its surrounds, she was stylish and immaculate in every detail. Her neatly coiffured auburn hair had been cut short, leaving her face framed by a pair of dangling black and gold earrings. She was not exactly beautiful – there was something hard about her eyes and about her mouth – but she was well dressed and extremely attractive. As the Jeep came to a halt, she focused on Trevor, her lips pursed with anger.

'Sorry, darling. Bit late. Got talking, I'm afraid.'

'You're not late, you're an hour and half late. Your lunch is ruined and I've sent the cook home – so don't expect anything to be prepared for you. If you're hungry, you'll have to look after yourself.'

'Sorry, sorry. Met a friend of mine. From the wine club. Darling, this is ...'

But that was as far as he got – he'd already forgotten Jarret's name. His wife folded her arms, her eyes narrowed and burning. She wasn't going to make it easy for him. He was on a hook of his own making and, as far as she was concerned, he could wriggle there. Trevor waved an arm in the direction of Jarret, as if his mere presence should have been introduction enough. But it had the opposite effect. Because, with a sudden toss of the head and cursing loudly in Spanish, his wife turned away and marched into the house – her green high-heeled shoes stomping noisily on the expensively paved *terrasse*.

'Sorry, darling. Oops. That was the wife, Maria. Venezuelan – from a good family. Lovely woman when you get to know her.'

From the little-boy look on Trevor's face, it was quite clear he worshipped her. That, when it came to the domestic side of his life, she was in complete control. And he apparently not only accepted, but welcomed it.

'Looks like I can't offer you much in the way of food. What do you say to a bottle of something? We can sit and drink it out here on the terrace.'

'It's too late to eat, anyway.'

'What was your name again? Got a large cellar, if you're interested in wine? Maria won't think I'm lying to her if you come down and select a bottle with me.'

'If I can be of help. And it's Jack.'

'What?'

'My name – Jack.'

'Oh, I see. Yes, your name.'

The *cave* was reached via a set of worn stone steps that led down from the kitchen. A metre-high stone wall and black wrought iron gate had been constructed to prevent anyone from falling down them by accident. At the bottom, there was a heavy, studded wooden door that

Trevor unlocked using a large, rusty key. On the other side of it was another door, an iron one, which this time Trevor opened by pressing a combination of numbers into an electronic keypad on the wall beside it. In contrast to the temperature above, the air inside the *cave* was cool and smelled of a mixture of spilled wine and damp. Intense fluorescent lighting illuminated every stone of a barrelled ceiling that appeared to stretch from far beneath the house, and every spider web that hung from it. On high wooden racks around the walls and in the centre of the floor, innumerable bottles had been arranged in dusty rows. The short time Jarret had been in the house, it was the first time he'd been confronted by something that wasn't perfect. He could only guess that Maria wasn't interested in wine or was never allowed access there.

'This must be worth a fortune.'

'Believe me.'

'How many bottles d'you reckon in total?'

'Two thousand, maybe more. Come with me. This is the interesting end. Where I keep all the old stuff. In the middle are the recent purchases that need to age a bit. And down the other end's the plonk I keep for cooking or a gargle at lunchtime. Forget about that, it's not worth looking at.'

'Then I'm honoured.'

Jarret followed Trevor past racks of Bordeaux, Burgundy, Rhône, Alsace and Champagne wines on his way to the 'interesting' end of the *cave*. It was the sort of place he wouldn't mind getting locked inside for a week or two. It was easy to understand why the iron door had been installed. If he didn't rush his new relationship with Trevor, maybe he'd get a few more chances to taste wines that otherwise he'd never afford. Not that such a relationship appealed to him. But its flowering, he suspected, lay not in the hands of Trevor, but with Maria.

'Choose one, anything you want. I'll go get the glasses. Red or white?'

'Red.'

'The racks you want are over there. Think you'll find them interesting. Close both doors after you. And don't take all day about it.'

Jarret crossed to the racks containing Bordeaux; he recognised the bottles by their shape. Bearing in mind Trevor's final words urging him to hurry, in no time he'd picked out a bottle of 1970 Petrus Pomerol. Too good for idle drinking midway through a boozy afternoon, but much too good to be missed. He carried the bottle carefully to avoid shaking it up. How could Trevor permit him to commit such a sacrilege? But as the opportunity had arisen, it was one he was prepared to make the most of.

Jarret was approaching the iron security door when his curiosity was attracted by the other end of the cellar, where the plonk was stored. He left the bottle of Petrus Pomerol balanced on one of the nearby racks. He was interested to see what Trevor classified as plonk. He gave the bottles a quick look over. None of the wines were bad; they were the sorts he'd choose for himself. Mainly produce from local vineyards with little ageing potential. Interspersed among them were cartons, again presumably recent purchases, of Bordeaux and Bourgogne, but he didn't recognise any of the vineyards printed on the labels.

He was about to hurry back to Trevor, when Jarret caught sight of yet another bulk purchase, stacked in the farthest corner away from the door in unopened wooden boxes. Either there was a party in the offing or someone, probably Trevor, was about to do some serious quaffing. Taking a box from the top of the stack, he turned it on its side and held it towards the light.

At first, through the haze of lunchtime beer, he struggled to make sense of what he was looking at. He rotated the box several times, minutely examining each of the sides. He hoped he'd find something to contradict what he'd discovered there. But nothing did. And when realisation dawned, he felt his flesh turn cold. Before him, inked on to two of the sides were the words Château La Tour Saint Briac, complete with logo – the same as he'd discovered on Alicia's wooden box of wine.

Jarret took out the Swiss Army knife he'd kept in his pocket since deflating the tyres of the Audi, and chose a short blade. He inserted it beneath the lid and carefully levered it off. Inside, the top layer of bottles seemed genuine enough – the red wine they contained sloshed audibly when he shook them. But when he shook one of the three from the bottom layer, it wasn't liquid which moved around inside it, but a fine powder. Clearly visible – even beneath the green of the bottle glass.

Panicking, he repacked the bottles and forced the lid back into place, hoping to make it look untouched. He'd lined up the nails with the holes but, because he couldn't hammer for fear of attracting attention, the result was not entirely satisfactory – so he buried the box beneath two others. Already, it felt like he'd stayed in the cellar too long. He was conscious of Trevor's instruction 'not to take all day about it'. To loiter around any longer would be unhealthy. He hurried over to where he'd left the bottle of Petrus Pomerol and slid it from the rack. Then, in his rush, Jarret misjudged the weight of the iron security door, slamming it behind him with a crash that must have resounded in the house above.

As he climbed the stairs to the kitchen, he could feel the bottle he was holding trembling in his hands. He was in a trap not of his own making. Or, more precisely, Lulu's making. And any imprudent action would cause it to spring shut and that would be the end of him. His annihilation was beckoning – he must betray no outward signs that anything had changed. That he'd learned nothing in the *cave* other than Trevor had impeccable taste in wine. And that if Trevor accused him of having been gone a long time, it was because he'd had difficulty choosing. He must act as if there was nothing on his mind. Only his shaking hands said different.

Jarret was halfway across the kitchen when he became aware that someone was watching him. In a corner, away front the window, vegetable knife in her hand, was Trevor's wife, Maria. She looked suspicious, her eyes suggesting that she knew everything; but that was only his imagination. Nevertheless, he felt guilty. On the kitchen work surface, beside her, was a chopping board with an uncut red pepper and onion on it. It appeared she was preparing supper, though Jarret didn't believe it. Not with her rings on and her expensive manicured hands. If she'd been standing there when he and Trevor had gone to the *cave* to search for wine, neither had been aware of her. But now he was aware, she made him nervous and he felt he had to speak. He held up the bottle of wine.

'Your husband took me to the *cave* to choose a bottle of wine.'

She remained silent. Jarret's indication of the obvious only led to her examining him with renewed distaste. She had no time for his empty-headed prattle. And when she came to reply, it was final.

'My husband is an intelligent man, but a drunken fool.'

And with that, she turned towards the chopping board, took hold of the red pepper and cut it in two.

Retreating outside, Jarret hurried back to the table, only too pleased to be back in the warm afternoon air. Trevor took the bottle of Petrus Pomerol from him with the gentleness of a man who'd just been handed a small baby. He held it myopically to his face, before giving up and taking out a pair of tiny gold glasses, which he balanced at an angle on the end of his nose. After studying the label for several seconds, he nodded. Then he looked inquiringly at Jarret.

'What kept you?'

'I'd difficulty arriving at a final choice.'

'You do know something about wine, then? Didn't think you bring back anything as good as this. Better go and fetch us a decanter and some proper glasses. A 1970 Petrus Pomerol, eh?'

Jarret settled himself beneath the shade of a dark green parasol. Though 'settled' wasn't exactly the word for what he felt. The discovery of the phoney bottles of Château La Tour Saint Briac had put paid to that. He'd have liked to get back into his Jeep and drive out of there right away. But being in too much of a hurry would compromise any trust Trevor had in him – only in that trust lay his safety. He'd drink the wine, make appreciative noises and, if possible, get Trevor to talk about soccer. He wished Maria would be true to her dislike of him and throw him out. But it wasn't going to happen. She played the part Trevor had allocated her. He was her golden goose and she'd never jeopardise the affluence of her luxury style. She might abuse him, but she knew better than to oppose his wishes.

'Nose like a dream – plummy and mellow. Take a look at that colour.'

Trevor's voice preceded him onto the *terrasse*. He emerged from the house carrying a flat-bottomed decanter in one hand and two large Bordeaux-shaped glasses in the other.

'Better nourishment than any salad the cook could've prepared for us. Bloody rabbit food.'

He poured just enough of the Pomerol to cover the bottoms of both glasses. Then, keeping one for himself, he slid the other across the table to Jarret. The moment for the tasting ceremony had arrived. This was one of the world's great wines from one of the smallest wine-growing areas of France. In normal circumstances, Jarret would've appreciated what he was about to taste. Mechanically, he swirled the wine around the bottom and side of his glass, then brought the glass to his nose to sample the bouquet. Part of the ceremony. He gave a single nod, intended to show his appreciation. Then, after one more swirl, he took a taste of the wine, letting it linger a long time on his tongue, before drawing air into his mouth and finally swallowing it. He may as well have been drinking sink water.

'Unbelievable. A real privilege. I've got to thank you.'

'Don't mention it. Good to share it with someone who really appreciates it.'

Trevor leaned forward in his seat and filled the two glasses a quarter full. He sniffed the wine again, with a far-away look on his face, and then began to sip it. As he did so, a white van entered the courtyard and drove slowly towards them. From its gleaming paintwork and black plastic trim, it was clear it had not long left the showroom.

It crunched across the gravel at a funereal speed, as if its contents might at any minute explode. When it was about ten metres away, it turned to draw parallel with the main house. Only then did Jarret recognise who the driver was. Also now visible, stencilled onto the side of the van, in red block writing, shadowed in black, was the business name, premises, e-mail address and telephone number of its owner, Monsieur Lageste.

Jarret was an occasional customer of his.

Monsieur Lageste owned a *cave* in a nearby village. What Lageste sold was fairly drinkable. Certainly of a high enough quality to supply to a number of cafés and restaurants in the area, which was how he made the bulk of his living. Though, with fifty per cent of the French population no longer drinking wine, that living was gradually shrinking. And here he was at Trevor's house driving a brand-new delivery van, presumably containing nothing but more 'plonk'.

Another time, Jarret might have been pleased for him. He came from an agricultural background, one of many children from a hard-pressed farming family – a profession that'd never been easy, but during the last part of the twentieth century had become progressively worse.

Lageste opened the door of the van and struggled out onto the gravel. His leg was refusing to obey him. He crabbed a few strides, before bending down to massage it. Jarret had heard there'd been an accident on his parents' farm, when he was younger, which had left him partly crippled. Eyes fixed warily on the gravel in front of him, he laboured towards the *terrasse*. He was embarrassed by his disability. Lageste and Jarret were no more than acquainted but, in such a small rural community, Lageste would not only know his name, but probably what he did and where he lived as well.

Jarret held the outsized wine glass in front of his face and pretended to drink. A pathetic enough gesture if the glass had been twice the size and opaque. But either Lageste hadn't seen him or, for some other reason, chose to ignore him. Nevertheless, Lageste looked distinctly uncomfortable, but having Trevor as a customer would more than account for that.

'I'm sorry to disturb you, monsieur, but I have brought the wine you ordered.'

'Good man. But wait a minute, weren't you supposed to deliver tomorrow?'

Making his best effort to spring to his feet, Trevor crossed to the kitchen door where, to one side of which, beneath a hinged, grey plastic cover was an electric bell. He gave it three long presses of equal duration. From where Jarret was sitting, it was barely audible, ringing somewhere within the depths of the house. After no more than ten seconds, a dark-haired man hurried out of a *porte-fenêtre* farther along the *terrasse*. He listened closely as Trevor gave him orders in a hushed voice. Then, both men walked to beside Lageste's van, where Lageste joined them and they began another whispered conversation, which grew more animated until Trevor's angry voice brought it to an end.

Lageste, looking crestfallen, limped off and began

rummaging frantically between the front seats of the van before returning with a battered clipboard containing some crumpled-looking paperwork. It was clear, from the way the two men looked at him, they had little respect.

Jarret had heard rumours that Lageste had once enjoyed a bit of a reputation as a ladies' man – which Jarret found hard to believe as he considered the sag-faced, overweight individual gesticulating beside Trevor. The only physical attributes surviving from his younger days were his thick black hair and a luxuriant moustache, which drooped weightily at the corners of his mouth. Too much sampling of his own product and too much food had seen to that.

Lageste slid open the side of his van and made a pile of three cardboard cartons, each containing six bottles of wine, and handed them to the man Trevor had summoned from the house. If the man found the cartons heavy, he gave no indication, but carried them quickly away and returned indoors. No sooner had he gone than Lageste began to arrange the rest of the boxes into piles of three. When it was apparent the man would be slow to return, he carried one of the piles over the *terrasse* himself and placed them near the front door. He was in a hurry to get away. Not to want to leave the cartons unattended, Trevor walked over and stood beside them. Gradually, the pile on the *terrasse* grew and Jarret watched as the assortment of Marcillacs, Gaillacs and Entraygues – reds, rosés and whites – were unloaded from the van and carelessly stacked by a limping, panting Lageste.

From Jarret's point of view, the sooner the unloading was over the better. He could afford to relax a little. He took another drink of the Petrus Pomerol, trembling to the extent that he now had to hold the glass in both hands. He tried to take a sizeable gulp, but had difficulty swallowing. It stayed in his mouth a long time before he could down it without wanting to retch.

As soon as Lageste had placed the final three cardboard

cartons of wine onto the *terrasse*, he limped to the back of the van and clambered inside. Jarret listened as he clattered about in the now almost empty vehicle before dragging the remaining cartons towards the door to unload them. As soon as they were stacked in piles of three, he climbed clumsily on to the gravel.

At first, Jarret failed to recognise what he was looking at because the unloading of wine was of far less interest to him than escaping from Trevor's house alive. All he wanted, at that moment, was for Lageste to hurry up and leave, so that in a short time he'd be able to do likewise. But the noisy activity from the back of the van inevitably drew his attention. The wine now being unloaded was no longer contained in cardboard cartons but in wooden ones. In itself that aroused little interest compared with his impatience to go. What did, however, was the identical dark logo scarred onto the boxes' sides. As soon as they were pulled from the van's dim interior into the daylight, he couldn't miss it. And his courage took another nosedive. Each bore the imprint of a chateau viewed through an arched gateway – and underneath, in black ornate lettering, the words Château La Tour Saint Briac.

And then he remembered the receipt he'd found in the car park in front of the Manoir Ivant, on the evening he'd gone there looking for Alicia. That too had come from the Cave Lageste. He recalled its sodden feel and smudged ink with clarity – almost as if he still held the soggy paper between his fingers. Somehow Lageste, an affable, simple man, had managed to get himself involved in something bigger and more dangerous than he could ever imagine.

Lageste carried the first of the heavier wooden boxes to the *terrasse*. Then Trevor's man reappeared to collect them for transferring to somewhere inside the house. Sweat patches had appeared under his arms and he was breathing heavily, but nowhere near as heavily as Lageste. Then a dark shadow of a thought crossed Jarret's mind – that something about the man seemed familiar, that somewhere he'd met him or seen him before. Only he couldn't think where.

Trevor supervised the completion of the operation like a diligent foreman, following the to-ing and fro-ing, watching both men as they went about their work, as if he trusted neither of them. Though he did little himself, other than to make the occasional remark, his mere presence imparted a momentum. Only when the last of the wooden boxes was being carried from the van did he look again at Jarret.

'Pour yourself another if you've finished; I'll be with you shortly. Damned inconvenient this.'

Jarret made it an especially small one. Then poured a little more. Only when the bottle was finished could he offer his excuses and leave.

With the van emptied, Lageste handed a battered clipboard and a pen to Trevor and indicated he wanted the top paper signed. But Trevor refused. A hushed exchange of words followed. Then, with a shrug of the shoulders, Lageste returned to his van, threw the clipboard inside and drove off.

Trevor watched him leave before returning to Jarret.

'Bloody man.'

And after taking a large sip of his wine: 'But bloody fine wine.'

Once again, Trevor's man emerged from the house to collect more boxes. But seeing Trevor was no longer close by, he looked around to see where he'd gone. It was then that Jarret knew without a doubt that there was something very familiar about him. And from the way the man was staring back, it was apparent he thought the same about Jarret.

For a brief moment, their eyes came into contact. And though Jarret quickly looked away, he'd witnessed the puzzled look on the other man's face. They'd seen each other before, but neither of them could remember where.

'After that interruption, I've half a mind to go and fetch another bottle. At least we'll be able to drink it in peace this time. Bloody man wasn't due to deliver here until tomorrow. What do you say? Another bottle?'

'I really should be going.'

'Rubbish.'

'There's something I've ...'

'Same again do you?'

It was then there came a shout from the other end of the *terrasse*. Though Trevor's man was still carrying three cardboard cartons of wine, he was now walking towards them, looking agitated and shouting.

'He's called Jarret. I saw him at his office. He was the one McBryde was using.'

And with those words, the context drilled into Jarret's mind. Before he'd had time to think about it, he'd risen to his feet and grabbed the nearly empty bottle of Petrus Pomerol by its neck. Because he knew the last and only time he'd seen the man carrying the wine was outside his office in Villefranche-de-Rouergue, where he'd been talking to McBryde – the man, with collar-length hair, who'd been standing guard. Dressed as he now was, in a T-shirt, his hair hadn't seemed so long. Now it all came back to him – but too late.

Trevor was also rising to his feet when Jarret hit him hard on the side of the head with the bottle of Petrus Pomerol. The thick glass acted as a club and Trevor's legs folded under him, as if they'd been made of paper. He fell awkwardly, knocking over his chair. Jarret didn't know why he'd hit him. All he knew was that he had. He should have made a run for it back to the Jeep, but not much of the rational was functioning in Jarret any more. It wasn't even instinct or terror that was driving him to it, just an insane impulse to be doing something, anything, other than standing there and admitting that he'd again fucked-up.

He'd got out of situations before. But never ones like now.

Then the end, when it came, came quickly.

Jarret had dropped the bottle and was in the act of turning to get away when, out of the corner of his eye, he caught sight of a movement. Maria, fist raised above her shoulder, was rushing towards him from the kitchen. He'd only a brief second to make up his mind – but he didn't want to fight with a woman. And then she was on him. She was faster or he was slower than he thought. So, as her raised fist was about to connect with his chest, he swayed back in an effort to avoid it.

At first, it seemed to have glanced off him – grating against the side of his ribs, leaving a tingling sensation. That was followed by what felt like a hard punch. He took a pace backwards to prevent it happening again. Only there was nowhere to go. Trevor's body was blocking the way and he fell, hitting his head hard on the *terrasse*, as he went down.

Somewhere, and for some reason it seemed a long way away, he heard wine boxes being dropped. Now McBryde's man was coming to deal with him too. He tried struggling to his feet, but it was more difficult than he thought. His arms had no strength in them any more.

It was then he felt the first kick against the side of his head. Maria was laying into him, her eyes blazing.

Jarret attempted to roll away, but his side had started throbbing and something prevented him. He put his hand down and his shirt felt wet. And on the ground, beside him, was a small warm pool. The next kick jolted against the back of his skull and made him dizzy. He tried raising himself on an elbow to see what was wrong. The right-hand side of his body was turning red and the handle of a knife stuck out, above the waistband of his trousers.

Maria had stabbed him.

The following kick connected with the side of his face

and his head hit the ground. He heard a sharp crack and a groan. But he couldn't tell any more whether the sounds came from him or another.

The final kick wasn't even felt.

25 (Saturday/Sunday/Monday)

First of all, there was a swimming sensation. Then it was as if he were floating. His eyes opened to a white room with a white light, which slowly began to turn yellow. His head hurt so much he thought it might burst, and lower down, on the right side of his body, there was a dull throbbing. With difficulty, he tried to look around him in order to recognise where he was, but it was nowhere he knew. Finally, he re-closed his eyes. Like being awake but in the middle of a dream. One that hurt. Hurt like …

\#

When he woke again, there was a nurse standing beside his bed. Dressed in white with white shoes. Her clothes were like a ghost's, but her tanned face and red lips were real. She checked the intravenous drip and adjusted the morphine dose that entered his body. He wanted to speak to her, but could think of nothing to say. Aware he was watching her, she moved to the bedside, leant across him and attempted to fluff up his pillows. Then she pulled the bed sheet to beneath his chin. In a quiet voice, almost a whisper, she asked him how he was feeling. He shrugged his shoulders, but didn't want to disappoint her – she looked kind. So he tried to say 'okay'. But couldn't. As she smiled, the sadness in her eyes depressed him.
    She left and he slept again.

\#

The next time he awoke, he was alone. If anyone had entered the room in the meantime, he couldn't say. Time passed, had passed, was passing – but without him. The blinds on the windows prevented him from knowing whether it was day or night. He couldn't remember the last time he'd eaten. Any nourishment entering his body was getting there via a tube in his vein. But how long he'd been fed that way – days, weeks – he had no way of knowing.

He looked around him, but learned little. It was clear he was in a hospital, in a private room. But it was a hospital that could have been anywhere in France. Villefranche-de-Rouergue? Toulouse? Even Paris. The blinds covering the windows saw to that.

Then, slowly, events began to return to him.

First an image, then a sound, an action, a connection – followed by the emergence of a narrative through which the procession of outrages and absurdities, that one by one drifted into his consciousness, could be strung together.

He remembered drinking wine with Trevor on the *terrasse* of his house. He remembered hitting him with the bottle. And that he'd been stabbed and there'd been a knife sticking out of him, just above the waistband of his trousers. And that there'd been a lot of blood. And, as he lay helpless, that Maria had been kicking him in the head. Over and over. And a man, McBryde's man, who'd been hurrying towards him carrying the cardboard cartons containing wine. What had he done to him?

He lay there, a swirl of events in his head. Attempting to progress from effects to discovering what the cause might have been. And the future. Why his life had been put at risk? And what now lay in store for him?

Until the effort of remembrance gave way to fatigue and he began drifting. The drugs once more returning him to that sphere between sleep and consciousness, relaxed and peaceful, almost euphoric. Then a ghostly image of Lulu slipped into his unprotected mind. And, though he didn't understand right away, he slowly began to. Desperately clinging to every shred of detail, as if clinging for his life to a rockface. To let go would be to recede into oblivion.

As the details gradually filtered through the fog of his brain, if it hadn't been for the feeling of euphoria, he'd have become angry.

#

He watched the doctor and nurse through sleep-encrusted eyes. Though their voices were soft, their whisperings seemed to echo round the room. His mouth was dry and his tongue felt heavy. He croaked as he tried to speak, though in what language he couldn't say. He lifted a hand in an attempt to gesture his need. It would hardly move. But the nurse understood and fetched him a plastic beaker of water, the type made for babies, and held it for him while he drank. The doctor looked on for a moment, then turned and left the room.

When Jarret had finished the water, the nurse went into the little private bathroom and refilled the beaker. She left it for him on top of the bedside locker; a kindly gesture, but where he'd no hope of reaching it on his own. The tightness in his right side saw to that. He uttered a sound that even he didn't understand. And the nurse, for a moment, seemed at a loss. She smiled at him weakly. She wasn't the same nurse he'd seen earlier; her skin was less tanned and her hair was darker. She looked at him with soft eyes as she waited for him to try to speak again. She looked pretty. He smiled. He was sure he was feeling better.

Then the nurse spoke.

'There's someone outside who's been waiting to see you.'

To reply was a struggle.

'Who?'

His voice was croaky and didn't even sound like his

own. His tongue felt thick and clumsy, and the word when it emerged sounded strangely elongated.

'Your sister.'

'I haven't … Alicia?'

'Mademoiselle Jarret. I don't know her first name. She's been back and forth to the hospital for the last few days. If you feel up to seeing her, she's waiting. If not, I can give her a message.'

'What does she look like?'

'Your sister. You've been very ill, Monsieur Jarret.'

'My sister?'

'Don't worry. She won't be allowed to stay long.'

'I haven't …'

'Shall I tell her she can come in? And remember, she'll be your first visitor, so don't tire yourself.'

Jarret nodded that he'd understood and she left.

So he'd gained a sister. He was curious to see her. If it was Alicia, then … Suddenly the pain in his side intensified. Did he actually ever want to see her again? After everything that'd happened? The answer was 'yes, probably'.

He heard the door swing open and turned his head expectantly towards it.

'Don't look so disappointed.'

He couldn't help it. It was Lulu.

'Unusual, I know, but I've been worried about you. You look terrible.'

'Pass me a drink of water.'

Lulu brought him the beaker of water and held it while he drank. When he'd finished, she fetched herself a chair from against the wall and positioned it close to the bed. Her serious expression returned. She wasn't visiting because he was sick. And certainly not to show him any sympathy.

'If you were hoping to see Alicia again, forget about it. It's not going to happen – so wipe her out of your life. From now on she belongs to us. In the short term, we can use her, just as once she made use of you. You served her purpose

– you kept her alive. Once McBryde had disappeared, she had no further need for you. For now, all she needs is us and what we can do for her. She's given us some very interesting information. Then when we finish with her, we'll disappear her, complete with a sum of money, a new passport and a new name. Bye, bye, Alicia. Only that's not her real name either, and neither was Julia Roberts nor Jennifer Taylor.'

'What is her real name?'

'You never need to know it.'

'I want to.'

'You'll get over it. The only women you'll have need for now are a bunch of nurses and me. They'll look after your health and I'll sort out the rest. Not your personal problems. Your fucked-up private life you'll have to deal with on your own. By the way, we have informed Trixie you've been hurt.'

'You know about her?'

'Naturally, we need to know about anyone who's likely to visit. She had a lot to tell us about you before we met. There's a man in the hospital vetting anyone who's likely to want to see you. We're not expecting you to be in any immediate danger, but with McBryde unaccounted for, it would be foolish to risk your safety. And there are still things we have to talk to you about. When you're feeling better, of course.'

'You don't give up. Can you get me some more water?'

'Sure.'

When finally he finished drinking, the beaker was empty. Without being asked, Lulu took it into the small private bathroom again and refilled it at the washbasin. She offered him more water, but this time he declined. Once again, he began to feel weary. His eyelids drooped and he knew it'd take a real effort to keep on concentrating. There were stories still to be told. But Lulu wasn't the sort of visitor an invalid needed. Her presence alone was making too many demands.

'But it still puzzles me what happened to McBryde and his associates. Nothing's been seen of any of them since you told us they left for the Far East. That many people don't entirely disappear like that. Are you sure they went away? Not staying under the radar screen until they can figure out what happened to Alicia? But, in truth, I can't see how either explanation makes sense. Alicia's saying nothing about it either.'

Jarret felt his heart leap, and an emotional electricity passed through him. So she wasn't the heartless bitch hell-bent on self-preservation that Lulu depicted her as being. She'd been trying to protect him. She'd once saved his life, now she was trying to prevent him going to prison. He could still be convicted of murder. But so, if he came to think of it, could she, being the one who shot McBryde. So perhaps her silence wasn't entirely for his benefit. But he would never know for certain.

'Are you okay? Do you want me to call the nurse back?'

'No, I have things I want to tell you. It may take some time, but you need to know them.'

'You look dreadful. I'd hate to be the one responsible for finally killing you.'

'No, I want you to stay.'

'I'll be back tomorrow.'

\#

The next day Jarret woke feeling better. His thirst had diminished and his body felt more like it belonged to him – he had a greater control of his movements. And though the throbbing pain in his side continued to cause him discomfort, he was emerging from the haze of painkillers.

Lulu arrived unannounced mid-morning. No nurse asked him whether he was ready to receive a visitor. It was presumed. And Lulu, he had no doubt, was the one who'd arranged the presumption. But it didn't bother him. Since he'd woken, he'd been expecting her. The things he had to say he wanted to get over with. She would be his confessor. And he'd make Alicia his very last gift – her innocence. Innocence of any involvement in murder. He didn't know whether he was thinking clearly, but hoped, for both their sakes, that he was.

Lulu pulled a chair over to the bed and sat down. Again she examined him before speaking.

'You don't look so crappy today.'

'No.'

'You had something to say to me.'

'Just listen and don't interrupt. If there's anything you don't understand, wait until I've finished. What I'm going to tell you will answer your questions.'

Lulu took a notebook with a pen attached from the side pocket of her jacket. She flicked through it until she found a blank page. When she looked up again, Jarret was looking away from her towards the covered-up window. After a minute, he took a deep breath and began.

Though he proceeded slowly, with many pauses for rest, Lulu never once interrupted. Half-way through, she closed her notebook and reattached the pen to it. Throughout, her expression remained serious; she betrayed no emotion.

He told her first about what had taken place at Didier's farm, the beatings and the rape, and how he'd responded. Taking the law into his own hands, but certainly saving the lives of two people whom he cared about. What else was he supposed to do? Stand there and watch? If he'd phoned for the gendarmes, they'd never have got there on time. He'd never killed anyone before. He hadn't realised he was capable of such a thing.

Lulu slid the notebook and pen back into her pocket and waited for him to continue.

He talked next about his relationship with McBryde and how, that Sunday morning in Villefranche-de-Rouergue, he'd entered into the contract with him, as if with the devil. He'd had little choice to do otherwise.

Lastly, Jarret told of the night at Le Papillon and the bloodbath that had taken place. And how it had concluded with him killing McBryde in an exchange of pistol shots. And how, all the time unknown to him, Alicia had been hiding herself away in the attic of his house. Which was why she'd returned to the same place when Lulu had arrived the next day. Why they'd found her hiding there. But as far as the previous evening's killings were concerned, she'd taken no part.

Once Jarret had made it clear that Alicia had been innocent of any of the killing, he suddenly ran out of steam. That had been his final gift to her; now he'd nothing left. His head fell back on the pillow and his eyes closed. For a moment, it looked as if he'd fallen fast asleep.

'Fuck me. That you were stupid I already guessed, but violent never. Fucking hell. McBryde, everyone, not one of them left. I suppose that solves one of our problems. But it means the French police will never arrest anyone over the death of Adams. Not the right person anyway. Fucking hell, you killed them all. Where are the bodies?'

'Pigs.'

'What?'

'Pigs. The pigs ate them. I fed them to the pigs.'

'Not by yourself, you didn't. That much I do know. You'd have needed someone to help you. Who was it? It must've been your neighbour? He owed you.'

'Didier knows nothing about it. I did it all myself.'

'Have it your own way.'

'What'll happen now? Will you leave me to the French police? Or will you get me extradited.'

'Neither.'

'Apart from shooting me, there's nothing else you can do.'

'Yes, there is – nothing.'

340

'I don't understand.'

'Where's the record of what you just told me? What I was sitting here listening to were the ramblings of a heavily sedated and delirious invalid. Not admissible in a court of law. If you've covered your tracks sufficiently well, no-one will ever discover a crime has been committed. And if the police ever did start to suspect you, then a word in the right direction might work wonders. But only then.'

'It's all a complete fuck-up.'

'It doesn't need to be, believe me. Just get on with the next part of your life. You're lucky still to have it.'

'Like I was trying to do before all this. Why are you suddenly prepared to help me?'

'You just want to hear me say it's because I like you. The truth is, if any of the killings get traced back to you, and you get linked back to us, then it'll truly be a fuck-up. Diplomatically speaking, anyway. The other afternoon at Trevor's was bad enough but, on that occasion, at least both sides ended up shooting someone.'

'What? Were you there at Trevor's?'

'Of course; ourselves and three French policemen from Toulouse sent to work alongside us.'

'So, you know what happened?'

'Yes, and in a weird way we're grateful to you. If you like, you can add that as a reason for keeping quiet about McBryde. But, personally, I've never been one to encourage incompetence.'

'You've arrested Trevor?'

'Yes.'

'You found the cocaine.'

'Probably the same consignment that the French police found traces of in Adams's wine cellar. And the same set of bottles that Alicia had with her. They had the same labels. All the time it was right under everyone's noses and we didn't see it. A previous background check on Lageste revealed nothing suspicious. In the end, what was he anyway, but just another greedy small-timer, who asked no questions and was only too pleased to get the money he was being paid. Or rather, that's the persona he's trying to present us with. If the jury's not prepared to accept it, then he'll go to jail. If it does, however, then that psycho, Zharkoski, is bound to believe he betrayed the organisation and have him killed. Either way, Monsieur Lageste will be a loser.'

'I don't understand how you knew what was happening at Trevor's. You agreed not to have me followed.'

'I agreed, yes. But that was never what was intended. The officer you call Curly was watching your back the whole time. Now you've got something to thank him for. Though when you were getting your head kicked in, I must say he seemed to be enjoying it more than he should have been. As soon as you and Trevor started drinking again, after Trevor's wife had stormed off, Curly contacted us. With both of you pissed, he'd a feeling things were about to become interesting. And he wasn't wrong, was he? Then Lageste arrived, and bingo.'

'So you saw everything?'

'Everything that took place shortly after Lageste had begun to unload the bottles from his van.'

'I was identified. I didn't have a choice.'

'You could have tried making a run for it. Your Jeep wasn't too far way.'

'It's a diesel. It doesn't start up right away. I'd have been caught.'

'You'd have had a chance. But not the way you played it. Trevor's wife was watching you the whole time. She's sharper than her husband. As soon as you hit him, she was on you. It was lucky you moved or she'd have nailed you for good. We had to shoot her to stop her kicking you to death. Or rather the French police did. It was one of ours who shot the other man. He had a flick knife and, where Trevor's wife might've botched it, he wasn't going to. The

French police reflexed their shot off after ours. Which was lucky, because if we'd been the only ones to fire there'd have been trouble. Lucky for you as well. Trevor's wife is now in hospital under police guard with a shattered femur and playing hell about it. The other one's in the morgue keeping nice and quiet, though requiring the completion of half a ton of paperwork. Still, everyone's pleased at the overall outcome. Superiors, that is. So that's all that matters. Though Trevor's still pretty pissed off, sitting in a prison and complaining of a headache. I hope you didn't damage him too much. We need to have a long talk to him.'

'I suppose I should thank you for taking no notice of me.'

'Thanks accepted. But don't run away with the idea it was because I cared. It was because I didn't trust you.'

'And all that crap about the Official Secrets Act?'

'Was crap.'

'Like the Whore of Babylon.'

'No, that was serious. Look who's been on top of things from the start. Certainly that was never you.'

'Without a dragon like me, you'd have had nothing to sit on. Who else could you have led by the nose?'

'Maybe you've a point.'

'What about the brown envelope then? Was that bullshit as well?'

'Ten thousand tax-free Euros ready and just waiting for you to get better. I love patriots like you. Queen and country above all else … not even upholding the law is a good enough reason for you.'

'Some law I upheld. It'll be some time before I'll be able to work. I need to get paid.'

'Point taken.'

'The doctors haven't given me a diagnosis yet. I don't know if they're going to keep me in here for months or days. Wherever here is.'

'You're in a hospital in Toulouse. And regarding your

injury, I just know what I was told. When you were attacked with the knife, you received two sorts of wound, incised and penetrating. The first was a superficial cut caused by the blade sliding down your ribcage. The second, the penetrating, was caused by the blade piercing the flesh and muscle on the right-hand side of your body – that was the more serious of the two. But let's face it, you were a lucky bastard. Though you bled a lot, the knife was angled downwards, cutting through muscle and tissue, but leaving your internal organs relatively unscathed. You underwent a laparotomy as soon as you arrived here, but the doctors are more or less certain there'll be no lasting internal damage. They want to avoid invasive surgery, so until they're certain they'll keep checking on you, which is probably why they've so far told you so little. As for your head, that too has undergone a scan and, apart from the deficiencies suffered by every member of the male sex and your abuse of alcohol, you seem to be fine. That Neanderthal skull of yours might have gone a long way to help.'

'So my immediate future is what? I'm not sure what you said exactly means.'

'That you're not going to die, that it'll be some time before you can ingest solids and if you were thinking of having sex, then you'll not be the one on top.'

'Perhaps I'll have to put a call through to Lulu.'

'So you're health is improving.'

'The problem is, I don't have her real phone number.'

'But she's got yours.'

'Does that mean I might be able to see her again?'

'Depending on the crisis, nothing can be ruled out.'

'So we'll get together some time?'

'Absolutely not.'

'No chance?'

'None.'

'Then I think I'm starting to feel better already.'

About the Author

Jack Alun is a freelance writer, whose travel writing, poetry and reviews have appeared in magazines, anthologies and e-zines throughout the world. He lives and works in both France and the UK.

Lightning Source UK Ltd.
Milton Keynes UK
UKOW05f1344260913

217995UK00001B/25/P